UNDER SUSPICIOUS CIRCUMSTANCES

BY GLORIA LAMBSTEAD

PAPERBACK PUBLICATION FIRST EDITION 2025

Edited by Kevin Anderson & Associates

Book Cover by David Ter-Avanesyan

-

Paperback ISBN: 979-8-9935649-1-3

eBook ISBN: 979-8-9935649-0-6

10 9 8 7 6 5 4 3 2

Instagram: @undersuspiciouscircumstances

TikTok: @undersuscircumstances

For the one who became my undoing. . .

You set me free.

CHAPTER 1

I

The casket was to remain closed; that was one of the instructions that had been left in the event of her death. She did not wish to be seen by those who gathered for the pitiful affair. To become the ghoulish sight of what was now a lifeless, loveless, unfeeling object. She wrote her instructions one afternoon in August, thinking that they would be carried out decades later. She had seen her father pass at eighty-three, and witnessing the quarreling and spitefulness that emerged among her brothers upon his death, she decided that she wanted no ambiguity, no vagaries, and no second-guessing. Her conviction, moved by dismay, compelled her to write these moribund instructions. Alas, she may have tempted Death's visit too soon . . . for she did not manage to live past her fifty-sixth birthday.

Her casket was to be black: piano black to be precise. Polished to the highest grade by the best cabinetmakers in France, it was to be so lustrous that its polish would resemble a black mirror. This was a decision made to spite the women who would certainly come to the funeral to gawk at her, so that in between their crocodile tears they would catch a reflection of themselves, reminding them that they too would someday meet a similar fate.

No recent photograph would be shown; instead, a large portrait of her would be moved from above the living room fireplace and displayed beside her.

This portrait, painted when she turned twenty-seven, was the only image of her past she wanted anyone to remember. *La terrible débutante*, as the portrait was nicknamed, showed her as a raven-haired beauty clad in a black chiffon ballgown draped with ornate black lace. She gazed away from the viewer, showing off fair skin, delicate rose cheeks, and deep red lips. Her determined and contemplative expression spoke of her independence, intelligence, and conviction of thought. She would never bow to the whims of any man, and she would never compare herself to any woman.

She had commissioned the portrait after the birth of her firstborn son, Maximillian. The black ballgown she wore in it had been made for her presentation at seventeen to high society at *Le Bal des Arts et des Sciences Industrielles* in Lyon, France, and her presence in it had caused quite the scandal. Her father, Magnus Deauvillier, had at first seethed with anger at the sight of his only daughter in black when all other debutantes were in white. But looking more deeply upon her noble stature, he realized that she was no longer some little girl among little boys. She had become a woman who commanded a respect usually only bestowed upon men. Her bravery drove scorn from the other young women, and fear in the eyes of her intended suitors. It was no matter; she was entirely her own person, and that ballgown was the embodiment of her. When there were those who thought childbirth would change her, she commissioned the portrait to prove that she was still in command of herself.

Above the casket's lid would be a voluminous arrangement of red bourbon roses, vibrant and dense with red petals. They were to cascade gently over the top of the lid and down to the bottom edge of the casket. No other flowers—no lilies, daffodils, or azaleas—just deep red roses. The lasting impression of her departure was that inside that raven casket and under those vermillion roses lay a bold and beautiful woman who had defied convention and held her head up high like her beloved father. She was Karine Juliette Deauvillier-Porter, the only daughter of the last great industrialist of Western Europe.

The intent of her instructions had been to celebrate herself as a great elderly matron. But her actual death came so soon and unexpectedly that it all read as post-mortem narcissism on her part. For all the grand pomp and drama, her last edicts for herself did not command any funeral regalia upon her mortal body. She wore a plain dress, her most comfortable; a coat she bought on her travels through Cambodia; her loafers, and some loose socks. She wanted her wedding band and her locket with its images of her children with her. Her hair was to be kept neat, and no makeup or embalming was to be used; her body was to be washed and sprayed with her favorite perfume. Before mortals she was to be sent off like a goddess. In the confidence of God and her family, she would simply depart into the beyond as Mom.

At the peak of her powers as a tastemaker and grand hostess, she was skilled at hiding her own humility and only presenting the image of the indominable socialite that she had become. But that was all that anyone would ever remember of her now. There was no climbing down off the ivory pedestal. Her memory was frozen like bronze upon that ether, her casket an unintentional epitaph to self-indulgence.

It turned out to be a blessing that the closed casket and the voluminous arrangement of roses shielding her body from view prevented anyone but the mortician and her husband from seeing what had happened to poor Karine. Her death was an abrupt and violent one, and her instructions did not call for any reconstruction. (She hadn't expected a need for any—why would there be?)

The sky that day was gray yet unnervingly bright; the sun was hidden behind clouds that enraptured the celestial dome, yet it seemed to refract and disperse light in all directions with no clear shadows to indicate its location. The sky itself made one's eyes hurt, and tears seldom provided any comfort from the harsh brightness. Color appeared to have drained from the world, and the priest, the mourners, the sky and the earth were now trapped in a black and white reality. The only color that stood out against this monochrome world was from the roses, pulsating in waves like a pumping heart, or a bludgeoned wound bleeding red.

That glistening casket, warping and contorting the faces of those closest to it, gave no reprieve from the equally warped reality that Mrs. Porter's immediate family felt staring at their now dead wife and mother within that reflective box. A father, two sons, and a daughter-in-law tried to remember the person inside, but met only their own perverse reflections staring back at them. They had to maintain decorum, stand stoically and quietly, when all they wanted to do was to release their anguish.

Mr. Henry Porter, the widower, stood at the far end beside the priest. So energetic and affable in happier times, he appeared to have aged several years in a few days—his brows wrinkled, his eyes sunken, his hair far thinner and more quickly receding. The financier was a man of few words; his resolute and resigned expression hid best the pain he felt undertaking this unthinkable task.

George, the younger of the two Porter brothers, was closest in spirit to his mother. Charismatic and independent, he carried in him a self-assurance that could not be matched by his fellows in university. Still a young man of twenty-three, he had much to learn on his journey into adulthood, but now maturity had fallen on him irrevocably. His new wife Isabel stood by his side, hiding her gentle tears behind her husband's handkerchief. She held onto George's hand, squeezing softly to signal to her husband that he had in her a companion who would stand beside him in joy and tragedy from now on. Mrs. Porter had much faith in Isabel to become the rock upon whom her son would rely, and Isabel was ready to take on this challenge. She was the new Mrs. Porter now. She stood resolute and composed, dignified in her posture, steady in her great role as the new matriarch of the family.

While Mr. Porter, George, and Isabel remained collected through their sorrow, they could see upon that black mirror the sight of the last member of the family barely holding on to his sanity. The elder brother, Maxim, fought feverishly to remain steady in his post and resist the urge to shatter into a thousand pieces. His legs shaking, his eyes swollen with tears, he tried to hold at bay the despair of seeing his beloved mother reduced to a black void.

Sadness had always amplified itself around Maxim. His gentleness and sensitive nature were no secret to his family, but he was aware that to acquaintances and relations of his mother's his behavior amounted to little more than "the fairy that could not keep his act together." Maxim knew he had to remain steady to avoid bringing embarrassment and shame upon the family. His mental state teetered upon the precipice of raw feeling and suffocating civility.

The priest continued his sermon, unending and vapid in both language and impact. The last rites he bestowed upon the deceased felt little more personal than those of a common housewife. Life built upon duty, family, marriage . . . it spoke little of the true accomplishments of the woman herself. The priest was not one Mrs. Porter would have chosen, but a last-minute evocation from Mr. Porter's less gracious American parish. The sermon entered its final praises; the casket slowly descended into the pit that would forever hold Mrs. Porter's body. It looked as though the family could finally release their anxious resolve, and that Maxim would pull away from the brink. Of all people at the burial, he must never see what had happened to his poor mother.

The six members of the French Legion slowly lowered the casket, their strong bodies holding taught the ropes that attached themselves to that grim box.

It came suddenly and viciously—a blurry mass darted downward from that blinding sky and struck the head of one of the legionnaires. Disoriented by the shock of the impact, he released his grip to clasp the side of his face, now bleeding profusely, a dead blackbird lying on the ground beside him.

The heavy casket became unbalanced as the other men struggled to keep it level. The mourners looked on in shock and confusion as the casket crashed with a thud upon the concrete bottom of the pit, the brute force shattering the hinges of the lid that opened to reveal the shifted body of Mrs. Porter within.

The congregants lurched back in horror, but Maxim sprang forward. His brother tried to hold him back but it was too late. Maxim looked down into that pit, and began to scream, the most unnerving and never-ending scream, as the last shreds of his sanity finally unraveled.

All Maxim could remember was the screaming. Even now, some thirty years later, the memory continued to haunt him. At least now he had medication that would keep it buried deeply in the back of his mind.

II

Maxim awoke from his bed in a state of chronic exhaustion. No matter how early or late he chose to go to sleep, he still would rise from his bed feeling like he had not slept at all. He had sought the advice of doctors and sleep specialists who found no physical issues. It could only be surmised that he was suffering not from physical exhaustion, but from exhaustion of the psychological kind. Still, he had to rise from his bed as he had every morning for the last eighteen years, to shoulder the responsibility of running his family's foundation.

He labored forward from his bed to his marble-festooned bath-room. In ritualistic fashion, he undressed himself before the floor-length mirror and proceeded to inspect his body carefully from the top of his head to his toes. He looked at every mole, mark, wrinkle, and wound that he could feasibly recollect upon his body from years past. He looked upon his face, worn and bedraggled. Bags under his eyes had become more pronounced, but despite his own insecurities, pragmatism forced him to accept that for a fifty-seven-year-old, one could not pretend to be anything other than past the point of no return—not that Maxim felt he had anything to return to.

He sighed as he stepped back from his reflection.

"Still looking like shit . . . at least I can still keep this body going."

Maxim had never had a positive view of himself, a character flaw he'd held with stubborn confidence from the emergence of puberty. He always fancied himself ugly, and no praise that could be posed to him would change this perception. He had on occasion looked back at pho-tographs of himself and thought, *Perhaps I was too harsh back then*, but the thought was fleeting and quickly reverted to him looking at himself, as he did now, as ugly.

For him, his physicality was itself no great exalt. He was an im-posing man, tall and broad shouldered. With long legs and a solid torso, he had inherited the best traits he could have gotten from the Deauvillier clan, a family of imposing and athletic men best exemplified by his ma-ternal grandfather Magnus. He looked like his grandfather, though in the back of his mind, he wished he didn't.

Maxim stepped away from the mirror and turned to the counter beside him to take his medications for the day: a steady cocktail of anti-depressants, beta blockers, and mood stabilizers he had been taking ever since the funeral. Maxim had grown afraid to talk about his mental state, clinging erroneously to the fear that any therapists and psychiatrists his family hired would secretly divulge his sexuality to his family, so instead of seeking therapy or counseling Maxim simply accepted his regimen of pills willingly, even after he had come out of the closet. They had become a substitute for processing the grief that was buried deep in his subcon-scious. The pressure to bury his emotions, to present a stoic and domi-nant facade, to be a "man," had been forced upon him by his family.

CHAPTER 2

I

"Good morning son! Did you sleep well?" chirped Mr. Porter.

Henry had stayed over the weekend at Gwenshill to visit his son. The two men greeted each other as Maxim walked into the dining room for breakfast, still unable to shake his tiredness.

"Morning, Father," Maxim responded wearily, holding his hand to his face. "I slept as well as always."

Their conversation carried itself through as it usually did—politics, news events, history, technology—for a good part of the morning. Their modus operandi was to exchange knowledge that was topical and engaging but never mounting to anything more personal that would truly forge a bond between father and son. Mr. Porter had little of the emotional intelligence needed for fatherly tenderness; he spent most of his life delegating others to address issues he could not resolve, but fatherhood was something he could not delegate. Maxim had largely accepted the cordial but detached relationship he had with his father, especially now that they were both adults, but at times the now eighty-seven-year-old Mr. Porter still came across as tone-deaf even through the veneer of civility.

"Father, someone must keep an eye on Gwenshill's maintenance. Houses like this one are going extinct and it takes a good eye and a tight ship to keep it from falling apart," Maxim was telling Mr. Porter now.

"Son, you've been keeping this tight ship for a considerable amount of time. It is only you, a skeleton crew, and the furniture. I know this house is your passion, but at your age, even I felt there was more to life than bossing around staffers and looking at invoices."

"Bossing around staffers and looking at invoices certainly kept your bank from collapsing every time the Standard and Poor's sneezed," Maxim retorted, sipping his coffee. "And it is not just the house that keeps me busy; I have the foundation keeping me productive."

He turned to his father, looking for a glimpse of his indignation. Mr. Porter knew that Maxim ran the charity from the reclusion of the old family office in the servants' wing. His son had little reason to leave the confines of the mansion.

Maxim finished the last bites of his breakfast and then offered an understanding overture to his father. "It is your fault I am this way— I am your son after all . . ."

"Oh yes, my son, certainly cut from the same cloth. If only you bothered to listen to my advice for once."

"Sorry, my stubbornness came from you too, so . . . your fault." Maxim softened further with a lighthearted grin.

Henry Porter chuckled warmly, knowing that he could rely upon Maxim to dish out a witty little jab at his expense.

"Well, I am going to the opera tonight with your brother and Isabel. Maybe you could take some time from being a ghost haunting these halls and join us." Mr. Porter rose from his seat. "It has been a while since we have all been together as a family."

"Sorry, Father, I have a function I am hosting at the Park Savoy and I will be busy there most of the evening."

"Oh right, I forgot. What's this event going to be about? Another one of those progressive causes of yours?" Mr. Porter turned back to prod further. "Should we contact the attorneys to dip into the trust?"

"No, Father, this time it will be organized by the foundation but not funded by it," Maxim replied in a mordant tone. "You can tell your boring little accountant that there will be no tax deduction this time."

"Fine by me!" Mr. Porter gazed out to the lawn outside the dining room. "It's a lovely sunny day, I think I will take the chance to stroll the grounds and get my steps in. My doctor has put me on new medication and it seems to be doing wonders."

"That's great, Dad, enjoy your walk," Maxim responded distractedly; his attention had already turned to reading over the emails that cascaded into his phone's inbox. Through the kitchen door, he called out for Luisa. She entered the room, a flurry of cream and blue in her apron and uniform, her dark curls tied back neatly in a tight bun.

"Luisa, you can take the dishes away. Father will be walking the grounds, so make sure to tell the staff to hold off on spraying the lawns until later today."

"Yes, Mr. Max." She nodded briskly, proceeding to move about the table collecting the plates. She suddenly paused mid-stride and turned to Maxim, still looking down at his phone.

"My apologies, Mr. Max, I failed to tell you this last evening. You had gone to bed early and—"

"That's alright, Luisa, what is it?"

"Mrs. Whitmer and her daughter Alice stopped by yesterday. They wanted to know if you would be available to see them for coffee."

Seeing the displeasure grow on Maxim's face, Luisa continued.

"They tried calling you, but they say that when they try, your number appears disconnected."

"That's because I blocked them, Luisa," Maxim retorted in frustration. "All they do is call me incessantly. Next time they come onto the property, tell them they can find me hanging from the rafters."

"Maxim!" Mr. Porter admonished. "Of all people, I never expected you to be the sort of person to speak like that to the staff."

"Luisa knows why I am annoyed; it is not about her," Maxim reassured them both, turning to Luisa. "I apologize for my temper, Luisa.

Just please continue with the dishes." She nodded once more and carried on with her task.

Maxim returned his gaze to his emails, but his annoyance persisted. "I don't know what's gotten into Carol and her daughter's head that I am interested in speaking with them. Let alone going to visit them in that peony palace of theirs."

"You were close to Alice when you were children," Mr. Porter reminded him. "Sometimes you had sleepovers, as I remember."

"Dad, I went to sleepovers at her house because she let me play house with her dolls. Don't you remember when Grandpa Magnus threw one of them into the fireplace thinking it was mine? Mom had to apologize to Carol and buy a new doll for Alice."

Henry shrugged. "I must have forgotten about that."

"It didn't help that she was my only friend. None of the boys from school wanted to hang around me, and none of them wanted to come here."

"You didn't put that much effort into making friends, son . . . what about the dances you invited Alice to?"

"Nobody wanted to see 'Maxine' and 'Fat Alice' at society dances, Dad. And after she lost weight, she didn't bother going anywhere with me, period."

Maxim rolled his eyes as Henry persisted. "That's all in the past, Maxim; why don't you go spend time with them now? They are two nice ladies, and Mrs. Whitmer was a good friend of your mom's. I'm sure that they just want some male companionship."

"They're rich enough, they can go get gigolos if they want company. I was sure that pool boy they hired was fucking around with one of them."

"Now son, you know that's not what I mean—"

Maxim pulled himself away from his phone to look up at his father with increasing irritation.

"—I mean someone more mature and intelligent. Someone more established. After all, you can't take this house with you when you die."

Maxim already suspected there was more to his father's persistence than merely being neighborly. Both men knew that Alice, who had always been a needy person, had divorced her husband after he ran off with a marketing VP back in April. He fixed his father with a scathing gaze. "Which is why this house will go to Charlotte," he snapped, referring to George and Isabel's daughter. "God help me if I live long enough to see her turn eighteen."

Maxim's indignation grew as he came to another realization. "And I am sure that I did not give them my cellphone number in the first place," he said pointedly to Henry.

"Now son . . ." Henry hesitated. "C-Carol and I just thought that since you and Alice were close once, and you're both alone . . . maybe it's time you reconsider your . . ."

"My what?" Maxim was reaching his limit. For decades, this rift had been ongoing but unspoken. When Maxim had first come out of the closet, Henry had accepted him, but the mores of Henry's generation dictated that it was not the sort of open and embracing acceptance that others younger than Maxim had enjoyed. While Henry Porter acknowledged that there were such people as homosexuals, he always maintained the infuriating notion that despite that, duty and family had to come first. After decades of not seeing any semblance of a companionship between Maxim and any man, Henry had begun to press Maxim in less subtle ways to conform to what was expected of him. Maxim at times was able to brush off his father's comments and asinine suggestions, but this morning he gave in to his anger.

"My what, Father? You go giving my details away without my consent to some withered old bat? So I can reconsider what? My preference for sucking dick over eating menopausal cunt?"

"Maxim! Crass language is not acceptable either."

"Neither is this ongoing desire of yours to keep pushing me to date people I have no desire to be with." Maxim stood up from the table in defiance. "You already have a straight son with a lovely wife and that wife gave you a grandchild. I am gay! And you need to get through your fucking head that nothing is going to change that."

Luisa having scurried into the kitchen sometime during the spat, the atmosphere in the dining room was now a disquieting low. After a moment, Mr. Porter shrugged his shoulders and sighed. He was not happy to have made his son so upset, but in his own mind he stubbornly believed he was doing the right thing.

"Alright, son. I just want you to not be . . . You never seem happy, that's all."

Maxim remained cold. "A woman is not going to make me happy the way you think she would. And frankly, if you do think that, then Mom's memory must mean very little." "As you're walking around the grounds, go tell the Whitmers I am not interested." With that, Mr. Porter was abruptly dismissed, and Maxim was left to bitterness.

Deep in thought, Mr. Porter descended from the terrace outside the dining room and began to make his way down the slope from Gwenshill, holding onto the stone parapet until he reached the gravel road at the foot of the hill. He just could not understand the life his son led. Though he felt himself so competent in the art of business, he remained baffled by the realities of his son's nature. Without the empathy and understanding of his beloved Karine, any dialogue between himself and his elder son would always feel transactional and tenuous.

The century-old mansion sprawled gracefully upon the hillside, its wings concealed behind clusters of mature trees. All one could see from afar was the main body of that auburn-brick edifice, so that it appeared less imposing than it actually was. Mr. Porter looked up at that manse upon the hill and reflected on the memories it had once held as the Porter family residence and as the domain of his late wife.

"Idyll" could little describe how those grand rooms were once filled with sunlight in the day and the sound of music at night. Karine had known how to instill an effervescent energy in every family gathering, every grand party, every society luncheon, and Gwenshill had served as her ultimate instrument as she held court with grace and poise. The house now seemed a hollow hulk, its curtains drawn tight, no flower beds blooming their fragrant delights into the warm breeze as they had in years past.

Mr. Porter never could understand why Maxim would continue to stay in that house, going so far as to short-change his inheritance for a home that was merely a mausoleum to dead memories. Henry had always believed Maxim remained there because of the trauma of Karine's death, but to Maxim it was more than that.

Gwenshill served as the crutch to the last vestiges of a legacy that, real or not, Maxim felt imprisoned to uphold. Maxim's truest misbelief of himself was that he had been brought to this earth to be more than another overthinking, anxious old queer living off a fortune that was in slow but terminal decline.

Why would fate have made him in the image of his grandfather, a man who had conveyed only ruthless ambition and enterprise? Out of all men, why did this man have to appear in the mirror every morning? A man who would have harbored obloquy to the son of his only daughter for not inheriting the family bravado? Maxim had always had more of his father's temperament: risk averse, lazy, and insular. This was compensated only by a natural intelligence that few peers could easily access. An intelligence that might have built more, created more, striven for more, but was impaired by a cowardice more suited to middle managers looking for steady incomes than trailblazers chasing great prizes at the risk of losing everything.

And then there was this heroic mansion built upon the aforementioned legacy. George and Isabel had made it clear to Maxim that they did not want Gwenshill to be passed to their daughter Charlotte. That the house and its contents would be sold off, and that every shred of the past would be tossed to the winds of time. Modern in the most indignant of fashions, never looking back or planning for tomorrow but simply existing in the here and now, they did not believe in holding on to the memories and vagaries of what had come before. Maxim did not have the strength to part from the past, and so he stayed put as Gwenshill's last custodian. Even as he felt a creeping sense of failure for not living up to the past that he now fiercely clung to, Maxim had become comfortable with the prison he had locked himself inside.

II

The New Mattachine Society Gala would begin quietly in the early hours of the evening. Maxim took the chance to go about the hotel's ballroom confirming with the organizers that all the food and refreshments were ready. He paced anxiously from one station to another examining each drink, each platter, and each giftwrapped prize for the charity auction that was to follow later that night. He would go over the servers one by one to ensure that their uniforms remained tidy and consistent, on occasion inspecting himself as well to ensure he was not becoming undone from the anxious frenzy of his final tasks.

The doors opened at 7:30, and the first bevy of guests made their way across the hotel lobby in the direction of the ballroom. Maxim, along with the head members of the society, stood vigil at the entrance welcoming guests as they came in. With each encounter he reminded himself to be friendly and even to appear meek; he was self-conscious that his size came across as intimidating and that when lost in thought, his face would rest upon an aloof and distant expression that sometimes strayed to the bitterness and even anger he felt inside. To counter this, he made an effort to keep his arms close to his body, lower his tall frame to the eye-level of each passing individual, and smile a welcome with the politeness of a caricatural grandfather. As the bulk of the guests made their way past him and only late-comers now straggled forward to the entrance, Maxim released himself from the anxious duty of greeting to wander about the event's swirling crowd. He paced slowly from one gathered cluster of patrons to the next, making small talk while sipping a glass of wine, picking canapés from passing servers as the conversations went on around him.

Fortunately, Maxim was not obligated to pitch or upsell the society, having donated resources for the gathering itself. Maxim felt more at ease talking to the Mattachine members than trying to persuade others to join or donate to the cause, an initiative he'd never been successful in, though the society members still honored his efforts in other ways.

The society's president, Elliot Newsham, came to shake Maxim's hand. "Thank you for the help with arranging this, Maxim. The venue and the list of guest speakers definitely raised the standards for us."

"Not a problem, Elliot," Maxim demurred. "I am just hoping all the effort will bring more funding for the charities. Some of these clowns just come for the food and the chance to get themselves a date by the end of the night."

"Of course they will." Elliot leaned cheekily into Maxim's ear. "We've got the best-looking boys chatting up the whales."

Maxim tittered, rolling his eyes. "Elliot, you are incorrigible."

Maxim saw a hand waving high above the crowd as his closest friend and confidant, Edward Cho, headed in their direction.

"Maxie! How lovely to see you again," Edward cheered at the sight of his friend. "Thank you for inviting me, darling."

"My pleasure, sweetie," Maxim replied, extending his arms to hug his friend. "We need to see each other more often these days. How are things with Paul?"

"Ugh. Terrible!" Edward scoffed. "He's been drowning his sorrow in booze over Dillon. You remember Dillon, right? Our ex-houseboy? He came out as poly a few months back and decided that just being in relations with both of us was *limiting his self-expression.*"

Maxim laughed. "What self-expression? It was not enough to be a kept man for two bears with a house in the Islands? Now he wants to fuck half the city's gayborhood?"

Edward smirked and helped himself to a cocktail from a passing server's tray.

"Well, you can never stop the young from coming up with new names and excuses not to call themselves sluts."

"We fought for sexual rights, Eddy. We can't complain about the eventual outcome."

"True," Edward shrugged. "Anyway, Paul is taking Dillon's departure badly. The guy reminded him of a lover he had when he was in his twenties, so he goes on about how he feels he's losing the same guy twice."

"How did the first one fall out of the picture?" interjected Elliot innocently.

"He died from AIDS."

Elliot's expression turned grim, and Maxim winced at Edward's deadpan response. Edward's dry humor had always tended toward the truly dark. With only the briefest pause, Edward continued unfazed, looking back to Maxim.

"But you know what, darling? Dillon's presence was wearing thin, to be honest. His constant use of tanning beds was aging him right out of his twink phase before he even turned twenty-five."

Maxim simpered. "There's never a dull story with you Eddy. Oh! I just realized that you and Elliot have not officially met . . ."

Edward and Elliot began with polite platitudes, but it took little time for the two men to begin exchanging stories of their escapades in Provincetown over the years. Maxim had noticed that anytime gay men met, especially in their age group, conversation would soon inevitably devolve into an unending list of conquests both successful and failed. It was the sort of topic that Maxim found little interest in following these days, having long dismissed the vapidity of such sexual one-upmanship. Edward could complain about his houseboy's escapism, but it reeked of a jealousy for the virility and vigor that all the older men in that ballroom longed to return to, instead having to settle for the transactional hedonism they could expect from obtaining a sugar baby.

Maxim checked out of Edward and Elliot's chatter and scanned the room around him. He could sense that the conversations in other parties were more of the same. The power dynamics, the talking points, the flattery and flirtatious grins had become white noise to Maxim. He had had his moment of existence as a sexual being in this community that celebrated sex so vigorously. But the fact that he had never found the love and tenderness he read from kin spirits like Housman and Forster, had never heard the voice of another man tell him "I love you," only added to his mounting burden of self-castigation. Was it truly better to have loved and lost than to have never loved at all?

"Max? Max . . ." Edward's voice echoed, breaking Maxim out of his lost thoughts. "Max, are your brother and sister-in-law coming? I've been dying to meet our new senator and his darling little wife."

Maxim hesitated briefly while he came up with a vaguely plausible excuse.

"Unfortunately, he can't make it. H-he's stuck doing a town hall after last week's mess with the senate housing committee. He sends his regards and hopes that our efforts are successful."

"I've heard! It appeared on my feed last night. Ugh, what a shame."

"Yeah . . ." Maxim muttered under his breath.

George, for as much as he loved his older brother, was never comfortable with the circle of people that Maxim involved himself with.

Not that it was a particularly disreputable crowd, but his brother had a prudishness around sexual orientation that Maxim considered excessively conservative. Still, if Maxim was stuck in the mindsets of the romantic era, how could he judge his brother for projecting the mores of the Great Society programs? George had won on a moderate platform, which was still more progressive than what he was running against.

Maxim could rely more on his sister-in-law as an ally to his community. Sweet, genteel Isabel had become as close to a real sister to Maxim as he could have ever wished for. Her petiteness did not sequester her into a passive role as wife to George; she was an outspoken believer in women's place in the workforce. Recognizing that tastemakers in fashion had always come from circles like Maxim's, she had developed a reputation as the kingmaker to several young and ambitious queer designers at the Maison de Caron, and she was the free-flying kite to George's square boulder.

The gala moved on to the dinner and awards ceremony. While Elliot took his place on the main stage with the guest speakers and other society fellows, Maxim and Edward sat on one side of the ballroom at a table populated with the younger cohorts of the New Mattachine.

"Are you Maximillian Porter?" asked a young man with streaks of blue teal hair bobbing neatly over a dark blond base.

"Why yes."

"I worked for your brother's campaign; we met briefly at his election offices? I just wanted to say it was a pleasure working for him . . ."

A surprised smile rose from Maxim's face; perhaps he had misjudged his brother's moral stonewalling.

". . . I had sent a resume to become a junior staffer in his administration. I am not sure if he has seen it, maybe you could help?"

As Maxim was about to respond he noticed the young man's knee press against his under the table. Maxim hoped this was going to be an innocent encounter, but he felt stuck in the realpolitik of a transaction where this twenty-something needed (or perhaps wanted) his patronage to further a political goal. Maxim's smile soured, and the person beside him recoiled their leg away from Maxim's with a pale expression hinting at discomfort.

"I-I-I'm sorry . . . I-I didn't mean . . ."

Maxim relieved the unease. "Look, just give me your contact information and I will talk to him. I'm sure there's an explanation why his office has not responded."

Maxim handed the young man his phone and they proceeded to write down their number and name, Daniel Herrods.

"I will call you whenever I can give you a response from my brother," Maxim promised. Then to break the tension, he added, "I promise you, it will not be for a booty call." Daniel smiled in relief, amity returning to the table.

Edward, overhearing the conversation, turned to Maxim, coyly remarking on his friend's demure rebuff.

Maxim shrugged. "Eddy, he's not my type. And I suspect I'm not his either."

Lesser men than Maxim might had taken the prurient opportunity, but he knew it would have been little more than a cheap thrill. He wanted something of value, not a price to pay.

III

A feeling took hold of Maxim as the speeches and awards ended and the gala moved on to couples swaying and swooning across the dance floor. Maxim sensed he was being watched. He could not quite make out who it was, or where it was coming from, but the notion that some shadowy specter moving about the crowd was keeping an eye on him festered in the back of his head. The older crowd waltzed inelegantly to the sound of the jazz band while the young'uns clustered at the perimeter of the dance floor in their own digital solitudes.

"Honestly, I've seen nursing homes with better footwork," Maxim quipped to Edward as they observed the swirling mass of joviality trying to match the wrong dance style to the genre.

"Well darling, this is a crowd more used to The Village People than Cole Porter," Edward pointed out. "Did you pick out this music? This is frankly more your style of party."

"No, I did not, but the default genre of music for the rich tends to be jazz standards ... not that they appreciate this music that well either."

"I guess upper-class gays like to pretend they are Nick and Gatsby."

"And we get to stand here being Stadler and Waldorf."

Edward tried to hold back his laughter, turning away from Maxim to avoid spilling the drink he held onto his friend. He paused abruptly at the sight of someone he recognized across the ballroom. His expression, shocked and somewhat bemused, drew Maxim's attention.

"What is it, Eddy?"

"I can't believe it's him. What is that trash doing here? Unless he's in the closet I would never expect one of them to be at a place like this."

"Who? I can't see what you are gaping at."

"It's one of the Grenvill spawn, I think his name is Jamie."

"Grenvill? Like, Oliver Grenvill?"

"Bingo," Edward declared.

The Grenvills were new money, their fortune built on real estate and private equity. Isidor Grenvill, the family patriarch, had been sent to prison for embezzlement and insider trading a decade earlier. The family splintered into two cantankerous factions. Oliver belonged to one of them: belligerent, imperious, and always thriving from scandal and bad faith. His fame as a podcast host was propped up by his family's money. The other faction was religious and withdrawn, and had remained out of the limelight as much as possible after the fallout of Isidor's conviction.

Maxim stared out attentively, scanning for a target that continued to elude him. He knew that the Grenvills were not an attractive family. Money and beauty are never mutually exclusive, but Maxim found it telling that all the money that family had was never spent on making its members appear less detestable. Perhaps fitting that bad company should always remain bad looking.

Seeing that his friend was struggling to locate the intended victim of their scorn, Edward pointed in the direction of a stout older gentleman, clad in a garish magenta colored suit and white sneakers. He was looking away from them, talking to someone still concealed by the crowd of dancers between them. Maxim was bemused. The man was no more or less ostentatious than any of the other guests at the party.

"Edward, you make it seem like I'm supposed to react to an ogre that just crawled out from under a bridge. He looks like Madam Mim in male drag—it's not exactly a crime to look like that in this crowd."

Edward turned again in the direction of his target and exclaimed, "Not *him*, Max, the young man he's speaking to!"

Once the crowd finally parted to reveal the source of Edward's ire, there stood a long and elegant figure, a midnight blue suit perfectly tailored to drape delicately upon broad and lean shoulders. No wrinkles or sagging fabric, the richest shade of blue flowing unbroken from his chest down his narrow hips and terminating upon unblemished navy-blue velvet loafers. His smile . . . how could Maxim ever describe such a smile? A smile so warm and unencumbered by pretention. A kind of smile that one longs to see at least once in their lifetime, the sort of smile that embraces so totally and unapologetically that little else in this world could ever matter from that point forward. Maxim could not help himself looking at that young man. His delicate blue eyes twinkled in iridescent brilliance, his dark brunette locks gently caressing a face that just crested beyond the hills of adolescence into the long and fortuitous road to manhood. But that smile, those eyes, that was all that Maxim could focus on.

"Ed, there's no way in hell *he's* a Grenvill," Maxim scoffed at Edward, his eyes still transfixed by that celestial being across the ballroom floor. "The Grenvills are some of the ugliest people in all of high society. Oliver Grenvill looks exactly like the sort of repugnant rat that one expects to appear in his podcast."

"I know! I know! It's difficult to believe, isn't it? Out of all the ugly men and women to come out of that family, he solely won the genetic lottery."

"I just can't believe it. What was his name again?"

Edward gaped at Maxim's dumbfounded state. "Max! You look like a deer in headlights; it's like you've never seen a twink before."

Maxim recomposed himself, his unconscious reeling that he had just ogled at another man like some lustful teenager. *Maxim, you fucking moron!* he thought. *You're fifty-seven! Get your fucking act together!*

"I'm sorry Edward, I-I'm not sure what came over me."

"You like him, don't you?"

"Don't be absurd!" Maxim laughed nervously. "I'm old enough to be his father! I never liked being hit on by older men who wreaked of expired cologne and hemorrhoid cream at his age. Not to mention he could be as odious as the rest of the family."

"Who knows? By his family's standards, he must be the fallen angel to be hanging out with 'degenerates like us,' as his relative puts it."

"I think he's a party crasher reporting back to Oliver. I'm calling security," Maxim said, turning to locate a guard.

"I would hold your horses if I were you . . ." Edward tugged on Maxim's shoulder, pointing across the room to where Jamie was now speaking with Elliott Newsham.

"I guess now we have the perfect excuse to go talk to him," Edward said with a sly smile.

"No sweetie, I'm not going to be another sad queen chasing after fresh meat so he can get himself a Birkin."

"Alright, Max," Edward groaned. "It was just a suggestion . . . and maybe you're right. After all, it's only with time you find out whether a twink ages like wine or sours like milk. I'm going to get one last drink before I head out. Paul is going to become insufferable if I get home late."

"I'll come with you."

"Nonsense, I'll get you something. It's the least I can do for you inviting me."

Edward left Maxim by the edge of the dance floor and headed toward the bar. Maxim returned to gazing out into the crowd of cheerful revelers, the music changing from jazz to house with increasing electronic beat. The younger crowd, broken from their digital seclusion, began to invade the floor. Maxim hoped to grab one last glimpse of that smile, that smile so enraptured it had briefly robbed him of his loneliness. One more glimpse might be enough to carry him through the rest of his week.

That feeling of someone watching him returned, taking his mind off of searching for Jamie in the dim light of the dance floor. The diluted light obscuring the dancers, the harsh music, it all brought Maxim back to the fetid demimonde of his youth. He headed in the direction of the bar, hoping to catch Edward.

As more people made their way from their tables to the dance floor, Maxim had difficulty snaking through the crowd, growing impatient and distressed. The feeling of surveillance, of a thousand eyes examining him, intensified, but wherever he looked he found only eyes facing in every direction but his. He vehemently pushed forward through the crowd, but invariably when Maxim passed one reveler, he crashed into another.

A darkened figure spilled the drinks they held upon themselves and Maxim. Maxim exclaimed in annoyance, "Look what you've done, you goddamn idiot! What makes you think you—"

In one blink Maxim's flush of indignation paled. Within that darkened and crowded room he had managed to come face to face with Jamie Grenvill.

"Oh! Excuse me, I'm terribly sorry," Maxim whimpered in anxious penitence. "I'm so terribly sorry. Oh dear, I ruined your suit . . . please let me pay for . . ."

"No thank you," Jamie replied sullenly. "Maybe it's for the best my night ends here."

The warmth of the smile Jamie had bestowed upon others would be denied to Maxim. Jamie turned away and disappeared into the mass of revelers, and Maxim stood alone in that maelstrom. That feeling of surveillance that had imprisoned his thoughts released him. It must have been a premonition, he thought. That when something wonderful happens, there was always a presence of doom standing beside him, watching him, his inadequacy transcending into another moment of failure. *Here it is again, Maxim, another glimpse of happiness walking away into darkness.*

"There you are!" Edward cried out. "I went back to our spot and you had left. What's the matter, Max? You look utterly defeated."

That was exactly how Maxim felt, but then what else was new?

CHAPTER 3

I

"Sorry, Max," George responded to Maxim's question over dinner about the young Daniel Herrods. "I think he may have slipped between the cracks."

A week had passed since the gala, and Maxim was visiting George and Isabel at their townhouse near the park. There were moments when Maxim felt he had to leave Gwenshill to escape from his thoughts, and when he was not staying at the Lafayette Club downtown, he would stay the weekend with his brother.

"Well, I'm just letting you know to check if the credentials are good. He seemed very respectable."

"Did you sleep with him?" George asked his brother bluntly. Maxim tensed up, gripping his steak knife tightly in contempt at the question.

"George! What an insensitive thing to say!" belted Isabel, coming to Maxim's defense.

"What? He's not married, and you know how that crowd is," George responded.

"No George, I did not sleep with him. Just because we are gay doesn't mean we think about fooling around every chance we get," Maxim said.

"Look Max, I didn't mean to sound like that. After all, using sex to gain political advantage is old news."

"But that assertion can be thrown at both straight and queer people George," Isabel pointed out. "Thinking that sexual manipulation is a gay men's game is insensitive."

George turned to his brother. "Max, even counting that your right to marry is a recent one, I have yet to see a gay man other than you who's shown any interest in being in a true monogamous relationship. I cannot take an open-minded view that gay men want the same stable lifestyle that you are looking for. And the fact that you're still alone tells me all I need to know."

"George, my dating pool is small just on the count of the gay population being small. And it gets even smaller because of our background. There have been men who've shown interest, but it was easy to tell they only wanted me for my money."

"Honey, I have to agree with your brother," Isabel intervened. "And people like Max are still being denied the opportunity to form the same emotional and romantic bonds as you and I have and express it publicly."

George paused briefly from his meal and looked at Maxim and Isabel.

Maxim continued, "The media and the right only ever fixate on the sexual aspect of gay love and nothing else. My friends and I are reduced to an act, not real people. We never had good role models that were neither tragic nor farcical."

"Maxim, I just can't buy into that reasoning. Straight couples in everything from art and literature to philosophy have shown how two consenting adults should comport with themselves for hundreds of years. What, just because it's two of the same genitalia together, you need to reinvent everything about what it means to be in a relationship? To not cheat on one another? Or to stay together when things get hard? Or boring? No, it looks like gay men just throw all set standards of conduct out the window just because they can't overcome their own urges."

"George, that's a very uncharitable view to have."

"Straight people have urges too, I don't deny that. But when we straights, particularly men, don't show discipline in how we exercise those instincts, we suffer hurting the people around us, and we will be met with whatever consequences society will throw on our heads for acting upon said urges. By that measure, gay men get a free pass."

"What free pass? To be sexually open?"

"No, Max, to behave without principle."

Maxim turned to his sister-in-law with a snarky grin. "Then I hope Isabel is double-checking all the women interns you decide to hire, George."

Isabel smiled slyly. "Oh, I'm not worried. Besides, I have my own company to keep if he decides to chase blue dresses."

Isabel and Maxim laughed heartily. George took the jest in stride.

"The only blue dress I'm chasing is the one you will be wearing for our vacation, Izzy."

Maxim sat back in his seat, appreciating the rapport between George and Isabel. He was glad his brother had a strong and supportive marriage and liked being a part of their circle, especially when their daughter Charlotte was around. Maxim adored his niece as if she were his own.

"Where is little Charlie?" Maxim asked.

"She's staying at her friend's house for a sleepover," Isabel replied. "Although if you had dropped in sooner, I bet she would have wanted to spend time with you."

"I know, I know, I didn't mean to come on such short notice."

"Max, you're always welcome to visit," George reminded him. "There's a spare room for you here for a reason."

"But you could always come stay at the house with me, I need more excuses to open up the rooms other than just clearing the stale air."

George and Isabel looked at each other with some trepidation.

"I don't know, Max. That house gets so cold. How has it been with the heating bill?"

Max felt himself deflate. *Here we go again.*

"The bills have been lower since we replaced the furnaces, but we still choose to keep the heat just warm enough so the pipes don't freeze."

"My, that house is such a hassle," said Isabel. "Maybe when the weather is warmer, Charlotte can play in the pool. The breeze that house gets in July is just lovely."

"Perhaps when Congress goes into summer recess, we can spend a few weeks at Gwenshill," George agreed. He realized he had not been in the house in over a year; he thought he should at least check that his brother was still okay living in that enormous and melancholy house.

"That sounds perfect," responded Maxim, contented with even a half-hearted promise from George and Isabel.

Dinner continued with little discord. Maxim stayed for a cup of coffee and then decided to depart for the Lafayette Club. He had to appear at the foundation's office in the morning, and the club was only a few blocks away.

II

The Lafayette Club stood as a grand pile of stone at the corner of Park and Jubilee Streets. A neo-Gothic castle that stretched itself twelve stories into the air, looming high like a distorted fantasy from the Brothers Grimm, it had been built in the tradition of the old gentleman's clubs of England but had since evolved into a hotel that catered to members of the city's oldest families. Maxim retained a private suite here, an inherited membership that descended from the Deauvillier line of the family. The Magnus baths had been a gift to the club from Maxim's grandfather over a century ago. Its swimming pool, steam rooms, and saunas were designed in the classical tradition. Entering the baths, one was transported to another time, to the time of Plato and Euripides, of Alexander the Great, of Nero, of Augustus.

Maxim returned to the club after a long day of conference calls and reading over donation requests. His chronic exhaustion grew more intense whenever he had to be in the office. It never seemed to end, the calls for assistance from organizations across the country. The more funds that were passed forward, the less impact it seemed to have. Maxim's employees still held high spirits for their cause, but he himself remained resigned. At least in the heat of the club's steam rooms he could dissociate himself from the feeling of rolling a never-ending boulder from his shoulders.

The club had entered new management earlier that year. There were calls to renovate existing spaces in the building, and the Magnus baths were to be torn down and replaced. Too expensive to keep up, the area was to be stripped of its Grecian aura in favor of the monotone banality of the corporate look. Maxim was in no position to object to the baths' defacement as he did not have the capital to restore the building himself. The family fortune was entrusted to charities, and the allowance he received from the trust was only enough to cover a comfortable life, made spartan by the upkeep of Gwenshill.

Thus, for the last months the baths would remain in their current state, he was spending more time at the club, reading over documents in the club's library and eating lunch in the founders' dining room with some of the other legacies. During one such lunch a club member looked over at Maxim's plate with a smirk.

"On a diet, Porter? Not often you see a member sticking to the lighter fare."

"I tend to eat light most days," replied Maxim. "The new menu they introduced is not suiting my stomach."

"I see," conceded the other man, then went on. "Did you hear there's a new batch of members joining the club? Those Silicon Valley types and the rest."

"What happened? Did that 'Soho House' of theirs get rid of naptime?" Maxim quipped.

The members around the table chuckled, another responding, "Apparently, it's just to bring in fresh blood to pay for the renovations."

Another member chimed in: "Don't forget the private equity jackals, fondling themselves with the brands and legacies half this table created."

"Well at least they are barred from this table so long as I'm alive!"

"Yeah . . . barely!"

The table roared with slightly contemptuous laughter. Maxim enjoyed the low-grade snobbery. It resembled the cattiness of his gay friends. Still, the decadence of the affair was telling. Many of the men around that table were no different than Maxim, fourth- and fifth-generation wealth whose reputations were built on money that had long ceased to make a difference. They were all dinosaurs, in denial of the asteroid heading for their seats in that ornate room, its walls covered in the portraits and photographs of their long-dead ancestors.

"Well, gentlemen .. ." the first member cleared his throat. "Times are changing and we have to accept that the Lafayette Club needs to change with it. Last I spoke with management, the Grenvills will soon be wandering through our halls."

The Grenvills? Maxim thought for a moment. It could just be a stunt for status or clout. It would probably be a senior member of that clan visiting the place, perhaps Oliver Grenvill looking to find more backers to fund his putrid show. Maxim couldn't imagine that Jamie himself would be wandering through those faded halls. He didn't think that he would ever see Jamie's smile again, but there was always a little hopeful but illusory spark in his mind that he might.

III

As the months passed, the date for the refurbishment of the baths grew closer and Maxim made the point of visiting them even more frequently. The spaces themselves were emptying of users in anticipation of the baths' closure. Maxim enjoyed this solitude. He could just inhabit these spaces and delight in looking at the mosaics on the floors, the ornate capitals on the colonnade that surrounded the pool, the murals of young maidens and athletes in classical dress, without the white noise and distraction of old men pontificating about their vapid entitlement robbing the spaces of their regal serenity.

The initial anticipation of the appearance of a member of the Grenvill family proved to be a non-event. Yes, a member of the more secluded Grenvills had joined the ranks of the club, but he was never to be seen using any of the spaces or amenities, or even entering the building. Things continued as normal, except for that recurring feeling Maxim had of someone or something observing him.

It came in waves, never in the same location or situation. He sat in the library reading Vonnegut and instinctively sensed someone standing behind him reading over his shoulder, only to turn around to find no one.

The feeling grew most intense in the main restaurant. Maxim usually sat in the center of the room, but began to request a seat in a sheltered corner so he could gaze out over the main space, hoping to see if anyone was watching him eat. Dementia could be the unsettling answer to this, Maxim had worried, recalling how his grandmother and one of his uncles had begun developing mental issues earlier than expected. He even fretted that having lived alone without a partner as long as he had could bring about the dreaded disease sooner. But he had received a bill of clean health from his doctor, and his diet and exercise routine were better than other men of his age. Still the feeling of surveillance persisted.

Maxim felt less uneasy inside the baths. Late at night, one could hear the echoes of footsteps bouncing about the marble and tiled surfaces, and the only footsteps he heard were his own. Maxim began at the edge of the swimming pool, the colonnade surrounding its enclosure forming a sacred grove from which he dove into the luminous blue pond at its center. He began to swim laps back and forth, each stroke a growing struggle that his long arms had to overcome. His upper body was better built to handle the arduous task of pressing and pushing against the force of the water; his legs would flap about in quick and compact movements but could not quite maintain the pace his upper body demanded. He swam a handful of laps before that surveilled feeling returned. There was someone in the swimming hall with him. He stopped his stride in the middle of the pool and called out.

"Hello?"

Silence persisted.

"Anyone there?" Maxim called out once more.

He heard footsteps behind the colonnade, but from the center of the pool he could not make out a figure walking in the shadow of those columns. He then heard the door to the steam room open, its creaking hinge screeching into the room beyond.

Perhaps it meant nothing; even though the baths were empty, the club itself was fully occupied. There was always a chance it was just some insomniac member deciding to sit in the steam late in the night. But Maxim had to find out. He swam to the edge and emerged from the pool. Grabbing his towel from the bench, Maxim proceeded to march to the steam rooms. He opened the squeaking brass door and entered that humid fog.

The room was large enough for two seating areas divided by a wall, but the mist in the room was so dense it was hard to make sense of the scale of the room or tell there was someone there. Maxim squinted his eyes trying to discern a recognizable silhouette, pacing through the dense cloud from one sitting area to the other. After a few minutes of seeing and hearing nothing, he shrugged his shoulders and conceded it may have been all in his head.

"I need to call Dr. Wells tomorrow," he said to himself, only to be jolted by the feeling of an unknown hand resting upon his shoulder.

Maxim leapt in fright and turned to face the mystery figure. He grabbed the person by the shoulders and pushed them against the parting wall of the steam room. Adrenaline fueled his alarm into a fury. Maxim jumped into a state of self-preservation, grabbing his assailant by the arm and pressing them forcefully against the cold tiled wall.

Maxim breathed rapidly in his anxious haze, but as he saw that his opponent remained still, he began to make sense of who he was holding by the arm. The dark and wet brunette locks, those blue eyes, and that face, so aloof and romantic, now so anguished by the tight grip of Maxim's clinching hand, belonged to none other than Jamie Grenvill.

"Please, you're hurting me," Jamie whimpered. "I couldn't hear you. I had my earbuds in."

Maxim's eyes widened in shock. "What the hell were you thinking?" he scolded Jamie. "You scared me half to death! And what are you doing here in this blasted building?"

Jamie pushed Maxim's hands away from him, breathing heavily.

"My uncle is a member—h-he lets me stay here under his name."

"How long have you been coming here?"

"Sorry?" Jamie responded blankly.

"How long have you been coming to the Lafayette Club without anyone noticing you?"

"For the last month or so. I only come during the night. My family kicked me out of the house."

"Why? Does your family know you're here?"

"No. I . . . I came out to them, and my family didn't want to hear it. I refused to go back into the closet to make them happy and they threw me out because of it."

"Threw you out? How old are you?"

"I'm twenty-six . . . look, it's complicated. My uncle is letting me stay here until I can find work."

"I see." Maxim found himself saddened by Jamie's circumstance. "I'm sorry to hear that."

"I'll be okay, this is just temporary."

Jamie sighed, looking at the floor as if searching for something.

"My earbuds fell on the floor, and I can't see them. Do you know how to shut this steam off?"

Maxim pulled on a lever by the door and propped the door open to let the mist dissipate. Within minutes the room was clear of steam and Jamie spotted the little white earpieces on the floor.

"Thanks," Jamie said, wiping at them with his towel. He leaned against the wall, his body glistening against the light of the room. Maxim saw the gentle ripples of sweat descend the lean and composed figure of Jamie's physique. With his towel tightly wrapped around his waist, Jamie resembled one of the figures that graced the murals just outside the room. Jamie noticed Maxim gazing at his body, transfixed, and his face turned playful.

"Come on man, you don't get with younger guys?" Jamie said with a grin. "I assumed you have the pick of the crop with shoulders like yours."

Maxim flushed with embarrassment, instinctively holding his own towel in front of his manhood. It was an uncomfortable realization that he was fully twice Jamie's age. He timidly responded.

"Forgive me, I keep to myself these days. And the flattery is nice, but I don't go for younger men."

"It's alright, I don't go for older men myself. Just something about you gives me the impression that there's still an energy within you that most men your generation lack."

"What do you mean?"

"Not every day you get a sixty-something-year-old man pinning you against the wall with their strong grip ready to fight," Jamie flirted with boyish mischief in his eyes. Maxim himself felt compelled; the thrill of being caught with a beautiful younger man was a long-forgotten fantasy of his. And Jamie's gaze spoke of that elemental urge, the most primeval and carnal of instincts.

"Makes someone wonder what they would do to someone in bed."

Jamie looked intently at Maxim, his eyes two iridescent portals that seemed lit from within. They beckoned Maxim like lighthouse beacons calling battered ships back to safe harbor. Or perhaps it was the way an anglerfish dangled its light before its prey, compelling it to surrender itself to its mortal fate. Maxim could not overcome the pull of those whirlpools of light. Paradise or perdition, he found himself pulled toward Jamie, his sight finally growing black as their lips pressed tightly together.

The crash of a distant door and incoming footsteps outside the steam room interrupted them, breaking the sexual tension that hung as dense as the mist that it superseded. Maxim realized that all this time the door had been open. Somebody could have walked in and seen the two of them; it could have become a scandal that Maxim could never live down.

Maxim pushed away from Jamie and walked nervously out of the steam room, leaving that beautiful young man behind without a word. All he could think was that he hoped the closure of those baths would happen as soon as possible.

CHAPTER 4

I

Just a block away from Edward's beachside bungalow, a small café sat on the main road that cut through the Islands. July had been a very busy month along the shores of that sheltered haven away from the city. It could not compare with the month prior, when the streets and beaches were swollen with tourists and locals wishing to revel in the celebrations and parades that carried on day and night. Still, there were hundreds of men of every age and complexion wandering around town, galivanting to the restaurants and bars that served more salubrious fares during the day to aid recovery from the decadent excesses of the night.

Edward had invited Maxim to stay at his bungalow on the Islands with him and his husband Paul. Edward and Paul were their own chaotic brand of steady companionship. Edward, always the more mature of the couple, had to keep an eye on Paul's wandering eye whenever young men would wander past their beachfront porch, looking for the gay clubs dotted along the coastline. Paul himself often behaved like a sulky teenager who never grew up, becoming needy and insecure after a few drinks whenever Edward would flirt with other men in the local shops. In the past the two had had their own circles of trysts and mutual acquaintances, but in their old age they preferred to remain exclusively with each other, watching old movies on lazy Sunday afternoons and tenderly falling asleep in each other's arms.

"Why couldn't they serve something less fattening?" Edward grumbled through his hangover as he scanned over the café's menu.

"You could have some eggs and grilled tomato," Maxim suggested while looking over his own.

"Max dear, you're not allowed to speak. You didn't drink last night."

"Yes I did, I had four gin and tonics."

"That barely constitutes drinking for a man your size."

"Eddy, do you have the seltzer tablets in your bag?" interjected Paul, rubbing his pulsating temples.

"Well, it's not like we can drink the way we did when we were younger," Maxim said resignedly. "I'm just glad we're not in nursing homes just yet."

"Not according to my new AARP card!" Edward laughed, pulling out the plastic rectangle from his satchel and waving it at Maxim. "I'm ready to take my place as the nursing home tramp!"

"Wow . . . sixty-five already?" Maxim had forgotten how long he and Edward had even been friends. Thirty years? More?

"Yep, it's about time. I hope the nurse that will be feeding me will be one of those gorgeous himbos. The Latin ones are always so sweet and bubbly."

"You, needing a nurse?" Maxim laughed. "I think Paul might have something to say about that."

"Oh, I don't know," Paul teased. "He's thinking of trading me for a newer model, I can feel it."

"Newer model my foot. I'm going to be driving you mad until the wheels fall off," Edward declared with a playful side-eye.

The trio carried on with their brunch as they discussed that evening's plans. Paul and Edward wanted to host a small gathering at their place with some of the old acquaintances in town. Maxim was game so long as it would not turn into a rowdy affair. He had never been keen on loud parties; the booming noise and hectic atmosphere of most clubs exacerbated his anxiety. After a few drinks he could tolerate the energy of a gay club, but finding more casual places in his circles was rare. He would usually just resort to hanging out in straight venues, even if he really wanted to be around other gay men.

Maxim noticed a group of dainty young men making their way toward the table. One of them, who turned out to be Dillon the ex-houseboy, waved and called out to Paul. What surprised Maxim, however, was that Jamie was among the group of babbling twinks.

"Hiii Pauly! Hi Eddy!" Dillon sang.

"Hey Dill, nice to see you here!" Paul replied cheerfully. "What are you boys doing tonight?"

Edward looked at Maxim, rolling his eyes in annoyance. For as much as Edward loved Paul, he had to accept that when it came to younger men, Paul could not override the brain that resided between his legs.

"We are heading over to The Rectory tonight, if you want to come along and have some fun with us?" Dillon chirped.

Maxim could see what Edward meant by the twenty-five-year-old looking older than he did. The use of tanning beds was doing a lot of damage to his skin. The crow's feet that were forming around his eyes were subtle but noticeable, though one would probably fail to see them in a darkened bar when the alcohol took its effect.

"The Rectory? I haven't been there yet. How is it, Dill?" Paul went on.

"Oh it's so great! Seriously, you should come with us tonight. We want to have some sexy daddies to dance with us."

"We'll think about it, Dillon. We had a lot to drink last night," Edward hedged.

"Oh *please*, Pauly," Dillon pressed on. "I have some friends that want to meet you, I showed them your profile on Instagram and they think you're super cute."

Paul gave Edward a begging look, like a little boy asking his mother if he could go play with his friends. Edward's disapproval was evident but he agreed that Paul could go if Edward went along.

"Yaass!" Dillon yelled out, then turned to Maxim. "What about you, Daddy? My friend here wants you to come also."

Maxim looked over at Jamie, who was the polar opposite of Dillon. His face still glowed with youth underneath a white Panama hat, his hair poking out in thick wavy locks. Maxim could not read the expression under Jamie's large sunglasses, but a faint smile poked through the stoic visage. Jamie wanted him to join them, though Maxim dreaded the idea of repeating their claustrophobic first encounter. Or the awkward ending of their second.

"Come with us, Max," Edward chimed in. "We can always leave early."

"Alright, I'll come," Maxim finally agreed.

"Awesome! Let's all meet in front, say 8:30? Great, we'll see you daddies later!" Dillon and his friends scurried away. Jamie trailed behind them, walking with stately poise as though purposely setting himself apart. He looked back at Maxim one last time, giving that playful smile.

"Nice seeing you again, sir."

II

Maxim dreaded the idea of going into the nightclub, especially when he felt the intense basal thundering that reverberated outside the entrance. Paul and Edward stood in front of Maxim, courted by the gaggle of young men they had encountered earlier that day. Jamie stood nonchalantly at Maxim's side, looking forward at the line ahead of them. Maxim and Jamie's hands grazed each other, creating sparks of attraction that made Maxim feel uneasy and yet titillated. What was this strange pull that rippled throughout his body and transformed into sparks of electricity that cascaded from his hand and into Jamie's? How had he never felt this with another man before? As the interminable line crawled forward, Maxim inwardly pondered the men of his past.

There had been Alister, the concert violinist whom Maxim had met at twenty-four while in his master's program at Yale. Alister was a dashing and eloquent gentleman who held court near the university in between concerts for the New York and Boston Symphonies. Alister embodied the most regal of British sensibilities, never mind that he had come from a Persian family. He took to afternoon tea, practicing Mendelssohn in the morning and reading Wordsworth into the late hours of the night. Alister was a tender and passionate lover, but his social standing and culture kept him from committing himself to Maxim.

There was Fernand, the Bohemian painter who lived in an endless daze of parties and narcotic abandon. Born to a Detroit aristocracy now long dead, he took to fretting away his inheritance in search of an artistic breakthrough, and Maxim had been his brief muse. But brief was all that became of the affair, as Fernand was destitute, drug-addled, and dead before the age of thirty.

There was Ethan, the tech developer who made his millions in the late nineties. Ethan was intense and calculating, a coldness that Maxim was empathetic to only because Ethan was what doctors would now call neurodivergent. Underneath that ruthless ambition, Ethan was a kind man, but time and ego had corrupted him. Richer than he could ever be, Ethan turned to religion and disavowed his homosexuality in pursuit of attaining proximity to God. (Or, in Maxim's opinion, more like Ethan desired to grow closer to God so he could one day usurp him.)

There was Carter. He had ambitions to work in the Treasury. He and Maxim were intellectual equals who enjoyed having long-winded conversations about anything that crossed their minds and sparring with one another over the dinner table and in the bedroom. Sharp-tongued and full of wit, Carter was the sort of man Maxim felt he could present for his family's approval. But Carter had been raised a southerner, and his ingrown homophobia crawled unevenly upward the same way his Georgia twang escaped his smooth Wall Street prose. Carter could not overcome his fear of holding Maxim's hand in the daylight, ultimately choosing instead to marry a woman whom he then gave HIV. He moved back to Savannah and ended up running the local gay bar.

Too many men had crossed Maxim's path. A few were memorable, but most were not: trysts that thrilled and chilled but went nowhere. Lengthy conversations and tender longings that died between bedsheets. Why had it taken so many decades for this kind of electric charge to build between himself and this twenty-six-year-old next to him? Could it have been what the universe called for? That perhaps your soulmate could have been held back in the universal assembly line of fate, or maybe you were the one who got pushed forward, ahead of your time in romance?

Jamie looked up at Maxim in brief intervals, giving a polite smile, his eyes twinkling behind those dark sunglasses. The sun was just setting on the horizon and the last of its light was striking the party's faces. It was then that the group arrived at the entrance of the club.

"Alright boys, let's see some IDs," barked the bouncer at the door.

One by one the group began to pull out their IDs and hand them over to be scanned. Jamie fumbled through his pockets and wallet, looking irritated. Maxim turned to him and asked what the matter was.

"I can't find my driver's license," Jamie said. "It must have fallen out of my pocket."

"Do you remember where you were last?"

"I was walking the boardwalk from the hotel. I think it must have fallen there."

Maxim could have said that he would wait for Jamie at the front door, or that he would see Jamie inside the club. He had no obligation to stay with him and go searching for that license.

"Then I'll come with you."

Jamie and Maxim broke away from the group. Maxim's friends, already passing the entrance's threshold, did not notice the two leave and head back toward the boardwalk.

The two walked along the shoreline as the sky finally grew dark, only illuminated by the lights that ran along the path. Maxim looked intently at the ground with each step, trying to notice anything that resembled an ID on the wooden slats of the boardwalk.

"I'm sorry Jamie, I'm afraid you may have lost your license," Maxim finally said, resigned.

"My license?" Jamie grinned. "My license is back at the hotel."

"I don't understand." Maxim stopped mid-stride.

"I just needed a convincing excuse to pull away. Techno just gives me a splitting headache." Jamie smiled. "And I also wanted to get to know you better."

"Know me?"

"After all, you know my name is James, or Jamie. I ran into you at the Mattachine Gala, and obviously again at the Lafayette. Yet I don't know your name."

"My name?" Maxim was taken aback that after all this time he had never bothered to introduce himself to Jamie. "God, you're right. I'm Maximillian, but you can call me Maxim or Max. I'm sorry. It must have totally escaped me."

"Maximillian?" Jamie chuckled. "Now that's an old-money name, surely beats Devon or Trystan."

Maxim chuckled back. They had found themselves at the end of the boardwalk, where the beach stretched out a few miles further toward the old lighthouse.

"Look," Jamie said with a mischievous smile. "Why don't you make it up to me? Let's walk to the lighthouse, and then we can get to know each other a little. You at least owe me a good story as to why you like to punch boys and then kiss them."

Maxim nodded and the two of them made their way across the beach, the moon rising above the night sky illuminating their path. They walked for hours into the night, past the lighthouse and all the way around the Island, then sat together by the shore. The night could have lasted for eternity, until the sun rose once more on another day.

III

"You're up early," Edward said as Maxim walked into the kitchen at six the next morning.

"Eddy, you're mistaken, I haven't slept the whole night," Maxim responded. "I'm exhausted . . . why are you up?"

"I left The Rectory early, the music was just too excessive, and I felt like a member of the walking dead among all the jacked-up twinks and hustlers." Edward took a deep sip from his coffee mug. "Paul is with

Dillon so I'm not too worried. But why didn't you sleep? I assumed you left earlier than we did. Weren't you upstairs?"

"No, I went walking along the beach with Jamie." Maxim sighed. "We spent the whole night talking to each other. He really is something special."

Edward gave a cheeky grin but then it dawned on him who his friend was referring to.

"Wait . . . the Grenvill boy? Max, I know I joked with you at the party that you should go talk to that young man, but seriously? Jamie Grenvill?"

"Oh, come on, Edward. He's actually a very nice person, and he can't help that he was born into that family. Something I can honestly relate to."

"Max, from what you've told me your family didn't come from thieving and cheating people. Didn't your grandfather make home goods? What is so evil about making electric toasters?"

"Ed . . ." Maxim sighed. "He's just a boy; he doesn't have a supporting family. We were lucky even by our own generation's standards. It's a shame that this mindset still exists in his."

Edward looked off to the side and huffed. His own upbringing had not been easy; he himself had looked for guidance from an older man in his youth. Maybe, he considered, this young 'black sheep' of the Grenvill family could become better with someone like Maxim to guide him. He turned once more to his friend.

"Look, I suppose you're right . . . even though I have my doubts, if you want to see where this goes with him than I guess I can't tell you no. Just be careful, okay?"

"I will," Maxim said with resolve. "At least he's not another sugar baby looking for his payday. He's ambitious, and he doesn't need my money to get his way."

CHAPTER 5

I

Maxim was experiencing feelings he had forgotten he'd ever had. The intense emotions came in both roaring mounds reaching upward into the sky and deep furrows where the only thing that he could feel was anxiety—an anxiety he had been struggling with for most of his life. Maxim felt out of place in this new relationship and was never sure how to behave around Jamie. Though Jamie carried himself easily, seeming unfazed by the realities of the thirty-year age gap between them, Maxim couldn't help feeling nervous walking around town on dates with such a dashing young man, the unnerving sense that all eyes were on them, judging him for taking away such a beautiful youth for his own private corruptions.

"Do you like getting called a daddy by younger men?" Jamie asked Maxim on one of their dates. "Or do you prefer being called sir?"

"No . . . not really," Maxim replied. "I never liked the implication of that word."

"Then what do you prefer?"

Maxim pondered briefly, looking back to his innocent companion.

"Just call me Max. I believe in being equal partners in relationships." Maxim paused. "I don't want you to feel like I'm above you in any way because of my age."

Jamie returned a sly grin. "You above me? Only in private I hope."

Maxim felt it a harsh hypocrisy that if he had ended up with a twenty-something woman, their union might not have read so pruriently. Or if Jamie had ended up with an older woman, it might have been seen as a feminist triumph. The crime of old age usurping youth in exchange for money was the one-dimensional mindset of those who looked at Jamie and Maxim so unfavorably. So Maxim refrained from holding Jamie's hand when the streets were crowded with people. On car and subway rides, Maxim grasped Jamie's thigh gently only when his hand was concealed beneath his messenger bag.

The quiet moments, like when they walked through the park in late October, saw the frigid anxiety thaw into a more tender affection between the two men. Maxim was comfortable being himself without pretense. Jamie would hold close to his partner's side, sharing stories of his childhood and of his time in boarding school, bestowing that gracious smile that gave Maxim such a thrill. Those early months filled Maxim's melancholy heart to its romantic heights, but winter proved to be an adversary to their budding intimacy. Jamie had found work at an investment firm that demanded more and more of his time. Maxim had his own schedule to consider; the family charities grew more hectic with the coming of the holiday season and he found himself needing to command the foundation from their city office more often than from Gwenshill.

Maxim saw less and less of Jamie, and even the text messages they shared were growing sparse, sitting un-responded-to for days on end. Maxim could not get used to this digital means of communication. There were so many things he wished to say, so many thoughts, feelings, and opportunities to connect he could not encapsulate in a block of text. He found it absurd that younger generations found this normal, the anxiety of using such impersonal means to maintain attachment to one another. Maxim felt like he was grasping at straws, but his own rationale conditioned him to think back to the novels he loved, in which lovers divided by space and time interacted via long letters sent to each other by chariot. They had the patience to accept that love by long distance could only travel as fast as the messenger's horse. But there was no horse taking days to connect Maxim and Jamie, only electrons flowing through antennas that promised instant relief.

Jamie was more pragmatic about their situation. He had to make a good impression at work, and to maintain the cost of living near the city center demanded a large salary. His family wealth afforded him a lifestyle he was accustomed to, and he was vehement that he did not want help from Maxim to maintain his lifestyle. Maxim was both understanding and frustrated. Jamie wanted to prove himself so fervently that Maxim could not help growing even fonder of him. Jamie embodied something that Maxim had always wanted to be, and in this small way, he lived vicariously through Jamie's drive and ambition.

Though their text messages were intermittent during those colder months, they did manage a few long phone calls that stretched late into the night. Maxim found immense comfort in Jamie's warm and mischievous voice; hearing its melodic tones helped bring to mind that gentle smile and those bright blue eyes.

"You worry too much about me, Maxim," Jamie told him. "I can handle the work."

"I just care, that's all. I miss you."

"You don't need to. I am always around, and I think about you a lot even when we don't see each other as much."

"I think about you too, my dear Jamie."

"I like it when you call me *your* dear Jamie."

"You do?"

"I don't know why, it's as if I belong to you in some way . . . I know we're equals in this. But . . . oh, it's just me being stupid."

Maxim chuckled. "It's okay, Jamie. I understand."

"Oh God!" Jamie broke in. "It's so late, we've been talking for hours. Why didn't you say anything?"

"Have we? Oh, you're right . . . wow, it's getting late."

"And me keeping you up like this," Jamie said with concern.

"It's not your fault, time flies when I talk to you."

"You're too sweet Max. But I should be more considerate."

"Then hopefully soon we'll see each other. Have a good night my dear Jamie."

"I can't wait to kiss you again, have a good night handsome."

Maxim would have remained talking to Jamie until sunrise if he could, he felt so young speaking to Jamie. It was a youth that only blossoming love could carry forth, a love that Maxim yearned for so long and was finally thawing his frigid heart.

II

"Are you going to marry me or what?"

The question, which Jamie put forth with coy indignation, had come so unexpectedly to Maxim's ears that he felt as if he had been hit by a freight train. Maxim and Jamie had been together for over a year at this point, and Maxim was deeply in love with Jamie. Though in the back of his mind he thought their relationship was never going to last, there had been many dates, holidays, and family events that spoke to the contrary. Maxim's family had learned, if not to accept Jamie, to at least tolerate the fact that he was the one man that had managed to stick around Maxim the longest.

"What?" was Maxim's eventual dumbfounded reply.

"Max, I'm not going to keep waiting for you to finally get on one knee and ask, 'Will you marry me?' . . . Don't you love me?"

Maxim was lost for words. Jamie, seeing in Maxim's gaze that his mind was jammed in anxious whirring, leaned forward and kissed Maxim as an antidote. It worked. Maxim, his mind cleared, was able to respond calmly.

"James, I do love you . . . but do you really want to end up married to an old man like me? Think of all the beautiful younger guys you could have. Men who could give you more passion, more energy, more everything than I can give you at my age. I am nearing sixty, after all."

"Maximillian, don't insult me," Jamie snapped impatiently. "I have been with men much younger than you. Do you think I would have stayed with you if I didn't think you were more than man enough for me?"

"This is still completely new to me," Maxim protested. "I've never had a relationship that has lasted this long. And at the same time, what is the rush?"

"Rush? We've been together for a year."

"You can't really know someone over the span of one year, James."

Jamie shrugged. "That's what marriage is for! A relationship is a journey, and marriage is a commitment between two people to go on the journey together."

"Jamie . . . my dear Jamie," Maxim sighed. "I'm already decades ahead in this journey."

"I'll catch up," Jamie teased. "Your family likes me, we have plenty in common, and—"

"Please understand," Maxim interrupted. "I've been alone for too long."

Maxim stood and began to pace about the room, avoiding Jamie's direct gaze.

"James, you know about all the medication I've been taking. Don't you want someone who doesn't need to consume pills like Tic Tacs just to process his existence?"

"You're being ridiculous," Jamie replied. "You suffer from trauma, which is nothing to be ashamed about. You're not an addict or an alcoholic; you're not controlling or abusive. My family is not supportive in the slightest, so I am not one to judge either. At least you are open enough to share your insecurities with me, and I love you more because of it."

"But James, I've never really loved anyone before you. There's just something about me that—"

"That nothing!" Jamie interrupted. "You're complex, that's all. If the men that came before me could not see the decent person you are, that's their loss."

Maxim persisted. "You don't want this, James. The time for me to love like a young man has come and gone. You don't want me."

Jamie crossed to the bar cabinet and poured himself a whiskey, taking a long pull before turning back to Maxim.

"Max. I know what I want, and I don't think I could say I've ever felt more connected to any other man than I have to you."

"But Jamie, we're three decades apart. My best years are behind me and yours are just ahead of you."

"Exactly." Jamie held firm. "My best years are ahead of me, and frankly I'd want to give my best to be with you. I love you, Maximillian, and if I can't be by your side as your husband . . . then frankly, why continue to be like this?"

Maxim was exasperated. "Jamie, please! Think of your future. It's pathetic that I am old enough to be your—"

"Don't say it!" Jamie interjected angrily, hurling the glass of whiskey to the floor, where it shattered into pieces. Tears began to stream down his face. "My own father cannot accept who I am. I don't need another man to tell me he doesn't want me."

Jamie covered his face with his hands and leaned against the wall. The sight of his tears finally broke Maxim's resolve to be reasonable. He could not bear that Jamie felt so lonely, or so intense a desire to be in Maxim's life. Maxim had cried his own tears over so many a broken heart; he did not want to be the one to inflict this upon Jamie. He grabbed a handkerchief from his pocket and began to wipe the tears from Jamie's eyes.

"Jamie . . . I'm so sorry for hurting you. I promise that I'll never hurt you."

Jamie looked up at Maxim, his eyes more glittering than ever.

"Jamie, there's no greater an honor than for me to ask you . . ." Maxim knelt to one knee, holding his lover's hands, never breaking his gaze.

"Jamie Grenvill, will you marry me?"

Jamie's body trembled and he began to tear up once more, but these were joyful tears as he ecstatically embraced Maxim.

"Maximilian Porter, of course I will!"

III

Maxim's family were less than enthusiastic about the announcement. George, always protective of his older brother, was most vocal in calling out the unsuitability of Jamie and Maxim's engagement, but his protestations fell on deaf ears. Maxim had already made up his mind, and he knew that George's objections, while coming partly out of genuine concern for his brother, were also tied to his own political career. Eventually Jamie met with Isabel and they worked together to persuade the two brothers to reconcile. Henry Porter, for his part, was bemused by the ordeal but remained mum about what he made of his son's soon-to-be husband. He knew only that his vain efforts at playing cupid had come to an end.

The true debacle of the pending marriage was between the families' lawyers. Jamie's family may have never approved of their son's homosexuality or his marriage to Maxim, but when it came to the division of assets, they butted in to make it clear their son would not sign any prenuptial agreement. Jamie had to embark on his own fight with his family over their hypocrisy and greed. Unromantic as it may have been, Jamie signed the pre-nuptials, and his family returned to their unrepentant exclusion.

The wedding was a small affair, with a handful of friends from both Jamie's and Maxim's circles. Though none of the Grenvills attended the ceremony, which did not surprise or faze Jamie, the immediate Porter family was present to see Maxim's happiness come to fruition. This blissful scene could not be a greater opposite to the memory that had haunted Maxim since the funeral. He had finally achieved the one goal in life he never thought possible, to be with someone he loved who loved him in return. Age meant nothing to Maxim now. He could live forever if he wanted to, because Jamie would be there by his side always.

IV

For their honeymoon, Jamie gifted Maxim an extravagant six-week tour of Europe: three weeks in the Mediterranean Sea followed by three weeks in Vienna, Prague, and Hamburg, with a return passage back to the United States on the Queen Mary 2. Maxim floated on a cloud of romantic exuberance at his new husband's gesture.

"Jamie, this is too much!" Maxim gushed as they boarded the plane to Nice for the first leg of the trip. "You should have let me pay for some of this. After all, I'm the established one of this pair."

"Don't be silly. I worked hard for the money, and frankly I like the idea of being the sugar daddy," Jamie laughed.

Maxim could only grin at the irony of his rich young upstart catering to the needs of an older escort. It was certainly the sort of story one could pass around the old circles of queens and fairies with haughty glee, perhaps even lowering Edward's skepticism of Jamie. *How comforting it is to see the shoe on the other foot,* Maxim thought. But Maxim had to show some restraint—he knew that Jamie was just out to impress, and that flights of fancy were something that could only be enjoyed on much stronger foundations. Still, the rapturous glee of being with someone so charming, vital, and self-assured gave enormous strength to his formerly weary soul.

Though Maxim enjoyed himself on their travels, he found that the specter of being surveilled had returned. It would creep here and there like an insect buzzing infernally around one's face only to fly away at the first swat. The feeling grew more intense in the evening, Maxim often awakening during the night to find Jamie sleeping beside him restfully. The door to their room was locked, the windows were drawn closed, and the city outside was quiet; eventually the feeling would go away as Maxim gazed at the serenity of Jamie's face beside him and drifted back to sleep.

"*Uno espresso doppio. Grazie!*" Maxim called out to the waiter as he and Jamie sat at a café outside of the royal palace.

"Maxie, I think you asked for two espressos, not a double," Jamie said between sips of his cappuccino.

Maxim paused briefly, covering his mouth with the back of his hand as he yawned.

"Eh, it will still be two of the same thing. More dishes for them to clean otherwise."

Jamie looked at Maxim with some worry as he yawned again.

"Are you okay, Max? You seem to not be sleeping as well. Besides those times I keep you up for a reason, that is." He winked.

"It's nothing, just that weird feeling of being watched. I spoke to the doctors already."

"I remember you telling me that, is it anything serious?"

"They don't think so, otherwise I'd be showing other symptoms."

"Other symptoms?" Anxiety crept into Jamie's tone. He placed his cup down on the table. Maxim held Jamie's hand to reassure him.

"I'm fine! Both sides of my family had sharp minds all the way into their eighties and even nineties. I promise you I will never need you to become my nurse."

Jamie smiled. "That's a relief then." He paused. "When did this feeling start happening?"

"Funny enough, during that gala when we first met," Maxim said unthinkingly.

"I see . . ." Jamie trailed off, took one last drink of his coffee, and turned to face the crowds of tourists passing by their table. His tone turned condescending.

"Honestly Max, tourists are so slovenly these days. It is like no one knows how to dress properly."

It was the first time Maxim had heard Jamie talk in such a snooty way. Though of course it wasn't unheard of within their class, it was uncharacteristic of Jamie to be mean-spirited. But he kept going.

"Look at that family over there, covered in brands like uncouth billboards. Talk about trash begetting trash."

Maxim tried a diplomatic approach. "If the clothes give them confidence why shouldn't they have the right to wear them? Class and taste are things that can't be bought."

"Max, these peasants like to pretend that they are like us. And yet their conception of how the upper classes actually dress is utterly distorted. Take that ogre over there with the Burberry flat cap and the Balenciaga sneakers. My God, I'd rather be caught dead than dress like that."

"Didn't your cousin Oliver appear on Fox News wearing a Versace shirt?" Maxim reminded Jamie. "Isn't that a bit hypocritical?"

"My cousin is a different story. He earned the right to dress like a clown to appear in that circus of fools."

Maxim noticed more moments of spiteful jest or unfamiliar venom from Jamie throughout the rest of the trip, but it was never directed at Maxim, and Jamie was still a very loving and kind partner to him. *A rose with thorns is still a rose*, Maxim thought; *one just has to be careful where to place their hands before appreciating its beauty.* But he couldn't help feeling a stirring of unease. Though his sense of surveillance had dissipated once again after that conversation at the café, this unease crept further, so indescribable yet so familiar.

CHAPTER 6

I

Gwenshill had been left closed off while Jamie and Maxim were on their honeymoon, kept to just a handful of staff, the windows and doors shuttered, all the furniture covered in cloth to avoid dust settling into the ornate fabrics. Maxim expected that he would return to find the mansion as they had left it.

"Home sweet home," Maxim sang as he and Jamie drove along the country roads that crossed through Gwendolyn Park to the house. "I hope Luisa has some food prepared. It'll be nice to return to a home-cooked meal."

"I find it so quaint that your housekeeper is also your cook," Jamie remarked as he looked out over the green parkland, his wavy curls blowing in the wind. "I think my family would go through a new chef every six months. My relatives were always so petty when it came to food."

"Why's that? Different diets?"

"Different fads. They only ate what was trendy."

"Well, you've had Luisa's food. And I'm sure she will be glad to see us."

Jamie stayed silent, and as they got closer to the property, it began to feel to Maxim like he was avoiding saying something important. When they reached the gatehouse, Maxim stopped the car, noticing that the wrought iron gates that led to their drive were now closed.

"That's odd." Maxim placed the car in park. "I haven't seen these gates closed since we had actual gatekeepers. One of the staff must have closed them and forgot we were coming back today."

Maxim turned off the car and began to unbuckle his seatbelt.

"Max, what are you doing?" Jamie asked, faking bemusement.

"What do you mean? I'm going to go and open the gates. You wait here."

"I don't think that's necessary," Jamie answered with a mischievous grin. Maxim looked at him with suspicion.

"James . . . what do you know about the gates being closed?"

Jamie smiled innocently. "Oh nothing, just say 'open sesame' and they will open by themselves."

"Jamie, don't be silly. I'm—"

"No, I'm serious. Come on, say it."

Maxim did not like to play games, but he entertained the gesture just for Jamie's amusement. And upon his call of 'open sesame,' the gates indeed opened automatically. Jamie pulled out a remote opener he had been hiding under the car seat and waved it at Maxim.

"That's a nice surprise. Any more surprises you're keeping to yourself?" Maxim asked.

Jamie grinned. "For that, my dear Maxim, I think we need to get home first."

Maxim drove on through the gates, a bit warily, but little else seemed different. Only after the first curve around the hill where the mansion stood did Maxim begin to realize something had changed. Or rather, many things had changed.

As Gwenshill came into view, they saw throngs of gardeners and landscapers, easily over a dozen, working across the grounds, trimming hedges, planting flowerbeds, cutting down overgrowth. The large trees that once concealed the mansion had been trimmed back, revealing its magnificent expanse.

Maxim stopped the car and exclaimed, "Jamie, what the hell did you do?"

Jamie put a hand on Maxim's arm. "I just thought you would like to come home to the life you once enjoyed."

Maxim didn't know whether to be excited or exasperated. There was nothing to do but continue on.

When he finally parked outside the front door they could hear further commotion coming from inside. Maxim rushed into the foyer and was greeted by a sight he had long forgotten: the sight of streaming sunlight reflecting gently onto freshly polished marble floors. The shine was so unexpected that he covered his eyes briefly, so used to a darkened and gloomy house. Once his eyes adjusted, he gazed into the other rooms surrounding him, all bathed in warm sunlight. Cleaning crews were moving about in rapid succession, rendering every surface spotlessly clean. Vases were back to being filled with luscious and fragrant flowers; perfectly crystalline chandeliers tinkled at the caress of the gentle summer breezes that once again flowed through the house. There was color, and light, and perfume in the air. Maxim had not returned to the Gwenshill of his present but the Gwenshill of his past.

"So, what do you think?" came Jamie's voice from behind him.

Maxim felt a vicious tug-of-war between wanting to strangle Jamie for being so profligate and wanting to kiss him for bringing back his family home from the grave. He chose to remain still.

"Jamie," he began when he could finally speak. "Where is the money coming from to pay for all of this?"

"My salary, of course," Jamie replied coolly. "I know that your family trust is stingy when it comes to personal expenses, so I might as well pull my own weight to keep this house running. This place needs lots of staff for sure."

"Jamie! You didn't hire staff, you hired an army! I know what your salary is, and even with my own allowance, we can't support all these people!"

"Of course not, Maxie," Jamie reassured him. "These are just temporary reinforcements. Half these people are just here to get the house up to the level it needs. Luisa and her budget crew were just not getting the job done for a house this big."

In an incredulous daze, Maxim walked slowly from room to room, pacing himself through each grand doorway as if seeing it for the first time. Jamie followed, an expression of benevolent mischief reigning upon his face. Rushing waves of memory flooded into Maxim's mind, decades of family moments, the long-forgotten whispers of a life that was bubbly and inviting.

"I can't believe this was all here," Maxim said in wonder. "I'd forgotten how beautiful these rooms used to be . . . how beautiful they are!" He rushed into Jamie's arms and embraced him. "Oh Jamie, thank you."

"I'm glad to see you so happy," Jamie replied. Maxim felt tears springing to his eyes at such an overwhelming display of care and sympathy from Jamie. Where had this beautiful soul been all his life? Maxim wondered. A dream had come true, and that happily ever after seemed as certain as Gwenshill standing tall for the rest of time.

Maxim got ahold of himself, dabbing at his eyes as he released himself from Jamie's arms.

"Right! I guess hunger is playing too much into my mood. Luisa probably has lunch ready. Luisa! Luisa!" Maxim called out, but nobody appeared.

"Actually . . . there's one more thing I should tell you," Jamie announced sheepishly. "I let Luisa go."

"You *what?*" Maxim's disbelief returned, flaring into annoyance. "Let Luisa go? James, she has been working in this house longer than you have been alive! Under what authority do you think you can just fire hardworking members of this household?"

"My authority as your husband and equal in this marriage," Jamie protested. "Luisa may have served your family well in the past, but the reality is that corners were being cut. And if we are going to keep this legacy going, then we need to change with the times."

"Legacy? I am the one with the legacy, not you," Maxim retorted. "Legacies are built on loyalty and trust, not on throwing out your staff every six months just because the vegan veal platter is not trending on TikTok."

It was the first real clash Jamie and Maxim had encountered in their relationship. The roller coaster of disbelief, euphoria, and indignation at the changes that followed Maxim's return home were a shock to his system. Jamie did not stand down in his stance that taking care of Gwenshill was not the same as that of a bungalow in some cul-de-sac. Once tempers finally cooled into a stalemate, Jamie admitted that Luisa was living in the apartment above the garage while looking for work elsewhere.

Maxim quickly made his way to the apartment and found Luisa sulking inside. He apologized, explained that it had been a misunderstanding, and offered to increase her pay, reiterating that the new staff would just be there to help her. Relieved, Luisa returned to the kitchen to begin preparing lunch for Maxim and Jamie. When the food was ready, the two men sat down for their meal and did not speak to each other. Jamie brooded silently as he ate, and Maxim felt nothing but exhaustion at this manic return home.

II

The afternoon transitioned into evening. Jamie and Maxim lounged in the library, listening to the sounds of the night streaming in from the open windows. Maxim was reading over emails on his phone while Jamie read a worn copy of *The Beautiful and the Damned* he had pulled from the shelf. Jamie turned to Maxim, whose face was still focused on the phone screen.

"I'm sorry," Jamie said. "I was carried away by the whole idea of changing things around. I should have asked for your permission first."

Maxim broke away from his phone and looked back to Jamie lying on the floor, the ornate details of the Persian rug radiating from the center of the carpet where he rested. Maxim sighed at the sight of those penitent eyes that glowed almost gray in the darkness of the room.

"I overreacted, Jamie. It's not your fault," Maxim replied. "I needed some shock therapy after all the years that I've spent just keeping this house a museum and not a home."

Maxim turned off his phone and tossed it upon a nearby table.

"Although, when it comes to important decisions, like hiring or firing people that work for us, we have to make those decisions together."

"I understand. I hope Luisa isn't that upset with me." Jamie sulked, gazing up to the ceiling. "Next thing I know I'm going to find rat poison in my protein shake."

Maxim chuckled. "I wouldn't worry, she's not known to hold a grudge."

"Good to know." Jamie smiled back at Max. "I love you so much, Maxim."

"I love you too, Jamie."

Jamie stood up from the floor and outstretched his arms, his gaze shifting ever so slightly. His backlit silhouette grew more intense from the light of the wall sconces behind him, his bright eyes the only light that stood out against the muted shadow of his body. Jamie slowly began to remove his clothes, one article at a time, keeping his gaze fixed on Maxim. With each piece of clothing, his silhouette grew more defined: his broad shoulders, his thin waist, his strong thighs. Jamie finally stood in the center of the room, all his clothes tossed aside, gazing ever more intently at his lover. Maxim, despite the sight of the beautiful body that he so intensely and passionately desired, could only focus on Jamie's eyes: those twinkling orbs of light that called to his innermost being.

He approached Jamie cautiously, never deviating from his line of sight. With only inches between them, their breath quickened, their hearts in tune with each other. Maxim placed his hand upon Jamie's cheek and gently stroked a lock of hair away from Jamie's face. Maxim fully felt the fire that he had denied himself back at the Lafayette. They trembled in ecstasy at the mere sensation of each other's breaths.

"I love you," Jamie repeated, his voice quivering with desire. "I love you so much I could die at this very moment."

CHAPTER 7

I

"Great. Just great!" Maxim exclaimed in frustration, looking down at a case of champagne bottles that had fallen from the delivery truck, all shattered on the cobblestone driveway.

"Our deep apologies, Mr. Porter. We will refund you for the cost of the bottles," replied the red-faced delivery man.

"I would prefer to get another case instead. Can the supplier ship another one right away?"

"I'm sorry, sir, this was the last case we had—the next shipment will only come by tomorrow."

"Bah!" Maxim exclaimed again. "My guests expect to drink from this vineyard exclusively! Ugh . . . well, I guess it's useless to cry over spilled champagne now."

Maxim approved delivery of the other drinks and food and headed back to the mansion. Luisa and the new kitchen staff began to sort through the items in preparation for the party that Maxim was hosting for the senior members of the New Mattachine. Maxim and Jamie had been living in Gwenshill for four months now, and Maxim was nervous about hosting a party at the mansion after so many years. He was particularly anxious because this would be the first-ever party where the guest list was predominantly of his own group of gay acquaintances. Maxim could only imagine what his relatives, let alone his grandfather, would have thought to have their ancestral pile filled with what they called "delicate fairies" prancing around the rose gardens and the antique furniture. Come to think, Maxim reflected with a snigger, it was his grandfather's fault for styling the house to be so welcoming to such tasteful fruitery.

Jamie descended from upstairs to find Maxim going over flower arrangements in the dining room.

"Hello handsome, I heard a crash and commotion outside the bathroom window. Did something happen?"

"Unfortunately, the champagne case fell from the truck and spilled everywhere," Maxim lamented to Jamie. "All we have are two bottles of the stuff and this crowd needs at least two dozen."

Jamie shook his head and huffed in agreement. He then turned to Maxim with a glint of mischief in his eye.

"I think I have an idea. How many bottles do we need?"

"Oh Jamie, you can't buy this champagne at the liquor store."

"Don't you worry," Jamie assured him with a rascally grin. "I'll be back in an hour, just wait for me and leave those two bottles in the kitchen."

Jamie rushed to the garage and took off in his car, kicking up a cloud of dust as he revved and roared out into the countryside. Maxim, not knowing exactly what Jamie was planning, anxiously began to rewrite the drinks menu for the party, discussing options for changes with the mixologist.

When Maxim planned for parties, he was used to intimate gatherings with his immediate family, and had only ever needed help from Luisa with cooking and prepping. Larger parties at Gwenshill had exclusively been the domain of the late Mrs. Porter. But those days were long gone, and Maxim feared he lacked the confidence to hold such events as his mother once did, a fear that led him to overthink every decision. The skies above were bright and clear of clouds, but part of Maxim hoped that a freak weather phenomenon would occur so he could call off the party. But then, he realized with a sigh, they would just move the party to the ballroom anyway. Either way, the only storm that brewed was the tornado of anxiety in his head.

Half an hour later, the food was prepared and lay across tables on the terrace outside the main living areas. Music echoed from the house out onto the terrace. A mix of popular genres from when Maxim was younger seemed like the safest option for guests around his age, but guessing that some of the older men would bring livelier dates, he'd mixed in some songs more in tune with Jamie's generation as well.

First to arrive was Elliot Newsham and his partner Marcus, followed by the news presenter Liam Leavesden.

"Why Maxim, this house is something straight out of a period drama!" Elliot commented as he wandered out onto the terrace.

"Yes, it's like I'm in Downton Abbey, just without the cute butler to serve me shade," commended Marcus in agreement.

Maxim flushed cheerfully. "The compliments are much appreciated, gentlemen."

Next to arrive were Dr. Benjamin Pratt and his husband Connor. Connor, a writer by trade, was used to attending parties like this one, which he tended to mine for gossip that he could later use in his books. Maxim was keen to avoid him; word about none of Jamie's family attending the wedding had stirred enough baseless chatter that Maxim was hoping to protect Jamie's reputation from Connor's creative license.

"Why Maxie, what a lovely castle for that little prince you snatched," Connor chirped with condescension. "Although maybe calling him Cinderella is more apt, considering his whole family is a gaggle of evil stepmothers."

"Why Connor, so very nice to see you. Are you still writing about sex workers who fancy themselves socialites?" Maxim fired back, unable to help himself even for Dr. Pratt's sake.

"No, sadly, turns out the socialites are far bigger whores than I give them credit for. So where's the little trophy husband?"

"He will be returning soon. He's running a brief errand."

"I can't wait to finally meet the lucky man who won the house-boy lottery. Sooo . . . how big is he?"

Maxim grew irritated. "Look here, you—"

"Yoohoo! Maxim darling!" At that moment Edward arrived with Paul onto the terrace, holding a bottle of wine in one hand.

"Sweetie! So good to see you." Maxim lauded, relieved at the interruption of Connor's spurious conversation.

"I know there would be plenty of booze, but I wanted to bring you this bottle of wine we got from our trip."

"Oh thank you Eddy, let's have it next time you guys are over for dinner. Oh wait . . . Paul has never been up here to the house! Paul, welcome to Gwenshill."

Other guests began to arrive and soon the terrace was full. As expected, most of them were older men, very few were under the age of fifty. The slow beginning of the party reflected the spirit of its guests: conceited and self-important, almost to the point of dullness. Some guests strolled through the gardens, others remained beside the food tables, gorging themselves like uncouth retirees at a cheap Caribbean cruise. Maxim took to walking about the guests, making small talk and checking if they were enjoying the food. Of course, some queried about the one item that was sorely missing at that moment: the champagne.

"Not to worry gentlemen, champagne will be provided soon enough," Maxim assured one guest.

"Well, Maxim dear, we are all waiting for this vintage that you have obtained," Connor interjected with a smarmy smile. "Everyone in the New Mattachine is dying to try it. You're certainly not going to try to sell us on the cheap stuff right?" His husband pulled Connor away with a scolding look.

"Don't you worry, Connor," said Maxim. "When the good stuff arrives, I will make sure to serve it to you personally . . . from your dog bowl."

The crowd laughed, even Connor's husband chuckling briefly. Maxim continued his rounds of the terrace until he ran into Liam Leavesden.

Liam, like Maxim, had come from an old-money background. Haughty and imperious, Liam enjoyed inflating his achievements as an adventurous war journalist and activist, though plenty of rumors swirled that he was little more than some opportunistic fruit whose career was only elevated by being born to a family legacy even grander than Maxim's. Still, it was a convincing enough fiction that it allowed Liam to expound to anyone who cared to listen about his two Pulitzer Prizes and his bestselling book, a history of his ancestors' escapades. Always sharply dressed, at times Liam took to wearing antique watches as a preamble to invite conversation about his family heritage. Maxim knew this trivia about Liam, and although Maxim saw that he was wearing a modern Patek Philippe today, chose to take the bait.

"Liam, thank you for coming to my party. Is that another watch from your family's vaults? It looks like it's never been seen by mortal eyes."

"Why Maximillian, no, this time I decided to go against type and I've bought a new watch to pass down to my son. Yes, it is a Patek Grand Complications. It may not have the pedigree of other watches in my collection, but like all the others, I hope that I will be passing it down to future generations just as my forefathers have done."

Maxim feigned being impressed. "Well, it certainly got my attention, and I'm sure your son will appreciate the gift. How old is he?"

"Little Jacob turned three last month. Yes, he will be inheritor of many a great treasure. I just hope that he will maintain the same humility and good judgement that I have."

"Then let's just hope that he keeps a steady financial ship like you. From reading your book, I got that many of the family branches diverging from yours just turned into dead ends."

"True, not all of us could be so fortunate. Though judging by your house, I guess that all this will be in the good hands of your niece someday."

"Yes . . . good hands," Maxim agreed halfheartedly. Their chat was soon interrupted by a loud commotion on the opposite side of the terrace. Maxim rushed to the other side, finding Elliot Newsham and Connor engaged in a heated argument.

"Connor, that filth that you wrote in your last book was unacceptable! I know that reference to the commodities trader smoking meth was my husband, you miserable bitch!" Newsham shouted.

"Elly, look, I don't know what you two like to do in the comfort of your bedroom," Connor scoffed. "But if what I have been hearing from the girlies down at the Eagle is true, there is an old queen named 'Marky the dump' who enjoys getting fucked around in that dark room when he gets his fix. But what proof do you have that it was your husband? Plenty of you Wall Street types fuck around with drugs the same way you fuck around with Grandpa's pension."

"Alright, enough!" Edward intervened. "You are behaving like a bunch of catty queers! Each one to his side and stop acting like children."

"This is a members-only catfight, sweetie," Connor sneered. "Fuck off, unless you want me to write about *your* drunk pervert of a husband."

"You leave my husband out of it!" Eddy yelled out, and pushed Connor to the ground.

Maxim was horrified; he wouldn't have believed that a party could go so horribly wrong in just the span of an hour. Dr. Pratt and Paul pulled their respective partners away before Connor and Edward began punching at each other. The other guests began to wail and shout, taking sides. Connor was obviously enjoying the unfolding chaos, which was just the sort of skirmish he'd been hoping for. Maxim came out of his state of disbelief and motioned for security to break up the raucous crowd before the party turned into a full-on nightmare.

Suddenly, the flick of a blade, the pop of a bottle, and the launch of a champagne cork halted the momentum of a skirmish that would have broken into an all-out brawl. Like a gunshot, it froze all in attendance, as they saw a cork landing at Maxim's feet. Following its trajectory, the guests looked up to the stone parapet, where Jamie stood holding a bottle of champagne in one hand and a saber in the other.

"That's one way to get everyone's attention," Jamie quipped with a smirk. The previously angry and loud crowd were disarmed by this charming rogue and began to laugh at their own behavior. Jamie looked down at the crowd, catching sight of Connor and then of Maxim.

"Pardon me sir, can you hold this bottle for me?" Jamie motioned to a nearby guest.

The guest took the bottle from Jamie's hand, and Jamie jumped from the parapet and made his way toward Connor. The crowd parted as he crossed the terrace in Connor's direction. As Jamie stood in front of Connor, he took the saber and pointed its tip at Connor's face.

"You, monsieur, were invited to this party on good faith and you have spoiled my husband's efforts," Jamie pronounced.

"That's cute," sneered Connor. "You must be Jamie the wunderkind. Where did you get the sword? Toys R Us?"

"No, though they do say a pen is mightier than this sword."

"Like the pen I'll use to write how you attacked me with a lethal weapon?"

Jamie affected contemplation. "More like the pen I'll use to write to every publishing house, from sea to shining sea, that you have profited from others' lives without their consent. I'm sure your current publisher, Mrs. Alice Whitmer, might take to the news well when our lawyers get a hold of Mr. Newsham's affidavit."

Connor's expression wavered between nervousness and anger. "You contemptuous little twink. How the fuck do you know my publisher?"

Jamie, still holding the saber to Connor's face, gestured in Maxim's direction.

"Oh, Alice?" Maxim replied smugly. "She's our neighbor. We're having her over for dinner tomorrow . . . perhaps I should also let her know about your behavior this evening?"

Sensing he'd lost the battle, Connor stepped back and gestured to his husband that they'd best be leaving. Jamie stood down with his saber and made his way to Maxim's side. As Connor and Dr. Pratt descended from the terrace, Connor looked back to the ogling crowd and gave one last juvenile quip.

"This party was fucking shit. You faggots can't handle a joke."

Maxim turned to Jamie, planting a gentle kiss on his cheek.

"You're my hero," he whispered in Jamie's ear.

"I told you I'd have it covered."

"Alright, gentlemen!" Jamie called out jovially to the crowd. "The champagne has arrived! What are you all waiting for? Your glasses are inside along with some fresh caviar!"

A cheer echoed from the guests as they made their way inside the mansion. Sure enough, there were dozens of glasses topped with champagne, their used bottles discarded in the back of the room, all from the vineyard that Maxim wanted. A narrowly missed disaster had become an unquestioned triumph, all thanks to Jamie.

II

"Are you sure you didn't feel it fall from your wrist at some point? Maybe while walking the grounds?" an officer from the Gwendolyn police department asked a despairing Liam Leavesden. Maxim had summoned the police to Gwenshill after the close of the party when Liam had realized his watch was missing from his wrist.

"No, I did not! You're the third policeman that asked this blasted question!"

"Apologies, Mr. Leavesden, we just want to confirm your whereabouts during the party; are you sure you didn't see anyone approach you that you were not familiar with?"

"I knew everyone except the servants and party staff. One of them must have stolen my watch!" Liam insisted.

Another police officer asked Maxim about security cameras.

"There are cameras inside, but most of the guests had been out on the terrace and in the gardens," Maxim told him. "There are no cameras immediately outside in those areas, just motion sensors."

"Were any new members of staff or servers at the party hired at the last minute?"

"No, the waiters are vetted in advance, and most of the staff have been working at the house for several months, some for years."

"Then can you take us to your security room? We must look at the camera footage."

Maxim obliged the officers and took them to the security room, then led them around the house to question the staff. The police departed Gwenshill around 1:00 a.m. after sweeping the grounds with metal detectors. They could not determine if the watch had been lost somewhere in the grounds or if Mr. Leavesden had taken it from his wrist in the bathroom, where there were no cameras, and had failed to notice walking out without it.

Liam was in sour spirits, suspecting that someone had swiped his watch from his wrist. But he conceded that he'd had work done on the band the day prior, so it was possible it had broken and caused the watch to fall off.

"Goddamnit Maxim! That watch cost me more than $300,000!" Liam steamed as he headed toward his awaiting motorcade.

"I will have the staff comb the grounds over one more time in the morning just to be sure," Maxim assured him. "If we can't find it tomorrow, I will let you know so you can call your insurance company."

"Honestly, this lowbrow thievery is unacceptable! At least that weasel Connor wasn't there to see it!" Liam huffed one last time as he stepped into his car.

The exhausted Maxim watched the motorcade turn the corner into the dark night and then returned to the comfort of Gwenshill's now cooled interior. He marched his way to his bedroom, finding Jamie lying in bed already undressed.

"So much for my act of bravado against that bitter fruit," Jamie commented as Maxim undressed.

"Not to worry," Maxim replied as he slid between the sheets. "I'm sure we will find it somewhere. Unless someone did actually steal it."

"What for? There are plenty more valuable things to take just in this house alone. Well, it hardly matters I guess; he can just buy another watch anyway."

"A watch that costs as much as a Bentley? Even the rich get upset when things get stolen from them," Maxim sighed, drawing down the light from his bedstand. "I'm exhausted. Good night, Jamie."

"Good night, handsome." Jamie leaned in and kissed Maxim one last time.

III

The following morning, Maxim woke up to the sun streaming through the bedroom window. Jamie had already awakened and was not on the bed beside him. Jamie must have reset the alarm by mistake, Maxim thought as he arose from bed and began to engage in his daily ritual before entering the shower. As he examined himself in the mirror, looking over his skin, he noticed something glinting behind him on the marble bench where he'd piled the clothes he was wearing the day before. As he rummaged through his clothes he pulled something from his back pocket; it was Liam's Patek Philippe, with a damaged link in the rose gold band. Maxim was stunned to find that the watch had been with him the whole time but could not comprehend how it had ended up in his back pocket.

Maxim showered and dressed, making his way to the dining room. Jamie sat eating brunch with Edward and Paul, who had stayed over after the party.

"Good morning Maxim!" Edward greeted him. "First time I've seen you sleeping in."

"Oh right!" Jamie exclaimed. "I forgot about the alarm, sorry—"

He stopped mid-sentence as Maxim pulled the watch from his pocket. Paul and Edward sat in stunned silence, while Jamie looked nervous.

"The watch! Max, where did you find it?" asked Edward.

"In the back pocket of my pants from yesterday," Maxim told them anxiously. "I can't remember how it got there."

"You had Liam Leavesden's watch this whole time and you didn't notice?" Paul asked incredulously.

"This is too bizarre. Oh God! What am I going to tell the police? What am I going to tell Liam? They'll think I stole the damn thing!" Maxim bellowed, fretting about the table.

"Calm down, Maxim," Edward broke in. "First of all, there's no reason for any of us to have stolen that damn watch, least of all you!"

"Then why was it on me?" Maxim countered. "Unless it was placed there."

Maxim turned to Jamie, who had not yet uttered a word.

"James, did you have something to do with this?"

"Me?! That's insane!" Jamie protested. "Why would I steal some other man's watch? I have a dozen of them in my closet!"

"The only person I let close enough to slip something into my pocket is you."

"Maximillian, I can't believe you! You think I would do such a thing? How dare you!" Jamie stormed out of the room; Maxim tried to apologize but Jamie had already rushed out into the house beyond, a door slamming shut in the distance.

Edward spoke once more, clearing the air from Jamie's departure.

"Look, at least the watch is safe and in good hands. We can call up the police and Liam and just tell them it was found in some rosebush or something."

"I suppose that will not create further questions," Maxim sighed. "But it still doesn't explain why I had the watch in the first place."

"I don't know, Max, maybe you found it and just forgot. That party started very badly with Connor behaving like a pest. And with all we had to drink, who knows?"

The affair of the watch was resolved and promptly forgotten by all but Maxim. Liam did not press for further investigation and the police closed the inquiry. Still, Maxim knew he was not one to be so absent-minded as to let such an expensive object go unnoticed on his person, and he kept puzzling it over in his mind. He remembered seeing the watch only once when he had been talking to Liam before the fight broke out. But he realized that from where Jamie had stood on the parapet, he would have to have gone around Liam to reach Maxim.

CHAPTER 8

I

The view of the countryside from Maxim's vantage point in the second-floor bedroom was framed beautifully by the turning leaves, but now it was spoiled partly by the sight of workmen and groundskeepers digging out the flowerbeds and lawns around Gwenshill.

Jamie had gotten the idea of creating a butterfly garden for Maxim's niece, Charlotte. The little girl had grown very fond of Jamie, and he wanted to gift her a "city of butterflies" for her birthday. George and Isabel thought it was a wonderful gesture, and Maxim reluctantly agreed to change the flowerbeds to make the garden bloom by the following spring. Maxim would look down from his bedroom at the workmen, hunched down on the soil, resembling bees rummaging around as they built their hive. He could see Jamie directing workmen, moving supplies, and getting his hands dirty with the various saplings and equipment being used in his pet project.

Maxim had found an old horticultural guide in the library and had given it to Jamie to read, but soon Jamie began to look up videos on the internet instead. Jamie was very meticulous in his planning, spending most of his weekends researching planting methods to understand how different plant species helped or harmed each other.

"This is no different than understanding patterns in the stock market," Jamie would tell Maxim. "The analysis of risk tolerance between different entities could determine the outcome of the whole economy. The acidity of the soil, the level of water demand, the impact of limited light, root structure . . . it could all affect whether this landscape thrives or wilts."

Maxim laughed. "I think you must run your theories by my father. He would appreciate the nuances of using daffodils to predict recessions."

"Ha, ha!" Jamie responded with joking enthusiasm. "You laugh, but one day I will be as rich as Rockefeller if I can make this garden thrive like my portfolio."

Maxim loved how committed Jamie was to leaving a mark on the grounds of Gwenshill. It was so refreshing to see a young man take on such endearing pursuits, when most men Jamie's age were more interested in going to bars and dance clubs. It reminded Maxim a little of himself, when he had been committed to studying art and architecture in his youth. A homebody even as a child, Maxim would read endlessly on the histories of great buildings and art movements, enthusiastically reporting his knowledge at the dinner table. Maxim's mother would indulge her son, planning trips to great landmarks on family vacations where he could sketch and study, much to George's and Henry's chagrin.

Maxim's passion, and his drive to pursue a degree in the arts, had been abruptly quashed when he turned sixteen and his grandfather, learning of his ambitions to become an architect, wrote Maxim a letter denouncing his dreams.

Maximillian,

You cannot imagine how exceedingly disappointed I am to hear that you want to follow this kind of profession. Only faggots become architects! Fey and inept fruits who can only draw pretty pictures and don't know how to build anything remotely physical. Engineers and builders are men of action, working with real materials and mathematical facts! Drop this nonsense or don't expect me to be paying for your education.

You are my grandson, and you will strive to become a man that commands others with fortitude and strength, not one who whimpers and whines because your prissy little drawings are illegible to the men who demand exacting instructions on how to build.

And you can forget about pursuing any idiotic endeavors like becoming a painter. Unless you want to become another useless vagabond eating grass and destroying the family name.

I will not be disappointed.

M.A. Deauvillier

Maxim had been so heartbroken at this letter that he would cry on his bed at night, but he never told his parents about it. So though they found it strange when he had a sudden about-face and decided to study civil engineering, but seemed defeated and sullen, they never questioned why.

After his grandfather's death, Maxim had quit engineering and decided to study history. He was still terrified of his homosexuality then, and had worried that if he had pursued architecture, he would have proven his grandfather right. He still wondered how his life would have turned out had he pursued his true passion instead of cowering in shame.

Maxim wanted to be supportive of his husband, but at times he would catch himself acting more like a father when he looked onto that youthful rogue, wiping dirt from his face with his forearm.

"So Jamie, is it all done?"

"I hope so. Now that the seeds and saplings are planted, we just have to wait until next year and see how it comes out."

Maxim smiled warmly. "I'm so proud of you. I'm sure Charlie will love the garden come next spring."

The days spent at the house were quiet ones. Maxim continued to run the foundation from the family office while Jamie would commute to the city during the week. Jamie would come home late at night, exhausted and stressed, at times only arriving to find the household fast asleep. Maxim would stay in the library waiting on Jamie's return, but at his age he would often fall asleep on his chair, only for Jamie to wake him to head to bed.

Maxim found himself in almost complete contentment at the outcome of his relationship. Comfortable in his marriage, comfortable with his surroundings, comfortable in his circumstances. The age gap no longer fazed him, though it did remind him that his body was facing new challenges as he approached his sixties. Maxim's daily ritual of staring into the mirror to analyze his body had become more draconian as he could not help comparing his declining physical form to Jamie's still ascendant manhood. Maxim awakened one morning before dawn to engage in his daily ritual, only to catch sight of a still-sleeping Jamie lying upon their bed in the mirror's reflection.

Jamie's skin was firm, his defined physique serenely reposed, that Grecian face hidden behind his curled hair unblemished by time. The sun's golden light cast a warm and tender glow upon that sleeping youth who resembled a hero of myth. Maxim could only counter such misplaced comparisons by staying evermore strict with his own diet and exercise. He pushed himself harder to maintain a modicum of athleticism, no longer just to remain active, but to keep up with the twenty-eight-year-old who now slept beside him.

II

Maxim and Jamie walked the trail that encircled the grounds of Gwenshill, deeply wooded and cooled by the dense canopy of trees high above them. The song of birds echoed in the air, singing melodies random and collective as the two walked along the gravel path to a stream that followed the edge of the property.

"I don't want to work anymore," Jamie blurted out suddenly.

"What do you mean?" Maxim replied. "You want to change firms?"

"No ... I am just tired of the stress and long hours." Jamie sighed, stopping a few steps behind Maxim. "I want to try something different."

"Like what?"

"I don't know, I have a pretty good amount of money saved up. I might want to strike on my own as a day trader."

"Day trader? Jamie, my sweet boy, that can be a risky thing to jump on."

"I'd rather take a chance, though. What else can I do? Just continue to be someone's obedient stooge and miss out on life?"

"You're young, there's still plenty of time to travel, make new friends. These investment firms just make it harder in the beginning, but you will get into your stride."

"And what about us?" Jamie retorted defensively. "What about the time we have together?"

"What about us? We have this house, and each other. I will always be here for you," Maxim reassured him. "I am not going anywhere anytime soon, my dear Jamie."

Jamie breathed deeply as tears came to his eyes. "I just get worried . . . I want to make the most of our time together."

Maxim extended his arms and embraced Jamie, his head resting on Maxim's shoulder.

"You think that I can do it? I just want to make you proud," Jamie said softly.

"I'm already proud of you. I just want to see you happy."

Maxim gently caressed Jamie's soft hair as he held him, looking up to the canopy of trees rustling in the winds as autumn leaves gently fell around them and thinking about how much Jamie mattered to him.

"If you want to take a chance on day trading, I'll support you."

"Thank you, Max!" Jamie gave a boyish smile. "And I promise that you don't need to do anything. I'll keep paying my half of the bills and before you know it I'll make sure that you won't have to spend another penny on your family home!"

"*Our* family home, Jamie," Maxim replied warmly. "You're my family now."

III

Luisa had served the Porter family for over fifty years, since Maxim was a small child. She had worked through the ranks, going from housemaid to head of the cleaning staff. As the years progressed, the late Mrs. Porter had taken the initiative to raise her sons to respect the people that served them. When Mr. Porter was away on business in the summer, Karine, George, and Maxim would take breakfast and lunch in the kitchen with the staff, where Luisa would cook for the cadre of other cleaners, gardeners, and handymen that maintained the house.

Karine's highbrow demeanor had been softened with a humility that was unusual for such a wealthy family. Maxim would observe that his mother, without her fancy dress, and her hair held back by a simple pin, still exuded a civility toward others that was becoming of a monarch. She had been a magnanimous aristocrat, thankful for the efforts of others, instilling a strong sense of loyalty in those who worked for her. Luisa had always been loyal to her mistress, and keeping Gwenshill organized and tidy was the best expression of her respect for her employer even after Mrs. Porter's death, even as the number of staff shrank with each passing decade.

To Maxim, Luisa was as integral a fixture to Gwenshill as any other antique in the house. But the truth was that Luisa was no longer able to perform her duties, even with new staff to aid her. Her sight was growing poor, her arthritis was flaring more frequently, and fatigue was making it harder for her to move around the mansion.

"Maxim, we need to talk about Luisa." Jamie approached Maxim as he worked at his desk.

"What about her?"

"I'm worried about her. I know you care about her, but you have to face facts," Jamie insisted. "She's in her late seventies; she can't go on like this forever."

"I understand that. That's why she'll only cook from now on because it is less intensive work than going around cleaning." At Jamie's frustrated look, Maxim continued. "Luisa is not just a housekeeper, she's family. And she enjoys cooking, in that respect she's like a nonna caring for her children. If things get harder for her, I will find her a nurse."

"Why don't you just send her to a nursing home then, where she can be taken care of properly?"

"Absolutely not!" Maxim responded bluntly. "If she needs help, she can ask for it."

"Fine." Jamie put his hands up in defeat. "But at the rate she's going, she'll end up hurting herself or someone else."

Another month passed in which Maxim was stubborn to accept that the woman who had stood by him and his family for so many years should be sent away to a nursing home where she would fade to obscurity. Maxim had known Luisa since childhood; he knew she was resolute and committed to her place in the house.

"Here is your tea, Mr. Max," Luisa said, handing over a piping hot cup to Maxim as he sat in the living room.

"Thank you, Luisa." Just before he could take a sip of his tea, he noticed her pressing the joints of her hands with her fingers, swollen and red with pain. A distressed expression crossed her face.

"Luisa . . ." He paused, reflecting on what he should say.

"Yes, Mr. Max?"

"How are your hands? Did you have the doctor give you new medication?"

"My hands hurt a bit, but I can manage, Mr. Max. Those pills from the doctor just make me sleepier."

"Are you sure? Maybe I can get Dr. Wells to make a house call."

"No thank you, Mr. Max, I'm perfectly fine." Luisa looked up to the portrait of Mrs. Porter hanging above the fireplace and sighed. "I do miss your mother. She was so pretty when I first met her."

Maxim looked back at the painting.

"Yes, she was." Maxim paused again, wondering how his mother would have handled such a difficult topic. He turned to Luisa once more. "Look, Luisa, you've served this family and myself for a very long time. And if there's anything you need from me, I just want to let you know that I care about you. And I will help you if you need it."

Luisa stood by Maxim's chair, placing her hand on his shoulder. She smiled back as Maxim placed his hand on hers.

"Thank you, Mr. Max. You don't have to worry about me. You are a good person just like your mother was." She looked once more at the painting and then at Maxim. "I will head back to the kitchen. Have some of that tea, and if you need anything else just let me know."

"Why don't you come and sit here with me? Just grab a cup, take a break from sitting next to that stove all day."

"If that's what you'd like, I'll join you, Mr. Max."

"Luisa, you can just call me Maxim. You've known me for long enough."

Luisa nodded with a small smile and made her way back into the kitchen.

Maxim nestled himself in the armchair, looking up at that portrait above the fireplace as his tea cooled undrunk. His eyelids grew heavy, the warmth of the room lulling him into a sleepy state. As he rested his eyes waiting for Luisa to return, Maxim's mind wandered from quiet contemplation to the solemn comfort of sleep.

He began to dream. Maxim was alone in a forest; he recognized it as the trail that led from Gwenshill to the stream. The forest was bathed in monochrome light, receding into muted tones of gray and taupe. There was no birdsong, no sound of scurrying woodland creatures, not even Maxim's footsteps made a sound against the gravel beneath him. But he could hear something that hid itself among the shadows of the trees that surrounded him.

As Maxim slowly paced along the path, with each footstep, the noise grew closer to him. He would stand still, as if remaining motionless would confuse whatever this was into thinking that Maxim was as static as the trees that surrounded him. But Maxim could sense that something was still watching him, that standing still was useless. He looked around trying to determine which direction led him back to the house and decided that he would proceed slowly and then begin to run.

By the time he could clear the wooded trail, he would be free of whatever was observing him. He stepped forward, one foot at a time, toward the route he could recognize. Sounds emanated from behind the trees far in the distance, slowly inching forward in his direction. He walked faster and faster along the trail that took him out of the forest. Hearing footsteps, Maxim began to run in fear, dodging overhanging branches and jumping over obstacles that stood in his path. The footsteps continued just behind him.

He was no longer being observed, he was being preyed upon, and whatever was hot on his pursuit could only mean certain death. His heart quickened, his breath grew heavier, adrenaline fueling every stride and leap his body could muster. The entity ran closer behind, now calling his name like an echo through the trees.

Maxim could finally see the end of the trail, where Gwenshill's gables poked beyond the tree canopy. He sprinted, the feeling of pursuit dissipating as he approached the house. Whatever was chasing him had kept itself in the shadows of the forest, calling out his name in an echoing roar that shook the ground beneath his feet.

He took one last step into the clearing, catching his breath as he stepped out of the forest. He looked at Gwenshill with relief, but as he took one last look behind him, the voice of the shadows reached a deafening shriek. Maxim awakened, startled by the sight of Jamie's face in front of him.

"Max!" Jamie exclaimed. "You were having a nightmare."

"Oh Jamie! You're home already? I thought you had to stay later tonight."

"I did. It's already past eight. How long were you napping?"

As Maxim shook off his disorientation, he realized that the mug of tea by his side had gone cold and was never taken away. "Jamie, have you seen Luisa today?"

"No, I just arrived home a few minutes ago. Why do you ask?"

Luisa Caldeira was discovered dead on the floor of Gwenshill's kitchen. Her body lay sprawled beside a broken mug shattered with remnants of her tea spilled out. It was determined that she had made dandelion tea with flowers presumably picked around the property. The flowers themselves, laced with herbicide, contained enough of the poison that it would have rendered the tea fatal. Luisa passed away at seventy-six years old, her death ruled accidental by the county coroner.

Maxim was distraught at the news; he knew now he should have heeded Jamie's concerns. But he hadn't listened, and now Luisa was gone. Maxim contacted Luisa's distant relatives, but they did not have the means to travel to see her. In the end Maxim sent her body back to her small village in Brazil for burial. It was difficult for Maxim to look at Luisa's now-empty bedroom, her belongings still hanging on the walls with mementos from her time at the house. Jamie was quick to find

Luisa's replacement, a professional house manager, and was also quick to transform Luisa's unoccupied room into his own office. Luisa's belongings were neatly packed away, to be sent back to Brazil. But the boxes, along with her memories, were lost in transit and in translation.

CHAPTER 9

I

The cold weather that February was unforgiving and long-lasting. There had been little snow, which was unusual for that part of the country, but what really stood out was the piercing wind, that struck one's face like a thousand needles of frigid pain. There was one concession that proved a reprieve to the cold halls of Gwenshill: a storm felled several trees on the property, and workmen arrived to transform the fallen logs into enough dried firewood to last the mansion for several months. The brutal cold required the fireplaces to be kept lit day and night. George and Isabel, along with their daughter and Mr. Porter, had come for a visit to enjoy the winter scenery, but the bitter wind kept them all barricaded in the house.

Afternoon tea was served in the library, the smallest of the rooms on the first floor and best served by its roaring fireplace. Judith, Luisa's replacement, brought a variety of baked goods and sandwiches from the kitchen along with two pots of piping tea and coffee. The Porters huddled together by the fireplace, partaking in sweet cakes, family jokes, and topical banter.

Mr. Porter was enjoying his position as the erudite patriarch, or at least that was how Jamie made him feel. The two of them talked broadly and well about economic theory and investment strategy, with Jamie firing round after round of inquiry upon the retired banker. Jamie was at his most charming and attentive talking to Mr. Porter, and Maxim was happy to see the two getting along so well. In Maxim's mind it was nice to see that his husband was integrating so naturally with the social dynamic of his family. George leaned over to Maxim, who sat beside him on the sofa near the fireplace, and gestured at the lively conversation between Jamie and their father across from them.

"He certainly found himself someone who enjoys his endless pontificating," George remarked.

"You should see how Jamie's eyes light up when he talks about finance," Maxim replied with a jovial grin. "That enthusiasm is hard to find with the young."

"I guess my concerns at seeing you two together were misplaced," George continued, grabbing a scone from the porcelain tray. "He's a breath of fresh air, and this house feels like a home again."

"It does feel like home. It's been a shock to my system, but change needed to come."

"I think it has done well for you. You seem happier, healthier, and in better spirits, barring this cold."

"I know. I can't remember the last time I felt this warmth here." Maxim outstretched his hands to the fire, the heat providing relief.

"And James has been helping with the upkeep of the house?"

"He has, but he left the investment firm back in November. We've been using some reserve funds until he's back on his feet."

"Oh that's right, you told me." George then turned to Jamie. "James, what was the firm you had worked for? I keep forgetting the name."

Jamie looked nervously at George, as if he had asked an intimate question. He waited a moment before he gave a hesitant answer.

"Kahn, Hastings & Aldrich. You know anyone at KHA?"

"I don't recall," George responded, turning to Mr. Porter. "Dad, have you heard of them?"

"Oh, they're a very old firm. They catered to our crowd in the past, but when the son took over he decided to change their strategy to invest in the tech sector."

"Oh? So Jamie, were you involved in these big mergers?" Maxim asked Jamie.

"I was not involved personally, but even if I were, my lips would have to stay sealed," Jamie said coolly. "If I divulge business secrets to George, it may affect his better judgement when it comes to government policy."

"I wouldn't worry, James, the nest of lobbyists that sit outside of my office already try to change my judgement on a daily basis," George replied, lying back on the sofa.

"Then I will invoke a sense of principle," Jamie tried again, giving a playful wink at Maxim. "My husband thinks too highly of you to partake in insider trading."

George and Maxim looked at each other and smirked. "Oh well, I tried!" George joked, tossing his hands in the air.

As the family laughed, Judith entered the library, looming somewhat ominously with her dark blue uniform appearing almost black in the fire's warm yellow light.

"Master James, Master Maxim, shall you be requesting more food from the kitchen or are you satisfied this evening?" She spoke in a dry, somber tone, her straight and angular hands clasped neatly together.

"No Judith, you can take this food away. Inform the kitchen to begin preparing dinner right away, a hot stew is in order," commanded Jamie with an assuring poise.

Judith moved about the gathered family soundlessly, picking up plates and placing them on trays. Maxim felt unsettled watching her as she resembled a dark shadow weaving its way around the family. It reminded him of the day Luisa died, and the nightmare he had about a dark being that stalked him from within the forest.

When Judith knelt beside Charlotte where she was coloring in a book on the floor, and moved to take her plate, they locked eyes for a moment. Something in Judith's gaze had disturbed the six-year-old, and she began to tear up and cling to her mother beside her.

"Mommy, mommy!" Charlotte cried, holding tight to her mother.

"What is it my dear? Why are you crying?" Isabel asked.

"I miss Luisa. That lady is scary."

"I apologize, Mrs. Porter." Judith said stiffly. "I am not used to being in contact with children."

"It's alright, Judith," Isabel reassured her. "Charlotte was just more used to Luisa, that's all." Judith nodded, collected the last of the dishes, and withdrew to the kitchen.

An awkward silence filled the room as the subject of Luisa's death hung over the gathered family. Jamie looked indifferent, but the other men and Isabel held a more somber expression. The crackle of the fire was all that relieved the silent tension in the air.

"Poor Luisa," said Mr. Porter finally. "She deserved better."

"She was a decent housekeeper, and her food was always a good comfort," George joined in.

As Maxim was about to agree, Jamie interrupted.

"I don't understand how you can feel sorry for her! Poor Luisa? How about poor Maxim? That old woman almost killed my husband!"

"Jamie, it's not that—" Maxim interjected, but Jamie cut him off once more.

"No, this is a joke! She should have retired long ago."

"Luisa had no other resources, no close family. Her options were limited if we had let her go," George countered. "In the end it was an accident, she did not mean any harm, she was just confused."

Mr. Porter added, "Never attribute malice to what can be adequately explained by incompetence. Her age and mental state were past their prime and it affected her judgement."

"We provided her with a steady income and a roof over her head, and she was dutiful to this family till the end," Maxim said finally. Jamie gave him a look of bemusement.

"Maxim, you could have died. Why are you still defending her?"

"Because if I had fired her like you wanted, she would have been an elderly woman with no place to go, living on a meager income from her social security," Maxim snapped. "You basically wanted her to be condemned to die in poverty."

"And you were living in the delusion that she was going to remain around forever!" Jamie shouted. Isabel covering her daughter's ears from their raised voices. George stepped in.

"Jamie's right, Max." George said calmly. Maxim turned to his brother in incredulity. "Luisa should have retired; she only remained here for your sake."

Maxim was shocked to hear this from his brother. "That's not true. She liked working here. She had a strong sense of duty to this house!"

"It is true," George said. "About ten years ago we offered Luisa the chance to retire in a warmer climate. Maybe a small condo down in Florida. We'd give her a modest allowance so she could take care of herself. Luisa considered our offer but chose to stay here."

"George is right," Isabel confirmed with a nod. "We offered the same arrangement to her every now and then, but Luisa would decline each time."

"I don't understand," Maxim replied.

"Max, it's not that difficult to understand," George continued. "She felt there needed to be someone here to look after you. That's why she stayed. She didn't want you to be left alone in this house."

"I can imagine why," Mr. Porter agreed.

Maxim sank into his seat, sullen. Jamie sat silently, his arms crossed, not wanting to look at his husband out of frustration.

With dinner prepared and laid out in the dining room, spirits eventually improved with the flow of the table wine. Maxim remained soft-spoken for most of the meal, while Jamie brooded in thought. To break the tension between the two men, Mr. Porter made a sardonic joke.

"Look on the bright side, James my boy—if Maxim had drunk the tea, you would have been stuck with this mausoleum."

"That's not funny," snapped George. Maxim rolled his eyes in irritation.

"Mr. Porter, if you must know, I love this house because Maxim is here. Without him it wouldn't feel like home," Jamie responded. He gave Maxim a wink and a forgiving grin. Maxim extended his hand across the table to Jamie's. Now that they had reconciled, the dinner continued more jovially with dessert and drinks.

Maxim felt grateful that Jamie's headstrong convictions, while they led to brief spats, never erupted into full fights. He was well-meaning, but against Maxim's abrasive stubbornness, there were bound to be moments when they would not see eye to eye. Maxim accepted this, thinking that a certain degree of friction was needed in a relationship. It never bothered him that these moments of friction occurred in front of others and not just in private.

Arguments between his parents, between his brother and Isabel, between Edward and Paul—he had observed these both directly and indirectly but lacked his own romantic experience of appropriate conduct in a relationship. George and Isabel hoped that with time Maxim and Jamie's relationship would mature, but they kept this opinion to themselves.

"Last call for drinks, bar's closing!" Maxim announced good-naturedly as he walked toward the cocktail cabinet, opening a decanter of cognac to pour. "Father, do you want something to drink before bed?"

"No thank you, son, my doctor said not to drink before I take my medication."

"Anything serious, Mr. Porter?" Jamie asked curiously.

"My ticker is one or two steps out of sync with the music," Mr. Porter joked. "My doctor says this medication will keep me in the beat."

"Is that working well?" asked George.

"Oh yes! I'm going to be swinging till I'm a hundred and twenty!" Henry laughed.

"Yes please," Maxim humored his father. "At this rate you'll outlive even Jamie."

II

Jamie was spending considerable time locked in his new office. Maxim thought that he would be seeing more of Jamie walking around the house, joining him for lunch, and spending more free time together during the morning and evening. Instead, Maxim only noticed more footsteps and the rolling of a desk chair coming from above his head, since Jamie's office was directly above his.

Maxim could not understand why Jamie needed to work in a separate room, since the Porter family office was large enough and had multiple desks. Jamie was adamant that he needed a separate space; he was used to working in an environment where his focus had to be fully dedicated to reading trading patterns and listening to non-stop news reporting. Maxim had briefly seen the office Jamie had created for himself in Luisa's old bedroom. A sleek and minimalist desk held an array of monitors propped together on two stands, forming a chaotic mosaic of graphs, ticker symbols, and data. On the opposite wall of the room hung additional monitors, each dedicated to a different news agency reporting twenty-four hours a day. It was not an office but a command center, orchestrated for Jamie to be continuously connected to the world outside of the provincial walls of Gwenshill. Maxim was impressed and overwhelmed by the setup, which had been expensive to buy and install.

"Trust me, Max, with this rig I can connect to every stock market in the world and move thousands of trades in seconds! We'll be rich beyond our wildest dreams," Jamie boasted.

"You mean *you'll* be rich," Maxim chuckled. "I'm already set."

"Max, if I'm successful, soon enough I'll be running your trust. Mark my words. Your family fortune will become even greater than it once was."

Those early days of Jamie working from home had an infectious enthusiasm that even Maxim was intoxicated by. But months had passed, and the upbeat momentum had waned during winter, and remained tepid into spring and early summer. Jamie was working far longer than he had at his previous job, his schedule consisting of twelve-hour days during the week. Maxim could see that Jamie looked considerably stressed, and at times ill-tempered.

He recognized the expression on Jamie's face; it reminded him of those days in his childhood when Henry had been overwhelmed with work. Spending days and nights locked in the family office reading over documents and attending innumerable meetings hosted in the house for board members and heads of different banks. Karine would instruct him not to disturb his father when he was in that frazzled state; when he was younger, he had never asked why, but he remembered the one time his brother had disobeyed their mother's command and barged into a conference call Mr. Porter was having with government officials. George would only recall that their father had given him such a menacingly enraged stare, that he went running out of the office back into his bedroom to hide.

Maxim adopted the old posture of not engaging with Jamie unless Jamie initiated contact. This extended into the late hours of the night, when Maxim would awaken to find Jamie out of bed. He would wander into Jamie's office, finding him awash in the glow of a dozen screens. Jamie's gaze would be transfixed on some data point on the monitor that from Maxim's sight only read as a singular harsh glare.

"Can't talk, the Nikkei opens in twenty minutes," Jamie would respond at the sound of his office door opening.

"Jamie, come to bed, you need sleep," Maxim would plead with concern.

"I can't; I'm under a lot of pressure to get this right."

"Jamie—"

Jamie would turn back to face Maxim, his eyes widened and bloodshot from caffeine. Jamie did not look at Maxim as much as he looked through him like he didn't exist. His gaze was as cold and dead as a corpse's. Maxim, unsettled, withdrew himself back to their bedroom. An hour later, Jamie would wander in and collapse in exhaustion upon their bed. Maxim would awaken once more to the motion of Jamie falling onto the mattress, facing the tired and haggard face of his husband in front of him. Jamie would only utter one phrase before he would promptly fall asleep.

"I'm sorry handsome."

There were moments of calm when Jamie would give himself distance from his work. The butterfly garden he had planted, driving into the city to visit his friends, the occasional gathering that was hosted at the house. He would put on a hoodie and sweatpants and go running around the grounds of Gwenshill for hours. And when they were locked in the house due to bad weather, he would make use of the heated pool by swimming lap after lap like he was preparing for the Olympics. Maxim could not figure out what was weighing so heavily upon Jamie's mind that he had to constantly force himself to remain active.

It felt to him like Jamie was obsessed with achievement, and when things did not go his way, he had to find other means to make it happen. This had a unique impact when Maxim and Jamie became intimate with each other. Their encounters would become prolonged and intense in passion and eroticism, with a voracity that Maxim in his advanced age found difficult to maintain.

Jamie's sexual intensity only strengthened with each encounter, like he wanted to release every fiber of his being to expel this anxious energy that emerged from his restlessness. Jamie was chasing some mental escape, and he began to take out this need upon his partner with no reprieve. At one point Maxim had to pull himself from Jamie's arms in the heat of passion, to try and console whatever force was presiding over his husband's restless mind.

"Jamie, stop. What's going on?" Maxim asked Jamie, their bodies interlaced within bed sheets.

"Why? Am I hurting you? We can take a break if you want."

"No, it's not that," Maxim sighed. "What is up with you lately? I barely see you around the house, and you're burning yourself out with all this activity."

"I'm fine," Jamie brushed him off.

"No, you're not fine. Tell me what's wrong," Maxim pressed. Jamie sulked, avoiding Maxim's gaze. After a moment, Maxim continued to push for Jamie to come clean. Jamie grew defensive and pushed back, like an animal cornered in his cage. He accused Maxim of not having faith in him.

"This is so typical coming from your kind!" Jamie cried out angrily. "You just go around all day lounging around and giving money away to pointless charities, pretending like things will change while you remain the same! You don't know what real struggle is!"

"Struggle? Your upbringing was as pampered and privileged as mine, you spoiled brat!"

"Unlike you, I still have something to prove! I can live outside of my family's shadow!"

"Don't give me that bullshit, Grenvill!" It was the first time Maxim had called Jamie by his last name. Jamie's eyes flared with anger.

They began to shout at each other as they sprang from bed and dressed themselves. Jamie paced the room, picking up objects and throwing them, his eyes filled with rage and hostility. Maxim chased Jamie around the room and finally grabbing hold of Jamie, gripping him tightly by the arms, forcing Jamie to face him. Jamie hurled one last insult, loathing and bitterness piercing each syllable.

"You are weak, a coward, and a failure!"

Something within Maxim snapped—whatever semblance of collected composure he had retained shattered within him. He was imbued with a fury more intense than he'd ever felt.

"You . . . miserable . . . SHIT!"

He swung his arm in full force, striking Jamie's face with the back of his hand. This sent the young man flying onto the floor. Maxim had become unhinged with rage and jumped upon his husband as he lay there still lost in the fog of what had just happened. Maxim gripped Jamie's neck tight with both hands, squeezing with all the strength he had to crush Jamie's throat shut. Maxim was fully absorbed in his rage, his eyes bulging, his teeth exposed and grinding so tightly that his jaw began to ache. Maxim could only see red, with Jamie whimpering and struggling to push against his weight.

A cloud had blocked the sun's light as it passed outside their bedroom. As it moved away, the sunlight reflected into Maxim's eyes from the broken mirror that stood across from him. Maxim caught his reflection in that mirror, a vicious and rageful beast hovering over a defenseless innocent. His rage ceased, consumed by an endless well of guilt as he looked onto Jamie's bloodshot eyes, glittering with sadness and fear.

"I'm sorry . . ." Jamie cried out through tears. "I'm sorry . . ."

Maxim could not comprehend what he had done. This fiery buildup of resentment and wrath that he had been holding for years had exploded like an atomic bomb on the one person Maxim never wanted to harm. He began to weep. He released his grip from Jamie's neck and pulled him from the floor to hold him close to his chest. Maxim cradled his husband in his arms, both clinging to each other and crying.

The release had come, not just for Maxim but for Jamie too. They sat together on the floor that whole afternoon, trying to process what they had gone through. Neither spoke, they just held each other silently, listening to the ticking of the clock, the call of birds outside, and the rustling of the wind. Maxim ran his hand across Jamie's hair while Jamie held Maxim's other hand, caressing it with his fingers, examining the folds and spots on the skin.

"I'm losing a lot of money," Jamie finally said softly.

"How much?"

"A few million. I'm just having bad luck."

"Why didn't you tell me?"

"Because I don't want you to think I failed." Jamie looked up to Maxim. "I want to prove to you I can do it."

"Oh Jamie." Maxim sighed, giving a gentle kiss on Jamie's forehead. "I just want you to be happy."

"I know . . . I grew up thinking happiness only came from success, and to not succeed was to fail at happiness."

"That's not true, my dear Jamie," Maxim comforted his young husband. "Happiness comes from those we care about most in the world, those that fill our lives with love, with tenderness, and with kindness."

"Then I guess you make me happy, Maxim," Jamie smiled, still nestled in Maxim's arms. "I need to be less stressed out about making mistakes."

"And being transparent about needing help," Maxim added.

"I will. Though, what do I do with my losses?"

"Well," Maxim breathed deeply. "I'll call our bankers tomorrow to talk about a loan, and you can pay it back over time. But you need to promise me not to take these risks again."

"Okay," Jamie agreed.

Maxim was still unsettled by their fight. It had escalated quickly, and his reaction had been so toxic. He wondered where it had come from, this instantaneous shift to rage on the threshold of psychosis. He worried if the medications that he had been taking for so long were losing their effect on him. Would he return to the night terrors, the hallucinations, the shrieking into a state of catatonia at the thought of what had happened at his mother's funeral? And, if the pills were failing, it may explain why he couldn't remember how the watch had gotten into his back pocket. Memory loss could have been the first symptom, and this rage another. For now, he had maintained his mental fortitude. So long as he stuck to his diet and exercise, he had to believe his medications would work as intended.

CHAPTER 10

I

"A Lady Wendell is at the door, Mr. Porter," Judith announced to Maxim, who was lounging on the terrace reading from his tablet.

"Who?" Maxim asked. He did not know any woman by the name Wendell, let alone a lady.

"She announces she is a friend of Master James. Master James is occupied with a phone call, sir."

"He didn't tell me we were having guests." Maxim looked at his watch; it was two in the afternoon. "Have the kitchen prepare an afternoon spread for the three of us on the terrace. I will meet our guest in the foyer."

"Yes Mr. Porter," Judith nodded.

Maxim had met some of Jamie's friends in the past. Most of them were of similar ages, young and cosmopolitan by most measures. Thus, Maxim expected to see a twenty-something young woman, though it was unusual to find Jamie's friends traveling this far from the city on such short notice. He envisioned some coquettish whisp of a woman, dressed in flashy and stylish clothes. Perhaps "Lady" was an actual name and not a title. The conventions of the nouveau riche produced veritable cacophonies of names and acronyms to set them apart from the staid conformity of the rest of the upper classes.

He rose from his sunchair, dusted himself off, and made his way to the foyer. He observed a rounded shape as he walked through the long gallery, colorful and vivid, adorned in floral prints under a large-brimmed sunhat. Halfway to the foyer he noticed some strands of silvery hair delicately revealing themselves against the bright bursts of printed peonies and lilacs. *Curious*, Maxim thought. This did not look like the sort of fashionable maiden Jamie would parade on his outings through town for Instagram.

The woman turned at the sound of Maxim's approaching steps clicking against the stone floor. She was about Maxim's age. She had a pleasant and breezy appearance, enhanced by a complexion that was fair and aristocratic. Jewels glittered and sparkled from her arms and neck, with several thick bands of gilded enamel studded with gemstones resting upon her wrist. Surely Maxim would have remembered this woman if she had been at the wedding, but the more he observed her, the less recognizable she appeared. Who was this woman who resembled a Fabergé easter egg?

"Lady Wendell, I presume?" Maxim asked shyly, not sure what to expect.

"Oh my word! What a dashing and handsome gentleman you are! My dear sweet Jamie has told me so much about you, but seeing you in person is a whole different reality. My word! If you were only straight, I would have snatched you for myself." Her glittering bangles clinked as she clasped her hands in enthusiasm, scanning Maxim from head to toe.

"Oh! Where are my manners? I am Lady Lillian Wendell, but you can call me Lilly. I am a dear friend of sweet little Jamie."

"Well, it's a pleasure to meet you. Though Jamie has never mentioned your acquaintance."

"Right! I do apologize for not attending the wedding. I unfortunately had to preside over the funeral of some ghastly relative of mine and could not avoid it at all! Absolutely horrid woman she was."

She briefly paused the flurry of her words, studied her surroundings, and turned to Maxim once more.

"My word, this house is so enchanting."

"Why thank you Mrs. Wen-, I mean Lilly," Maxim smiled. "Why don't we wait out on the terrace. Jamie will join us soon."

"Oh, the view must be quite charming from up here. Reminds me a bit of home." Lady Wendell beamed.

Maxim found her an enchanting woman, the bright and peppy spirit of a little girl outshining her age. They made their way to the terrace where a table had been prepared with an assortment of baked goods and fresh bread delivered that morning. Maxim and Lillian continued with a lively banter as they waited for Jamie. She carried on most of the conversation, talking endlessly about the gossip she came across from her local village back in England. She was an American who married into nobility, having spent most of her life in the British Isles and Europe. Her eldest son inherited the title of Baron Aysgarth from his father, and Lady Wendell was in the habit of traveling around the world after her husband's passing. She was visiting the United States and had decided to stop at Gwenshill to see "her little Jamie" before heading to California.

"How did you meet Jamie? If you don't mind me asking," Maxim inquired curiously.

"Well!" Lillian took a deep breath. "I know dear Jamie through my youngest son Cyril. You see, Cyril and Jamie were friends in boarding school. They were very close, and amusingly enough they looked very much alike."

Lady Wendell reached into her purse, pulling from her wallet an old photograph, its edges worn from frequent handling. Maxim looked at the faded picture to see Jamie in his childhood along with Cyril. Maxim was struck at how similar the two boys looked, almost like brothers.

"It is quite uncanny," Maxim commented. "What happened to your son?"

"My little ray of sunshine passed away," Lady Wendell explained, sorrow echoing in her words. "Jamie and Cyril were part of a school field trip to the Alps. I was told that my Cyril was coerced by one of the schoolboys to descend some advanced trail. He took the wrong direction, and he fell into a ravine."

"I'm so sorry, that's terrible to hear," Maxim said in sympathy.

"You should have seen poor Jamie's reaction. That boy was traumatized by losing his friend." She sighed, bringing a cup of tea to her lips as she gazed out into the countryside.

"I do feel your sorrow. My mother died unexpectedly, and her loss was also devastating."

"My dear man, no tragedy compares to a mother losing her child. If choosing between your own life or your child's, a mother will always sacrifice herself first. My eldest . . . well, I never had the opportunity to be a mother to him, but my word, Cyril was my baby to the end."

A stillness lingered in the air. The two sat looking out onto the horizon, observing the birds that flew past them and anticipating Jamie's emergence from the house. Maxim reflected on the relationship he'd had with his mother. Karine would always try to show equal affection to her two children, but Maxim would look back and think he had demanded far more attention from his mother than she would give to George. There was guilt that came from being so needy, and taking her presence for granted. Though maybe she knew that George was going to turn out more adept at handling life struggles than himself. Maxim lived in denial most of his youth that he was like his father, but Karine understood instinctively how to navigate the emotional needs of her firstborn, simply by recognizing the inner nature of her own husband. She had a blueprint, a strategy to help guide her son to become better than his father. She had admitted as much to Maxim, weeks before she died.

Karine had faith that her son could be strong and independent on his own, that he didn't need to feel so afraid and insecure of himself or his own accomplishments. But Maxim continued stubbornly to fear navigating life alone. He was like his father in that way; they both needed someone to provide comfort and support. In a twist of circumstance, it was Maxim's father who was able to move on, becoming independent and self-reliant after Karine's death, while even after thirty years Maxim had only become more entrenched in his need to have someone there to hold his hand.

Lady Wendell broke the silence. "I must say I am very happy that Jamie met someone like you."

"How so? I always worry that I am too old for him," Maxim responded softly.

"Oh nonsense!" she scoffed. "Jamie is an old soul; he always preferred the company of older people. But he told me that you are the first one that viewed him as an equal."

"Did he?"

"Why yes! Oh my word! All old men are the same, including my dearly departed husband. Always with a wandering eye for the young, never for substance but all for artifice. But Jamie tells me how respectful you are of his inner person. That is quite refreshing to hear."

"Well, that's a lovely thing for him to say."

"And I mean every word of it." Jamie's voice came toward them as he walked onto the terrace, grinning at Lady Wendell's presence.

"Lilliput!" Jamie exclaimed.

"My sweet Kinder Egg!" She rose from her seat and embraced Jamie, holding him tightly like a mother and son. 'It's so good to see you! Let me look at you! Oh, my word! You're just as I remember you!"

"Oh Lilly," Jamie chuckled. "To you I may as well be ten years old forever."

"Oh, I just can't help seeing you and my dear Cyril playing leap-frog in the great hall during the summer holiday. You too were so adorable together."

"Very adorable, Kinder Egg," Maxim teased Jamie.

Jamie laughed sarcastically. "Only she can call me Kinder Egg, got it?"

The three sat together on the terrace eating carrot cake and sharing memories, with Jamie and Lady Wendell discussing the shared impact of Cyril on both their lives. It gave pause to Maxim's thoughts of how his mother would have felt about Jamie being the person he ended up with. Would she have treated him as tenderly and comfortingly as Lady Wendell did? Or would she have echoed Henry and George's hesitancy over him marrying someone so young?

He observed how Jamie behaved with Lady Wendell, laughing and smiling earnestly and without pretention. They were two friends, though to Maxim it echoed the friendship one would see from an adult child and their parent. They were so comfortable in each other's presence, Maxim could see that she saw Jamie as a simulacrum of Cyril. And though Jamie's mother was still alive, Maxim could sense that Lady Wendell had become a mother-figure in her own right to his husband. At one point during the afternoon, Lady Wendell looked down at her phone to check the time. It was a quarter to six.

"Oh my word!" she exclaimed. "I have to go, my dear Kinder Egg. My flight to San Francisco leaves in two hours and I must depart at once!"

"Lilliput, don't tell me you're flying commercial. What happened to the family jet?" Jamie asked.

"Oh, my eldest son decided to lease it to a charter company. He says it's to save money on the upkeep. I don't know what he goes on about, seeing that the money is mine to use until I'm dead. Don't worry, Kinder Egg, I'm flying first class, not steerage."

Lady Wendell hugged Jamie one last time and said her goodbyes. She did not say when she would be returning but hoped to visit them soon. They watched her car disappear around the bend of the hill. Jamie turned to Maxim.

"If you must know, I used to be obsessed with Kinder Surprises."

"Oh really?" Maxim chuckled.

"When school was back in session, Cyril would bring me boxes full of Kinder Eggs from England. We would open the surprises inside and collect as many of the toys as we could."

"That was nice of him. I'm surprised you kids didn't grow chubby from all the chocolate," Maxim teased.

"Oh, we didn't eat it . . . we would feed it to the dogs in the village." Jamie said in a deadpan tone.

Maxim's face turned pale at this detached admission of malice, until Jamie burst into laughter at Maxim's expression.

"No, you doofus! You should see your face. We would eat all of it, we were just active kids." Jamie smiled with his mischievous grin.

Maxim's shock gave way to an uneasy smirk. He had heard of student pranks that went on in private schools like Jamie's, but something about Jamie's tone did not sit well in the back of his mind. Why admit so easily to feeding chocolate to dogs? Did Jamie know it could kill them? No, Maxim thought, it was just a morbid joke. A joke convincing enough to feel like an admission of unabashed guilt.

II

"Did Jamie recover from his money problems?" Edward inquired, sitting at the poolside with Maxim. It was a hot July morning, and Maxim had invited Edward to stay at Gwenshill while Paul was visiting family.

"He's repaying the loan installments, but whether he's making money on top of that is yet to be seen," Maxim replied wearily, their fight remaining fresh in his mind.

"I don't understand why you helped bail him out."

"Why wouldn't I?"

"He chose to leave his job; he was careless or greedy or whatever. It sets a poor example."

"Sweetie, he's my husband. And he is young and starting out, so some mistakes are expected."

"Some mistakes? Didn't you say he lost three million dollars? Boy, what luck it is to make mistakes with a rich daddy's bank account."

"Eddy . . ." Maxim looked at his friend with annoyance, but Edward returned his gaze with a look of disapproval.

"Don't Eddy me. I'm nowhere near as rich as you, but I know that if Paul tried hiding any secrets like that from me, I'd be livid and demanding divorce."

"It's not something I would accept either, but taking risks was kind of the family mantra."

"Your family Max. Your family." Edward plunged into the pool and began to swim to the other end. Maxim followed his friend, walking by the pool's edge to the other side. When Edward's head emerged from the water, he was met with Maxim standing in front of him at the pool's edge.

"You still think he's trouble, don't you?" Maxim looked down at Edward.

"Not necessarily, but I don't think keeping big secrets like that is healthy for a relationship."

"Me losing my temper wasn't healthy either."

"Max, two wrongs don't make a right. You guys cannot keep secrets from each other." Edward immersed his head once more in the cold water and swam back to the opposite end of the pool.

"We don't, I promise you!" Maxim shouted. "He's learned from his mistakes!"

Beyond the enclosure of the pool room, they could hear the roar of an engine in the distance. It appeared to be Jamie's car approaching the house, but the roar sounded different. Maxim looked out from the terrace doors as Edward climbed out of the pool. The distinct noise emerged from the woods in a blurry flash of red that sped along the road leading to the house.

"What the hell?" Maxim wondered aloud.

He made his way to the motor court with Edward in tow, still drying himself with a towel. The revving of the engine grew louder and louder, rattling the windows outside the front door.

Outside the door they were met by a shining new sports car. Jamie turned off the engine and emerged from the car's interior, a self-assured smile emanating from his face as he encountered his incredulous husband.

"Surprise! Isn't she beautiful?"

"Jamie, what on earth is this? Where did this car come from?"

"From the dealership, where else?"

"James! You can't go buying new toys when you're still in debt!"

"About that . . ." Jamie's smile grew as he placed a small slip of paper in Maxim's hand.

"Here's the remaining balance of the loan. Thank you for believing in me, handsome." Jamie winked.

Maxim looked down at the check; it was indeed all the money left to be paid, down to the penny. Maxim could not believe this turnaround in Jamie's fortune.

"Jamie! This is amazing! How did you do it?"

"Well, I was paying off my creditors and I came across an opportunity to invest in a futures contract. I took some of the loan you gave me to invest, and I made six million!"

"Jamie, how much of the loan did you use to play in futures?" Maxim prodded; he was under the impression Jamie was not going to use the loaned money to keep playing the market.

"Just 1.7 million. Look, it was a gamble, and you told me not to play fast and loose. But my chances were so good that I could not pass it up."

"Jamie, I cannot believe you!" Maxim cried in frustration. "You can't be irresponsible with other people's money! I know enough about futures to know that if your bet had gone wrong, you'd have gotten yourself in a hole twice the size!" Maxim paced around the court with his hand to his face. Edward side-eyed the exchange; his displeasure at Jamie's actions was evident and unsurprising.

"And what was wrong with your car?! It was only two years old!" Maxim continued. "Yet you go off buying a hyper car that will sit around in the garage unused!"

"But Max, this car is not for me . . . I bought it for you," Jamie answered, some of his enthusiasm deflated by Maxim's disapproval.

"For me?"

"Yeah, this is my apology for how I behaved that day. I'm sorry again, I promise not to keep anymore secrets from you."

"Oh Jamie." Maxim sighed as he hugged him. "Thank you for the car, but you didn't have to."

"I know, I just love you too much. I'm sorry." Jamie pouted.

"Okay, okay, enough!" Edward interjected, shaking his head. "Frankly, I will never understand this class."

"Oh, don't worry, Eddy," Jamie replied with a cheeky grin. "I didn't forget you."

Jamie walked to the trunk of the car and pulled out a large box and presented it to Edward.

"I knew you were visiting, and since you are Max's closest friend, I thought you should receive something special."

"Oh no Jamie, your shenanigans will not work on m—" Edward stopped mid-sentence as he caught glimpse of the contents within the box. He continued to loosen the wrappings to reveal what looked like piles of signed photographs.

"Ohhhh ... MYYY ... GODDDD!" Edward cried out. "They're signed autographs of Bette! Of Joan! Of Mae WEST! OH MY FUCKING GOD, STREISAND IS IN HERE!"

"I have a friend who's an antiques merchant and deals in Hollywood memorabilia. I asked him for signed photos only addressed to Eddys, Edwards, and any variations he could find."

"These are all addressed to ME?!" Edward exclaimed excitedly, beaming like a child on Christmas morning.

III

Gwendolyn Township was no different than other villages with upper-middle class pretentions and historic charms. It was a ten-minute drive from Gwenshill, on the opposite side of the park it was named for. It was a picturesque town, with quaint red-brick buildings and tree-lined streets. There was a café, a few boutique restaurants, an antique shop, and a fitness club. The town had originated to serve the households of the many mansions that made up the northern end of the county, but now instead of carpenters and butchers, it was full of affluent types who adopted blue-collar affectations with white-collar budgets.

Dr. Amos Wells, Maxim's physician, kept his practice in the heart of the township. A modest and courteous man in his mid-forties, his salt-and-pepper hair was combed over to help conceal a prominent widow's peak. He was a very competent doctor, and Maxim had been his patient for several years after the family physician had retired a decade prior.

Dr. Wells spoke clearly and directly, having conducted his regular checkup of Maxim.

"Alright, Max, your lungs and heart sound normal. Have you been experiencing any other issues?"

"Well, Doctor, I haven't experienced the paranoia I had over the last few months. But I am getting a bit forgetful, and having mood swings also."

"Have you been taking your regular medications?" the doctor continued, writing into his notes.

"Yes, Doctor."

"How are you sleeping? Have you been having trouble maintaining a regular eight hours?"

"I've been experiencing more nightmares. They used to be under control with my medication, but they don't seem to be working anymore."

Dr. Wells took a deep breath as he scanned through Maxim's records and his own notes.

"I don't know what to tell you Maxim, beyond the fact that at your age, some forgetfulness is not unexpected. The issue of night terrors, and the paranoia, may be your body developing a tolerance to the medication you're taking, since your regimen has gone unchanged for several years."

Maxim looked about the room from his chair, avoiding direct eye contact with the doctor. Anxiously he asked whether there was something that could be done.

"Well Maxim, I'm surprised that you have been taking all these medications for as long as you have. With counseling and non-medical therapy, you could have weaned off this stuff decades ago. My concern is what kind of psychological impact it would have if you tried ending this regimen cold turkey."

"So I'm stuck like this? Go insane with, or go insane without?" Maxim pressed his fingers against his knees and rocked in his seat uneasily as his anxiety grew.

"Your other tests came out normal, so I would argue you are healthier than most. It could be the case, all other indications considered, that if you start going to therapy, and lower your dosage, it may help with your symptoms. You might not completely stop taking these drugs, but you can minimize any increasing issues that may arise as you grow older."

Dr. Wells rose from his seat and pulled a card from his desk, handing it to Maxim.

"You can seek counseling in the city if you prefer, but some patients of mine recommend this therapist. Her practice is just a few streets over."

"But you are cutting back on my medication?"

"Some of it we are going to cut, but in small dosages," Dr. Wells responded as he wrote Maxim's prescription on his medical pad. "Come back in three months or otherwise call us if symptoms worsen."

"Thank you, Doctor."

Maxim stepped outside; the heat of the afternoon air felt invigorating compared to the clinical chill of the medical office. He looked down at the card the doctor had given him and walked through town looking for the therapist's address. He walked past several little shops and the occasional pedestrian. Turning the corner to the street noted on the card, Maxim came across a dotty little Victorian house, its brick walls painted over in delicate blue, with navy shutters and front door. He walked tentatively toward the house, his hands shaking.

In front of him was a simple wooden placard painted with white and silver trim.

"Anette Alcindor – Licensed Therapist"

Maxim stood in front of the door tentatively, holding the card in one hand and slowly moving his other to grab the door handle, its worn brass knob shining faintly from years of use. Maxim gripped the door, fearing what he needed to do. He wanted the nightmares to stop, but he did not want to admit that he was seeking help. *Deauvilliers are not weak-minded, and Deauvilliers do not need help*, echoed the voice of his grandfather in Maxim's head.

"I'm not crazy. I'm not crazy!" Maxim repeated to himself over and over. He twisted the handle, each degree of rotation feeling like an immeasurable struggle.

"I'm not crazy . . . I'm not crazy . . . I'm not crazy . . . I'm—"

Maxim was startled by the sudden opening of the door. A young woman stood on the other side, equally surprised by the sight of Maxim looming just in front of her.

"Oh! I'm so sorry!" she yelped. "Didn't mean to frighten you."

"Oh no, it's my fault . . ." Maxim mumbled hesitantly. The young woman's concerned face just made him more anxious, and now he worried his presence was frightening her.

"I'm sorry, I must have the wrong address."

Maxim turned around and quickly walked back to the main street. He rationalized that he would seek counseling in the city where the therapists were used to his class. He would try out the lower dosages first, and maybe he would not need any further help. Maxim kept circling through this reasoning for the remainder of the day. He walked to the pharmacy, picked up his prescriptions, and then drove back to Gwenshill. Jamie was waiting for him; it was their first wedding anniversary. Jamie had asked the kitchen to make red velvet cake for them, Maxim's favorite.

IV

Jamie felt like he had the world on a string when he recovered from his losses. The accountants, on the other hand, had a different take on his windfall. After paying the money he owed, and the taxes that he failed to report on his payout, he did not have much left. To the average man it was still a considerable sum of money, but for Jamie it was cold comfort having to surrender the bulk of a six-million-dollar payout. Maxim had a more pragmatic take. He thought that the whole ordeal would teach his young husband to understand that fast money was easy to make, and easy to lose.

In the meantime, something had gone wrong with Jamie's garden, and the flowerbeds had failed to bloom. Jamie tried to rush a process that required more than just one planting season to work, proving himself impatient with both horticulture and markets.

Jamie still put on a humble presentation when George and Isabel visited Gwenshill with their daughter. Jamie sweetly told Charlotte, kneeling to her level and greeting her with his signature smile, "Charlie, the butterflies were busy packing the flowers in their luggage. Next spring they will begin moving into our city."

Jamie could put on a convincing act for Charlotte, but Maxim saw in his eyes that disappointment was an emotion Jamie did not like to experience on a regular basis. Another summer had passed, and fall's cool breezes returned once more. Maxim was content in how their marriage was settling into a quiet rhythm that flowed from morning to night. He could see that a little restless spirit in Jamie's manner remained. But in his mind, Maxim believed that Jamie would settle into his groove sooner or later. Jamie maintained a balance between his work and his new hobby. Some evenings he worked late, but for the most part he tried to keep himself level-headed.

Maxim saw parallels in their life and that of his parents. He was the dutiful husband working from the family office, while Jamie was the spouse who commanded over the running of the house, dictating instructions to the hired staff from his own command center. There were regular visitors from both Maxim's and Jamie's circles, with intimate gatherings on a weekly basis, and the occasional big party once a month. In a welcome difference from the past, Maxim planned the gatherings at the house, and Jamie served as entertainer and master of ceremonies. The two of them worked well together and complemented each other anytime they had to appear in public. The reputation and outward success of their marriage shone like a beacon in the night. To the world outside, and in Maxim's eyes, he believed that he had begun a revival of his family's legacy as great tastemakers.

Maxim saw how Jamie's presence lit up the room with every person he spoke to. His charm, his wit, his smile . . . Jamie reminded Maxim of his mother at those parties, the grace and elegance of someone who conducted himself with the dignity of noble birth. It painted a wholly different picture of a person who early in his social provenance had been known as the "black sheep of the blackest family in high society."

"You know, you never gave me an explanation as to how you got all those bottles of champagne at the Mattachine party," Maxim pointed out to Jamie as they took reprieve from their latest gathering at the house.

Jamie gave a sly smile. "A magician never reveals his secrets."

"Oh come on, there is no way that you were able to find all those bottles of that exact champagne on such short notice."

"Alright, alright, I'll tell you." Jamie relented, smiling through the whole confession.

"You see, there *was* champagne in those glasses, but not from those bottles. I just called up every fine restaurant from here to the city and they willingly parted with their empty bottles. I bought the cheap stuff to fill the glasses in the kitchen and put the empty bottles in the dining room for show. After all, I only needed the two bottles we already had. One to open with the saber, and the other for the two of us to drink."

"You sneaky devil." Maxim snickered in amazement. "But then how did no one notice the difference in flavor?"

"Max, please, everyone knows that price tag and flavor mean nothing when it comes to wine. And champagne is just fizzy wine." Jamie giggled. "Though I will not take responsibility for that near brawl. That was just serendipity that aided in the slight-of-hand."

How clever Jamie is, Maxim thought. He always knew how to take advantage of a situation when the opportunity appeared before him. When chaos erupted, Jaime maintained his cool when things appeared to be falling apart. Maxim had been so hesitant two years ago when he first encountered that young man in the midnight-blue suit, and now that young man was in his living room laughing and smiling at the most innocuous of conversations.

But when the guests had long departed and the parties were over, there remained a friction as Maxim attempted to overcome his demons. The nightmares were becoming more frequent, and more vivid. He would wake up in the middle of the night in a cold sweat, at times jolting awake in his bed. He never screamed awake, but the commotion was at times forceful enough to wake his sleeping husband. Jamie showed understanding for Maxim's condition, but the frequent nights of disturbed sleep resulted in Jamie becoming fatigued and irritable.

"At least it's not snoring," Jamie remarked one morning as the two of them sat having breakfast. "I would have smothered you with a pillow at this rate."

"I'm sorry, Jamie; if you want to take up one of the other rooms I would understand."

"Don't be silly. If the doctor says it's necessary then we'll work on this together."

Jamie sat scrolling through his phone, when a flash of inspiration came across his mind.

"Why don't you take up boxing again?"

"Me? Box? I haven't boxed since I was your age," Maxim replied, reluctant at the idea of returning to such a taxing regimen.

"I don't know, I think it is kind of sexy," Jamie flirted. "After all, maybe releasing some of your stress and anxiety on a punching bag would be good."

"Well . . ." Maxim paused. "I suppose that would help with my temper."

"That's the spirit!" Jamie chirped. "We can buy up some equipment or start looking for a boxing gym."

"Actually, there's some equipment in the downstairs gym we can use. It's old at this point, but when we bought it, it was all Olympic-certified equipment," Maxim replied without looking up from his breakfast plate.

"What downstairs gym?" Jamie asked in confusion. "I've been living here for over a year, and you never mentioned a gym."

Maxim looked up at Jamie, his brow furrowed. He was certain he had told Jamie there was a gym underneath the ballroom.

"The gym in the basement? Of course I did, how else do you think I keep myself in shape?"

After breakfast, Maxim walked Jamie along the servants' stairs into a long corridor that ran underneath the length of the house. Sure enough, at the end of the hall through a set of double doors, there was a large basement space filled with gym equipment and an unused boxing ring, worn with use but still in good condition.

"Maximillian, I can't believe you never told me this existed!" Jamie uttered in astonishment.

"Jamie, I swear to God, I told you this when I first gave you a tour of the house."

"Max, if that were true, I wouldn't be wasting my time doing calisthenics in the woods."

"I'm sure of it. I . . . I . . ."

Maxim found himself lost mid-sentence, trying to remember when he had given Jamie a tour of the mansion, but his mind was blank. It felt like a fragment of his memory had been clipped from his mind like a deleted scene in a film reel. Maxim became distressed at this lapse; the fact that he could not recall taking Jamie into this exact location caused a twinge of fear. Jamie didn't notice Maxim's concerned expression.

"You know what Max, whatever," Jamie responded, throwing his hands in the air. "At least we can just buy new gloves and hire a trainer to come over."

Maxim kept attempting to recall this lost memory, but the more he pondered, the hazier it became, and the more fearful of his mental state he became by consequence. Though maybe Jamie was right. He had been right before, Maxim thought. Maybe some new activity would help him clear his mind of its fog.

CHAPTER 11

I

A year had passed; it was now re-election season for George's senate seat. Maxim had orchestrated a charity function at Gwenshill to help raise funds for his brother's campaign. There were private donors flying in from across the country, and strict security had been hired to keep reporters and party crashers from entering the grounds.

Maxim was feeling confident in his ability to keep the festivities in order. He had made mistakes in the past and learned how to plan for them; he was sure he could guarantee a party that would paint his brother in the best of lights. Jamie was asked to remain reserved and stay in the background throughout the function, something that he found irksome, but he agreed to be on his best behavior for Maxim.

"I think it's unfair. I am not like my cousin; I voted for your brother in the last election," Jamie vented to his husband as the two dressed for the party.

"I know it's unfair, my dear Jamie. But I want my brother to succeed, and your cousin has been a vicious little shit talking about George on his podcast."

"Again, that's not my fault. I'm a Grenvill in name only."

"Look, it's just for today. After this you can return to being the life of the party," Maxim assured his husband with a cheeky grin.

Jamie smiled, fastening tight the bowtie onto Maxim's shirt.

"You look handsome," Jamie flirted.

"You too," Maxim returned with a kiss.

The mansion was awash in wealth, more splendid than it had ever been in the past. The men wore black tie, suave and smart down to their cufflinks and oxfords. The women were draped in diamonds that fell elegantly upon graceful dresses and gowns. It was the sort of gathering that many of the more progressive would have decried as bourgeois and decadent. But the public rooms had been crammed with some of the biggest names and fortunes that could ever be assembled for the benefit of the democratic cause.

It was the sort of party, old-fashioned but not extinct, that had been the métier of the philanthropic classes for much longer than the current members of the Porter family had been alive. These were Maxim's people, and Jamie was the fish out of water among the old-money establishment. He remained quiet and observant, watching how Maxim comported himself with the other guests.

"Maximillian my dear!" called out a voice from the chorus of socialites. And it continued this way for most of the afternoon. Parades of bankers, magnates, lawyers, and patrons ingratiating themselves with the likes of Maxim and his family. The men would crowd around George, courting for favors and negotiating influence for their continued support of the senator. The women congregated around Isabel, wearing a dress provided to her by the fashion house. An avant-garde outfit that had appeared on last year's runway, it had been modified and toned down for her stature. She stood beside her husband as a symbol of progressive yet tasteful femininity.

"My dear Izzy, your dress is magnificent," Maxim praised his sister-in-law.

"Why thank you Max. Magnificent is this party. I hope you and James are enjoying your efforts."

"I can't take credit; Maxim is the mastermind behind the whole affair," Jamie responded candidly.

"Karine would have been proud. It's like being at one of her parties when I first met George."

"Oh God," Maxim laughed. "Remember when Uncle Reggie got drunk and got hold of Grandpa's accordion? George was so red in the face with embarrassment I thought he would explode."

"Oh yes!" Isabel snorted in laughter. "Your mother gave such a look at Reggie, it was like she had lasers coming out of her eyes. It was hilarious."

"Don't get me started. Mom had to talk circles around Mitterrand to not get Reggie sent back to the foreign legion for face-planting into his wife!"

"Mitterrand? Like the president of France?" Jamie asked.

"I think he was no longer president then," Isabel commented, pondering the timing of the events.

The open cocktail hour proceeded to dinner. George and Isabel sat together with his biggest donors, while Maxim and Jamie shared a table with other guests. A familiar youth with a dark blond haircut sat to the left of Maxim.

"Herrods? I didn't recognize you without your blue hair."

"Yes Mr. Porter, it's me Daniel."

"What are you doing here? I don't recall seeing your name on the guest list."

"I drew the short straw between your brother's staffers to attend the party. I think I was listed as just 'Staffer #1,'" Daniel said a bit sheepishly.

"Oh I see. Nice to know my brother hired you after all. This is my husband, James."

"Hello James, nice to meet you," Daniel greeted Jamie politely.

Jamie took measure of the man, who was no younger than he was. He gave him a shifty look.

"Likewise, Danny boy."

Daniel and Maxim talked pleasantries during the dinner, telling one another of what had transpired during the time they last met. Jamie remained quiet for most of the dinner, listening to Maxim's conversation between bouts of small talk with other guests at the table. Daniel was a polite and decent young man, still learning how to operate in the politicking of Washington, too young to be another jaded operator of the political machine.

Daniel had kind hazel eyes, which complemented the tie he wore; a slightly crooked smile, and a small nose on a round face. He had a pleasant disposition that Maxim had not fully noticed on their first encounter. He was the veritable opposite of Jamie, whose beauty was instantly disarming, while Daniel's looks were a slow burn. They shared some common interests, which expanded the conversation through the various courses. At one point during the meal, Maxim turned to Jamie, noticing his curious silence.

"Everything okay Jamie? Usually you're so talkative."

"I don't know," Jamie huffed. "The food is upsetting my stomach."

"Do you want me to get you some seltzer tablets?" Maxim asked with concern.

"No, I think I'm going to head inside."

"Oh. Well let me know if you need anything."

Jamie left the party and headed upstairs. Maxim was worried; it was unusual for his husband to leave in the middle of the action. Maxim told himself he would drop in to check up on Jamie after George's speech to the donors.

II

When Maxim came to bed that night, Jamie was already asleep. It was nine in the evening, and the party had carried on without his presence. Maxim felt like he had abandoned his husband; he certainly felt odd enjoying a gathering without him. George's speech had been grandiloquent and vapid. Maxim had imagined the sort of witty comeback Jamie would whisper into his ear during the whole oration. He felt lonely without his other half beside him.

The following morning was unseasonably warm. George and Isabel had stayed over, and Maxim met them for breakfast wearing a pair of shorts and a linen shirt.

"This is unusual weather for October. It feels like spring!" Maxim exclaimed, helping himself to the breakfast buffet.

"Well, it must have been a good omen. People danced late into the night the moment the doors to the rose patio opened," George replied, sipping his coffee. "The donors had nothing but praise for the whole party."

"Well, I'm glad to hear it. Senator Porter for round two!" Maxim cheered heartily.

"Where was James?" Isabel asked. "I saw him leave during dinner."

"He felt ill and went to bed early. Something about the food didn't sit well."

"That's a shame."

Jamie walked into the dining room not long after, still wearing his pajamas. He had a glum expression on his face as he joined the others at the table. They exchanged greetings, Jamie dismissing his absence as a simple stomachache before sitting down to eat his food.

The family continued with their meal, Jamie remaining quiet through the remainder of breakfast. Late in the morning, George and Isabel departed Gwenshill to return to Washington. They had another event to attend before the election. Maxim waved his goodbyes from the foyer; recalling he had some emails to answer, he headed to the family office. He walked back through the dining room, finding Jamie still sitting in his chair.

"Jamie? Do you want me to call the doctor?"

"No." Jamie sat unmoving. "How was the party while I was gone?"

"It was okay. It would have been better if you had been there."

"How was it talking to the blondie?" Jamie asked bluntly. Maxim was confused.

"It was fine. We talked a bit more but that was it."

"Did you fuck him?" Jamie retorted, his voice full of contempt.

Maxim was floored by the question. It took him a moment to overcome the shock of hearing such an inquiry coming from Jamie's lips.

"What kind of question is that?!"

"You heard me. Did you fuck that blond tramp?"

"Have you lost your mind? No, I did not sleep with him!"

"I saw how he looked at you with those deadbeat eyes. That prissy little fruit, drooling over the opportunity to get fucked by his boss's gay brother!"

"Are you listening to yourself? I can't believe I'm hearing this!" Max was beside himself. "I'm married to you! Why the hell would I fuck anyone else?"

"Because you're not fucking me!" Jamie griped bitterly. He was acting like a jilted and jealous teenager.

Maxim grew quiet, at a loss for words on how to respond. He had grown weary in bed for the last several months, as his medications sometimes lowered his libido. He had hoped it wouldn't matter, being that Jamie could perform dual roles, but perhaps he had been placing too much responsibility on Jamie to be the active partner. He felt awkward expressing the reason why.

"I don't know Jamie. I didn't think it mattered."

"Mattered? Of course it matters! I like being the one who gets overpowered! That gets dominated by the bigger man! I want a man to fuck me! And fuck me hard!" Jamie's voice grew louder as his anger built.

"James, stop yelling! Do you want the whole county to hear it?"

"I don't give a fuck if they hear it! I want you to pin me against the wall and fuck me till I'm screaming for you to stop!"

"James, you're delusional! What does this have anything to do with Daniel?"

"Because you spoke to him the whole night! Being all cutesy and flirty with that whore and ignoring my needs! It's so typical, you wrinkled old fucks chasing fresh meat when you're bored with what you've got!"

Maxim did not know how to deal with this conversation. To him, this argument seemed so preposterous and immature he could not comprehend how to proceed with or end it.

"I don't have time for this," Maxim said plainly. "I have work to do, and you have your own shit to deal with. Get your fucking act together."

Maxim left the room and returned to the solemness of the office. Sitting at his desk, Maxim started to work. He opened his inbox, organizing his thoughts to start writing his responses. His hands hovered over the keyboard, ready to type an answer to a donation request. His hands remained frozen in the air, yet to strike a single letter key. But Maxim's mind was blocked by a cloud of anger and disbelief. He thought aloud, his ire growing with each syllable.

"Me? Cheat on him? What is that brat possibly thinking? The nerve to think I would sleep with anyone else! That insecure, miserable, entitled little—" Maxim slammed his fists upon the desk.

He was deeply insulted, to the point he could not mentally overcome the need to berate Jamie for such an outrageous indictment of his loyalty. He stormed out of the office, slamming the door as he cut his way through the kitchen back to the dining room. Jaime was no longer at the table; his dishes were already gone. Maxim stalked the rooms on the first floor, looking for his husband. Maxim suspected that Jamie was hiding, and an animalistic furor possessed him at the thought that Jamie was playing more childish games to avoid him. He barged into each room, yelling Jamie's name, until he entered the library.

Jamie was sitting on a chair with an opened book on his lap, his eyes turned to Maxim.

"What's the matter Max? You look upset," said Jamie in a worried tone, as if oblivious to their altercation.

"What do you mean 'What's the matter'?" Maxim yelled. "You miserable brat! You accused me of cheating on you!"

Jamie's eyes widened, his face growing pale.

"Max! When on earth did this happen?"

"Don't play fucking dumb with me Grenvill! You literally threw a temper tantrum in the dining room just now and accused me of fucking that blond next to me!"

"What!?" Jamie grew confused and concerned. "Max, you left the dining room to say goodbye to your brother, and I came here to read after the three of you left."

"Do you think I'm that stupid? Do you think I'm making this up?" Maxim continued to yell, throwing himself onto Jamie, pulling him from his chair by the arms and violently shaking him.

"Max! Let go of me!"

"How do I know that *you're* not fucking around? Like you're an innocent party, throwing yourself in front of every greasy rich queen that looks in your direction! I'm not the fucking cheater, you are!"

Jamie pulled himself apart from Maxim, slapping him across the face. Before Maxim could strike back, Judith rushed into the room.

"Is everything alright?" she called out, breathing heavily.

"Ah! Here's proof!" Maxim declared. "Did you hear the altercation between myself and James in the dining room just now? How he was screaming I wasn't fucking him, for the whole world to hear! Master James and his delusional rape fantasies!"

"MAX!" Jamie shrieked, gasping in shock.

Judith stood there awkwardly, frightened by Maxim's escalating temper. Avoiding eye contact with either man, she grew pale and distressed. Maxim's temper dissipated at her reaction; he felt his rage regressing and being replaced with an overwhelming sense of puzzlement.

"M-Mr. Porter," Judith muttered, "I was in the pantry just outside the door to the kitchen. After I heard you escorting Senator and Mrs. Porter out of the room, I entered to clear all the dishes. Master James left just after you."

Maxim's face flushed as a feeling of horror overcame him. It had been a hallucination, one that appeared so vivid he had thought it was real. Jamie was now the one whose anger began to bubble over at the incident.

"I don't understand . . . I saw him sitting there . . . it was like he never left the room . . . I . . . I . . ." Maxim began hyperventilating, desperately trying to make sense of what he had seen.

"Maximilian, that's enough!" Jamie proclaimed angrily. "I've never encountered someone so utterly insecure of himself in my entire life! Accusing me of throwing a childish tantrum, when you are the one pulling things out of thin air!"

"I'm sorry Jamie! I swear, it felt as real as us standing here!"

"I'm going to stay with friends. You are becoming unhinged. I don't care what you need to do, but you need to get your fucking act together!"

Jamie stormed out of the library. Maxim followed suit, a torrent of apologies and pleas for understanding pouring from him along with his tears, but Jamie would not tolerate it. Jamie remained angry but calm, determined to get away from Maxim and the suffocating energy of his jealous paranoia. He took off in his car, driving furiously away from the grounds of Gwenshill. Maxim remained in the motor court, struggling to make sense of his behavior, and trying desperately not to break down into a groveling mass of sorrow.

III

A week passed before Jamie returned any of Maxim's stream of apologetic messages on social media, text messages, phone calls, and voicemails. Maxim had avoided reaching out to Jamie's friends, as he did not want to drag more people into another symptom of his unresolved trauma: hallucinations. He also avoided contacting George or Isabel, in the fear that they would end up sending him to a mental facility. And calling Edward was out of the question. Would the police be arriving at Maxim's front door? Would Jamie have Maxim committed? Maxim's mind was spiraling. The scandal would be the end of all his grand dreams, and the end of a romance that had begun so unexpectedly and had blossomed into a love that felt so genuine and real.

Perhaps the implosion was a good thing, Maxim reasoned. He was still hopelessly insecure, and the age gap would always be the barrier that divided them. A love divided by one, maybe two generations was preposterous to contemplate—the different music, culture, mores. He was going to be sixty in no time; fate had taken too long to resolve Maxim's loneliness, and his age would be his undoing, and Jamie's departure was proof of that. Maxim was feeling physically ill during that long week of uncertainty. Fatigued and weak, his mind a blur of painful longing and absent focus. Maxim would sulk in his bedroom, only coming out to answer emails and delegate work when the family foundation would call the house begging for direction.

"Maxim, you need to return to your prescriptions from before," Jamie demanded when he finally answered Maxim's pleas.

"I'm developing a tolerance to the pills. I need to cut back. Please, I'm so sorry for doubting you, my dear Jamie."

"There's no way I'm coming back to that house with a man who is on the brink of psychosis," Jamie reiterated more forcefully.

"I will go to therapy; I will seek help."

"Maximillian, you've been saying this for months and I'm sick of it! Go tell your doctor to increase the dosage of your pills or I am filing for divorce."

Divorce. Now the hammer had fallen. The final humiliation of seeing his home torn apart, and his spiraling madness being exposed for the whole world to see. And after all the destruction he would just be remembered as another demented old man dying alone in his own ruinous haunted house. For as much as he feared his medication ravaging his mind, the fear of being alone at the end of his life held greater sway.

"Okay. I will call the doctor and tell them the lower dosages are not working," Maxim relented. "Just please come home."

Maxim called Dr. Wells the following day, lying that he had been going to therapy, but the prescription needed to be increased again. Jamie returned to Gwenshill that afternoon. The first dinner in the house was a tense affair, and Jamie returned to sleeping in the other bedroom for the night. The healing would progress through winter, mending itself with the first showers of April.

CHAPTER 12

I

The butterfly garden had finally bloomed with a triumphant explosion of color and fragrance. It was as though fate had conspired to celebrate the healing of Jamie and Maxim's relationship by turning the grounds of Gwenshill into a feast of visual delight. Maxim's symptoms had diminished considerably from the previous year; he reasoned that the lower dosages had acclimated his body into accepting the previous amount of medication. Jamie had forgiven Maxim for their fight. The couple invited Maxim's family to attend a "grand opening" of Jamie's butterfly metropolis.

'I love it! This is absolutely breathtaking," Isabel proclaimed as she entered the terrace with Charlotte. The once precocious little girl had grown less enthused about the endeavor over time, but still made an act to express admiration for her young uncle's delayed birthday present.

"It is quite pretty, Uncle Jamie, and there are butterflies everywhere," Charlotte said.

"I'm glad you like it, Charlie. It was an effort of love. Look at the variety of butterflies. And we have so many songbirds flying around, it's a chorus of melody!" Jamie gloated.

"It surely is beautiful," agreed Mr. Porter, who was walking on crutches as he recovered from an operation.

Judith prepared lunch to be served on the terrace, where the family carried on in the usual custom of jovial pleasantries and the occasional joke. Maxim did not speak during the meal. He remained reserved and determined to put on a brave face for his family and his husband. The other members of the family did not notice Maxim's silence as Jamie remained at center stage for his latest achievement.

"How are you doing with your day trading, James?" asked George.

"It's going well," Jamie responded. "I am actually thinking of taking on some outside investors."

"Is that so?" Mr. Porter chimed in.

"Yes, I have worked out a new strategy. Futures contracts are becoming too risky with the current climate; I need to rethink what's the next step."

"Are you looking into derivatives? Mutual funds perhaps?"

"I'm looking into fintech, maybe digital contracts. I'm writing a prospectus for now."

"Well hopefully you don't get burned from the risk taking," George replied.

Jamie hesitated briefly before responding. It was imperceptible to George and Henry, but Maxim suspected that Jamie may have been playing fast and loose again.

"With every investment there is risk. Though it would be nice if I could get some more investors to share it. Mr. Porter, what do you think?"

"I don't see why not. I'm an old man, losing some pocket change won't make a difference." Mr. Porter laughed. Maxim became uneasy at the idea of Jamie taking money from his father.

"At least the payoff from this garden was worth it in my eyes," Isabel commented. "I would love to have some of these varieties in our garden."

"Hear that James? If Wall Street fails you can make a living as a professional landscaper," George joked, the table chuckling in unison.

"What about you, Maxim?" Mr. Porter asked innocently. "I had a conversation with a trustee in the foundation recently. He says you have been having difficulties with your tasks."

Maxim felt himself growing anxious and defensive. "I have been doing a perfectly competent job; I just had been dealing with some health issues, that's all."

"Health issues? Nothing serious I hope?" said Mr. Porter.

"I have been pushing him a bit hard in the gym and exercising outdoors," Jamie intervened. "I forget at times that he's not the same age as me and the soreness leaves him drained physically. He has wonderful stamina though."

"Well, the best part of Gwenshill is the fresh air. Please push him hard, it helps with his sour mood," Mr. Porter teased.

"Ha, ha," Maxim retorted in annoyance.

"If anything, James, if you can prove yourself adept with your investments, you could help take some of the load off Maxim's responsibilities. Those charities are always begging for money," Mr. Porter laughed.

Maxim wanted to rebuke his father, but with his mental state still fragile, he didn't want to give his father any ideas of surrendering the family foundation to Jamie.

II

"Creatine? All that does is bloat you with water," Maxim said as he looked over the supplements Jamie had selected for him.

Maxim and Jamie had been exercising together since Jamie's return. Maxim had kept a regular exercise routine that rarely changed, but he agreed to work out with his husband to help mend the rift the fight had created. It went so far as to adopt taking the various sports supplements that Jamie kept in the kitchen.

"Out of all the sports supplements, this one is the best at maintaining muscle mass and recovery. And it helps with the nervous system," Jamie replied keenly.

"Fine, I guess it wouldn't hurt taking it before the gym."

"It's recommended to take it every day."

"Every day?" Maxim scoffed. "As if I'm not getting enough chemicals as it is."

"Don't worry Max," Jamie smiled. "This one has my seal of approval."

Jamie's one concession to Maxim was that a boxing coach would be hired to help train Maxim, and Jamie was to join in the classes also. The reasoning for having Jamie box was twofold in Maxim's mind: to serve as a sparring partner, and as self-defense against himself. Maxim was still dealing with moments where a rageful energy bubbled from his subconscious. They mostly happened when he was alone, but a couple of times a month they happened in the presence of others. Jamie didn't seem to notice, but Maxim believed Judith had taken note of them on one or two occasions.

Maxim retreated to the office or the garden when he had the chance. Work was an easy pretense to remain sequestered away. There was a side door from the office into Jamie's new garden. Maxim would walk out of his office and sit in the carefully planned meadows and flowerbeds, and in that brief respite he found himself not as an old man but a young boy, immersed in the calming sensibility he had felt as a child playing in the gardens his mother once tended, smelling the rich scent of deep red roses and counting petals from the sunflowers that grew in the grounds. It was an unorthodox garden, but in those days walking through the grounds was like wandering through an impressionist painting. Jamie had created his own work of art with the garden, different but beautiful, and now it was filled with monarchs, Maxim's favorite butterfly.

CHAPTER 13

I

Mr. Henry Isaiah Porter III passed away in his sleep at ninety years old in the early hours of the fifth of July at the home of Senator and Mrs. George Deauvillier-Porter. Maxim and Jamie, along with Henry, were visiting George and Isabel at their townhouse for a barbeque. Jamie insisted that a grand party at Gwenshill would have been more befitting, but Independence Day weekend had always been George's domain; he was obstinate that when it came to barbeque, only his townhouse would do, since he had a smoker and an outdoor kitchen.

"His last meal was your beef brisket, George. He died a happy man," Maxim consoled his brother with deadpan humor. George, still teary, tried to hold back from laughing.

"Max, you're such a prick," George responded, hugging his brother tightly.

The funeral did not have the pomp and ceremony of Karine's funeral. There was a church service in the city's main cathedral and a mass. Directors and former coworkers of Mr. Porter's bank attended, along with business leaders and politicians. The mood was melancholy yet held a sense of relief for the brothers who mourned their father's passing. Henry had lived a long and fulfilling life, and despite the sadness

George and Maxim felt, his death was not as tragic and unexpected as the death of their mother had been decades prior. Though George had become emotional during the eulogy, Maxim was surprised to find himself not any more mournful at the passing of his father than he would be by any other death. He thought that maybe he had already expelled the entirety of his grief for the death of one parent, which had depleted his feelings for the other.

The procession of mourners made their way to the open casket to see Mr. Porter one last time before he was to be cremated, his ashes to be split between the family crypt and France to be with his late wife. George and Isabel kneeled together, each quietly praying over the departed patriarch. After their turn, Maxim and Jamie approached the box. Jamie kneeled, silently looking over the body. Maxim did not kneel but just stood beside his husband.

"He was like a dad to me," Jamie said softly to Maxim. "My own father never had the patience to listen to me."

"Sadly, that's the case between a lot of fathers and sons. Headstrong men sometimes don't recognize when they are just repeating a pattern," Maxim replied, gently placing his hand on Jamie's shoulder. "He thought of you as a son."

"How do you know?"

Jamie looked up to Maxim, waiting for his answer, but the right words never emerged from Maxim's mind.

"I just know." He sighed, patting Jamie's shoulder.

Maxim noted how waxen his father looked; there was no question that what he saw was not a person, just a body that used to be so. The gloom frozen in Mr. Porter's face did not convey his once upbeat and irreverent self, or even resemble the stern and deeply thoughtful banker. The photo that stood beside the body was of a younger and more determined man, with his flaxen golden hair and large rimmed glasses. If there had been a moment when Maxim looked up to his father, it had been during the time that photo was taken. Here was the embodiment of duty and conviction to his work and career, the model of someone who believed deeply that his profession was a vocation that required absolute earnest. Those were illusions that quickly fell by the wayside as Maxim grew older. And now his father was no man at all, but a lifeless object.

"Can you give me a few moments alone before we go?" Maxim asked Jamie, who nodded and went to stand with George and Isabel. Maxim kneeled by the casket, the light padding of the kneeler digging into his shins as he rested his body weight beside his father. Maxim did not believe in prayer, in a God, or gods, or whatever fictions that his family so willingly believed and obeyed. He just kneeled, looking intently at the face that looked even more unreal from this vantage point than from afar. The makeup used to disguise decay was too thick and discolored and Maxim felt a sense of disgust at the sight. *They made you look like shit*, he couldn't help thinking.

Maxim lingered, processing the defining moments of his life with his father: the tone-deaf comments, the lack of tenderness, the emotional absence, the missing moments where he wanted to hear "I'm proud of you." Maxim had felt his father's pride only when he achieved what his father expected of him: high grades, awards, diplomas, and certificates of worth to society; he hadn't felt the pride of his father's love. Maxim still resented that failing, that irreconcilable sense of not being worthy if not certified as such by others, even as his father now lay surrounded by white lilies and orchids. In this final moment between father and son, Maxim could only gaze at his dead father with anger and contempt.

Maxim stood up once more, still facing the casket. Leaning close, he whispered into the dead man's ear the only words he could muster after a lifetime of being made to feel inadequate by a father who was not there to comfort him in sorrow or support him in happiness, leaving all the burden of loving his child to Karine.

"You failed her, you failed me, and you're the reason she's gone."

Maxim walked away from his father, relieved that Henry was gone, yet bitter with the lack of emotional closure. George took half of the ashes to be buried with their mother. The remainder, Maxim took to the Porter family crypt; it was the last time Maxim would allow himself to think openly about his father.

II

The Deauvillier family fortune consisted of a tangled trail of shell corporations and trusts. After the death of the patriarch, Magnus Deauvillier, the estate was divided equally between his four sons and only daughter.

The empire they inherited was a conglomerate that spanned home goods, textiles, consumer electronics, telecommunications, shipping, industrial chemicals, and military defense.

The four brothers fell into bitter dispute over which brother would inherit which industry, in a time when the Deauvillier empire was losing its prominence in continental Europe, facing the risk of nationalization of key industries by the French State. Karine, being the female heir, was not awarded any direct stake or roles in the industries her father had built. Instead, she inherited minority shares in each of these industries. In this way, Magnus believed he had secured the future of his daughter; should any of the branches of his empire fail, the others would remain strong under her brothers' combined leadership.

But his faith in the business acumen of his four adult sons was misplaced, each brother wrestling furiously to control the entire family legacy rather than to build on the business together. Each brother wanted to be the sole leader, the new patriarch. And like immature children, they each attacked and sabotaged their siblings' efforts to run their shares in the family business. When Karine met Henry Porter, her family's empire was on the threshold of permanent stagnation.

Henry had gone through the dissolution of his own family's business, brought down by family ego and hubris. He began planning to transfer Karine's stake in her family's industries to other investments. He did so secretly, to ensure that his wife's fortune would not be sabotaged by her brothers. What was left was a similar tangle of assets and accounts spread around the world, but Henry was successful in his scheme. When the Deauvillier family empire collapsed under the weight of lawsuits, scandal, disinvestment, and mismanagement, its industries nationalized or sold off to foreign corporations, Karine's wealth remained, now contained within the zombie shells of the companies her father had once created. All of them became vehicles to maintain an estimated six-hundred-million-dollar estate in perpetuity for their sons, Maxim and George.

After Karine's death, Henry had become the trustee of his wife's estate, providing monthly stipends for his sons as per the rules of the trust. But with Henry's death, the estate was once again divided between the two heirs, each left to decide what assets and accounts would be allocated to whom.

On top of Karine's family money, Mr. Porter had amassed his own fortune of some fifty million dollars in government and corporate securities along with a penthouse near the city and a summer villa in the lake district. Henry's will was read a fortnight after his death; the villa was bequeathed to George, the penthouse to Maxim, and the securities to be divided between both. What neither brother had expected was that Henry instructed the charitable foundations to be split in two after his death, with Isabel and Jamie each responsible for one of the new entities.

"This is ridiculous, I have been running the foundation for over twenty years! Why did he decide to split it in two?" griped a confused Maxim at the attorney.

"Well Maximillian, according to this testament, your father believed that the resources of the foundation needed to be better divided to reflect the interests of the whole family."

"Please explain," George joined in. "Even I think this is a strange request coming from Dad."

"Senator, it is unusual I grant you, but not uncommon. The deceased cites how your brother Maxim tends to support causes that do not align with your values and interests."

"He split the foundation because I spend money on gay causes?!" Maxim exclaimed, growing even angrier.

"That's not what he meant." The attorney cleared his throat. "You can support causes you deem noble and in line with your principles Mr. Porter, but now there will be a charitable organization that will be aligned with your brother's own principles."

"With half the funding! I can't believe it! And I am not even in charge of what is supposed to be *my* charity! Why did he appoint James then?"

"The deceased did not specify. But be that as it may, you and your brother now have equal control of your shares of your mother's estate. You can make determinations of what assets you'd like to designate to the foundation without restriction."

Maxim was furious but remained quiet, sulking as he looked out the window of the attorney's office. George did not dare utter any words at the revelation, not wanting to upset his brother further. Though he enjoyed the idea of Isabel having the ability to support causes that she cared about with his half of the Deauvillier estate, Maxim still felt betrayed by his dead father. *May he rot in hell, that bastard,* Maxim fumed. And although the bond between him and his brother would always be strong, he could not help feeling resentment at George for continuing to view Maxim's life as unseemly and thus undermining the causes he cared about most deeply.

III

"That's fantastic!" Jamie exclaimed when Maxim revealed the details of Henry Porter's will to him.

"So, how much is my salary for running the new foundation?" Jamie asked jokingly, sounding almost frivolous.

"Zero," Maxim replied sternly. "I'm in control of the purse now, and I'm not giving a salary to someone who's already comfortably wealthy."

"Oh damn, such a killjoy," Jamie replied.

"I'm serious. I will not have my spouse living on money that's supposed to go to youth shelters and AIDS research. You have your investments."

"But Maxim, don't you see the opportunity we have now? I can create an endless source of income for your causes."

"What are you going on about?"

Jamie proceeded to divulge an elaborate scheme to entrust the charity funds through different financial instruments, pitching that he could relocate funds to new investments and securities that would pay out to the charities of Maxim's choosing. The premise of Jamie's grand plan was that he would use the stock market to continuously fund the charities, outlasting the funding that would come from his husband's estate completely.

As Jamie reiterated the logistics of his plan, Maxim tried to follow, but the more he listened, the less it made sense to him. Jamie would proceed to get into further details with each repeated explanation in the hopes of convincing Maxim that he would be looking out for the best interests of the charities. Maxim was not versed in the sort of financial machinations that Jamie pitched to him with great enthusiasm. He could only see how Jamie's eyes would light up as he explained complex financial instruments. Jamie's pitch continued over the following weeks—over dinner, during their workouts together, and on the occasional trip to the city. Steadfast in his concerns, Maxim only agreed to allow Jamie to work on his plans as a separate effort from the charity function.

"I promise this will work out, Max. The group of investors and traders I'm talking with know how to make your charities piles of money."

"Jamie, I am confident that you will do a great job. But we cannot have a repeat of what happened last time," Maxim responded skeptically.

"Last time, I recall, it worked out so well I gave you a new car!" Jamie fired back, frustrated.

"What new car?" Maxim asked, confused.

Jamie's brow furrowed. "The car I bought you? We drove it just last night back to the house?"

Maxim looked back at Jamie with mild bewilderment. Then, like a lightbulb, the memory flashed before him.

"Oh! Right!" Maxim hesitated.

Jamie paused. "Are you okay, Max?"

"I'm fine Jamie. I just forget sometimes. You shouldn't worry."

"How can I not worry? This literally happened yesterday!" Jamie grew annoyed, the twinkle draining from his eyes. "I don't know what is happening with you, Max!"

Maxim did not like when these episodes happened in front of Jamie. Their severity and frequency had lessened, but it still distressed him.

"It comes and goes, it's fine," he persisted. "It's a part of growing old, that's all."

"Max, this is serious."

"Believe me, everything is okay." Maxim tried to ease Jamie's concern. "Show me what you can do in the next month or so. You'll make me proud I'm sure."

Jamie's eyes sparkled once more as he lunged forward and landed a kiss on Maxim.

"Thank you Max! I love you so much."

CHAPTER 14

I

Maxim hated his birthday. He was born on Valentine's Day, and since the age of eight, he had resented that the one day of the year when he was supposed to celebrate his life, he would be reminded that for everyone else it was the day to celebrate the one you cared most about romantically.

But now in his sixtieth year, he finally felt he had a reason to enjoy his birthday. Jamie had planned a party for Maxim, inviting all his family and friends. Wanting to make up for all the years that Maxim had not received a Valentine's Day card, Jamie hand-made fifty-two different cards in various colors and covered in hearts. He invited Charlotte to help, writing "Happy Valentine's Day Uncle Max" in each one, dotting the 'I's with hearts and putting lipstick on Jamie to apply kisses for some of the cards. It was a wonderful gesture from Jamie, showing an innocent generosity that Maxim wished he had experienced as a schoolboy. Maxim wanted to show his appreciation for Jamie by making him a valentine of his own.

Maxim drove to Gwendolyn to peruse the local crafts shop, giving Jamie the excuse of a visit to Dr. Wells. The little shop carried an assorted collection of colored papers, ribbons, and other crafting tools.

It was a small store attended by an elderly shopkeeper, her wiry gray hair held back by a series of hair clips in the back of her head. The shopkeeper had known Maxim for many years.

"Is your niece making a Valentine's Day card?" asked the shopkeeper cheerily.

"Actually, I am making one for James," Maxim replied, embarrassed. "It's cheesy I know."

"Oh, there's nothing wrong with that!" she assured him with a comforting smile. "Nothing wrong with being young at heart. I think it is wonderfully sweet."

"Thank you, I'm glad you approve." Maxim smiled.

Maxim paid for his purchases and proceeded to the exit but was called back by the shopkeeper.

"Before I forget. What was the name of your housekeeper? The one from . . . oh, where was she from? Brazil?"

"Luisa, you mean? She passed away a few years ago."

"Oh! My condolences. My sister used to sell her different varieties of tea and was wondering why she never came to pick up her order."

"What order?" Maxim asked, curious.

"Oh, I wouldn't worry Maxim, it was so long ago. I say, she showed my sister and me that yerba tea they used to drink back in her village, it was quite strong!"

"I see . . . where is your sister's shop? Maybe I'll pick up something different." Maxim felt an urge to find out more; any mention of Luisa after her death called on his psyche.

He walked a few blocks south to a shopfront whose windows were filled with various bags of tea leaves and the ornate canisters they were packed in. Maxim walked in to the strong aroma of allspice and bergamot floating in the air, and saw the sister behind the counter mixing spices for a customer.

"I think this combination will make for a great immunity booster. Yes, I've used it myself during a cold and it worked wonders!"

She turned at the sight of Maxim walking into the store. "Why hello! Welcome! How may I help you?"

"Hello, I am Maximillian Porter. I live on the other side of Gwendolyn Park, and my former housekeeper used to buy your tea. A Luisa Caldeira?"

She paused for a moment.

"Why yes! The Brazilian woman, I do remember her. Lovely lady, she used to buy a regular variety of tea for her employer. Oh wait, you're Mr. Max! She used to talk about you a lot."

"Did she?"

"Only good things I assure you." She chuckled as she finished packing up the other customer's order. "Whatever happened to her?"

"She passed away a while ago."

"Oh dear, I'm sorry to hear that."

Maxim and the sister were now alone in the store. Maxim felt compelled to ask more about the matter, though he could not explain why. A feeling of being watched crept nervously in his mind, and he glanced at the door to be sure no one was coming in or out.

"I was wondering what kinds of tea you used to sell to her; I mean, to my family."

"Well let me think . . . oh wait, I keep records of large orders. This shop has been around since the time there were still lots of big houses on your side of the park."

She turned around and walked to a large cabinet lined with books, scanning the rows until she found what she was looking for: a worn spiral notebook, its cover inscribed with the words "Gwenshill – Deauvillier Porter."

"Let me see," she said, flipping through a dozen or so pages, hundreds of dates, quantities, and notes from decades' worth of orders. "Ah yes, right here. She would usually buy chamomile, allspice-lemon, green, Earl Grey, dandelion, ginger peach—"

"Dandelion?" Maxim interrupted.

"Yes, we get it from a reliable source. All organic and from a protected meadow down south."

"You mean she would buy dandelion tea from you?"

"Why yes. The petals must be separated from the stalks due to their bitterness," she continued, Maxim listening intently. "It's a very time-consuming process, so the supplier does the work of separating and sends us the washed and dried petals."

"Couldn't she just pick them from the ground and make it herself?"

"Anyone can, but since they are viewed as weeds it is not safe to do so in settled areas. The herbicides they get sprayed with can be very toxic."

"I see." Maxim's mind filled with dread. He did not know what to do with this information. "Your sister mentioned Luisa's last order was not picked up?"

"Hmmm . . ." She once again looked down at the notebook, flipping through multiple pages, halting at the point where the page was half-empty with the most recent orders.

"Interesting." She paused, Maxim's mind racing. "It looks like the last order was for dandelion and mint . . . yes, it was dated to September three years ago."

"Thank you," Maxim said, his mind a whirl of anxious activity.

What could this mean? Why would Luisa go picking dandelions for herself if she had an order of them waiting in Gwendolyn? Maybe the weather had been poor? But they had a van for staff use—couldn't she have asked someone to take her to the shop?

"Did she usually come down by herself?" Maxim asked.

"She did. Though now that you mention it, someone else from the house was going to pick up the tea for her, she told me."

"Did she say who?"

"Sadly, I don't recall."

II

"Max, I'm starting to get bored of these gardens," Jamie said as he gazed out from their bedroom window.

"Already? You put in so much effort to make them a 'butterfly metropolis,'" Maxim replied, surprised at Jamie's ambivalence.

"Yeah, but butterflies were more impressive to a seven-year-old than a ten-year-old. I could tell from Charlotte's *enthusiasm*," Jamie pointed out with a sarcastic tone. "One year it's butterflies, the next it's ponies, soon enough it'll be boys at this rate."

"Good thing that'll be George's problem, not ours," Maxim joked. Jamie tittered, then turned his gaze once more to the gardens, his face contemplative and serene.

Jamie would be facing his own milestone of turning thirty in a few months, his visage still youthful but with less fullness in his cheeks. His jaw had grown more defined and manly, his body stronger, his body hair more pronounced around his chest and arms. Jamie was turning fully into a man in Maxim's eyes, the ideal man he had foreseen in that steam room at the Lafayette. Masculine yet beautiful, youthful but mature. He avoided the fate of other gay men, who took their beauty for granted in their twenties but then became inelegant worn-down husks of their former selves. In his mind's eye, Maxim could see Jamie grow into his forties and fifties, an Aurelian embodiment of manhood and strength with those Grecian curls crowning his evolving imperial face.

"I am going to plan for a new garden, maybe plant some lavender."

"Whatever you like. Maybe some sunflowers also?" Maxim suggested.

"I don't know . . . I always thought they were goofy looking," Jamie answered. Maxim thought he had told Jamie sunflowers were his favorite, but maybe he had imagined that conversation also.

"Well, you pick what you think works best."

"Alright handsome." Jamie winked.

Maxim was seeing his control over his environment diminish over time. He could not determine whether it was a result of his willingness to make Gwenshill a home for himself and Jamie, or if it was just the evolution of their relationship with his younger husband taking a more dominant role. Jamie was doing a good job as the head of the new foundation made with Maxim's half of the inheritance. He had reorganized the funding strategy, delegated new roles, and streamlined the transferring of funds between Maxim's trust and the NGOs. Jamie's fresh perspective was moving more funds to the people and charities that Maxim cared about.

Jamie had a higher degree of responsibility now; he worked with a group of other men of his age. They never came to the house, only connected over livestream to talk to each other from their own workstations. Sometimes Jamie would leave Gwenshill for the day, going to meetings with his teammates or going to the foundation offices on Maxim's behalf.

Maxim, on the other hand, found himself without responsibilities for the first time. He was going through highs and lows with the symptoms; at times he would remain lethargic and his mind blurred. He would wake up with exhaustion, but it would linger later into the day. He became more sensitive to sounds, and the feeling of paranoia ebbed and flowed during the week. He took creatine daily on Jamie's advice, though Maxim still was not convinced. *Creatine or not, I will never recover as easily from exercise at this age as you do, Jamie,* Maxim thought to himself.

But there were other days he felt completely normal, his mind clear and his energies elevated. It also helped that Maxim's mood improved during the warmer months. Maxim would take his car and go driving through the countryside, heading into the city just to have a reason to get out of the house. Although truthfully, he had another reason to leave Gwenshill—he was becoming uncomfortable with the impersonal nature of his relationship with Judith, the house manager. She was very reserved and professional to the point of seeming officious, never sharing any anecdotes of herself or her past. She walked quietly through the house, in her dark uniform, commanding the other staff and answering to Jamie's requests and instructions. She had a disquieting way of looking directly at people; Maxim found it stern and condescending. He also felt there was a strange familiarity to Judith's gaze, but he could never pinpoint with any certainty where he had seen it before.

The car that Jamie had given to Maxim was a powerful and fast machine, and Maxim had reservations about speeding around in it. The women in Gwendolyn would shower him with praise, and the occasional young man halted in his tracks to post images of the car for their social media. Maxim enjoyed the image of himself as the dashing older gentleman with the fiery sports car, strong and powerful like the machine he drove. It was a relieving contrast to the forgetful and witless old man who spent his mornings trying to remember if he had brushed his teeth already.

He had yet to take the car through the Snake Head, a stretch of country road that ran along the mountain ridge of Gwendolyn Park. Its winding road was made up of a series of hairpin turns and twists that followed an older native trail, and at its end was an observation outlook with views of the county. You could see Gwendolyn and Gwenshill from its summit, but the main draw was the winding road itself, and in the summer, it was not uncommon for there to be accidents and even the occasional death.

"Why don't we go for a drive?" Maxim asked Jamie as the two lounged about in their bedroom.

"Sure, why not?" Jamie agreed contentedly. "Are we taking my car?"

"I was thinking my car."

"Oh, you mean the invisible one?" Jamie teased.

The two left the comfort of Gwenshill and embarked on the journey up to the outlook, Maxim driving and Jamie in the passenger seat. They turned onto the exit from the state road and began the ascent up the Snake Head. Maxim was pacing his way around the curves and narrow bends, only accelerating when he was in the straight segments and could see no oncoming traffic. Maxim was pushing the car to what he believed was its limit, but he was still being very cautious. He did not want to make a fast turn and come face to face with another vehicle or drive off the road. Jamie simply looked out into the scenery, dense with conifer trees, his long curls fluttering in the breeze.

"Isn't this a great road? This car loves all these twists," Maxim reveled.

"It sure is. Can I be the driver on the way down?" Jamie asked.

Maxim was nervous to allow Jamie behind the wheel, but he figured there was no harm. After all he thought, Jamie had already driven the car off the lot when he got it for him.

"Sure, why not?" Maxim answered with some trepidation.

The scenery when they reached the outlook was far more picturesque than usual, with the bright blue sky and the occasional clouds floating past. Gwendolyn appeared as a rust-colored cluster to the west of them and Gwenshill a single mass surrounded by its lawns and Jamie's gardens.

The two of them were immersed in the view, breathing the fresh mountain air. Maxim came behind Jamie and held him close, while Jamie rested his head on Maxim's shoulder.

"This is a nice view," Jamie said, taking a deep breath.

"Glad you like it. It's even better in the fall, when the whole county is one explosion of colors. You can barely tell where the town begins or ends on those days," Maxim gloated good-naturedly.

Maxim clung tenderly to Jamie, suspended in the tranquil silence of their embrace, looking out into the horizon. In that blissful moment, a creep of insecurity came over Maxim. Still holding to Jamie, he asked him quietly, "Would you ever leave me?"

Jamie lingered briefly, taking another deep breath, then answered, "Don't be silly. I am not the type of guy who runs away when things get tough."

"I just hope that what's happening to me isn't pushing you away."

"No, Maxim. There are worse things that can divide us. After all, what's happening to you is not your doing," Jamie comforted Maxim, bringing his hand to Maxim's face and kissing him gently. "Would you leave me?"

"Never," Maxim whispered, kissing Jamie once more.

Jamie and Maxim clung together for a few moments longer and then headed back to the car, Jamie taking over the steering wheel.

"Although I will say Max, you didn't push this car hard enough," Jamie said as he turned the ignition.

"Really? I think it was—" Maxim could not finish his sentence as Jamie pressed hard on the accelerator, the wheels squealing as the car launched forward. Maxim was thrown into his seat.

Jamie began to speed down the road, a flurry of signs and warnings of falling rocks whizzing by them. Jamie gripped the steering wheel tightly, his gaze focused and intent, a boyish grin plastered on his face. Maxim was still processing what was happening, each hairpin curve pressing its G-force squarely at Maxim's body. Flushed with fear and thrill, Maxim could only process the fear.

"James! You're going too fast! Slow down!" Maxim shouted.

"We're just getting started, handsome. Hold tight!" said a jubilant Jamie.

The winding two-way had a sharp drop heading down and a mountain face heading up, so that with any false move the car could be sent flying down the mountainside. One remained cool and focused, the other flush with fear, both overwhelmed by the flowing adrenaline of the speed and risk of death. The engine roared, the wheels screeched, the bodies of the passengers pressed tightly to the floor of the car. Maxim could only scream as he saw a car approaching them from a blind corner, but Jamie remained collected, throwing the wheel hard left, inches from where the shoulder gave way to a sheer drop.

"James! Are you trying to kill us both?!" Maxim shouted once more, but Jamie did not respond. He was consumed by the speed and ignorant of his husband's pleas. The descent was a fast one, but for Maxim it felt like an eternity. The car made it down the road, returning to the country exit they'd started from.

"Woo! That was wild!" Jamie exclaimed excitedly. "Best purchase I've ever made."

Maxim, still flushed and breathing heavily, just stared at Jamie, incredulous and enflamed with anger.

"Jamie, I thought we were going to die up there! Is that how you want to go, careening down a cliff?!"

"Your face is priceless, Max." Jamie laughed. "Come on. I'm starving, let's get lunch."

Maxim could not help but go from ire to laughter at Jamie's response, so unconcerned and breezy. The fright of the experience gave way to a rush he had not felt since the roller coasters of his adolescence.

"I swear Jamie, the stunts you pull . . . I can't figure out whether to kiss you or slap you." Maxim laughed nervously, wiping tears from his eyes.

"Then good thing you're with me till death do us part, as they say." Jamie grinned with a glint of mischief in his eye.

CHAPTER 15

I

Maxim had come to attend the local congress of the New Mattachine. The hosting of the gathering had been relegated to another member of the society, and Maxim was relieved to be given a reprieve from planning and funding another event.

"Nice to see you again, Maxim," Elliott Newsham greeted Maxim with a handshake. "Glad not to be in the spotlight this time?"

"I don't know, Elliot, if the food isn't on point, I might have to rescue the next gathering," Maxim warned with a sardonic grin.

"Of course, no one can compete with a Maximillian affair," Elliot smiled graciously. "We will just have to make do with less."

The meeting was being held at the Modern Art Museum, the main exhibition hall having been populated by rows of chairs, buffet tables, and an open bar. The exhibits on display were an assortment of works by queer artists and painters that were on loan to the museum collection, along with pieces recently donated by members of the society. The scale and breadth of the collection was of great intrigue to the society members, who unsurprisingly congregated around those works of art that veered more to the profane than sublime. Some could not help themselves from giggling like teenage boys when looking at the newest donation, a collection of original negatives and prints from Andy Warhol's *Body Parts*. Maxim rolled his eyes at their juvenile spirit.

"I swear, why do gay men behave like they've never seen another man's dick before?" Maxim quipped.

"Max, I don't think most men are up to your moral level," Elliott remarked with amusement.

"Seriously Elliott, we are exposed to dicks all the time!"

"Fuck me, who brought the moral police?" a voice echoed behind the two men. It was Connor, his condescending smirk and mocking gaze more pronounced than ever.

"Connor, I thought I barred you from attending New Mattachine gatherings," Elliott said, his upbeat demeanor souring at the sight of Connor.

"You did, but being that Benji donated *Body Parts* to the museum I have the privilege to view our donation at any time, even during private functions," Connor retorted smugly.

"Why am I not surprised that this is your doing? You own DeKoonings and Pollocks, why donate this smut?" Maxim sniped.

"Art is art," Connor shrugged. "If the straights can paint women's tits and asses for two thousand years and not call it porn then why should we be any different?"

Maxim huffed in displeasure, and he and Elliott took their leave of Connor's asinine assertions, pacing around the gallery and viewing the works together until it was time to host the meeting proper. Elliott took his place at the head of the meeting with the senior members going over the minutes from the last meeting. Maxim found himself sitting next to Connor and his husband near the middle row of seats. Maxim dreading having to sit next to them. During the meeting, Connor kept gesturing for Maxim to lean in next to him, trying to tell Maxim something. He tried to ignore Connor at first, but eventually relented.

"What is it Connor? I don't want your stupid gossip," Maxim whispered.

"I think you might want to know what I have to tell you," Connor whispered back.

"Connor, I am not interested." Maxim repeated, trying to contain his vexation.

"Even if it is regarding that little bastard husband of yours?" Connor countered. Maxim turned to face Connor, livid at his insult of Jamie.

"Connor, I swear if you make another defamatory comment against my husband I will throttle you in court." Maxim held back from yelling at Connor so as not to cause a scene, but he was growing more agitated in his seat.

Connor continued pressing, a self-satisfied grin forming on his face.

"You could take me before a judge Maxie, but you'd lose your case if what I have learned turns out to be true."

Maxim knew Connor loved getting a rise out of people, and Maxim was not letting him play games just to get fodder for his trashy books. Maxim and Jamie had put him in his place before; they could do it again if they had to.

"Considering last I checked you still have the same publisher, I would bite your tongue," Maxim sniped one last time.

"Look Maxie, I know that I take great pleasure in being the bitch of the group, but in this case, I am doing you a serious favor."

"And why am I being given said honor?" Maxim replied acerbically.

"Because sometimes the genteel pushover needs a dose of the truth," Connor answered.

For once Connor seemed earnest enough that Maxim agreed to listen to what he had to say. When the general meeting ended, Connor pulled Maxim into a side vestibule leading to another gallery

"So, about the little bastard—"

"Connor, I said enough with the insults!" Maxim yelled. Connor quickly hushed him to keep them from attracting attention.

"Quiet! Your husband is not what you think he is."

"What are you implying, you rotten fruit?"

"Simply that your sweet Jamie is lying about his life story."

Connor finally got to the point, divulging a rumor that Jamie was not the son of either of the dueling brothers in the great Grenvill family rift, but was in fact the illegitimate son of Isidor Grenvill, the incarcerated patriarch. The pretense of his being a spawn from the religious side of the family was just that, pretense. They took responsibility for Jamie as their own in order to avoid the obloquy of having the head of the family be known as an adulterer.

"Bravo Connor, bravo," Maxim responded with contempt. "This makes me wonder why you haven't been hired to write for daytime soap operas."

"Oh, laugh if you want, but it would certainly explain why he doesn't look like any of the other members of the family. A blessing on his head, surely."

"I've had enough. I am heading back to the meeting." Maxim turned but Connor grabbed him by the arm.

"Maxim, I'm not being flippant. Every family has its skeletons, figurative and literal. Why do you think none of the Grenvills came to your wedding?"

"What kind of stupid question is that? Because they are religious and don't believe in gay marriage."

Connor gave him a look of disappointment, shaking his head. "You really don't know, do you?"

"Know what?" Maxim retorted, still skeptical.

Connor pulled his phone from his pocket, rapidly fiddling and swiping gestures onto its screen until he found the image he was looking for. He handed the phone to Maxim.

"What is this?"

"That's Oliver Grenvill, his sister, and *her* new wife. This was sent to me by someone who worked for the wedding photographer."

Maxim was dumbstruck. He refused to believe what he saw, as it would mean that Jamie's whole backstory was nothing more than a charade.

"From what he tells me, the whole Grenvill clan was jubilant during the event," Connor continued. "Though when the other bride is the daughter of a hedge fund manager I imagine you tend to overlook scripture and focus on the mammon."

"This is absolute lies. This is fake! Oliver Grenvill—"

"Oliver Grenvill is a grifter," Connor interrupted. "They all are! Money is their religion, not some stupid book. You really think our class gives a shit about who's fucking who? We only care about holding onto our money. The only difference now is that we don't worry about our precious daughters marrying closeted fairies and causing scandal later."

"What a horrid view of people you have Connor—you always have! This could be a fake picture for all I know."

"And you are a blind old queen," Connor snarked. "But I guess that's expected from a hopeless romantic with a middle-class vision of love."

Maxim handed the phone back to Connor and turned away, looking into a painting hanging behind him. The fury of rich brushes of paint, swirling red like an ocean of blood in the middle of a storm. He focused on one point in the painting, staring until he slowly disassociated from the room, from Connor, and from himself. But Connor kept talking.

"The reason no member of the Grenvill family came to your wedding was not because of our *abominable ways*, but because they don't see your husband as one of them. He is a Grenvill, yes, but a Grenvill in name only."

A Grenvill in name only, just as Jamie had said himself. What were the chances Maxim would hear that expression from someone else? Connor must be lying, Maxim thought. Jamie would never conceal such a secret, be so deceitful, so two-faced. Connor was just creating drama to compensate for his humiliation at the party at Gwenshill. Jamie, his sweet, charming, witty, dear Jamie, would never break Maxim's trust. Maxim turned back to Connor.

"Connor, frankly I can't understand why Benjamin married you. You are an insufferable, contemptuous parasite, and you give all gay men a bad name."

Connor was unfazed by Maxim's words. Looking satisfied, he took a step closer and leaned in close, whispering one last retort into Maxim's ear before leaving him alone in the empty gallery.

"But at least we are honest with each other, which is frankly more than your husband is willing to do for you."

II

Maxim left the suffocating gallery space full of gawking and now-drunk society members and wandered the streets of the city alone. The words of Connor's revelation, or fabrication, swirled in his head. He walked aimlessly, going up the main avenue block after block without thinking about where he was or where he was going. Time both stood still and accelerated simultaneously; he could not make out what time of night it was, only that the streetlights were on. The sidewalk was filled with young people pacing about, laughing and chatting as they made their way to the bars and restaurants that lined the avenue. The city's chaotic sound became like a white noise machine drowning the thoughts that bubbled in his mind.

Jamie a bastard, an impostor? How ridiculous a claim, Maxim repeated to himself. *He went to boarding schools, he knows people in high society, he is as blue-blooded as they come. He is not some penniless influencer faking being an heiress, he's ambitious and hardworking. He did not marry me for my money!* After all, Maxim reminded himself, there was a prenuptial agreement! Even if he died, Jamie could not inherit anything from the estate that wasn't written in his will.

Maxim began to feel ill, dizzy and short of breath. He found himself in the park in the center of the city. His mind had been so consumed with his singular desire to keep moving that he had walked several miles without stopping for a drink and must be dehydrated. Water? No, Maxim wished for something stronger in the middle of that manicured grove. Nevertheless, he could not locate a vendor or water fountain around him; the park was empty. He stood by himself, looking around, lost in a haze of confusion and denial. He shrugged his shoulders, his mind and body exhausted from the unplanned trek. Finally he sat on a bench to rest, closing his eyes, breathing deeply, and clearing his mind of all distractions.

The roar of the city in the distance, the sound of the wind rustling the trees–Maxim began to think of happier times with Jamie, the dates they'd had together walking through this same park. The deep conversations, the jokes, the stolen kisses, Jamie's warm smile and those twinkling eyes. He recalled how they had embraced each other in the cold winds of winter. "You're so warm, let me get close to you," Jamie would say to Maxim, wrapping himself around Maxim's waist, shrouded by the heavy coat Maxim wore. But the trail of memories, so perfect in Maxim's mind, now held a crack of distrust.

His phone beeped, breaking Maxim's contemplation. It was a message from Jamie, asking when he would be back home. Maxim typed that he'd had too much to drink and was going to stay at the Lafayette overnight. A small white lie. Maxim looked up at the skyline of the city. The metropolis had its own chaos of lights and colorful signs blasting energy into the night. He scanned the horizon briefly, not thinking much of the cacophony of towers he looked upon, until something odd caught his eye.

He spotted the building that held his father's penthouse. He expected it to be dark, no one having occupied its rooms since Henry's funeral. But Maxim could recognize that the lights of the living room and bedroom were aglow in that crystalline box high above the city. Maybe they had been left on by mistake? Isabel had been in the unit to pick a suit for Henry's funeral, or maybe the cleaning staff had neglected to turn them off. Maxim kept thinking how strange it was, until he saw the living room lights turn off—someone was inside the penthouse at that very moment.

He stood up, intent on exposing the miscreant; it was not unheard of for some opportunist staff member to occupy the empty apartments of their bosses, thinking they would never appear at a property whose only worth was speculative and not sentimental. If Maxim were to catch the louse red-handed and throw them out into the street, it would certainly be a good story to tell the members of the Lafayette the following day. He crossed the couple of blocks that separated the park from the foot of the building and walked briskly through the lobby. The receptionist greeted Maxim instinctively, but as Maxim entered the elevator and the doors began to close, he saw the same person running to the elevator doors with a panicked expression. The doors closed and Maxim began his ascent to the penthouse.

"If it turns out it's the superintendent his ass is gone," Maxim scoffed as he reached the penthouse level.

As the doors opened onto the foyer, a muffled sound of music echoed through the unit, loud and basal. The telephone rang unremitting from the lobby, a useless warning to whoever was in the apartment. Maxim walked into the living room and saw two unfinished glasses of wine and an empty bottle fallen over the cream-colored rug. *Someone thinks he can bring a date over?!* He paced slowly across the apartment, trying not to make his presence known so he could catch the intruder and their partner in the act. A trail of clothes led from the living room down the darkened hallway and into his father's former bedroom. The music was blaring and harsh, the heavy techno that Maxim absolutely despised. He remained careful as he walked toward the bedroom door, the loud music proving a convenient cover for his footsteps. The door was unlocked— the intruders were truly confident they wouldn't be caught.

Maxim burst through the door. In the darkness of the room, he could make out two figures upon the bed in the act of intercourse. They were startled by the sound of the door smashing against the wall, Maxim banging his fist against the switch to turn on the lights. The lights briefly blinded Maxim as he faced the two upon his father's bed.

"Party's over—" Maxim began to shout angrily, but his fury instantly gave way to horror as he encountered Jamie's eyes staring back at him.

"Max!" Jamie hesitated, in his own state of shock.
"I can explain!"

Maxim was frozen in place, feeling like he was about to have a heart attack, his illusions so brutally shattered at the sight of his beloved Jamie in bed with another man.

"James! What is the meaning of this?!" Maxim demanded, at the brink of becoming utterly consumed by his rage.

The other man concealed behind Jamie's body revealed himself, the stench of alcohol and sex reeking into the air. Maxim's eyes widened once more, his heart wrenching at this further betrayal.

"Paul?!"

CHAPTER 16

I

"I'm not surprised," George said matter-of-factly from his office telephone in DC.

"Couldn't you be more supportive than that, George?" Maxim moaned, still in tears from the events of the previous night.

Maxim thought he had suffered a nervous breakdown; he could not remember what had happened with absolute certainty, only that he had left the penthouse sobbing incoherently. He somehow found himself at the front stoop of George's townhouse, not completely sure of how he got there, his hands bruised as if he had endured a fight. Isabel had opened the door to find him slumped on the steps, and had called George.

"Maximillian, you married someone half your age, kept him in that house in the middle of nowhere, and you expected that he would not get bored out of his mind just playing dollhouse and sleeping with you like you wanted?" George was saying. Maxim and Isabel were surprised at his cruelty.

"George! That's no way to talk to your brother," Isabel protested. "He had his trust betrayed, his home ruined!"

"And I'm still not surprised. Maxim, I know you're upset, and it is a terrible thing to happen to you. But you know you should have been with someone more appropriate, in both age and stage of life. You got swept up in being with a young man and he took you for a ride."

"That's not fair! Old straight men ruin decades-long marriages to chase young blonde tramps all the time, and they don't get castigated for it."

"That's different, Max—" George halted his train of thought, knowing Isabel was still on the other end. "I can't get involved in this discussion; I have a confirmation hearing to attend."

"You and your double standards! That's all you're good for! Forcing double standards on everyone else just to make yourself look like the bigger person!" Maxim shouted.

Isabel grabbed the receiver before George could respond. "George, he's upset... I know, I know ... Just ... Just call back when the hearing is over... bye honey." Isabel huffed with frustration, turning to Maxim. "We will talk about this more later. You need a shower and sleep."

"Izzy, why is he always like this? Why can't I get my brother to be on my side ever?"

"It's not that he isn't on your side. You know George, he just wants you to find someone who cares for you deeply and that would never do anything to hurt your feelings."

"What am I going to do, Isabel?" Maxim asked, exhausted and exasperated. "I have been searching for someone my whole life, and I thought Jamie was the one. He was the only one who cared about me enough to stay. Enough to put up with my nonsense."

"Max, that's not true. Think of all the men who are in the same boat as you," Isabel responded, "Look, you deserve to be with a companion that is on the same level as you are emotionally, mature and caring."

"I don't know," Maxim sighed. "I just don't want to be alone when the time comes."

"I know, Max. But we will always be here for you."

Maxim headed upstairs, took a long shower, and slept in the guest bedroom for a few hours. Later in the afternoon, George called back to the house and he, Maxim and Isabel began discussing how to proceed. Maxim, feeling more grounded in his emotions, agreed with his brother and Isabel that he needed to file for divorce from Jamie, and that Jamie should be immediately removed from his role in Maxim's foundation. Maxim, so steadfast of his husband's innocence the day prior, marveled at how much had been changed by that fateful trip up the elevator car.

The fallout in Maxim's friendship with Edward was more explosive. Edward accused Maxim of unfairly attacking his husband when Jamie had initiated the affair. Maxim berated that Paul was a drunkard who had lured Jamie into cheating. Edward eventually threatened to file assault charges if they ever saw each other again. Maxim could not believe how his whole life had seemed to come crashing down in the span of twenty-four hours. Jamie, meanwhile, was nowhere to be found; he had not returned to Gwenshill and had made no effort to contact Maxim. No text messages, no phone calls—Jamie had become a ghost. Maxim called into the foundation's offices and instructed the employees that Jamie was no longer allowed on the premises.

Maxim remained at George's townhouse for the rest of the week, only requesting that his medication be brought to him from Gwenshill. Night and day he waited for a response from Jamie; night and day he heard nothing. Even Jamie's social media profiles showed nothing, having remained inactive ever since that night.

Maxim debated whether he should tell George and Isabel about the rumor Connor had shared with him, but it was already humiliating enough for Maxim that he had married an adulterer, he did not want to be doubly condemned for having married an impostor as well. Reluctant to do anything at all, depressed and drained of his energies, he sulked in bed watching old movies, coming downstairs for meals and to read documents for the foundation. He wanted to spend the rest of his life just lying on that bed, waiting for the day he did not have to wake up again. He was constantly afflicted by nightmares of Jamie's eyes twinkling in the darkness, reliving the memory of finding him in bed with Paul.

"I have to head back home," Maxim announced one night over dinner with Isabel and George.

"Are you sure you don't want to stay longer?" Isabel offered.

"Yes, stay a few more days; Gwenshill is not going anywhere," George joined in.

"No, I know when I'm overstaying my welcome," Maxim insisted. "I need to make cutbacks at the house. But thank you for helping me through this."

Maxim returned to Gwenshill to find its staff engaged in their duties as though nothing had happened. Even Judith didn't know where Jamie had gone. Maxim informed her of the separation and instructed her to collect all of Jamie's belongings and put them into storage. He proceeded to announce that the bulk of the staff would need to be let go. Gwenshill would return to the way it had operated before Jamie's influence, with the exception that Judith would stay on.

Gwenshill's windows were curtained off, the furniture and antiques covered, the gardens only minimally maintained. The house returned to the gloom of a mausoleum, and to the melancholy of its owner's loneliness.

II

It had been several weeks since Jamie was last seen. The lawyers had prepared the divorce papers, and process servers were hired to deliver the divorce documents to Jamie, but they could not track him down; Maxim was becoming concerned that Jamie might have done something rash. Though Maxim was still experiencing a great deal of anguish over what Jamie had done to him, he couldn't help worrying about Jamie's well-being. George recommended the services of a private investigator, a friend of his from college who had experience tracking people while working for the FBI.

Maxim contacted the investigator, Detective Fred Catinella, who came to meet him at Gwenshill.

"There is something that I did not tell my brother," Maxim revealed to the detective. "I have heard rumors that James, my husband, may have been lying about his background. Could you confirm whether this is true?"

"Mr. Porter, Maxim, I will confirm whatever I can about your husband in order to ascertain his whereabouts. Is he operating under a different alias, do you think?"

"Not that I am aware of, but the rumors seem serious enough to investigate his family ties. They say he may be the illegitimate son of Isidor Grenvill."

"I see . . ." the detective paused, taking notes on his pad.

"Please, I do not want my brother to be made aware of this," Maxim stressed anxiously.

The detective gave Maxim a steely look.

"I will be discreet when I can, but I will report anything that can be a detriment to your family."

"Thank you, Detective."

Maxim returned to his routines, the worry now out of his hands. He resumed examining himself in front of the mirror, sequestering himself in the family office to work, taking meals by himself in the dining room. His symptoms of fatigue, mental fog, and memory loss persisted along with even more paranoia and hallucinations.

Maxim once again felt he was being observed, watched over by some force that creeped about like a shadow. He believed he could see a glimpse of this force, scurrying behind the threshold of doors and out of the corners of his eyes. His paranoia took hold most prominently during the night, when the few staff were asleep and no one was supposed to be wandering the halls of Gwenshill. His symptoms would linger for days, then go unnoticed for the same amount of time.

Maxim suspected he was developing dementia; it was the only thing that made sense to him. He was aware that something was happening to him, something random and troubling. How long would this go on? He knew he needed to seek medical help; he did not know how long he would remain lucid before the symptoms returned. But Maxim was afraid, he did not want his fear to be confirmed or let his suspicions prove him a fool. Instead, he imposed a stricter diet on himself: no red meat, sugar, seed oils, or alcohol. He pushed himself harder in his exercise, treating his body as a machine to keep his mind clear of anxiety.

But his nightmares persisted, growing worse, and now he had the added torment of seeing Jamie in his sleep. The betrayal haunted his mind so that he was afraid to close his eyes, and the disappearance of the real Jamie only added to his torment.

One night, Maxim awoke to another nightmare. He decided to leave the disquiet of his bedroom and head to the kitchen to make himself coffee to remain awake. When he was a young boy, the darkness of Gwenshill's corridors had scared him—a pitch-blackness so deep it seemed that only demons and malevolent ghosts could reside there. The only light that glowed was from a halogen light that hung just outside the main staircase window, its diffused shine rendering an ominous orange flame through the curtained opening.

Maxim no longer believed in ghosts and demons in the halls, but the neurosis that now manifested from his own deteriorating mind was not that different than his childhood fears of the dark. He paced through the dark hallways, about to cross the threshold of the kitchen when he stepped on something sharp on the floor and yelped in pain. He pulled his phone from his pajama pocket and pointed its flashlight on the ground; an old nail popped out from the wooden floor.

Maxim heard a noise coming from the other side of the kitchen door. He entered slowly, pointing the phone's light around the room before turning on the light switch. The kitchen seemed empty, clean and orderly for the following morning. Maxim waited to hear any other sound, shrugged his shoulders, and went about preparing a carafe of coffee. He was sluggishly fighting back the urge to yawn when he felt the glass carafe bang against something in the sink. He looked down into the sink to find a mortar and pestle, half washed, with some white residue still on its surface.

"What's this doing here?" Maxim asked himself, grabbing the mortar, its residue smudging his fingers.

He looked at what was within the vicinity of the sink, only noticing a pot of creatine. Curious, he opened the pot and looked inside it, finding nothing unusual other than white creatine powder, though it appeared as if it had been shaken recently, the plumes of powder wafting out of its container. Maxim thought it strange, but in his half-awake state, he couldn't tell if he had handled the pot too harshly or whether the sink's contents had something to do with it. He made himself his coffee, drinking the whole carafe before heading back to his bedroom to wait for sunrise.

The following morning, he walked into the kitchen, feigning he had forgotten something in the family office. He noticed that the mortar and pestle were gone, and the pot of creatine was no longer on the countertop.

"Judith, wasn't there a pot of creatine here last night?"

Judith paused and turned to face Maxim, her face devoid of expression other than a rapid twitch of her eye.

"The pot indicated it was expired, Mr. Porter. I will see that it gets replaced," she said somberly.

Maxim did not press the point. To him it looked like the pot was half full, but tossing out old supplements seemed the least of his concerns.

III

"He has left the country; he's been jumping around Europe from what my sources could tell me," Catinella informed Maxim over the telephone.

"How? His passport is here," Maxim replied, confused.

"He's been flying on a private charter, reporting a stolen passport when he landed in Malta," Catinella explained. "It appears he doesn't want to be found. I'm sorry, Mr. Porter."

"This . . . this is disappointing to hear."

It had been three months since Maxim had seen Jamie, and it was bittersweet, knowing he was actively avoiding Maxim. Could Jamie be running from more than the divorce papers? Could he be running from the rumors? Connor wouldn't keep a story like that to himself. Maxim was deflated, and still in the throes of depression when the detective revealed what he had found about Jamie's background.

"He is the son of Isidor Grenvill," Catinella confirmed. "The story tracks that his brother posed as his father, and his biological father posed as his grandfather. He was kept out of the country for several years in various boarding schools to conceal the infidelity. At some point there was a falling-out between himself and the bulk of the family, and he was briefly supported by his other brother, posing as his uncle, until he became self-sufficient."

So the rumor was true. *Oh Jamie, my dear Jamie,* Maxim lamented to himself.

"What was the falling-out about?" Maxim asked the detective.

"Something about his biological mother, but it cannot be made certain," Catinella replied.

Maxim ended the phone call, slumping upon the living room sofa in distress.

"At least he's alive," Maxim whispered to himself.

Maxim appointed an interim head for the foundation so he did not have to work. Instead he walked through the grounds of Gwenshill, the gardens turned up and replaced with gravel, the bushes and trees untrimmed. He meandered through the wooded trail to the stream, and on his return, he would stop at the edge of the woods looking up at the house in its return to unending gloom. Though he once could not imagine parting from Gwenshill, now Jamie's presence was everywhere, and the memory of Jamie kept pushing Maxim away from his home. His mind stood trapped between the memories of the distant past and the pain of the immediate present. The cold wind of winter returned, its frigid embrace adding to Maxim's frail disposition. He decided to close up Gwenshill for the winter and to begin living, temporarily, in his father's old penthouse. Maxim left Judith to keep the house in order while he was away.

His father's penthouse was a different kind of spatial reclusion. Henry's sensibilities had been defined by market forces, hence the apartment felt cold and corporate. It was finely appointed but detached from any semblance of personal charm, not even personal photos; it was an asset rather than a home. Maxim did not venture into the bedroom where he had discovered the affair; he locked the door so no one, not even himself, could enter without its key. Instead he slept in the guest bedroom, a minimally furnished room with a large bed and a television mounted upon a wall dividing the room from the dressing area. Maxim felt uncomfortable in that room. It may have belonged to him on paper, but like Gwenshill, it was an architectural representation of the parent and not the child.

On the first morning of Maxim's stay, he continued with his ritual inspection. His hair was becoming grayer, and the receding of his hairline was more prominent. He looked more haggard, the bags under his eyes increasing in size from the sleepless nights. He pulled open the vanity drawer looking for a hair trimmer. An empty bottle of medication rolled out from the back of the cabinet. Maxim grabbed it and glanced at the label; it was digoxin, his father's old heart medication.

"Honestly," Maxim thought aloud at his father, "you had to forget you took your medication already. Maybe you would have lived to a hundred and twenty, old man."

CHAPTER 17

I

"You are looking good Max, buzzing your hair was a nice change," Isabel complimented Maxim while the two of them were having lunch in the city.

Maxim's decision to remove all the hair from the top of his head had been an impulsive one. He'd never particularly cared for his hair, and he was not sure what he expected from seeing his scalp for the first time. He thought he looked more menacing, his permanent scowl complementing the defined shape of his skull. Maxim used to avoid looking menacing in public, but now he wore his intimidation without regrets. His dear Jamie had abandoned him and broken his heart; he wanted to become a stone wall.

"Have you heard anything from James?" Isabel asked.

"No," Maxim sighed. "He started posting on his socials again, and he acts like I never existed."

"How immature," Isabel scoffed. "I'm sorry it ended like this, Max."

"He is still avoiding signing the divorce papers. He posts where he is all the time, but the servers can't seem to get a hold of him."

The waiter appeared at their table, a tall and handsome man with dark red hair and a short, trimmed beard.

"Is there anything else I can get for you?" the server asked.

"No, that's all; thank you for the meal."

"Please come back soon, sir." The waiter left the check and gave Maxim a wink as he walked away. Isabel noticed the flirting, but Maxim did not.

"He's cute," she remarked innocently.

"He is, but I'm still married," Maxim countered.

"Well . . . why don't you get back at James?" Isabel asked, a hint of daring in her smile.

"What do you mean? By taking a lover?" asked a confused Maxim.

"Well, the designers at the fashion house talk endlessly about *poly* this and *open relationship* that. Why should James get to fly around Europe being indecent while you gloom about in that penthouse all by yourself?"

"Of all people, I never expected this kind of talk from you, Isabel," Maxim teased.

"Max, you're not obligated to be just like me and your brother, as much as George wants you to do so. Why don't you give meeting someone a shot?"

"I don't know . . . I don't want George to think less of me."

The waiter returned with the receipt for Maxim to sign. When he opened the holder, he saw a telephone number and note written on the customer copy: "Daddy, call me ;D"

Maxim blushed and showed the receipt to Isabel, who returned a coy look to her brother-in-law.

"I think you deserve to be mischievous, Max. I'll handle your brother." She chuckled.

They paid the bill, Maxim leaving a large tip. He was flattered; the interaction had helped him feel desirable again. Maxim and Isabel walked the several blocks between the restaurant and her office building; before they separated, she invited Maxim to attend a fashion show later that month. She believed it would be a nice break of routine for her brother-in-law to meet some creative spirits. Maxim agreed, and began to look forward to coming out of his shell of seclusion.

Maxim returned to the penthouse; he walked out onto the terrace and looked out into the park and city beyond. The view was a different beast to the serene landscapes of Gwenshill. He gazed out, listening to the muffled roar from the streets below, the occasional horn and siren breaking the monotonous rumble. He remembered the receipt with the waiter's number, pulling it from his pocket and debating whether he should call. He brushed his hand against his torso without thinking, and the feeling of his hand triggered the memory of Jamie's skin against his. The intrusive rush of thoughts of how Jamie felt again his body, lips interlocked, hot breath against their faces, hearts that beat in unison—it froze Maxim in thought upon that terrace. He looked out into space, then at the receipt, and out into the city once more. Maxim wanted to call the number, but something was holding him back, telling him maybe it would be better to wait until later. In the end, he forgot about the phone number entirely.

II

The spring/summer fashion show was organized outside of the performing arts center, with several pavilions representing each fashion house. The Maison De Caron, Isabel's employer, was hosting its show inside the grand foyer of the state opera. The swirling staircases and mid-century light fixtures served to promote the new design language of the fashion house. Maxim and Isabel sat just behind the front row full of fashionistas and magazine editors invited to rate and review the show. Maxim observed the behavior of the women and men invited for the event. Their aggrandizing poses, their air of erudite conviction, their wardrobes reaffirming their aura of privileged arrogance.

By comparison Isabel was more classically dressed, her composure more tasteful and refined. She was not one to pretend to be up-to-date or trendy; for her style was the ultimate designation of how one accomplished good taste. And Isabel could never be described as anything other than stylish. The show ended with the main designer walking down the runway to generous applause. Maxim thought the clothes were too gauche, but he was of similar temperament to Isabel when it came to fashion. The designer was an older man, of exuberant tailoring and a contrived hairstyle. Maxim hoped he would not have to strike up a conversation with him.

A cocktail party was held on the opera members' mezzanine for the attendees of the show. Isabel and Maxim headed there to mingle and gossip; Maxim found himself not thinking of Jamie for the moment, a reprieve from the torment of betrayal that still swirled in his mind. Maxim enjoyed Isabel's company, and the feeling was mutual. In moments like this, Isabel felt more like an upbeat little sister than merely his brother's wife. She introduced her colleagues to Maxim, all of whom shared their condolences for Maxim's treatment by Jamie and the occasional compliment on Maxim's appearance.

"Fuck that guy, you're a hot daddy!" a queer assistant exclaimed, tipsy from too much drink. Maxim chuckled, while Isabel was chagrined.

"Okay Lolo, I think you've had one too many 75s for tonight," Isabel directed the assistant. "Will you excuse me Max? I need to get Lolo to cool off."

"It was nice meeting you Max!" Lolo called, being escorted by Isabel to a bench.

Alone, Maxim meandered casually among the crowd of fashionable guests. He found himself within the vicinity of the bar, comingling with other attendees trying to get the attention of the bartender. As he waited for his turn, his face slipped into its resting scowl.

"You look so disapproving—didn't like the shows?" a voice next to Maxim called out. He looked down to see a shorter man with jet-black hair parted neatly behind his ears. He had a gentle face with a sharp jawline, a serene smile, and reassuring gray eyes behind large thin-rimmed glasses. He wore a black cardigan with gray slacks and a gray dress shirt. He was clean shaven, and Maxim could tell he was probably a few years younger than he was. He had a calming presence, which resonated with Maxim.

"Oh! Forgive me, I sometimes don't realize I'm making that face. I'm actually enjoying it a lot; my sister-in-law helps run one of the fashion houses." Maxim smiled at his new acquaintance. "Do you work in fashion yourself?"

"Not exactly; I was hired to design the pavilion for one of the houses on show. I'm an architect by trade."

"Oh really? I wished I could have been an architect," Maxim said with a smile. He extended his hand. "I am Maximillian by the way."

"I'm Victor; nice to meet you, Maximilian." Victor shook Maxim's hand.

The bartender turned to acknowledge them. "Apologies, gentlemen, what can I get you?"

"I would like a gin and tonic please; what would you like, Victor?" Maxim asked.

"Make it two," Victor replied.

They continued to talk as they enjoyed their drinks. Victor Delaney was fifty-two years old and had been a practicing architect for several years. He ran a boutique studio in an old bank building on the east side of the city, designing high-end homes and working on historic restorations. Maxim was delighted to learn of Victor's background, especially about how the firm was responsible for the renovations to the state opera. He felt somehow reassured by Victor's quiet demeanor. Victor felt so approachable and non-judgmental, Maxim thought. Conversation came naturally between the two of them, and they shared many of the same interests and sense of humor. But a concern had crept into Maxim's thoughts: was Victor straight? That would prove an embarrassing gaffe for Maxim, and he did not want to make Victor feel awkward. He hoped the subject would be broached in some inconspicuous way, though the opportunity continued to evade him. Maxim then realized that he had lost track of Isabel.

"Oh dear, I completely forgot about my friend. I need to go looking for her."

"No worries," said Victor. "I will be around. I should go check on my ex."

"Your ex?"

"Yeah, he's around here somewhere. Hopefully not too tipsy."

They smiled shyly at each other. Maxim felt so relieved and comforted to have made this connection with Victor that it brought out a tenderness that he had never felt before, apart from Jamie. Maxim, not wanting to leave Victor, pulled out his phone and texted Isabel that he had met someone. She replied that she had to make sure the assistant was okay anyway, and wished him luck with a winky face.

"She's busy with something, so if you want to go find your ex then I can just stick around here," Maxim said to Victor a bit anxiously.

"You can come along, I promise he doesn't bite," Victor said with a chuckle.

Maxim and Victor wandered through the gathering looking for Victor's ex-husband, who was the designer that hired Victor to design his pavilion. After exchanging greetings and seeing he was fine, Victor motioned for Maxim to follow him. They left the mezzanine and descended the staircase to the lobby. Victor took Maxim into the auditorium, walking along the aisles to a side exit. They climbed the empty stage and were standing at its center. Maxim did not know what to expect. The space was unoccupied, with props and set dressing stored away for the next season.

"Wow, it's so strange seeing it from this angle," said Maxim, looking out at the rows of seats and the soaring space from the stage.

"Takes your breath away, doesn't it?" Victor pointed up to the chandeliers that hung from the ceiling.

"You know why the lights are shaped like clusters of spheres and starbursts?"

Maxim shook his head.

"The architect was having a tough time designing the look of the lights. His daughter was blowing bubbles in his studio one day and the way the light hit the floating soap bubbles inspired him to replicate it," Victor explained. "There are no lights in them; there are projectors hidden in the rim of the dome. Their light hits prisms inside the fixtures, mimicking the light bouncing from a bundle of soap bubbles floating in the air."

Maxim observed the fixtures with curiosity.

"Unfortunately, it didn't work for long. The mechanisms back in the day were very fragile; they stopped working after a few seasons and the lights were abandoned. We worked to get them to operate correctly again."

"That's amazing. I have been coming to the opera since I was a child and always wondered why they didn't light up."

"Well, restoration sometimes is not just about preserving the past, it is about preserving the whimsy of life," Victor said with a gentle smile.

Victor continued to walk Maxim through the auditorium, telling him the story of its restoration. Maxim was transfixed by Victor's knowledge, the way he so patiently explained how all the efforts made to restore the building had been met with discoveries and missteps. Maxim also felt an attraction to Victor's enthusiasm; here was a man who enjoyed telling people of his expertise. Victor's manner was so mature and gentle, Maxim noticed. He seemed like the sort of man who never shouted, never got into angry quarrels. Maxim realized he was thinking of Jamie less and less, almost forgetting him entirely.

At one point the two men found themselves ascending into a hatch concealed in the uppermost balcony. They moved gingerly through the small space, coming to the rim of the auditorium dome where the projectors were held.

"Watch your step," Victor cautioned, grabbing Maxim's hand as they arrived at an opening in the ceiling. The two sat on the floor of the scaffold, looking down at the stage below.

"My dad was once the janitor of the theater," Victor explained. "He told me of this spot when I was younger. We would watch Puccini and Gershwin together, and later when I was a broke-ass student I would bring dates here sometimes." He chuckled. "A date once brought popcorn and dropped some of it on the orchestra seats below. I always wonder why we were never caught."

Maxim began to laugh, until a flash of memory from long ago came to his mind. He looked at Victor in astonishment.

"That was you!" Maxim's eyes widened. "I remember it now, I was here with my family for *Tristan and Isolde*, and I noticed something falling on my head—it was popcorn!" The two men burst out in laughter.

"I thought it was being tossed from the balcony, but where I sat it didn't make any sense." Maxim continued, still laughing at the realization that Victor had been over his head this whole time.

Maxim leaned forward to see if he could find his old seat, but Victor pressed his arm against Maxim's chest to stop him. Their laughter paused as they realized they were still holding each other's hands. Maxim looked into Victor's gentle eyes as their lips met in a kiss. Maxim had not been this intimate with anyone in months.

CHAPTER 18

I

Maxim and Victor began to see each other regularly. To Maxim the courtship felt like when he was younger; there were no social media posts, no long-winded dialogues of text messages, no digital anxiety. Maxim would call Victor and vice versa; they talked briefly but daily, meeting up at restaurants and other spots in the city for their dates. Maxim was straightforward with Victor about the complication of his separation from Jamie, and Victor understood.

Being with Victor was a different kind of attraction than Maxim had felt for Jamie. It was not charged with an electric current of passion, it was the long and sustaining warmth of a stable relationship, albeit one tempered with pragmatism. Maxim was now sixty-one, and although there was still an age gap between himself and his new partner, it was not so excessive that they could not connect through their shared life experiences. They had been influenced by the same life forces and milestones. And in the long run of their lives, their age difference did not appear so extreme.

Jamie still hadn't attempted to contact Maxim for several months. Maxim held on to the divorce papers symbolically but didn't care to retain the process servers and left the paperwork unsigned, thinking it moot without the other party to complete the final termination. Maxim did not have to worry about the divorce affecting his inheritance, but he thought perhaps as a magnanimous gesture he could part ways with the car Jamie had bought him.

Victor, meanwhile, was a very thoughtful partner, sometimes to a fault. He would plan out every detail of a date in advance, which Maxim valued greatly, but there were times that the planning would be bogged down with minutiae. Maxim also realized that in this relationship, he needed to give more consideration to class distinction in terms of what tastes were affordable.

"Max, could we make a concession?" Victor asked one evening over dinner. "Could we select a different bottle of wine?"

"Why, don't you like its taste? Sometimes vintages don't mellow out as some expect," Maxim replied unthinkingly.

"It's just that the bottle will cost more than the whole meal for the two of us," Victor pointed out.

"You do make a good point," Maxim conceded. "Price and taste don't always match."

It was one of the few snippets of wisdom he still retained from Jamie.

"Victor, I want to ask you something else. Do you ever think about getting married again?"

Victor paused and looked out across the restaurant. His face was contemplative and calm, his eyes unflinching but quiet in reflection. He turned back to Maxim.

"I don't know; my line of work doesn't really allow for good marriages."

"How so? I would think architects are very eligible husbands, divorced or otherwise," Maxim teased.

"Sometimes the long hours get in the way, and stress can sometimes create friction. In the end architects usually end up marrying each other," Victor joked. "The devil you know and so on."

"Such a shame! If I were not stuck in my own mess, I would marry you," Maxim joked back, but beneath his words was a hint of genuine desire.

Maxim could see himself with Victor, living together in a house built just for the two of them. It would allow Maxim an escape that he had never truly considered, of leaving the shadow of Gwenshill and freeing himself from the past. It seemed so promising, but it was still escapism. He still stubbornly refused to imagine actually parting from his home.

"And if James ever does sign the divorce papers, would you marry again?" Victor asked.

"I don't know," Maxim answered. "I was with James for four, maybe five years? And I haven't had any other meaningful relationships since my twenties. I think I would go back to being by myself. I mean, I would want a partner still, but marriage . . . I don't think so. Not after all that has happened." Maxim hoped his honesty did not send the wrong message to Victor.

Victor maintained his thoughtful gaze, giving a pleasant smile to Maxim.

"Then let's just enjoy the ride. Cheers to the journey." Victor raised his glass.

"Yes, let's," Maxim agreed.

II

Maxim was no longer experiencing the worst of the symptoms that had dogged him for the last several years. Some forgetfulness had taken root, but the memory loss and chronic fatigue were not affecting him. He took it as a sign that being with Victor was disconnecting some underlying impasse in his mind. Maxim continued to rationalize his conditions, and still did not seek counseling. He still suffered from nightmares when he tried to curb his medication, and the mental exhaustion persisted.

Maxim did not tell Victor of his condition. They had been together for three months at this point, and Victor was unofficially Maxim's boyfriend. They conducted themselves as though they were an established couple, and though the question of Maxim's separation was unresolved, it didn't change that Maxim loved Victor, and he did not care how others perceived it.

Maxim remained living in the penthouse, having not returned to Gwenshill since closing up the house. He began to feel for the first time that Gwenshill no longer held a huge sway over him. Being with Victor was slowly changing how Maxim viewed his relationship with the past. Maxim was now feeling like he was living in the present, and it was not as intimidating as he used to believe; though sometimes he would catch himself indirectly talking about Gwenshill through the lens of Jamie's time at the house, and Victor could sense that Maxim was not completely over his previous relationship.

"Max, do you want to be with me?" Victor asked one evening when they lay entwined together on the bed at Maxim's penthouse.

"Of course I do," Maxim replied.

"I can't help but think there's something else that occupies your thoughts."

"I promise you that there's nothing else."

Victor sighed. "You seem to always refer to James when you talk about your home in the country."

"Do I do that?" Maxim hadn't fully realized he had been doing this and wondered why.

"It gives an impression, that's all."

"I don't know why I do that. I'm sorry," Maxim responded, giving a gentle kiss to the back of Victor's neck. "I don't want you to think there's anyone else besides you."

Victor turned around in bed to face Maxim. His gray eyes looked a muddled green against the fabric of the bedsheets. "Maybe we need to make new memories. We have a lot ahead of us still."

"You think so?"

"I think so. I want to be with you, Maxim, and I think that for as long as you will have me, we should make the best of it."

"I want to be with you too," Maxim sighed. He paused once more and began to think about what he wanted. He needed to test something before he could make a decision that would affect him for the rest of his life. "Look, why don't you come to Gwenshill with me?"

"You really want me to go with you?"

"Yes. I need to make a decision; there's something I need to know for myself, and I need you there."

"Okay Max, if that's how you feel."

III

Gwenshill remained frozen in time as Maxim and Victor drove along the road that circled about the grounds. Spring was coming into bloom, but no flowers were to be found after the gardens had been cut back. The trees and hedges were growing new leaves, still bright green in their fresh emergence from the cold of winter. The house looked gloomy and cold, even with Maxim having ordered Judith to prepare it for guests. Maxim had been gone for so long that seeing the house in its current state felt almost like seeing it for the first time. It came as a true shock. The house appeared haunted, even with its manicured grounds and maintained facade. He could finally see that it was a house devoid of life, a home in name but not in spirit.

"It's quite beautiful, but melancholic," Victor said as they pulled into the motor court. Judith stood outside by the front door, looking as solemn as Maxim remembered.

"Judith, have you prepared a room for Mr. Delaney?" Maxim asked.

"Yes Mr. Porter. Will Mr. Delaney be staying for long?"

"Please, call me Victor." Victor inserted, his placid demeanor unbroken.

"Victor will be staying for a few days. Please have lunch prepared."

"Yes Mr. Porter," Judith answered, returning to the house like a shadow.

The house was prepared for their visit, albeit sparsely. The interiors were clean and cold, no fresh flowers to perfume the air, just the stale smell of cleaning products. The curtains were drawn open to let the sun's light stream through, but there was no warmth to be felt from its rays. Maxim suggested they lounge in the library where the fireplace could warm the room, but first he took Victor on a tour of the house as they waited for lunch to be served.

Victor was slow and attentive in scanning the details and character of each room. He examined the spaces like a doctor examining a body during surgery. Maxim in turn observed Victor, looking at how the machinations of Victor's mind echoed in the subtle expressions of his eyes. Maxim was anxious to gauge what Victor would make of his childhood home. Would Victor discover some secret of Maxim hidden in the rooms of Gwenshill? Would the walls literally speak of Maxim's trauma and madness? Maxim fretted, but Victor would only comment simply and humbly.

"This house was built with great care, but it is an echo of another time."

Maxim looked at Victor, his manicured yet understated presentation contrasting against the grand drama of the rooms, and realized this was not a house for reasonable and modest men like Victor. Maxim then understood why he kept referring to Jamie when speaking about Gwenshill: this was a house that amplified personalities and temperaments. It stood against the truth that comes from being of calm demeanor and only partaking in simple pleasures.

"Yes, it does feel like it belongs to another time . . . another place even," Maxim agreed thoughtfully.

"Do you feel at home here?" Victor asked.

"It used to be home, but now it's just a house," Maxim answered, slowly realizing he was telling his innermost truth.

As the day went on, while Maxim and Victor ate lunch and discussed walking together around the grounds, Maxim began to feel certain that it was time to start his life anew. It was time to part ways with Gwenshill. Victor was the partner that Maxim needed. And to be with Victor, Maxim needed to unshackle himself from the memories of the past, of both Gwenshill and of Jamie. The divorce remained in limbo, but Maxim would move on with his life. Jamie could just disappear as far as Maxim was concerned.

CHAPTER 19

I

Victor had been working late for several days, rescheduling dates and deferring phone calls from Maxim. Maxim remained flexible with the shifts, but it began to come across as though Maxim was still not a priority in Victor's life. His career had to come first, Maxim reasoned, but he could not help but feel frustrated. He had already contended with Jamie's constantly shifting schedule in the early months of their relationship. Having to experience this with Victor felt like an uncomfortable repeat of the past.

"How's it going with Victor?" Isabel asked one afternoon when she and Maxim were having coffee at the townhouse.

"It's going well," Maxim sighed. "But Victor's been working late again. Another deadline for a house he's designing."

"Oooh, intriguing," Isabel chirped. "Is he designing for anyone important? I saw his name come up in a house magazine the other day."

"He wouldn't say. Only that the client is very demanding," Maxim replied.

Isabel heard the note of dissatisfaction in Maxim's voice, and could see in his face that he was not getting the attention he felt he needed.

"Max, he is a business owner after all," Isabel reminded him. "I don't think it is fair of you to ask him to put his career second to your relationship."

"It's not that," Maxim told her. "I would just think that when you run your own office you could let others do the work for you. Like my father and his bank."

"As I understand, his clients come to him for *his* ideas. Maxim, you must understand that in creative circles it's sometimes the designer that is more important than the label. I think you're still used to James' influence," Isabel asserted innocently.

Maxim turned to her and reflected.

"He knew how to make me feel wanted. But I will admit, he never made me feel comfortable being vulnerable."

"I understand," Isabel comforted Maxim, placing her hand on his, giving a caring smile.

Later that evening, Maxim had plans to go to dinner with Victor. An hour before they were to meet, Victor called Maxim. Victor's fatigued tone of voice was all Maxim needed to know that their date would have to be rescheduled again.

"I'm sorry, I hate having to do this. My client keeps making changes last-minute before we meet with the city and it's just driving the office nuts."

"Don't worry, I understand." Maxim replied. He was frustrated, but he had to adhere to Isabel's advice. "When do you want to meet next?"

There was several seconds of silence at the other end of the line, until Maxim became nervous. Was he pushing Victor away? Maxim's anxiety bubbled up, and he called Victor's name into the phone, only for the call to hang up with no response.

"How could he hang up on me?" Maxim thought aloud, his mind spiraling into fear. "No, it must be a mistake. The line must have cut."

Maxim called Victor back but got only a "this number is not in service" reply. Maxim spiraled further into insecurity. Victor had blocked him . . . Victor was ending it . . . Victor did not want to continue dating an insecure old queen . . . Maxim collapsed onto his armchair trying to comprehend what he did wrong. There was no other explanation—he had pushed Victor away and now he was back to being alone.

Maxim's mind furiously began to rethink every conversation, every message, every phone call, date, event, intimacy, everything they had done together for the last several months. Maxim became irritable, angry at the sudden betrayal. *Fuck him*, Maxim thought in his nervous delirium, *I can move on . . . I am not going to be played again.*

"Who the fuck does he think he is? I can get any hot young man I want. I don't need this shit!" Maxim said aloud.

He paced about the room, letting his irrationally racing mind disconnect Maxim from the real world. He turned to the bar cabinet, pulling out a bottle of cognac. He poured a glass and drew it to his lips, only to throw the glass across the room in rage. He grabbed the bottle and proceeded to drink it straight, but Maxim felt instantly sick. His irrational haze dampened and the strength of the alcohol knocked him back into his seat.

At that moment he finally recognized the ringing of his phone, looking confusedly at its blinking screen. He did not recognize the phone number, and assumed it was a spam call. When the phone ceased ringing, he saw it had been trying to call him multiple times. He called it back and went pale at the sound of Victor's thoughtful and fatigued voice at the other end of the line.

"I'm so sorry Maxim. My phone battery went dead, and I had to call from my office line. I feel bad rescheduling again, why don't you come over to my office and I'll give you a tour?"

Maxim was now the one who began to hesitate, wincing as he realized how utterly deranged he was behaving. He could not believe that he blew up into such outrage over something so banal and understandable. Maxim replied calmly, almost meekly, trying to maintain whatever semblance of composure and civility he could muster.

"Oh! That's alright. I'd love a tour, but . . . I can't come right away."

"Well, I still have some staff in the office, if you don't mind coming late when it's just us two," Victor responded.

"Of course. Are you hungry? I can bring us dinner."

"That would be great, I haven't eaten all day. See you at ten?"

"Sure, I'll see you then. Bye Victor."

"Great, see you then. Bye Max!"

As Maxim hung up, he became violently ill, running to the bathroom to vomit. It was not simply the excess of the cognac, but the purging of the violent energy of his anxiety that forced him into the bathroom. Maxim was riding a storm of chaotic emotions, becoming weak as he kneeled in front of the toilet. He lay there on the bathroom floor, breathing heavily as his nerves cooled. He had three hours to compose himself before he was to meet Victor. Maxim was glad that Victor never got to see this side of him; surely Victor would have ended their relationship right then and there at the sight of Maxim's deranged insecurity.

II

"I'm sorry work drains so much of my energy. At least I get to burn the rest with you." Victor smiled cheekily as he looked up into Maxim's eyes, his head with its smooth black hair resting on Maxim's broad chest.

Maxim took a deep breath. "You work too hard. I'm sure you could get someone to step in for you. Make some time for the two of us," he suggested. Victor's cool tone hardened slightly

"But we are together now. Are you not enjoying it so far?"

Maxim turned to Victor, timorous and hesitant to answer.

"Uh . . . well, yes, I am enjoying this time with you. I was just thinking we could do something different, explore new things. We haven't left this city since I took you to Gwenshill. Why don't we go on a trip to Europe? Maybe Africa?"

"That sounds like a lovely idea Max, but I can't leave the office. I have too many projects to oversee and too many clients to answer to," Victor replied.

"Then drop some of them. You're not their whipping boy—you are your own person."

In his mind Maxim believed he was making a reasonable assertion. But Victor sat up on the bed and looked at Maxim, his gaze turning stern.

"Max, that's not how this works. I've worked up my entire life to get this far and build my reputation, and right now is the most productive time of my life. If I simply ignore or drop my clients, all that I've built will just go undone."

"But you are successful," Maxim countered. "Your name is in magazines and news articles. Surely you've earned some time off."

"Yes, but if I want to continue to be recognized for my efforts, I need to keep at it. I know you're disappointed, but that's an unglamorous aspect of being an architect."

"I think you are being unreasonable on yourself. We are together, eventually you will not need to work so hard."

"Maxim, I don't want to live off your money." Victor stated resolutely. The air in the room became tense with feeling. Maxim was taken aback by Victor's words.

"I mean nothing of that sort. It's just that I can help take some of the edge off, keeping your office going so you can pick only the projects you want. It'll be like I am your patron."

"Max, I managed to stay afloat without a patron when I was younger, and I plan to keep it that way." Victor got up from the bed. "I think it's getting late, I need to get up early for a site visit."

"Then stay overnight. You can go to your project from here."

"I can't, I need clean clothes and my work notes at home."

"Fine, then I guess I'll see you around," Maxim blurted out, allowing his irritation to show. Victor stared back at Maxim for a moment, his own frustration breaking through his usually demure expression. They did not raise their voices, or fight, but it was sharply telling that they wished to be apart for the remainder of the night.

III

After two weeks with no word from Victor, Maxim went from feeling guilty to feeling ambivalent. They were entering a third week of no contact when Maxim received a phone call from Victor's number.

"Hello stranger," Maxim responded innocently.

"Maxim, you haven't talked to me in weeks." Victor spoke directly. "I know I have been occupied with work, but I don't appreciate the radio silence from you."

Maxim was taken aback.

"I'm sorry, I thought you needed some space. I was feeling like I was demanding too much from you, and I thought it was better if you engaged first."

There was an awkward pause, until. Victor broke the silence with a frustrated sigh.

"Max, I'm sorry. The stress is just affecting me. I prefer when you're the proactive one."

"I don't know what to do with this information," Maxim said. "You tell me your career is important and that you can't make time for us, at least for the time being. So, I give you some space to power through your work, but that doesn't work for you either?"

"No, it's not that. I just need you to be there and be supportive."

"Victor, I am supportive. But this relationship limbo is not working. We're stuck in a routine, and it's taking away from new memories we could be making together," Maxim insisted.

"Maybe you're right," Victor replied after a moment. "Maybe . . . we should think about moving our separate ways." Maxim was uneasy.

"Separate ways? That's not what I was asking for. I don't want us to break up. I just want some clarity in when this work will be over."

"That's just it, Maxim, I can't give you that," Victor protested, though he remained calm. "There are times when I have no projects, and times I get overwhelmed with them. And I need to work during the latter to compensate for the former. I know it seems unfair, but I need to know you are there for me when the work is piling on my head. I can't always make time for my personal life when things get this crazy, and I need you to understand that."

"Victor, of course I understand. Please forgive me," Maxim replied, growing meek. "I wasn't avoiding talking to you, I was just trying not to become an imposition for you."

"Max," Victor sighed once more. "Then maybe we should just take a break. This is what it's going to be like dating me, and I understand that it's unfair to you."

"I don't think your commitment to your work is unfair," Maxim answered softly. "But if you think a break may be best for us right now, then I support it. I love you, and I am here to support you in any way I can."

"I love you too Max, I know we'll get through this together." Victor responded, still calm and composed.

The two of them agreed to stop communicating with each other until Victor was able to pull himself away from his work. In the meantime, Maxim had to contend with not hearing from his boyfriend for an indefinite amount of time. Maxim could only imagine the worst coming from this arrangement: that he would only hear from Victor after several weeks, if not months; that when he was able to hear Victor's voice again, it would be to announce that he had moved on and left Maxim for someone more sensitive to Victor's needs. Maxim could only blame himself for setting this situation in motion.

Maxim once again became absent-minded and inactive as he worried about his future with Victor. He procrastinated on his duties to his foundation and avoided communication with anyone outside his family. Maxim's idleness only served to magnify his distracted nature; though at moments he felt like time stood still, he soon realized that a full week had passed in his distracted haze.

IV

"So, how are things going with Victor?" Isabel asked Maxim over dinner with him and George one evening.

"We are taking a break at the moment," Maxim said resignedly. "His work is just taking too much of his time right now."

"That's good!" George interrupted. "A man with a work ethic. Now that's the kind of guy you should have been with in the first place."

"How? He's constantly working, he's a slave to his office and his clients," Maxim complained.

"Max, that's the real world. He has discipline, is committed, and doesn't run away from responsibility," George pointed out.

Maxim gave George a disapproving stare. "George, you leveled the same praises at James. At least he learned to balance his life and work."

"And look how that turned out?"

"George, enough," Isabel scolded her husband, turning to Maxim. "Max, it's understandable. Sometimes even your brother forgets that there are more important things than work and politics."

George huffed. "Look, all I'm saying is just don't let this guy fall by the wayside."

"I'm not," Maxim muttered, cutting into his meat, the knife in his hand scratching harshly against the plate. The more he fixated on the food in front of him, the more difficulty he had cutting. His anxiety grew, combining with anger at himself, with every screech of the utensil. Locked in on his plate, he didn't notice George and Isabel staring at him in concern.

Isabel was about to speak when Maxim, erupting with irritation at his failed task, tossed the knife onto his plate.

"George, you gave me the worst cut!" he exclaimed to his brother. "This beef is only nerve endings!"

"Max, just use the steak knife," George replied acerbically.

"You didn't give me a steak knife!" Maxim was nearly shouting now.

"It's right in front of you, Maximillian! Stop making a scene!" George retorted, his raised voice adding to the tension.

"Maxim," Isabel interrupted calmly, indicating the knife next to Maxim's plate. Maxim was still oblivious at first, then noticed the unused knife to his left. He gave a deep exhale and placed his hand on his forehead in exasperation.

"I'm sorry George, I don't know what is wrong with me," Maxim said.

"Is everything okay Maxim?" Isabel inquired, at the same time that George asked more bluntly, "What is the goddamn matter with you?"

Maxim looked at the two of them, Isabel concerned, and George irritated. Maxim could tell even in that moment of emotional distress that he was not going to receive the support he needed from George. He could see that George was losing his patience with Maxim's temperament, his constant state of dissatisfaction, his dramatics, the way he sabotaged his own happiness and dragged George and his wife along with it. In the end, he offered the weak excuse that he had just had a rough night. Isabel attempted to diffuse the situation by changing the topic.

"So Maxim, have you received many offers for Gwenshill?" she asked curiously.

"Yes, there have been some offers," Maxim replied, "though they are mainly only interested in the land. Most of them would raze the house itself."

"That's a shame," said Isabel.

"It is expected, I suppose," George put in, his irritation fading. "The land would make for a good subdivision."

Maxim looked back to his plate. With the serrated knife now in hand, he cut through the stubborn piece of meat. In a sullen mood, he bit into the lukewarm morsel of food on his fork and ate.

V

Maxim began packing his luggage to spend a weekend in Gwenshill. An appointment to show the property to a prospective buyer had been set for the following Monday, and Maxim wanted to be present to give a history of the house to the visitors. The trip to Gwenshill was also an opportunity for him to complete the layoff of the remaining few staff that still worked in the house. Maxim did not take satisfaction in these tasks, but he made a commitment to himself to leave the past behind and look forward to a new life with Victor.

"Max, I'm so glad that the worst is behind us," Victor declared joyfully. "Now I can have my managers take over and we can go back to having fun."

"That was a difficult time for us. But we survived it," Maxim said proudly as he passed between his bag and the closet.

"I'm sorry if I seemed difficult through this time Max. I really am."

"Oh Vic, it was I that was setting unrealistic expectations. Can you pass me that bag over there?"

Victor grabbed the small bag from the dresser, walking toward Maxim and placing a tender kiss on his lips.

"So, now that I have the time. Where are you thinking of going on our date?" Victor smiled.

"How about Greece? Maybe Italy? You architects love a tall doric column," Maxim teased.

"Ha, very funny. I'd bore you out of your mind with architecture."

"With you? I'm never bored." Maxim smiled.

Having Victor in his life once again was one of the few joys that stood out in Maxim's life. He was happy, happy in a settled and contented manner. He wanted to continue this happiness for as long as he could, maybe until the end of his life.

"Do you think we will run into your ex?" Victor asked.

"I don't know, and don't care. If we do see him, though, I'll have the divorce papers with me," Maxim joked.

Jamie was a distant memory to him, a blip in Maxim's personal history. Maxim could finally breathe a sigh of relief that he would have someone truly there for him. Victor departed the penthouse with one last kiss and a promise to call Maxim later that night.

As Maxim loaded the last bag into his car, he noticed that he had forgotten his gym supplements. He returned to the penthouse and pulled the pot of creatine from the upper kitchen cabinet. He looked at the container, one he had taken from Gwenshill a month prior when he visited with Victor. He recalled that he was supposed to be taking the creatine daily, but his mental fog and lethargy had him only taking the supplement on clearer days.

"I guess I should take it now," Maxim told himself, grabbing a glass from the cabinet and pouring some water into it.

He grabbed the scoop from the container, pouring a serving of the fine white powder into the glass. He turned behind him, searching for a spoon to stir the mixture. Spoon in hand, he stirred the mixture of powder, turning the water translucent. Maxim noticed something in the bottom of the glass, something hard and undissolved. He brought it closer to his face, examining the strange clump, then scooped the detritus out with the spoon to look at it further.

It was a pink clump, crumbling into the water. Maxim could not determine what it was. It resembled a pill of some kind, he thought; he would take his medications with his creatine on occasion. Maybe he had dropped a pill into the powder without noticing? None of the medications he consumed were this pink color, though. He tried to pick up the clump with his fingers to get a better look, but it instantly crumbled in his hand.

Maxim thought of the night he'd found the mortar and pestle in the kitchen sink of Gwenshill, next to a container of creatine, and wondered if the two were connected. He shrugged the matter off, reasoning that he must be going through another bout of paranoia; he threw the container of creatine in the trash and dumped the contaminated glass into the sink.

Maxim returned to his car and drove to Gwenshill, arriving at the property late in the evening. He felt even more detached from the house than he had on his previous visit. It loomed menacingly in the dark, its floodlights turned off to save electricity. Judith stood by the entrance to the house, ready to receive Maxim. Maxim did not see Judith at first, her dark uniform rendering her nearly invisible in the shadows. He could only see her face, with her stern and unforgiving gaze peering out into the night. Maxim took a bit of comfort that at least he would not have to contend with Judith's cold gaze for much longer.

"Good evening Mr. Porter; it is good to see you again," Judith said in her reserved and calculated manner.

"Hello Judith. Is the house ready for the viewing on Monday?" Maxim asked, unsettled by the gloom that had seemed to descend upon the house.

"Yes Mr. Porter, the interior has been thoroughly cleaned. The florist will arrive tomorrow morning to provide arrangements for the public rooms."

"And the grounds?"

"The lawns have been cut Mr. Porter. Also, I took the liberty to have the kitchen prepare dinner for your arrival."

Maxim hesitated, feeling an uneasiness he couldn't explain as he spoke to Judith in the quiet dark of night. Her piercing eyes seemed to not be looking at Maxim, but right through him.

"I could use a light meal, thank you Judith," Maxim said eventually, and she nodded in accordance. The two made their way into the house, closing the door behind them.

"And Judith? Please have the floodlights turned on when I visit. Gwenshill looks like the house of the living dead coming up the driveway."

"Yes Mr. Porter."

Maxim waited for Victor's call as he ate in the dining room. The silence of the room disquieted Maxim, his appetite lessened by the unsettling sound of Judith's steps along the stone floors of the long gallery just outside. Each step of her hard-soled shoes broke the silence with a loud reverberating thud. She must be checking each room for any issues before the viewing the following day, but at times the sound of her footsteps appeared random and unexpected.

It was surprising to Maxim how detached from his family home he now felt. Gwenshill had become divorced from any semblance of joyous memory and familial warmth. As he retired to his bedroom and looked up at the ceiling from his bed he mused that this no longer felt like *his* bedroom, but simply a room for him to sleep in.

VI

Maxim's real estate agent was running late; he had agreed to meet an hour earlier to brief with Maxim on last-minute preparations and about the buyer. Maxim tried calling his number several times, but the calls kept going into voicemail. At a quarter past nine, he called Maxim back, sounding distressed.

"Mr. Porter, I apologize; my car is having mechanical problems. I've called a rideshare to collect me while the mechanics determine what happened."

"Just great!" Maxim yelped. "I don't have a clue what this buyer wants, or who it even is! How far are you from the house? Can I pick you up?"

"I am not sure. I am deeply sorry, Mr. Porter."

Maxim heard a car horn on the other side of the line; it was the rideshare, and the agent informed Maxim he would be there in half an hour. Maxim looked at his phone to see it was already 9:30 in the morning; the agent and the buyer would now arrive around the same time. Maxim instructed Judith to have champagne and hors d'oeuvres ready as the staff finished cleaning. The agent emailed a dossier on the buyer to Maxim, and Maxim rushed to the family office to read it over. He was about to turn on his computer when the doorbell rang.

"Shit," Maxim said, looking at the time once more. "They're early. Shit!"

Maxim marched back to the main house, thinking what sort of person would be walking through the doors. Probably another developer, or a new-money family lowballing the house. Maxim walked down the gallery, noticing from a distance the front door was open and unlocked. Now he had to face some affluent stranger who would raise a fuss about having to walk in themselves and not being greeted at the door. He heard footsteps slowly pacing toward the living room. Maxim quickened his stride, announcing himself as he closed the front door and headed into the living room.

"Hello!" Maxim chirped, "I do apologize for not greeting you at the door—"

Maxim froze mid-sentence at the doorway to the living room, dumbstruck at the silhouette that stood before the fireplace, facing the portrait of Karine, then slowly turned around to face him. Those gentle locks of hair, those twinkling eyes, that smile.

"Hello handsome," Jamie said humbly with an innocent smile.

"Jamie!" Maxim gaped.

It had been eight months since he last saw that elegant and youthful face. He had cut his long curls back to a military style, short and neat, but with some waves still gently caressing the top of his forehead. Jamie wore a light pink suit that gave a gentle glow to his face and skin, his eyes still bright blue and twinkling with light, complemented by that same warm and inviting smile. He was still as beautiful as the day Maxim had glimpsed him across that ballroom.

"It's good to see you Maxim," Jamie said softly. "Nice to see you are still as dashing as I remember."

"Jamie. Oh, my dear Jamie . . ." For a moment Maxim was lost in the thrill of seeing Jamie again, that charming face returning to him as if in a dream. Then, with the impact of a piercing bullet, Maxim was jolted out of his reverie.

"James! What the hell do you think you are doing here?" he exclaimed with anguish.

Jamie's smile faded, his expression becoming repentant.

"Max, I know what I did was wrong. I—"

"*Wrong?*" Maxim interrupted. "You destroyed our marriage! My closest friendship is gone! And you dare show up unannounced after disappearing for months on end?!"

"I know, it was horrible. I wish I could change what happened."

"I can't believe you would do this to me. We made a vow to each other!"

"I was immature and restless. I wanted more; I didn't know how to tell you."

"So you went running to the arms of another man? And with one of my friends of all people!"

Jamie began to pace about the room slowly. "You were becoming someone else, something else . . . I was worried. I went to talk to Eddy about it, but instead I ran into Paul. We got drunk, and things escalated."

"Escalated? ESCALATED?!" Maxim shouted angrily, his ire now pouring out. The wounds he thought had scarred over reemerged with force, festering and pulsating. He turned away, unable to even look at Jamie as he continued.

"James, you ran away! And you were gone for months!"

"The guilt was eating me alive for what I had done. I didn't want to face you . . . I *couldn't* face you."

"I tried to reach you! You ignored me!"

"I wasn't ready! Please believe me when I say that I never stopped loving you Maximillian, but I needed to flee to find myself again."

"You tore us apart! You abandoned me!"

The room grew quiet as the two men stood looking at each other, Maxim in anguish, Jamie remorseful. The light of the sun streamed through the windows that flanked Jamie on both sides, appearing to embrace him in a glow of forgiveness. Maxim marveled at how perfectly Jamie seemed to belong in this house, yet he remained determined to tear this false comfort out of his life.

"James, apologies will never undo the damage you have done to me. You left me in ruins, and went running off like a coward."

"Max, I was afraid," Jamie replied timidly. "You were so mad, and what you did to Paul . . . I worried about what else you might do." Fear emanated from his eyes as tears began to gently fall down his cheeks.

Maxim stood there quietly. He could never recall exactly what happened that night in the bedroom, and he worried about what Jamie had witnessed. His hands were still marked with the wounds left behind from attacking Paul. In some ways it was a relief that part of his memory was a blank, so he didn't have to relive the entirety of that awful night, but he could not avoid the fact that he had been consumed with rage. He had attacked Jamie, then Paul; would he lash out like that again? No, Maxim did not want to believe it, a chill running down his spine.

"I don't remember any of it," Maxim said coldly, squeezing his fists tight. "All I remember is you on top of my best friend's husband."

Jamie gazed out onto the lawns, his voice quivering.

"Our garden was so beautiful."

"James . . ." Maxim took a deep breath. "You broke my trust, you broke our vows. Worse, you caused me to lose all sense of what was real between us. I want a divorce."

"Max, I'm sorry," Jamie pleaded, tears flowing from his eyes. "Max, I love you . . . I always loved you."

"Your tears no longer work, James," Maxim said tiredly. "I shed enough tears for you, after you ran away."

Maxim walked to a cabinet beside the door, pulling out the divorce papers from its drawer. He tossed them onto the coffee table.

"I want you to sign the divorce papers, and I want your things out of this house," Maxim commanded.

Jamie began to sob. "Maxim, I made a mistake. I swear there is no one else."

"No James, it's over."

"I just want to go back to the life we used to know . . . our home, our garden, our memories, the love we shared for each other."

"Clearly my love for you meant very little, for you to do what you did."

"Maxie. Please . . . it was a horrible mistake. I still love you. Please." Jamie continued sorrowfully.

"James, I met someone else," Maxim said firmly. "And this house is going to be sold, and that's the end of it."

"Wh-what?" Jamie whimpered, wiping a tear from his face. "Do you love him?"

"I do. And I want to build my life with him."

Jamie ceased his tears, sitting on the sofa and hunching over to the divorce papers before him. He looked up at Maxim, his face consumed with sadness. Maxim could only give a cold stare of disdain at Jamie's broken trust.

"Maxim, is this what you really want?" Jamie asked.

"Yes James, it is."

"But you didn't sign it."

"What would have been the point when the guilty party wasn't here? Sign the document and get out."

Jamie slowly pulled a pen from his jacket. He committed his signature to paper, handing the documents back to Maxim. Maxim grabbed his own pen and took his turn to sign,

"Well, I guess that's it," Jamie said, tears returning to his eyes. "I hope he makes you happy, Maximillian. That's all I ever wanted for you . . . happiness."

Jamie stood, looked around the room one last time, and proceeded to walk out. Maxim stood alone in the room with the signed papers. It was finally over, he thought; now he could begin his new life with Victor. He looked at the signatures and thought of the opportunities that lay ahead, the new memories he could have. The world was his and Victor's to explore. Tomorrow was going to be the grand adventure that Maxim had always wanted. Here was his freedom from rage, from loneliness, from sadness, from . . . from . . . *Jamie*.

"Oh Jamie . . ." Maxim said, Jamie halting his stride at the threshold of the door. Jamie looked back to Maxim, his saddened face now placid. "Only you could ever make me happy."

Maxim turned to Jamie. In one sweep of his hand, Maxim tore up the papers, tearing the bundle into smaller pieces. He dropped the torn fragments on the floor, tears of joy now streaming from Maxim's face. Jamie's smile grew radiant as he ran into Maxim's arms and kissed him tenderly.

"Oh Maxie, I could only love you!" Jamie exclaimed, pressing his lips hard upon Maxim's.

"Oh Jamie, I missed you my dear Jamie," Maxim sighed. For all the misery and hurt Jamie inflicted, he was the only one that Maxim could ever imagine being with. There was no other that would ever replace his dear beloved Jamie.

CHAPTER 20

I

Parting ways with Victor was a challenge that Maxim wouldn't have thought himself capable of. But he returned to the city the following day resolved to accept whatever Victor's reaction would be.

Victor was surprised and obviously upset at the news, but maintained his composure as Maxim reassured him multiple times that it was not because of him that they were breaking up. Maxim still loved Victor, a love that was placid and easygoing, but with Jamie's return, he had to try to repair their rift. In Maxim's own mind, he felt that his love for Victor lacked the fire, the effervescent energy he felt with Jamie, the kind of romance that made old men feel young again.

Victor admitted that he would have had to cancel their planned trip regardless, as he'd been called to start a project for a new design client. The reality stood that whether they remained together or not, Victor had to place his work and career ahead of his personal life. Maxim and Victor ended their relationship amicably, with the possibility that if Jamie and Maxim could not work through their issues after all, Maxim would reach out to Victor once more.

Jamie, for his part, spent the following weeks doing damage control. He contacted George and Isabel to ask for their forgiveness and

make amends. Isabel was unmoved by Jamie's overtures and peace of-
ferings, reluctant to accept him back into the family. George was more
welcoming, an about-face that perplexed both Isabel and Maxim. Maxim
would soon discover why: Jamie had been singing George's praises to
well-connected businessmen in Europe so that when international interests expressed desires to invest in the country, they would call Senator
Porter to be their friendly ear in Congress.

"Jamie, I expected better from you. Whatever happened to pro-
tecting my brother's integrity?" Maxim protested.

"I did protect his integrity—why do you think they started
reaching out?" Jamie winked.

Reconciling with Edward and Paul proved a more difficult task
for Jamie. He pleaded to Edward to forgive Maxim but was met with
silence. Eventually Jamie persuaded Paul to get Edward to meet with
Maxim in person. Maxim did not press the manner of how Jamie was
able to achieve this, happy to be able to see his close friend once again.
Their first meeting was an awkward one, seeing each other for coffee
near the park in the center of the city.

"Eddy. You look . . . different," Maxim commented, taking in
his friend's altered face for the first time in nearly a year. Portions of
Edward's face were frozen in place, and others had been stretched to
conceal his crow's feet.

"I had Botox injections done," Eddy admitted.

"Botox? Sweetie, you never needed Botox, what's wrong with
you?" Maxim exclaimed.

"Oh, look who's talking, grandma. You look like shit," Edward
fired back.

After a brief pause, both men burst into laughter. Over the span
of the afternoon, they began to rebuild the pieces of their friendship. It
was nice to have a friend like Edward back in Maxim's life. Paul still
avoided speaking with Maxim, keeping his distance beyond a bit of small
talk at the door, despite repeated apologies from Maxim. Maxim felt great
guilt for what happened that night, but Edward assured him that it was
Paul who had stepped out of line. Maxim was still remorseful, but equally
grateful that Jamie was willing to repair the broken fragments of
Maxim's past.

They took Gwenshill off the market and tasked the real estate agent with selling the penthouse instead. Jamie returned to his projects at the mansion and to his day-trading in his office. Jamie's smile beamed through the halls of Gwenshill; he was more attentive to Maxim than he had been in the past and Maxim took great satisfaction in seeing those happily glittering eyes each day and night. Maxim saw his home come alive once more with light and color, as if Jamie's presence had expelled the darkness and gloom that loomed over the house.

The one secret still hanging over them was that Maxim had yet to confront Jamie about what Detective Catinella told him. Maxim wanted Jamie to reveal why he kept this hidden, yet the bliss that Maxim felt for having his home and soulmate back kept the difficult questions in the back of his head. He did not want to spoil this wonderful moment; he wished this happiness would last forever.

II

A week after his sixty-second birthday, the sale of the penthouse cleared. Maxim took reprieve from the harsh winter weather in the Lafayette Club's renovated saunas. Maxim's memory of the previous classical interior still pressed upon his mind as he sat in the sauna, the heat warming his lungs and relaxing the tension in his muscles.

There were two other men and a woman in the sauna with Maxim; one of the men and the woman were talking casually about finance, interrupting the polite stillness of the air.

Maxim rested his eyes with his earbuds silent in his ears as a ruse to listen to their conversation. Maxim enjoyed being a voyeur in the lives and turmoil of strangers, mostly as an amusing distraction; he seldom overheard anything particularly humorous or salacious. He listened to the woman speak, discussing the imminent dissolution of some bank with the other man, who only offered vague commentary.

"There are talks of a buyout by one of the big three," the woman was saying.

"With the current S.E.C. investigation? Pfft. They'll only agree to a buyout if they can buy the firm for pennies on the stock," one of the men scoffed.

"The old man must be pissed that his son brought the whole firm down while he's still recovering from his stroke."

"Yeah, I've seen him walking around the club."

"Who? Aldrich Senior?"

"No no, Junior."

"Benny Junior? He's a member here?"

"Yep, he joined last year. Lately I've seen him stuffing himself stupid in the buffet."

"Shit, I'm not surprised. He's probably enjoying the high life until KHA goes under. The fat ass."

Maxim's interest piqued at the mention of Jamie's previous employer. He remembered a few instances where Bernard's name had come up in conversation with Jamie, but Jamie never spoke in much detail of his time at the firm. Maxim remained silent with his eyes closed until he eventually left the sauna and returned to his suite.

Later that evening, Maxim descended from his room to the founders' dining room. Glancing into the main dining hall as he passed, sure enough, he saw a portly gentleman in his late thirties sitting near the buffet tables. Multiple plates of food sat in front of the man and he took bites from each plate at random. Maxim did not want to assume that he was Bernard Junior, but if he came across him in the public rooms, he would attempt to prod into the man's backstory.

The cadre of club members Maxim sat with at dinner contributed only the same old talking points. Maxim asked if anyone knew what was happening at KHA; beyond bemoaning the inexperience of the young, they did not reveal much. Maxim gave up the inquiry and made his way to the library to finish a novel, but on the way he serendipitously ran into the man he believed to be Bernard. Maxim gave an innocuous lie to get the man's attention.

"Pardon me, I am looking for the library. My memory is a bit foggy, is it this way?"

"I believe so. But I—" The gentleman paused, his expression growing nervous as he looked more closely at Maxim.

"You're Max Porter, James's husband."

Maxim feigned ignorance. "Oh! You're a friend of my Jamie?"

"Actually, he worked for our firm. I am Benny Aldrich."

"Yes, Jamie mentioned you a few times. Though his time with your firm was somewhat brief."

"It was best that James and the firm moved our separate ways," Bernard said with resentment in his voice.

"I'm sure it was a shame losing such a steadfast employee; he was so dedicated to your firm," Max said.

Bernard's face turned stern. "Mr. Porter, to be blunt, that comment is in very poor taste."

Maxim was bemused. "What do you mean?"

"The NDA James signed clearly states—"

"NDA? What NDA? Jamie resigned so he could strike out on his own."

It was Bernard's turn to look confused.

"Resigned? That's absurd. Is that what he told you?"

"Well, yes. He never mentioned an NDA to me. He now helps manage my foundation," Maxim replied.

Bernard grew pale. "He *what?*" he exclaimed, his gaze moving frantically around him. Quickly scouting the corridor, he grabbed Maxim by the arm and started marching him down the hall. They passed by club members, at times bumping into them as Bernard quickened his pace. Bernard halted when he came across the sight of a single-use restroom with a bolt lock, dragging both men into the room and locking the door behind them.

"Aldrich, what is the meaning of this?" Maxim cried.

"Shhh! Will you be quiet!" Bernard whispered. "Give me your phone."

"Excuse me?"

"Just give me the phone!" Bernard demanded. Maxim handed his phone to Bernard, who left it with his own next to the sink, running the faucet to muffle the sound of their talking.

"What is going on, Aldrich? What has this got to do with my husband?"

"Hush!" Bernard whispered once more. "I don't need any more reason for the Feds to fuck me over!"

Maxim fell silent as Bernard continued.

"James was very charismatic and knowledgeable when we first hired him. He brought many clients to KHA, and we were making huge returns from their investment."

"So?" interrupted Maxim.

"Let me finish. He was a great salesman, but a lousy trader. He would execute bad trades all the time. The senior members would try to help, but the kid kept playing fast and loose with our clients' money and losing."

Maxim stood perplexed.

"There was no question he was smart, but the more he lost the more he would double down to try and pull himself out of his spiral. He was not being transparent with what he was doing, just making excuses and talking out of his ass about 'trusting his process' until he got lucky."

"Then what happened?"

"He doubled down on a short-sell order and sank millions more into a hail-Mary pass, betting on some rumor he had heard. If it had failed, our gains for the whole year would've been wiped out! But the little shit was right, and he was able to recover from all his losses. We were going to fire him when we discovered how he almost brought the whole firm down."

Maxim was incredulous, but something did not feel right about Bernard's story.

"Going to fire him? That doesn't make any sense. Why an NDA? He recovered all the money he lost, and I've never known you Harvard Business School idiots to have qualms with treating clients' money like a night at Ceasar's!"

Bernard hesitated, growing flustered.

"Well . . . you see . . . James was privy to some *irregularities* in our operations that he threatened to reveal to our clients. Nothing illegal, as our attorneys will point out. We offered instead to effectively pay him off if he remained quiet."

"So, you silenced my husband so you could conceal what? Your greed, or your incompetence?" Maxim prodded. "How rich."

"Mr. Porter, I am warning you that your husband is not who you think he is," Bernard whispered. "If I were you, I wouldn't trust him with a penny of your money, or anyone else's."

"Considering the whole club is talking about the shitshow your father's firm has become, you're one to talk."

Bernard grew red, out of both embarrassment and irritation at the truth of Maxim's assertion. He nervously grabbed Maxim's phone from the sink, handing it back to him.

"I have made my bed, Mr. Porter." Bernard murmured. "But it is you who sleeps with a dangerous bedfellow."

Bernard unlocked the restroom door, peeked outside to confirm no one was around, and walked out, leaving Maxim behind. Maxim returned to his suite. Sitting on his bed, he pulled out his phone to look at his pictures of Jamie. He then realized he had deleted them all, and had to switch to social media to look at old photos. He scrolled through the posts, many of them happy images of Jamie and him together; Jamie's smile so enchanting and warm, and Maxim's own smile so unconcerned and genuine.

"What a load of nonsense," Maxim scoffed. "My dear Jamie, I believe in you."

III

"My old boss was arrested," Jamie announced by the poolside a few months later. Maxim was swimming laps while Jamie read the news report from his phone.

"Who?" Maxim asked, holding onto the edge of the pool near Jamie as he caught his breath from the vigorous swim.

"Benny Aldrich? He was my boss before I set out on my own," Jamie continued. "Bloomberg is reporting that he is in custody for tax fraud and mismanagement of client funds."

"I remember now," Maxim responded.

"Poor Bernard, the guy wasn't cut out for it," Jamie chuckled.

"It's a shame the firm will go under," Maxim said. "All those decades in business."

"Max, having worked there I can honestly tell you they were a bunch of morons," Jamie sneered, taking a sip from his drink. "Do you remember what your dad once said? Something about malice and incompetence?"

Maxim looked up at Jamie from the edge of the pool.

"Jamie, it's very ugly when you talk like that about people. It doesn't suit you."

Jamie looked back at Maxim, his aloof expression giving way to diffidence.

"I'm sorry Max, I forget how I come across at times." Jamie smiled. "So, what are we doing for Father's Day?"

"Next week? I'm not sure yet. Do you want to travel somewhere?"

"Travel?" Jamie pondered. "I can't, I have a call with new investors on that Monday. Let me plan something special for us and I'll let you know."

"Sounds good Jamie."

Maxim returned to swimming laps, pushing his body hard against the water with each stroke as he travailed the ends of the pool repeatedly, while Jamie sat watching Maxim swim between checking his notifications. Maxim felt more fatigued than usual. He would linger with each lap at each end of the pool, becoming more breathless. Jamie noticed Maxim's struggle and called out to him.

"Max! Don't push yourself too hard! That's my job!" Jamie teased.

"I'm fine! Always had a strong heart!" Maxim replied, breathing heavily. He swam up to the edge in front of Jamie. "Only a few more laps and I'm yours." Jamie leaned down and planted a kiss on his lips.

"Did you take your creatine today?" Jamie asked.

"I forgot, sorry."

"Max, you need to take it every day!"

"Oh, come on Jamie, that stuff doesn't work," Maxim protested. "Maybe for a young man like you, but not for me."

"Maximillian, it has lots of health benefits. You need to take it every day for it to matter," Jamie insisted.

"Okay okay, I'll take it," Maxim relented. "Can you go ask Judith to bring it over? And mix it with juice or something?"

"I'll bring it over, don't you worry handsome," Jamie chirped, kissing Maxim once more before heading back into the house.

Maxim got out of the pool to wait for Jamie's return. He sat by its edge, his feet still submerged in the cool water. He looked out through the French doors into the sunny clear sky of early summer, enjoying the birdsong and the rustling of trees against the warm breeze. He thought of how caring Jamie was, always looking out for his wellbeing, especially now that they were back together. Jamie was also taking a more active role in the township: joining the local historical society, buying organic foods from the farmers' market, and giving gardening advice to some of the old ladies. He was now an instantly recognizable fixture in town.

Maxim gazed up at the glass roof that covered the pool, noticing the hazy film of dirt from years of the glass canopy being left unwashed. It triggered the memory of a different haze, the strange experiences with the creatine powder—that pink clump, the mortar and pestle, and the way Judith had discarded a full pot of the stuff the following day. Thinking it over, he realized that there were times his mental haze and fatigue were worse after he took the creatine, when he would spend days in this strange fog, and when he was stressed, he would begin to see shadows and feel paranoid. No, he reasoned, there was no immediate effect, and he felt some of these symptoms even when he didn't take the creatine (sometimes at night, and other times in the early morning). It could still be due to his other medications, his increasing tolerance to them manifesting physical ailments, or maybe the creatine was interfering with the medication in some way.

Jamie returned and handed him a glass of hazy yellow-green juice. "Here you go Max. Judith bought this new citrus medley, I mixed the creatine in it for you."

"Thanks Jamie, I was getting thirsty," Maxim acknowledged, drinking the entire glass down without stopping.

"How does it taste?"

"It's good, have you tried it?"

"Not yet. I'm going to grab some champagne from the fridge and see if it works as a mimosa," Jamie said. "I'll be right back."

Maxim was left by himself once again. His thirst quenched, he jumped back into the pool and returned to swimming. The first laps felt easier as he was energized from the brief reprieve. He increased the power of his strokes, pedaling his legs against the water as he propelled himself forward with his long and powerful arms. His breath quickened as he dove and rose from the surface in great plumes of splashing water. He was mid-way through another lap when he began to feel dizzy. He stopped, trying to catch his breath, but the dizziness increased.

He floated about the pool, his vision going blurry and his mind becoming ever more disoriented. Something was wrong, and Maxim could feel that he was having difficulty keeping himself afloat. He looked frantically around him but could not ascertain where the edge of the pool was. His mind spinning, his arms flailing against the water, Maxim gasped for breath as his head flopped above and below the water line. Fully panicking now, he tried to scream, but water entered his mouth and the more he struggled the more he felt he was about to drown. Maxim could feel the pull of some force dragging on him. This was it, this was death pulling him to his end—he was not ready to die, not this way. He called for help, he called for Jamie, he called for anyone, but all it did was push more water down his throat.

"Max? MAX!" A voice called out, followed by a large splash. A pair of arms wrapped themselves around Maxim's flailing torso.

"Max! You need to stand up!" the voice cried, but Maxim could not understand the command; he continued to wail incoherently as the arms surrounding him kept trying to lift him out of the water.

"Max! Stand up!" the voice cried out again. "Help! We need help here! HELP!"

Maxim heard another splash, and felt another set of arms grabbing him. He could no longer discern what was happening around him, and then everything went black.

IV

Maxim awoke in a hospital bed in Gwendolyn. He was met by the worried sight of Edward, Jamie, and Dr. Wells.

"Where am I?" asked Maxim, unsure of what was happening.

"Oh my God, he's okay!" Edward yelped in relief.

"Eddy? W-what are you doing here?"

"You invited me to come over, remember? My audition got canceled so I decided to come earlier. Thank God I did!"

"Bu-but what happened?"

"Maxim, you were drowning on the shallow end of the pool. We kept shouting at you to stand up, but you were incoherent," Jamie said.

"I . . . I . . . don't know what happened," Maxim mumbled, distressed.

"Fortunately, we confirmed you did not suffer a stroke," Dr. Wells told him. "But I am recommending you stay at the hospital for observation."

"Is that necessary, Doctor? I would rather have Maxim rest at home," Jamie objected.

"It will only be for a few days, just to make sure his condition is stable. Were you doing anything unusual before the incident?"

"No, only that I drank some juice with creatine in it," Maxim responded.

"Well creatine is completely harmless; what else was in the juice?"

"Nothing else, Doc. Just citrus, our house manager bought it in town this morning," Jamie replied.

"Wait. Was there grapefruit in the juice?" Maxim asked, Jamie returning a blank expression. "I get bad reactions with grapefruit when I'm on my medications."

Jamie hesitated, anxious, but Dr. Wells intervened.

"Max, although grapefruit can interfere with your current medication, it does not result in this kind of mental episode. Just to be safe, we will keep you at the hospital for the next few days," the doctor asserted once more.

Maxim remained bed-bound that evening, with little to do other than watch the television and sleep. He had the hospital room to himself, the nurse's station a few doors away. Jamie and Edward returned to Gwenshill, assured by the doctor that Maxim's condition was not serious and they could come back to see him during visiting hours. Maxim flipped through the television channels, bored; his only welcome distraction was the young nurse who would come to his bedside to bring him his meals and his cocktail of pills.

"Good evening Mr. Porter, how are you feeling?" asked the nurse, her uniform neatly pressed with some colorful pins on her lapel. Her nametag spelled "Charlotte" in large block letters.

"Bored but good," Maxim replied. "My niece's name is Charlotte also."

"That's nice, my parents named me after where I was born."

"Oh, good thing you weren't born in Plattsburgh then," Maxim teased, earning a smile from the nurse. "What's for dinner?"

"Some pasta, bread, and fruit. Doctor said your medication is more effective with carbohydrates."

"Oh goody," Maxim replied in jest. As the nurse shuffled the trays around inside the cart, looking for Maxim's medication, he noticed one small cup with a pink tablet inside of it. It looked familiar.

'Nurse, what's in that one over there?" Maxim asked, pointing to the cup in question. The nurse looked at the little container.

"Oh, don't worry, Mr. Porter. That one is not for you."

"I understand, but what is it though? I think I've seen it before."

The nurse pulled out the cup of Maxim's medications and placed it on his tray next to his meal, then looked once more at the little pink pill.

"Does a family member have allergies? That's what the pill is for," the nurse told him with a shrug. "You can buy it at any pharmacy; you don't even need a prescription."

"Really? I think I may be getting some hay fever from my husband's garden," Maxim fibbed. "Should I be taking this kind of allergy medication?"

Curious, the nurse picked up his medical chart.

"I'd ask your doctor first, Mr. Porter. He tends to avoid giving that specific one to patients that are under the same regimen as you."

Maxim sat back in bed, puzzled at this information. Suspicion was growing in the back of his mind, but of what?

"I see . . . I'll ask Dr. Wells," Maxim said and thanked her. After she left, Maxim sat in silence for a long while as he slowly began to digest what he had just experienced in that swimming pool.

CHAPTER 21

I

A heavy summer storm befell Gwenshill in the middle of the night. The freak weather event had pulled off several slate shingles from the roof of the mansion, and heavy downpour entered the attic. The damage was only reported early that morning when staff noticed water dripping from the ceiling on several bedrooms in the north end of the house. An emergency contractor was called to the house to repair the damaged roof, while Maxim and Judith sifted through water-logged boxes to check for damage. Much to Maxim's dismay, many of the ruined items had once belonged to his late mother.

"Fucking fantastic!" Maxim exclaimed angrily, pulling water-logged documents from one box. The ink was bleeding into the pages from being soaked for several hours.

"How can I assist, Mr. Porter?" Judith asked, her gaze stern and intent.

"Check through the boxes of clothes; anything wet should be sent to be professionally cleaned."

"Yes Mr. Porter," she replied, going through the marked boxes that were closest to the roof leak.

The fetid heat of the attic, which had never been insulated, made the task of sorting through the boxes more difficult. Maxim was sweating and panting, and Judith was equally struggling. They decided to carry the boxes to the ballroom where the space could better ventilate and dry the wet items. The large terrace doors were opened; the breeze from outside combined with the cooling shade of the tall ballroom ceiling made the sorting of items more bearable.

"All of this might need to be tossed for all we know," Maxim lamented, looking at the considerable pile. There was almost a whole life's worth of items that had belonged to Karine that were soaked from the storm. Some items were so old they disintegrated in his hands. Letters, photographs, family film from his mother's childhood; Maxim could only feel disheartened at the sight of the memories of his mother crumbling into dust and wet mush.

Judith was more efficient and less sentimental as she sifted through the boxes that contained Karine's dresses, sleeping gowns, and undergarments. In one box, she encountered a large leather-bound travel case, big enough to fit several dresses. The case was wet from the outside, so she instinctively opened it to inspect what was inside. She froze, stunned.

"This is beautiful," she declared softly.

Maxim had never seen Judith express any emotion before, and it only piqued his curiosity as to what Judith was looking at. He stood over Judith as she pulled out his mother's black chiffon ballgown, its delicate black lace still preserved over a half century later. Maxim felt an almost supernatural presence the moment Judith pulled the gown from its container, an unwitting time capsule of his mother's most prized possession. Judith was mesmerized by its beauty, her eyes transfixed, her hands gently feeling the texture of the intricate lace pattern on the bodice of the dress.

"Judith, put the gown back in the case," Maxim commanded bluntly. He hadn't even known the dress still existed. Thinking it had been lost long ago, he was determined to keep it preserved. "Judith, I said put it back!" he barked once more.

Judith was startled by the command, breaking her from her trance. "My apologies, Mr. Porter. What shall I do with this?"

"Take it to the family office. I will ask Isabel if she knows a conservator."

Judith placed the dress back into the travel case, wiping the wet surface of its exterior with a dry cloth. She took the box with its precious contents and placed it on Maxim's desk. She lingered briefly, caressing the travel case, then returned to the ballroom to continue her task. The organizing took several more days; what could be salvaged was left drying on makeshift racks, and the rest Maxim ordered to be cleaned by professionals. At one point Maxim wandered into the living room and looked once more at his mother's portrait.

"Mom, why this now?" he sighed to himself.

"Hey handsome," came a sudden voice, startling Maxim. He turned to see Jamie just behind him.

"What are you going on about?" Jamie asked.

II

"My word, what a wonderful dessert. And so exotic!" Lady Wendell marveled. "How extraordinary!"

Maxim and Jamie were holding a picnic at the edge of the woods that surrounded Gwenshill. Lady Wendell had brought pastries made in her estate, and Maxim offered to make a dessert in kind for the three of them to enjoy. They lay underneath a large ancient tree whose branches shaded them from the harsh sun.

"I'm glad you like it, Lilly! It's our late housekeeper's recipe; she took great pride in her take on a fruit tart," Maxim gloated.

"It's very good, Max," Jamie agreed. "You could have been a baker." He chuckled, helping himself to another slice.

"You just have to buy the papaya melon when it's just ripe; too soon and it might give some people indigestion," Maxim continued.

"How so?"

"There's an enzyme, I think? I can't remember what it was. Luisa told us her mother would wrap papaya leaves around tough meat to make it tender."

"How interesting. I wonder if that works with game meat," Lillian pondered.

"Why, Lilliput? The deer on the estate too tough to eat?" Jamie asked in a cheeky tone.

"Oh Kinder Egg, it's either that or the cook not letting it sit in the sherry long enough," Lillian huffed.

"You know Lillian, you could—" Maxim found himself suddenly at a loss for words. "You could . . . you could . . . damn it, what was I going to say?"

Jamie and Lady Wendell sat in their folding chairs staring back at Maxim, waiting for his question, but he remained stuck.

"It will come to me. Nothing serious." Maxim brushed it off. Jamie continued to look at him, a hint of concern in his eyes.

"Are you okay Max?"

"I'm fine Jamie," Maxim assured him.

It had been six weeks since Maxim left the hospital; his forgetfulness was now a daily occurrence, and Jamie was becoming over-protective when Maxim would find himself going blank. It made Maxim more self-conscious of his condition, feeling that his grasp over himself was slipping ever so slightly. His other symptoms of paranoia, fatigue, and detachment still appeared sporadically, and his nightmares persisted, but seldom did they antagonize Maxim anymore. He would wake up from them in the middle of the night feeling simply defeated, learning to keep his body still so as not to disturb Jamie sleeping beside him.

"Max, why don't you increase the amount of creatine you're taking? It will help keep your mind sharper."

"Jamie, please, I am just growing old. I am already following every new-age health gimmick you give me," Maxim protested.

"Okay mister stubborn, I just want you to keep healthy," Jamie conceded.

"I am healthy! I'm eating fruit right now aren't I?" Maxim joked. Jamie rolled his eyes.

"That reminds me. This fruit tart would go wonderfully with the sorbet we have," Maxim said as he dug through the cooler beside him.

"Oh my word, how decadent!" Lillian raved with girlish glee.

"Just great!" Maxim grumbled. "Judith forgot to pack up the sorbet with the drinks."

"I'll go get it," Jamie offered.

"You don't have to, we can save it for later."

"No, I insist. The cooler needs more ice anyway."

Jamie walked back to the house, leaving Maxim and Lady Wendell lounging underneath the tree. In the brief silence of Jamie's departure, Maxim looked up at the long sinuous branches that fanned out into their thick canopy of leaves. He listened to their gentle sway, closing his eyes and retreating into his thoughts. Taking comfort in the happy moments of his childhood, he recalled the times when his boyish curiosity would carry his imagination into the forest trail. Swimming in the stream, riding his bicycle around the gardens, playing with his brother George, the visiting of distant relatives and the parties that accompanied their stay. Underneath this tree, Maxim could escape into the purity of more innocent times, sheltered from the realities of the present and the unknown of the future.

"Is there going to be a new flower garden, Maximillian?" Lady Wendell asked, interrupting Maxim from his quiet meditation.

"I would ask James, Lilly. The last garden was his pet project."

"Oh, that's right. I missed seeing them when it was in peak bloom," Lady Wendell reflected.

"It was quite beautiful, and there were so many varieties of butterflies flying around," Maxim replied, looking back at the house to see Jamie's silhouette still making its way up the hill.

"How marvelous! Leave it to Jamie to be so clever," Lady Wendell chirped merrily.

"Yes, he was very clever," Maxim sighed. "I even saw monarchs, my favorite butterfly from when I was a kid. There were so many of them, it was a pretty sight."

"Monarchs? How interesting!" Lady Wendell commented. "I'm wondering if Jamie planted milkweed."

"I'm not sure, I suppose so." Maxim replied. He knew Jamie had kept a list of saplings he ordered, but he had not seen the list in many years.

"Well, I hope the gardeners took great precaution."

Maxim's brow furrowed in curiosity. "Why? Are the saplings difficult to plant?" he asked.

"Well, my gardener back in England tells me that the . . . what is it, sap? Oh my word, I will probably get this wrong. He told me the sap or serum or whatever is poisonous. You must be very careful when handling the plant and not get any of the sap on you."

"Like a poinsettia?"

"It is worse than that. So much so, even the butterflies themselves are filled with it when collecting the nectar." Lady Wendell nodded, taking a drink from her cocktail glass.

"Then what does it do?" Maxim inquired further.

"It can stop the heart," she replied.

Maxim felt uneasy at the thought that they'd overlooked something so serious, though Maxim concluded that since it hadn't grown on the grounds of Gwenshill in a couple of years, it was no great concern now. Perhaps next time Jamie would know to choose less dangerous plants.

Lady Wendell pulled a large folding fan from her bag and flapped it gently. She looked back to the house and began to wave to a returning Jamie, ice bags and sorbet in hand.

"Phew, the sun is so brutal," Jamie moaned, wiping beads of sweat from his forehead. His chest, partly visible where his linen shirt was unbuttoned, also glistened with sweat.

"Our brave knight returns with refreshments. Hurrah!" Lady Wendell joked.

"Here Jamie, let me make you a drink," Maxim offered. "Lilly, would you like to have another one?"

"I'd love to try something else," she suggested.

"Then let me make you one of my favorite drinks. Jamie?"

"No thank you Max, just throw me a seltzer," Jamie replied. Maxim handed him a can and Jamie pressed it on his head to cool off as he lay under the tree resting his eyes.

Maxim probed the cooler, pulling out bottles of gin, orgeat, bitters, and lemon juice. Grabbing a handful of ice, he dropped it into a cocktail shaker followed by enough ingredients for two glasses. Maxim shook the steel vessel rigorously and then poured its cold contents into two clean coupes. He handed one glass to Lady Wendell, keeping the other for himself.

"Cheers, I hope you like it." Maxim smiled, raising his glass.

"What is it? It has a lovely color."

"It is called an Army and Navy. I learned to make it back at Yale," Maxim responded.

The two of them clinked their glasses. Jamie lay beside them unconcerned, until he opened his eyes suddenly and with a look of fear, he turned to Lady Wendell as she was about to take her first sip.

"Lillian, no!" Jamie yelled, slapping the drink from Lady Wendell's hand. Its contents spilled onto the ground.

"James, what is it?!" Maxim exclaimed.

"She's allergic to almonds! Lillian, you didn't drink any, right? You have your epi pen on you?" Jamie's eyes darted between Maxim and Lady Wendell. Lillian sat startled and somewhat confused.

"I have the pens in my bag. But what do you mean, almonds? Maxim didn't put any almonds in my drink."

"Yes Jamie, what's with the overreaction?" Maxim was confused and irritated.

"Max, orgeat is made with almonds! It could have killed her!" Jamie snapped back in disbelief at Maxim's carelessness.

"How was I supposed to know? I pulled out all the bottles and she didn't say a word!" Maxim exclaimed.

"Dears, please calm down." Lady Wendell spoke in a calm but shaky voice. "I didn't know orgeat was made with almonds, so how would he? Do not blame your husband for this. He was just being gracious."

"My God Lilliput, good thing I know what Max's drink was. If something happened to you—" Jamie cried, visibly shaken, hugging Lady Wendell tightly.

"I am so sorry Lillian, I feel absolutely mortif—" Maxim began.

"No, no," Lady Wendell interrupted him. "I am sure it would have been a lovely drink. Don't cry my dear Jamie, don't cry."

They continued their picnic, Lady Wendell remaining jovial and bubbly despite the unexpected shock. Jamie sat close to Lady Wendell, his head on her shoulder, still recovering himself from the ordeal. His gaze was serene, but Maxim could sense some melancholia in it. Maxim knew that gaze; it reminded him of himself when he was younger. The fear of losing Lady Wendell felt as real to Jamie as the fear Maxim had of losing his mother, whenever there had been a surgery or a mishap during her life. Even when she had recovered, and the worst was behind her, Maxim would still fear her loss. Looking at Jamie, now thirty-two, he still saw a scared little boy who feared losing the woman most important to him.

"Oh my word! I almost forgot. Kinder Egg, were you careful with planting that milkweed in your garden?" Lady Wendell asked Jamie.

Jamie looked back at her with a surprised expression. "Milkweed? What milkweed? Who told you I planted milkweed?"

Lady Wendell continued, "Maxim was telling me how he was delighted with all the monarch butterflies that flew about your garden. My gardener back home told me that you need to plant milkweed for them to appear."

Jamie turned to Maxim, giving him a strange look, as if he had been caught doing something wrong. He turned back to Lady Wendell with a nonchalant response. "Maxim must be misremembering; there were many different butterflies, and many different flowers planted, but milkweed was not one of them."

"But Jamie, I was sure there were monarchs flying around, more than any other," Maxim insisted, but Jamie continued to dismiss the idea.

"Maxie, I planted the garden. There were no monarch butterflies and there was no milkweed."

"But—"

"Max!" Jamie interrupted, annoyed. "Enough of this. The mental roller coaster ride you put me through was bad enough."

Maxim refrained from speaking further; he did not want to antagonize Jamie after what had just happened.

III

That evening, Maxim found himself having difficulty falling asleep. His mind kept whirring, like an old computer that continued to run calculations, yet failed to produce an answer. Something did not add up. Maxim's memory may be failing him in his day-to-day life, but he could not drop Jamie's assertion that what he saw a few years ago was just a figment of his imagination. Maxim knew what he saw, and he had to prove what he saw was true to himself if not to Jamie. Maxim tossed and turned in bed, disturbing Jamie from his sleep.

"Max, are you having a nightmare again?" Jamie mumbled.

"Sorry," Maxim whispered. "I'm just going to get a glass of water."

Maxim left their bedroom and decided to go to the family office as Jamie returned to sleep. He paced through the darkened corridors, following the muted light from the staircase window. Instead of descending the main stairs to the first floor, he continued down the hall toward the servants' wing. He walked past the staff bedrooms; each door locked with sleeping staff members within. Noticing that Judith's room was unlocked and the door ajar, Maxim peered into it briefly, seeing that she was not in her bed. She must be in the bathroom, he thought, turning the corner and descending the service stairs to the kitchen. Maxim walked into the darkened room, thinking no one was there. He flipped the light switch and found Judith standing in the middle of the kitchen. Startled by the sudden brightness, she dropped something that rolled across the floor and landed at Maxim's feet.

"Jesus Christ!" Maxim exclaimed in surprise, holding back his voice to not awaken the rest of the house. "Judith! Why are you standing there in the dark?" he asked angrily, catching his breath. Judith stood frozen in place, her face pale like she had seen a ghost.

"Mr. Porter, my apologies. I didn't mean to frighten you."

Her eyes drifted nervously to the object she had dropped. Maxim looked down, picking up a bottle of pills.

"Aspirin?" Maxim asked.

"Mr. Porter, I can explain—" Judith hesitated, looking uncharacteristically anxious. "I-I have a migraine, and I needed to grab some water to take my aspirin."

"But then why come down here? There's a water dispenser upstairs," Maxim pointed out.

"There were no cups. I came to grab one from the kitchen."

Maxim looked back to his hand at the bottle of aspirin. He noticed how light it was, opening the cap to peer in and see there were no pills left.

"This bottle is empty," Maxim stated.

Judith continued to hesitate. "Is it? M-My migraine is that severe Mr. Porter, I didn't even notice."

She continued to stand frozen in place. To Maxim she looked more nervous than pained with discomfort. Nevertheless, Maxim walked to an upper cabinet, reached for a bottle of ibuprofen, and handed it to Judith.

"Just don't wander around the house in the dark," Maxim commanded, still irritated.

"Yes Mr. Porter. Have a good evening Mr. Porter." She began to scurry out of the kitchen.

"Judith," Maxim called out. She froze once more and looked back anxiously at him. "Your glass?"

"Yes of course." She nodded, returning to the room and grabbing a glass from the cabinet. She walked briskly out of the room and disappeared back up the service stairs.

"I swear ..." Maxim griped to himself, looking around the kitchen. "She gives me the creeps."

Maxim rested his hand on the counter in frustration; he was met by the sensation of something granular. He turned his palm to see it, and noticed some white powder stuck to his fingers.

"What the . . . ?"

Maxim opened the closest cabinet, which was full of the containers of creatine powder he was supposed to be taking. Coincidence? Perhaps . . . but this odd encounter with Judith robbed Maxim of his attention, making him forget he was heading to his office computer. He looked about the kitchen, trying to remember through another bout of mental haze why he was even there to begin with. He poured himself a glass of water and returned to bed. Maxim hoped he could process what he had witnessed with a clear mind the following day.

CHAPTER 22

I

Edward was cast in the role of Lady Bracknell for a revival of *The Importance of Being Earnest* at the main city theater. Maxim decided to surprise Edward by buying a ticket in the front row to watch his friend where Edward might possibly notice him from onstage. Jamie could not attend the show with Maxim, having to host a video conference with clients, but it did not bother Maxim that Jamie was not with him. It had been two years since they reunited, and during that time, they had worked to rebuild the trust between them to the way it had been before the affair.

Maxim had returned Jamie to his post as head of his charitable foundation, giving even greater trust to Jamie to manage the funds he received to gift the various charities. Jamie had developed a reputation of his own, running his own investment fund with an expanded group of international clients. Maxim offered to surrender the family office to Jamie outright, but Jamie politely declined. He still preferred to have an office just to himself, assuring Maxim he did not want his colleagues invading their shared home.

Maxim's body was slowing down, but he continued to push hard on himself to remain active. There were times the exercise was too much for Maxim, and he would begin to feel lightheaded and weak. He took to walking the trails around Gwenshill, and at times hiking through the forest preserve. Jamie insisted Maxim install a GPS tracker on his phone, so Jamie would feel at ease when Maxim wandered around the forests. In equal measure, Maxim could use the tracker to see where Jamie was, but he did not feel the need. Maxim had complete trust in Jamie, and that trust was the bedrock of their relationship.

Arriving at the theater, Maxim was directed to his front-row seat by the usher, where he nested himself snugly in the tufted chair. His long legs felt cramped already, his knees pressed awkwardly by the raised stage, but Maxim wanted to be there for his friend and opted to bear the discomfort.

The auditorium filled quickly with people, most of whom were of similar ages to Maxim. He felt sad not to see younger patrons; he had been seventeen when he first saw this play, and already a great fan of the works of Oscar Wilde. He had been very tall for his age, and Maxim liked to think he could have modeled himself after the great poet—sophisticated and witty, able to brush off hateful insults with erudite quips. (Unfortunately, rather than embrace his idol, he had opted to join the basketball team over the poetry club in prep school. It was a poor choice regardless, because his height was no substitute for the reality that Maxim was a lousy athlete, but in an all-boys school, it was better to be a failure at being a jock than to be a failure at being straight.)

The lights dimmed, and the audience quieted itself in preparation for the curtain to rise. Maxim was curious to see what energy Edward would bring to his performance. His friend was a master of camp and a virtuoso of comedy, and Maxim was excited to get to experience it in action.

Act one began, the initial dialogue between Algernon and Ernest flowing effortlessly and whimsically. The audience was enamored, chuckling with ease at the extravagance of the dialogue. Maxim was blissful, cramped but content in his seat, smiling brightly at the performance before him, enjoying every turn of phrase from one character to the next. He paid close attention to the play, following the sparring of prose, until the "gaps" started happening again.

As Maxim sat in the darkness, the longer he observed the show, the more fragmented the performance became. The words from the actors splintered and cut mid-sentence, their choreographed movements interrupted and robotic. This was not the fault of the performance. For several months now, when Maxim was made to stay still and fixate on a task, his mind would begin to forget segments of the immediate present happening before him. Time would jump in Maxim's mind, as if skipping forward. Information was, by Maxim's own understanding, being omitted by his own brain. He would notice this when watching movies; continuous scenes seemed fragmented and chopped, like they were jumping ahead without the context of what came before. But when he looked at the clock, time itself would skip forward.

It began with movies, but this new corruption of his mind showed itself in lectures, concerts, and any other events that required Maxim to sit still and focus. Maxim didn't reveal this to anyone, but he tried to find ways to overcome it; if he exerted other stressors, his mind would fixate on something else, hence he could maintain continuity of memory. He would watch movies on the treadmill, take frequent breaks from looking at his computer, record lectures with his phone to listen while walking. But most disturbingly, when nothing else worked, he would sometimes purposefully induce pain on himself, which would distract his mind enough to force it to stop creating gaps in his stream of consciousness.

Maxim did not want his mind to skip over this performance; he did not want to see Edward become a scattered collection of broken speech and sporadic movements. But the discomfort he was feeling huddled in that seat was not enough for his mind to overcome the disruptions. He began to think, looking at his immediate surroundings, what he could do to incite pain.

He looked at his knees, compressed uncomfortably from his big frame poorly fitting into such confined space. He pressed them harder against the metal edge of the stage in front of him. The discomfort and pain increased, but time continued to skip forward in his mind. He pressed harder, the nerve endings of his knees shooting back to his brain in agonizing distress. Maxim was in anguish, grinding his teeth as he pushed his knees harder, slumping and pressing his back to his seat to increase the force of his body against the hard edge of the metal in front of him.

This agony created the stimulus his brain needed to keep from short-circuiting his memory. Through this self-imposed torture, he watched the remainder of the first act as one continuous sequence of events. As soon as the lights came up for the intermission, Maxim released himself from his protracted position. His knees ached merci-lessly; for the first few minutes Maxim could not stand up from the pain. He sat in his chair breathing deeply before attempting to rise again.

"Are you alright?" asked the theatergoer beside Maxim, noticing his pained expression.

"Oh! Don't mind me, I suffered a leg cramp during the show," Maxim lied, returning an embarrassed grin.

He thinks I'm deranged, Maxim thought to himself, embarrassed at the lengths he had to go to, to maintain not just his sanity, but his grasp of time itself. Maxim stood in front of his seat, waiting anxiously for the call to return to the second act. He didn't want to go through the pain again, but he was not going to miss Edward's moment in the spotlight. Maxim needed to remember this play, even if it meant permanent dam-age to his knees.

II

"I'm so glad you came to the show! Thank you Maxim, you are a true friend," Edward praised him as the two men sat together at the bar across the street from the theater.

"Eddy, you were wonderful! Lady Bracknell was your best per-formance ever."

Maxim's knees pulsated with pain from sitting through the whole play. He tried to mask his condition, lying to Edward that he was sore from exercise.

"Oh stop, they only cast me because I'm an old queen. But nice to know that this fat ass still gets butts in seats," Edward joked.

"I am sure that Oscar would have called you the toast of Mayfair."

"*C'est la vie* . . . but thank you again for coming. We don't see each other often enough."

"It's true. You should come to Gwenshill sometime," Maxim offered. "Jamie's planted a new flower garden, and in a few months it will be in full bloom."

"Sure, I'll come. The first garden was very attractive."

The two friends carried on with their conversation, relaying new stories and revisiting old ones. Edward spoke of his plans to travel with Paul for their long-delayed second honeymoon after the show ended; Paul had given up alcohol and was taking better care of himself. They had worked through their own relationship struggles to become even closer.

"Jamie still feels extremely guilty for the whole affair," Maxim told Edward. "He hopes it hasn't changed your opinion of him."

"Maxim, your husband and I are on good terms," Edward assured him. "In fact," he added nonchalantly, "he even recommended a new exfoliant for me not too long ago."

"Really? He didn't tell me. What was it?"

Edward turned back from his seat, pulling a bottle of lotion from his bag.

"Jamie told me that he uses this on his face. Your house manager sent over a bottle to try, and it works pretty well," Edward boasted.

Maxim looked at the label, which didn't look familiar from what he remembered of Jamie's products in their bathroom. It was a foreign brand from South America, with a papaya fruit in the center of the label.

"Jamie said it was the best in the market. I use it on my face and neck daily," said Edward.

"Did he give you this recently?" Maxim asked curiously.

"Oh no, the first bottle I went through it in a month, then I started buying it for myself online."

Maxim shrugged his shoulders, not thinking much more about it, though he did find it odd that he couldn't recall having seen that lotion at all.

III

"Uncle Max, I'm thirteen. I can take care of myself." Charlotte said, annoyed that her parents still expected her to be chaperoned by her uncle.

Isabel had a work obligation and George was still in DC, so Maxim had offered to pick up Charlotte from a recital being held on the other side of the park across from their townhouse. Charlotte had grown considerably from the last time Maxim had seen her. She carried herself with a determined conviction, walking fast and upright, her face intelligent and confident.

"Don't you like spending time with your Uncle Max?" Maxim asked teasingly.

"It's not that, I just think it sucks that I can't do some things by myself," she groaned. "I know how to take the subway from my school back home. I look both ways when crossing. My dad took me to learn taekwondo so I can defend myself."

"What belt are you now, Charlie?"

"I'm a red belt. My teacher said I might get my black belt next year."

"That's great!"

"Yeah, I'm the best fighter in my class, but still my parents won't let me hang out with my friends without family or security."

Charlotte continued her pace, expedient and determined. She was taking her frustration out on the sidewalk, walking with an impatience that only came from being a child raised in the city. Maxim was also a fast walker, but at his age, he struggled to maintain the same speed, at times pausing to catch his breath and almost bringing himself to run. Charlotte was focused on getting home quickly, lost in her own world.

"Charlie, you must understand that there are dangers that come with your dad's work. He's just trying to keep you safe from the nutjobs that are constantly harassing him," Maxim explained, stopping once again to catch his breath.

Charlotte turned back when she heard Maxim heaving, his hand resting by a nearby tree.

"Am I walking too fast, Uncle Max? I'm sorry."

"No my dear, I just need a break," Maxim reassured her, still breathing heavily. He pointed to a park bench nearby. "Why don't we take a seat and you can tell me a little more?"

The two of them sat, surrounded by the colors of fall. Leaves that had gently descended to the ground were soiled by the footsteps of passing pedestrians and sopping from the watery remnants of yesterday's cold rain. Charlotte blew on her cold ungloved hands to keep them warm before stuffing them back into her jacket.

"It's going to get worse, Uncle Max," she was saying. "I heard my parents talking last weekend. Promise me that you won't tell them? It has to be a secret."

"Alright Charlie, I promise."

Charlotte sighed deeply. "My dad told my mom that he wants to run for president," she revealed. Maxim could see that his niece wasn't happy about this news.

"Oh, my sweet Charlie, it could be an exciting new adventure for you. If he wins, you get to see the world, live in the White House . . ." he nudged her shoulder gently with a smile. "And your dad is a good man. He has his heart in the right place."

"But then I *really* can't be myself," Charlotte countered. "I will never be alone, always watched wherever I go, always under the eyes of my parents. I want to be normal, go to school, hang out with my friends. I know when other kids are being stupid, but I still want to do what I want without my parents knowing. I don't want to be treated like a porcelain doll that never leaves the shelf."

"You want to be your own person," Maxim echoed. He knew what Charlotte meant.

"Yes! Uncle Max, my parents are so protective. Were your parents like that too?"

Maxim thought for a moment, then told Charlotte about her father when he was younger, how he was also rebellious and independent. He told her of the times when George would get into trouble at school, when he would upset Henry and Karine with his antics. George rebelled against the suffocating nature of their upbringing; it took him going to university and meeting Isabel for him to come into his own. He recalled to Charlotte how her grandmother would at times get frustrated with George's behavior, but that was because she knew he was intelligent and capable. Maxim told Charlotte that, with time, she would also move outside of her parents' shadow to find herself.

"You are a lot like your grandmother," Maxim commented, hugging his niece tightly. "She also wanted her dad to stop getting on her nerves."

"I wish I had known her," Charlotte replied.

"Me too Charlie, me too."

Maxim's phone began to ring. It was Isabel, wondering where they were. Maxim apologized, letting Isabel know they were only a few minutes away.

"Well, your mom is now mad at me," Maxim joked. "We better get going."

"Thank you for talking to me, Uncle Max. Out of all the adults, you don't treat me like a dumb kid," said Charlotte, leading the way back to the pathway.

"Unlike most adults, I still remember what being a kid felt like," Maxim replied with a smile.

They walked along the asphalt trail, the sun setting slowly behind the city skyline. Two generations, side by side; one ready to journey forward, but unsure of what lay ahead, the other sharing wisdom from a path already traveled.

Their comfortable silence was interrupted by Maxim's voice echoing in the cold wind.

"What belt are you now, Charlie?"

IV

From: Andrew Wright <a.wright@lgbtmetro.org>

To: James Porter <jamesporter@mdpfoundation.org>

Cc: Maximillian D. Porter <maximillian.d.porter@mdpfoundation.org>

Received: February 28 – 1:02 PM

Mr. James Porter,

I hope this email finds you well. We are saddened to hear that after twenty-four years of generously aiding The LGBT Metropolitan Society, the MDP Foundation (formerly the Porter Family Foundation) is opting to direct its resources toward funding other charitable opportunities.

Your patronage will be missed. We hope that in the future, the MDP Foundation will reconsider providing funding to The LGBT Metropolitan Society to help our organization with its ongoing efforts to provide outreach and support to LGBTQ+ communities across our metro region.

Regardless, we thank you for your many years of support.

Andrew Wright

Head Trustee and Board Member

The LGBT Metropolitan Society

CHAPTER 23

I

Maxim sat at his computer, trying to write responses to emails his lawyers had sent regarding his trust. He stared at the screen, his mind struggling to compose the sentences he wished to type. Maxim knew what he wanted to say, or at least, he knew that there was an answer to the questions he had read. But his continuing mental haze clouded Maxim's faculties, causing him to type words and instructions that were confusing, at times almost indecipherable. Maxim would reread his responses and find that what he had typed made no sense, so he had to delete what he had written and start over. The more he rewrote, the more confusing his assembly of words became.

Maxim pushed himself away from the computer, his chair rolling back as he pressed his hands against his face. Closing his eyes, Maxim tried to cut through the mental scramble and focus on a coherent string of thought.

"Not even when drunk do I have this much trouble writing a lousy email!" Maxim told himself.

A knock came from the office door, and Judith stepped into the room holding a tray with a cup of coffee and a glass of water, its contents cloudy.

"Thank you Judith, I was just thinking I needed some coffee," Maxim replied. He looked at the glass beside it. "What is this? I already drank that creatine crap."

"No Sir, Master James said that you left the glass undrunk at lunch," Judith replied.

"I had that stuff in the morning with my orange juice."

After a pause, Judith blurted out, "My apologies Mr. Porter, I failed to mix the supplement with your juice this morning."

Maxim looked at Judith with a disgruntled sneer. He was beginning to grow tired of Judith's presence at the house. She may have been professional and dutiful, but her personality continued to give Maxim a deep sense of unease. It did not help her case that Maxim detested the texture of the chalky powder Jamie made him drink every day (particularly when he had to drink it with tap water), since she was usually the one to bring it to him.

"Fine Judith," Maxim barked, taking the cloudy glass and drinking it down. "Blergh, this tastes awful every time. And you forgot to bring the cream and sweetener," he huffed.

"My apologies Mr. Porter, it will not happen again." Judith bowed in atonement and returned to the kitchen to fetch what Maxim requested. Soon after she left, Jamie walked into the office holding a bundle of papers.

"Hello handsome. Why the grumpy face?" Jamie asked casually.

"It's nothing, I'm just procrastinating answering emails from the lawyers," Maxim lied.

"Good, because their office called and informed me they need your signature on some forms." Jamie placed the documents on Maxim's desk, a neat stack of paperwork with a dozen or so tags sticking out from them.

"They need me to sign for all of this?"

"They said it's urgent, that it will clear up the matter with the trust," Jamie said with a shrug. "I offered to print all the documents and send them back signed."

"Well tell them I need at least an hour, maybe two, to read over all this," Maxim instructed Jamie. Judith walked back into the office with the cream and sweetener. Maxim turned to Jamie as Judith walked out of the room.

"What do you think of Judith?"

"I don't know, in what sense?"

"There's just something about her that never sat well with me. Maybe we could look for another house manager?"

"Don't be silly," Jamie said, growing defensive. "I've had—I mean—we've had her for years and she has never done anything wrong."

"No, but she is so distant and frigid."

"Maxim, she's a trained professional. These days it's not common for staff to be personable to their employers. You got too used to having the same staff for decades."

"Granted, I don't expect her to become Mary Poppins, but I didn't sign up for Mrs. Danvers either."

Jamie rolled his eyes, unconvinced. Maxim shook his head, looking back at the stack of documents before him and worrying over whether he'd be able to read through that stack of papers and recall its details. His lapsing attention span could handle a few documents at a time, but to read and remember them all required more than the couple of hours he had.

"Let's talk about this later, Jamie. I need to get on these papers," Maxim said. Jamie nodded and left him alone.

Maxim grabbed the first set of documents from the stack, a substantial prospectus of ten pages. He began to read through it, finding it comprehensible and concise. Maxim took his pen and signed the document, setting it on a separate pile. The second document, some six pages, was about the transfer of assets between shell companies. He signed it and continued onto the next document. Soon he began to struggle with reading through the large unbroken blocks of text. He signed the third and fourth documents and set them with the rest. He knew he needed to take a break, feeling suddenly drowsy; instead he drank from his coffee cup to remain alert and pushed through to the next set of papers. It was twenty pages long, but he couldn't read past the third sheet. Maxim was only a third of the way complete, and an hour had already passed.

Maxim lay back in his office chair, thinking maybe a short nap would help. Setting his phone alarm for fifteen minutes, Maxim rested his eyes and quickly fell asleep. He began to dream he was a child again, meandering through an empty Gwenshill. His voice echoed out through the second-floor corridor, calling for people he knew, but met with only silence.

"Mom? Dad?" Maxim called out. "George, are you there?"

Maxim heard a whooshing sound behind him. He turned around, seeing something run into a bedroom. Afraid, he continued to call out for his family.

"Mom? Is that you? George?"

He stepped toward the room, his childhood bedroom, and heard what sounded like faint whispers coming from inside. When he reached the door, the whispers grew louder, but when he opened it, he found no one there.

He looked around his room, the walls covered in painted stars and planets. On his bed, his stuffed elephant had fallen gently over to one side. His construction blocks, arranged into a city skyline, stood opposite his bed. He looked around the room, the whispering voices remaining.

A low rumble began to overtake the whispers, and the room began to shake. Maxim stood still, watching all his things begin to fall onto the floor. The room creaked and groaned. A black sludge seeped down the walls, covering everything in a dark void of nothingness. He ran out of the room, the whole house shaking underneath his feet.

The sludge spread from the room out into the corridor, following Maxim. He raced down the stairs, still calling out for his family. The floors heaved, the plaster cracked, light fixtures crashed onto the ground as the sludge continued to seep through the house.

Maxim tried to open the front doors to escape but they would not open. He rushed to the living room but the sludge covered the doors to the terrace. The house was collapsing around him, the void consuming everything as the walls and floors gave way.

He ran through the house, desperately looking for an exit. He saw the door to the kitchen and remembered the service entrance. He lunged into the room as the house collapsed behind him, the door clicking shut as he fell to the floor.

The shaking ceased, and the kitchen appeared undamaged. Maxim stood up, catching his breath, thinking the worst was over. He slowly turned to see a figure by the kitchen sink. It was Luisa, hunched over cleaning dishes as if nothing had happened.

"Luisa! Luisa!" Maxim called out in tears. "The house fell down! I can't find my family!"

"Oh, don't worry Mr. Max, your family went to get you a present," Luisa said sweetly without turning around.

"Luisa, we're in danger! We need to go!" Maxim rushed to her side, trying to pull her out of the room.

With one strong tug, he pulled her away from the sink. Luisa turned to face Maxim, her eyes blackened, her face swollen, her apron stained red with blood and vomit. Her voice was distorted and warped and sludge seeped from her mouth as she spoke.

"Don't worry Mr. Max . . . let . . . me . . . make . . . you . . . some . . . tea."

Maxim awoke from his nightmare in a scream of absolute terror. The sound of a metal tray crashing onto the floor, broken glass and porcelain shattering to pieces on the ground, broke his hysteria. Judith stood there in fright, having dropped the tray at the sound of Maxim's screaming.

"Mr. Porter! Are you alright?!" Judith exclaimed.

Maxim sat in his chair, scanning the room and realizing that the bundle of documents was gone from his desk, his alarm having gone off two hours prior. At the point of tears, still processing what had happened, he grew irate at the sight of Judith standing there in the middle of the office, looking at him in shock. His nerves completely frayed, he shouted at her in anger.

"What the fuck you are looking at?! You have lived here fucking long enough to know what fucking hell I have to live with! Fucking clean that mess and GET OUT!"

II

From: Carolina Tavares <tavares@aidsrescenter.org>

To: James Porter <jamesporter@mdpfoundation.org>

Cc: Maximillian D. Porter <maximillian.d.porter@mdpfoundation.org>

Received: May 12 – 9:35 AM

Mr. Porter,

It is unfortunate to hear that the MDP Foundation will be withdrawing its funding commitment to the AIDS Research Center. We are considerate that during times of economic hardship, charitable organizations must reduce their funding initiative to continue providing support to other NGOs and charitable institutions. We hope the MDP Foundation will consider continuing their commitment at a reduced level rather than terminating the funding completely.

Please reach out to me in person so that we may help in coming to a new funding goal that best suits your organization's needs and your financial capacities.

Sincerely,

Dr. Carolina Tavares

President

The AIDS Research Center

III

Jamie's thirty-fourth birthday party was a raucous affair, with hundreds of guests descending upon Gwenshill. Maxim had invited Edward and Paul to the party to make sure he'd have his own company in case the festivities proved too much for Maxim's sensibilities.

Judith walked onto the terrace looking for Maxim, calling for the three men to be present for the arrival of the cake.

They walked into the ballroom, resplendent in gold and blue decorations, the antique chandeliers replaced with disco balls and balloons covering the entirety of the ceiling. Jamie sat at one end of the ballroom on a gilded throne, surrounded by friends who held court before him as if he were the Sun King at Versailles. Jamie was enjoying every moment of his festivity, his expression filled with confident and buoyant jubilation.

"Max! Max!" Jamie called out from across the ballroom. Maxim and Edward went to him, Jamie rising from his throne to plant a kiss on Maxim.

"Are you enjoying yourself, Prince Jamie?" Maxim asked, basking in Jamie's warm smile.

"This birthday is the best one yet. Thank you for the party, Maxie," replied an elated Jamie. "I hope all the noise is not too much for you."

"So long as you're having fun my dear Jamie, I'll manage," Maxim smiled.

The cake was rolled out, a towering mound of confectionery made to look like a renaissance castle. A candle stuck out from each of thirty-four fondant chimneys. The guests sang together, the voices spreading about the house as more people joined the chorus to celebrate Jamie. Maxim was astonished at the veneration of his husband. Jamie blew out the candles to a roar of cheers and applause. Grabbing a knife, Jamie carved into the cake. Placing a slice on a plate, he climbed upon the seat of his throne and called everyone quiet for a speech.

"My dear friends, clients, and all present. I want to thank you all for coming to my birthday party. It is so wonderful to see how many of you have made me a part of your lives and have been a part of mine. I just want to thank you all for your support, your love, and for some of you, your money . . ."

Jamie paused at his guests' laughter and continued, now turning his gaze to Maxim.

"But on a day where it is all about celebrating me, I must return one gift. In my family, it is custom to gift the first slice of cake to the person whom you most treasure in this world. It is a symbol of humility, that one must remember they would not be there without the love of others. So this gift, I give to the most important man in my whole life. My beloved husband Max. I love you Maxie; thank you for everything."

The crowd applauded, Maxim moved by Jamie's declaration. Jamie gave the slice of cake to Maxim and kissed him once more. The party returned to its energetic celebration; the music blasting, the guests prepared to dance the night away.

Maxim and Edward stepped away from the party, walking through the gardens. The sky became a brilliant swirl of oranges and magentas as the sun set behind the trees, the hues of ending daylight surrendering slowly to the blackness of night.

"That was a beautiful gesture coming from Jamie," Edward commented. "I never thought his family would follow such a tradition."

"That's because it's a tradition from my family—my mother's family actually," Maxim revealed.

"Then why did he say *his* family?" Edward asked in surprise.

"Come on Eddy, didn't you notice that none of the guests were actually from *his* family?" Maxim pointed out.

Edward shrugged his shoulders; Maxim had never told him, or anyone, that Jamie was an illegitimate child.

"You're right, he is part of your family anyhow. At least there was never an argument over whose in-laws you're visiting for Thanksgiving," Edward joked.

"At our ages, Eddy?" Maxim scoffed with a chuckle. "Sooner or later we'll be visiting our in-laws in hell."

They continued to walk along the garden path through rows of wildflowers. Maxim made a turn toward the tall hedgerow, going through a gate which led the two of them to another enclosure. Within the tall hedges stood a more intimate garden, with a fountain at its center. The two of them sat by the fountain's edge and continued to talk.

"What are your plans for the summer?" Edward asked casually. "Paul and I will be slumming at the Islands as usual."

"What happened to your second honeymoon plans?"

"We had another fight. We patched things up, but we had already canceled our trip over it."

"I'm sorry to hear."

"Paul has unresolved issues," Edward confided with a sigh. "He's treated alcohol as a sedative for a long time. I love him still, but at times it's just too much." He pulled a packet of cigarettes from his pocket and lit one, taking a long drag from it and blowing its smoke into the cool night air.

"Are you guys seeking counseling?" Maxim asked innocently.

"Why? We're in our seventies. The time to seek help was long ago." Edward took another drag, exhaling deeply. "I accept Paul as he is, he accepts me . . . we have our bungalow, and we can be ourselves there. I think we'll just move out of the city and go live in the Islands full time."

"And give up acting?"

"There's a small community theater now. I can always teach, and I've directed a few plays, you know," Edward replied.

Maxim paused, looking back to the garden gate at the daffodils that bloomed all around them. Their bright yellow flowers stood out against the others, whose colors appeared muted against the light of the moon. He soon became lost in thought. He kept trying to remember something, something he had forgotten to do, something that troubled him but was only faintly appearing in his mind. Something about a flower? Maxim thought. He felt himself entering a mental blank, dissociating from the world around him. Eddy kept calling to him, finally breaking Maxim from his state of oblivion.

"Max . . ." Edward looked at Maxim, worried. "Are you alright?"

Maxim sighed, at first trying to think of a convincing excuse but settling on being truthful with his friend.

"Eddy, I think there's something going on," Maxim said finally. "I'm not feeling myself. I haven't been feeling myself for a long time."

"What do you mean, what are you feeling? Have you been to a doctor about it?"

"I haven't, I'm afraid to go alone. And I don't want to worry my dear Jamie about it."

"Oh Max," Edward consoled him.

"It happens in waves; I feel fine some days, but I get so lost in others. There are weeks when I'm in a complete fog, feeling groggy and weak, not being able to focus or remember anything."

"But surely Jamie would have noticed this by now. After all, you're married and living together," Edward pointed it out.

"I keep it to myself, he thinks I'm just forgetful. But I know there's something seriously wrong with me."

"Max, how long has this been going on?"

"A few years, but it's been getting worse. Ever since that time in the pool when Jamie jumped in to rescue me."

Edward turned to him with a look of confusion.

"Max, I'm the one who pulled you out of the pool."

"What?"

"When I arrived, you were struggling in the pool while Jamie just stood there. It wasn't until he noticed me that he started to tell you to stand up. I jumped into the pool to pull you up; he only jumped in after I started calling out for help to lift you."

"I didn't remember any of that," Maxim admitted, confused and distressed at the revelation.

"After we left you in the hospital, Jamie told me that he was frozen in shock and did not know what to do. To me, he looked like he was waiting for something."

"What do you mean? Like what?" Maxim asked.

"I don't know, Maxim. Only your husband can tell you."

CHAPTER 24

I

Maxim no longer felt safe getting behind the wheel of his car. He now relied on a rideshare service to take him from Gwenshill to the township and back. Sitting on a bench outside the doctor's office, Maxim waited for the car while he listened to a lecture on architecture through his headphones. It reminded him of Victor, and made him wonder whether Victor still thought about him.

Maxim wondered what it would have been like to have met Victor when they were younger: Victor, a struggling architect, Maxim, the sheltered and wistful heir . . . maybe it would have worked back then. To think that in some alternate life, Maxim could have looked up to the dome instead of the balcony and caught sight of Victor. It could have been a romantic beginning, Maxim thought, though their real meeting had been equally unexpected. It was such a different experience from meeting Jamie, passion and abandon all mixed into one. Maxim dreaded the thought that one day his mind would corrupt itself to forget all those tranquil memories. The idea of losing them was inconceivable.

A horn beeped. Maxim looked up to realize it was his ride, and scurried over to enter the car. As the vehicle sped off through town,

Maxim looked out at teenagers on bicycles, parents with their kids, people in various dress and uniform going about their lives.

Maxim was saddened to think of how his most important memories were becoming as fleeting as memories of the strangers that walked the streets of Gwendolyn. How his birthdays, his family, his loves, his sorrows would become as meaningless to his corrupted brain as the sight of some random little boy holding a butterfly backpack at the street corner. How could he? It was as unimaginable as—wait.

"Butterflies," Maxim whispered to himself.

His mind flashing suddenly, he grabbed his phone and typed into the search bar the few words he knew had some importance: *monarch butterfly, milkweed, heart*. It took less than a second for the prompt to reveal the answer.

> **Milkweed**, a common member of the Asclepias family, are a common type of wildflower popularly used in gardens for their ability to attract monarch butterflies. Milkweed sap, present in its roots, leaves, and stem, is known to harbor cardiac cardenolides, which mimic the behavior of cardiac glycosides, commonly prescribed under the pharmaceutical name of digoxin.

Maxim looked at the string of text. Surely it was just a coincidence? He looked at the images of the plants themselves, little clusters of orange flowers emerging from a single stem like a little bouquet. Maxim could faintly recall seeing these flowers in the garden, but also recalled seeing them somewhere other than Gwenshill.

"Judith, is Jamie home?" Maxim inquired upon his return.

"No Mr. Porter, Master James drove to the city."

Maxim remembered a box containing the invoices and receipts for Jamie's garden; he knew it was stored somewhere in the house. Maxim had thought it strange that Jamie would have stored the receipts in a different place from the general expense files for the property, but at the time, hadn't thought much about why. Jamie had insisted that it was his project, and it was to be paid for by his work. Maxim searched through the house, checking the basement rooms and ascending to the attic; he could not find the box. Judith approached Maxim as he continued searching through the house.

"Mr. Porter, is there something I can assist you with?"

"Yes Judith. There was a box containing invoices for James' butterfly garden. Do you know where it has gone?"

"Is there a reason you ask, Mr. Porter?" Maxim paused. Why was she asking this?

"Judith, I need to look at the files," Maxim said firmly. "Do you recall where they were stored?"

"I believe Master James returned them to his office, Mr. Porter." Judith hesitated. "But I believe that Master James locks the door to his office when he is not home."

Maxim turned back toward his room. "That's fine; I keep copies of every key in this house."

Judith followed behind him as he entered his bedroom, and he ordered her to stay in the hallway. Maxim walked to his closet, opening a false panel that concealed a safe, from which he pulled out a large ring containing dozens of keys. When he emerged from the bedroom, Judith was still waiting at the door.

"Judith!" Maxim barked in irritation. "Don't you have tasks to undertake? If I need your assistance I will call for you."

"M-My apologies Mr. Porter," Judith stammered, and hurried off.

Maxim made his way through the house to Jamie's office. He unlocked the door and stepped into the room, scanning the space for sight of the box. Even after going through file cabinets, drawers, and Jamie's desk, Maxim could not locate the invoices. He walked to the closet and peered in, initially not seeing anything of note. He glanced up to the closet light, looking for its cord to pull, when he noticed a small cardboard box buried deep in the back of the uppermost shelf. Maxim reached up to the box, struggling to grip it briefly before pulling the box from its high perch.

He took it to the desk and opened it, finding the invoices at last. There were page after page of approved invoices, with intricate lists of every item purchased and the cost of all the labor. He flipped through until he noticed the Latin name of the milkweed buried within a list of plant selections. A note marked in red ink beside the name read "by owner's request" and at the bottom of the document was Jamie's signature confirming the final list. Maxim pulled out his phone to take a picture of the pages in question. He had only managed a few images before he heard the roar of a car parking just outside the window. It was Jamie, returning unexpectedly.

Thinking fast, he captured a few more images of other pages and stuffed the papers back in the box. He could hear a commotion from the corridor outside, as footsteps descended the hallway toward him. Maxim jumped from his seat, rushing to the closet to place the box back on the shelf.

"How did he get in? Why didn't you stall him?!" Jamie's voice echoed, his steps quickening as he approached the office.

Maxim closed the closet door just moments before Jamie entered the room. Jamie was out of breath and irate. It was the first time Maxim had ever seen Jamie's face twisted into such ugly anger, an unsettling contrast to his typically charming and breezy demeanor. Jamie visibly calmed himself as he took in the room and Maxim.

"Maxim, why are you in my office?" Jamie asked, his voice a monotone cut with disapproval.

"Oh Jamie, you're here early," Maxim said, aiming for indifference. "I was looking for the receipts for the butterfly garden. I can't seem to find them."

"Why do you need them, handsome?" Jamie asked with a nervous smile.

Maxim held his own, maintaining aloofness. He lied, curious to see what Jamie's response would be.

"Well, you see, I had a member of the Mattachine ask how much it cost to build the garden. Since the invoices are not in the office files, I went looking for them here."

"Max, I would appreciate if you didn't go snooping around my office. I could have emailed you the receipts," Jamie replied. "How did you get in anyhow?"

"I have a copy of the key," Maxim replied.

Jamie let out a huff of indignation, but Maxim had already walked away, returning to his bedroom to replace the keys in their hiding place. Jamie forwarded over the garden receipts not long after. When Maxim returned to his desk in the family office, he looked over what Jamie sent him. Comparing them with the images on his phone, he noticed that the mention of the milkweed was missing. Maxim checked the dates of the purchase orders; they were the same. Why would there be two versions of the same order? Maxim looked over the handful of images he had managed to take. Most of them matched with no revisions or notes, but there was one charge that did not; a charge from the landscaper for a bottle of herbicide that had gone missing.

II

The following morning, Maxim was having a great deal of difficulty recalling what he was doing. He could not remember why he was at his desk, why he was in his office, why the sound of the paper shredder coming from Jamie's office bothered him.

He stepped out of the office and walked around the first floor. Wandering through the rooms, Maxim paced slowly and carefully with no finishing point. He could not understand why he was doing this, he only felt that he needed to keep walking through the house. He did not focus on any object inside or look out at the scenery beyond. His mind was so consumed by a confused haze that his body demanded that it could not remain still.

"Hello handsome." Jamie's voice appeared from behind him. Maxim turned, looking back at Jamie giving him his warm and tender smile. "How are you feeling?"

"I'm fine," Maxim responded slowly, his mind not processing what he was doing. Maxim looked intently at Jamie and found that his smile was the only thing Maxim could process.

"I'm fine Jamie. You're looking so nice today Jamie," Maxim said meekly.

"Why thank you handsome. I am done with work for today," Jamie continued. "Why don't we go sit on the terrace together?"

Maxim felt even more bewildered; the room around him seemed alien and removed from reality. Maxim understood that he was indoors, but didn't know where in Gwenshill he was standing. His only comfort from the uncertainty his mind created was that Jamie was there beside him, his smile and twinkling eyes the only sights that still tethered him into the real world. This was the worst episode of mental disruption Maxim had experienced yet. Maxim was afraid to keep walking alone, and so he grabbed onto Jamie's hand, and sheepishly nodded his approval.

"Let's go to the terrace then." Jamie spoke softly, guiding Maxim to the terrace.

Jamie is so kind, Maxim thought. *What a caring man Jamie is*. Maxim and Jamie sat on a bench on the terrace looking out onto the countryside, the sun shining bright, the birds singing sweetly just out of view. Jamie rested his head on Maxim's shoulder, holding his hand while they talked together. Maxim's mind was spiraling into a haze of conflicting and disjointed thoughts and emotions, but in this quiet moment, he could still hold onto the presence of Jamie beside him. Even though he could feel his mind slipping out of sanity and composure, with Jamie's smile and his tenderness, Maxim felt safe. Maxim could not think Jamie capable of anything other than to love and care for him.

III

To Monsieur Maximillian Deauvillier Porter,

We are mailing you this courtesy receipt for the approved transfer via electronic wire of **$763,879.22** from the MaximDPorter Trust S.A. Luxembourg to the MDP Foundation effective June 1st of this year.

Tax documentation has been forwarded to your accounting firm, Olds-Newman Accountants LLC.

For a breakdown of total values and assets affected, please view your private account documents with your digital client key at BambergerFreres.lux.

With utmost service,

Jacqueline Fontaine

Private Banker

Bamberger Frères

Banque Privée

Luxembourg

CHAPTER 25

I

George and Isabel opted to host this year's fourth of July barbecue at the family's villa in the lake district. Maxim and Jamie would stay there for a few days away from Gwenshill. There were to be other guests just for the barbecue, including many of George's friends. Isabel and Maxim took to preparing the side dishes in the kitchen while George and Jamie manned the grills in the courtyard. Maxim could not remember the last time he had visited the villa, which George and Isabel had redecorated since they took possession of it. The earlier decor, designed to Karine's taste nearly half a century ago, had been replaced by the eclectic mix of Isabel and George's opposing styles. Like George and Isabel, the villa was an expression of an ever-changing present, rather than a staid repetition of the past.

"You know Max, George loves sleeping on that chair more than our bed," Isabel joked. "Never have I felt more insecure from a piece of furniture."

"Don't take it personally, Isabel," Maxim chuckled. "Every man has that one place in the house where they instantly go unconscious after dinner."

Maxim stood over the kitchen sink, rinsing and washing vegetables for the salad. He was interrupted by a sudden flash of memory from the nightmare he'd had of Luisa, her face and body convulsing before him. Maxim forgot what he was doing, his memory of the task in front of him a blank.

"Izzy, are the ribs seasoned already?" George asked, entering the kitchen.

"I left them in the trays ready for you George, but I did not spread any sauce on them."

"Why not?"

After a brief spat over the food, George took the meat with him outside to finish prepping it while Isabel gave a frustrated sigh as she worked on the coleslaw.

"Everything okay with you guys?" Maxim asked.

"Oh, it's nothing Max. Just that we decided to give the staff the day off *and* your brother decided to invite a bunch of people at the last minute."

"And you were okay with this?"

Isabel huffed, "I'm choosing to let it slide this time."

"Who's coming over then?"

"He invited some fraternity brothers from college. His detective friend is also coming; Fred, I think?"

"Fred Catinella?" Maxim asked, looking back to Isabel as she nodded.

"He's retired now, but George and I listen to his podcast. It's interesting," Isabel continued. "It's about suspicious deaths."

Most of the guests that George had invited turned out to be previous donors to his campaigns. The group of wealthy businessmen and attorneys took turns ingratiating themselves, gathering around George to bargain for support and vice versa. Maxim could only imagine it was to build enthusiasm for George's presidential run, which had yet to be announced to the press. Jamie partook in the banter between George's friends, throwing his charisma at them, hoping to attract more clients to his own sphere of investors. Jamie stayed in the periphery of their attention, purposefully attempting to keep a spotlight on himself without outshining George.

The outlier of the group was Detective Catinella, not having come from money or a vaunted heritage. Catinella was of a military background, maintaining a stoic and reserved demeanor among the other guests. Those who spoke to him were mostly the spouses of George's friends, the new crime podcast being the other topic of conversation that consumed the gathering. Maxim was intrigued by the detective's new career path, listening closely to Catinella's telling of some of his guest speakers and their stories.

"There was the story of two competing morticians out in California," Catinella said of one case. "One of them was suspected of killing the other by spiking his food to induce a heart attack."

"Suspected?" asked one of the wives.

"The victim was found to have trace amounts of a compound similar to a heart medication. The victim did not take any such medications at the time of death, but the coroner discovered there were traces of other compounds commonly found in oleander leaves."

"Oleander, good gracious. I have oleander growing in my garden!" another woman exclaimed.

"The accused was arrested for other charges, but not for murder," Catinella told them. "There was no conclusive evidence that he had spiked the victim's food, just hearsay."

Maxim listened to the detective's story with an uneasy feeling in the pit of his stomach. He had his own questions for the detective, but he did not want to ask them with Jamie present. Maxim still had the photos of the lists and expenses from Jamie's garden, but the originals were no longer in the closet where he'd found them. Maxim needed to find an opportunity to get the detective's attention.

Jamie approached Maxim just then. "Maxie, your brother needs a couple of tanks of propane from behind the garage."

"Do you need help getting them?" Maxim asked.

"Actually, I'm in the middle of a pitch to one of your brother's friends," Jamie told him, then asked reluctantly, "Do you really need me?"

Maxim saw his chance.

"Don't worry Jamie. Detective, could you help me with the tanks?" Maxim turned to Catinella, indicating with a tip of his head that he needed to talk to him. The detective excused himself and accompanied Maxim away from the gathering toward the garage.

"I take it you and your husband have worked things out?" Catinella asked casually.

"We mended things, yes," Maxim said once they were out of sight. "Listen, um, he doesn't know I know."

"After all this time?"

"What he doesn't know won't hurt him. But I wanted to ask you about that story you told of the two morticians. Was the drug that the plant mimicked digoxin, by chance?"

"Yes, do you know this story?" Catinella asked, surprised.

"I saw it in a YouTube video," Maxim lied.

"So what about it?"

"You said that there was evidence that the victim did not take that drug, but what if the victim did? Would the police have considered it suspected murder?"

The detective walked silently, pondering the question as they approached the shed that stood behind the garage.

"I suppose it's possible, but there are a lot of variables that this killer would have to know in advance," Catinella replied.

"Like what?"

"For one, the killer would have to know the victim was taking the drug. Second, they would need to introduce the plant substance in a way that the victim would not know they were taking it. The victim could in fact commit unintentional overdose if they were to take their medication without knowing it was already in their system."

"That's all? Surely the police would catch this in the autopsy?" Maxim asked with concern. He directed Catinella to where the propane tanks were.

"Not every police precinct is equipped like that of a major city," the detective pointed out. "Some small-town or, worse, lazy coroners won't suspect anything unusual if the circumstances of death can be plausibly explained. For example, death by heart attack at twenty-three with no history of medical conditions will raise more suspicion than that of a seventy-eight-year-old who does have that history."

"Could a killer really be that calculating?"

"What you're suggesting is both too vague and too specific a target," Catinella told him. "It's like being the only one who knows Achilles' weakness is his heels, and then choosing to plot from afar to get him to break them on his own. In my years of experience, no killer was ever that patient. At some point, they all aim the arrow to strike the heel."

"And what if they were that patient?"

"Wait for a possible lifetime just to get away with murder? It'd be easier to plot for your own death by that logic. Be your own killer."

The two men trekked back to the party, each carrying a tank of propane. Maxim was left wondering if his suspicions were for naught. Did Maxim really think it was more likely that his father and Luisa had been murdered, than for there to be a series of morbid coincidences? And if so, who would be the murderer? Jamie? That must be irrational paranoia. After all, they hadn't even died in the same way, or in the same location.

Maxim and Catinella returned to the courtyard to find George fretting over how long they'd taken.

"Guys! I'm losing heat here!" he barked in frustration.

"Sorry George, the tanks are very heavy," Maxim said snidely, handing over his full tank to George to swap for the empty one.

"All that size and you can't carry a tank of gas?" George asked with an acerbic tone.

"Says the politician whose head is filled with hot air," Maxim countered.

The barbecue continued into the evening, followed by a fireworks show over the lake. Jamie returned to Maxim's side for the spectacle, the two of them sitting by the water's edge with the other guests. Catinella sat drinking a beer and talking with George and Isabel. Jamie pulled out his phone, readying himself to take pictures of the fireworks. Maxim pulled out his phone to do the same, and found himself reminiscing over how his father had passed away just after the fireworks display back in the city. So cheery and upbeat he had been that night, with no indication that it would be his last. Maxim looked through his library of images, searching for a picture of his dad from that night. He found a good photo of Henry, smiling along with a younger Charlotte on his lap. In the back there was a bouquet of flowers, an impromptu gift from Jamie to Isabel for having arrived at the party late that night.

He looked through other photos of that day, showing a happy and united family enjoying the holiday: George at his station making steaks and brisket with Isabel beside him, Charlotte playing with Henry, Jamie making cocktails, and Maxim absorbing the festive mood. Maxim scanned through the images mindlessly until his scrolling halted at an earlier, closer photo of Jamie's bouquet. It was a voluminous assortment of flowers, already in a watered vase when Jamie gifted them. It held daisies, lilies, tulips, carnations, along with some branches of . . . *milkweed*.

Fireworks began to explode in the air, illuminating the dark summer sky. Maxim grew pale; Jamie didn't notice, holding out his phone unconcerned to capture the show happening before them. Maxim looked out into space, his gaze affixed over the lake's surface as it glowed from the light of the fireworks high above the water. *Could it be possible?*

"Max. Max!" Jamie called out. Maxim looked back at his beloved Jamie.

"What's the matter Maxie? You look like you've just seen a ghost."

Maxim remained quiet, realizing he had to reel in his emotions before he could respond. He snapped himself out of his incredulity and took a deep breath.

"I'm sorry Jamie, I was just thinking of my father."

II

Maxim lingered at the door, wondering how things could have ended so horribly. The last they spoke, things seemed to have been going so well for Edward and Paul. They had sold their place in the city, they had moved to the Islands permanently, they were enjoying taking life easy, cuddling in front of the television, watching old movies. There had been no hint of anything wrong.

The stillness in the air became suffocating to Maxim. The humid heat of summer, unrelieved by a breeze that had ceased the moment Maxim was given the wretched news that August afternoon: Edward was dead, and Paul was in custody as a suspect in his murder.

Maxim could barely process what he was being told. The police officers stood just beyond the threshold of the front door, their uniforms neat and orderly, their expressions stern and dispassionate. Maxim's knees felt weak; he wanted to fall to the floor and weep. He looked away from the officers, looking back into the inner recesses of the house trying to bring himself to speak. His eyes teared up and he held his hand over his face to cover his anguish. The officer explained that they wanted to speak with Jamie, who was away visiting Lady Wendell's estate.

"He is not in the country right now," Maxim told the officers. "Why do you need to speak with him?"

"We need to confirm his whereabouts on the night of the incident."

"Well, he is in England, I can assure you," Maxim replied. "I have this app on my phone that shows me where he is at all times."

Maxim pulled out his phone and showed them the blinker that marked Jamie's location. The officers leaned forward, studying the screen, before returning their firm gazes to Maxim.

"And you can account for your whereabouts on the night?" asked one officer.

"Me? I was here."

"By yourself?"

"No, there are always some staff present. Our house manager was visiting a sick relative, so I had to stay to keep things running," Maxim replied, his voice trembling.

The officer pulled out a card from his breast pocket, handing it over to Maxim.

"Well, Mr. Porter, when your husband returns, please tell him to contact us."

Maxim nodded and watched as the officers departed.

Maxim closed the door and paced slowly to the living room. The shadows that lurked in the corner of his eyes moved feverishly, always out of his direct sight. They were more numerous than usual, specters of death so it seemed, making themselves more visible with each erasure of life that occurred around Maxim. Maxim lived with these shadows, hallucinations or ghosts whatever they may be, as a permanent fixture of his mind now. There was also something else, something that Maxim did not want to acknowledge but had been forced to when the police arrived at his door.

The previous night, he had received a phone call from Edward. It had gone to voicemail, registering a message that was twenty-three seconds long. When Maxim checked his voicemail that morning during breakfast, he had been met by the sound of grunts and gasps coming from the speaker. Maxim rolled his eyes, thinking that Edward had called him by mistake during a night of sex, and deleted it. But then the police arrived, and now Maxim wondered if that last message had been a cry for help—the last desperate gasps of his friend being killed, and maybe also the grunts of his murderer. Maxim's regret only deepened his depression, and his own dread.

Apart from the voicemail, he was struggling to believe that Paul could have done this. Paul could never commit so vicious a crime, Maxim thought. Maxim needed to get answers that he knew he would not get from the police. He did not know how to go about it, but first, he needed to call Jamie.

"Hello handsome. How's my dear Maxie doing? Lilliput says hi!" Jamie's upbeat voice echoed through the telephone.

"James, something has happened," Maxim said, his voice timorous and small.

"What is it?"

"Edward is dead."

There was a pause, the silence only broken by the sound of what appeared to be static on the other end.

"What? What do you mean he's dead?" Jamie replied.

"James, you need to come back now. The police are asking for you."

"Me? What on earth for?" Jamie exclaimed, the sound of thunder echoing in the background.

"I don't know, Jamie. Paul is in custody. You need to come back to the country."

"Max, you can't be serious."

"James. They think Paul killed Eddy! I've known them for half my life. I know Paul would never hurt anyone."

"But I can't leave England now. I-I-I need to help Lilliput with something."

"James, you need to come home."

Jamie agreed reluctantly to return from his trip early, and arrived at Gwenshill two days later. The police returned for questioning, speaking with Jamie for over an hour in the confines of Jamie's office. Maxim waited anxiously in the living room until the officers descended the stairs.

"Is that all, officers?" Maxim asked.

"That's all, Mr. Porter. We will reach out to you and your husband if we have any more questions," one officer replied. "Have a good day."

The officers departed, leaving Maxim and Jamie alone. Maxim still felt distraught at the loss of his best friend. Jamie sulked quietly, angered at the outcome of the interrogation.

"Those classless arrogant pigs," Jamie said with derision.

"What did they ask you?" Maxim queried nervously.

"They asked me if I was meeting with Paul. The nerve of these clowns!"

"What? Were you?"

"Of course not! I was in London and at Aysgarth Hall with Lillian."

"James, that's not what I asked," Maxim retorted. Jamie grew angry and rebuffed Maxim.

"How dare you. If you think I was back to fucking that old bitch you must be losing even more brain cells than I thought."

"James, my best friend is dead!"

"And I had nothing to do with it. It was Paul who strangled him!" Jamie exclaimed.

"How do you know he was strangled?" Maxim asked. The police had not revealed to Maxim the cause of death.

Jamie hesitated. "Th-they told me! Some homeless beach bum claimed to have seen me there that night. Which *obviously* I was not! I showed them my passport stamps and Instagram to prove it!"

"Why would anyone claim you were there? James, *were* you seeing Paul behind my back?!" Maxim exclaimed.

The argument soon exposed old wounds on top of the escalating trauma of Edward's death. Maxim was emotionally overwhelmed, his mind retreating to a state of stress-induced confusion and paranoia. The shadows appeared to fly around the room like wasps that swarmed around Maxim, while Jamie stood there angrily arguing, oblivious to the mental havoc that his husband was experiencing. Maxim could not handle being in Jamie's presence, wanting to step away from the fight with every fiber of his being.

Maxim began to leave the room, only for Jamie to follow him, continuing his defensive and irritated diatribe. Jamie would trail Maxim across the mansion, the two of them going from room to room berating and yelling at each other. Maxim walked upstairs, heading back to the their bedroom, but Jamie would not cease. Maxim took a sharp turn, walking into another bedroom and locking the door behind him before Jamie could enter.

Jamie banged at the door, shouting slurs and insults at Maxim about his insecurity in order to antagonize him even further, but Maxim was emotionally drained. Maxim pushed a dresser against the door to barricade it, then collapsed onto the twin bed trying to clear his mind. The shadows only swirled more, the hallucination intensifying. Jamie stood outside the door, still screaming, while Maxim resorted to just sitting at the corner of the bed in tears.

"Oh Eddy . . ." Maxim cried in grief, "my dear friend . . ."

Jamie's shouts finally ended, followed by the sound of his car taking off into the night. Maxim remained confined in the room he was in. It was a familiar feeling lying on that bed—this had been his childhood room, now stripped of all its cherished wonder and whimsy, as stripped of happiness as Maxim was in that moment. Edward had been the closest thing to an older brother that he could have asked for, and now he was gone. The shadows swarmed before Maxim's eyes, growing ever more intense until he finally surrendered to an exhausted sleep.

III

It took five months for the trial to be held, and another sixteen minutes for a jury to convict Paul of murder. The prosecutors called it an open and shut case; Edward had been found strangled to death by their housekeeper in the beach bungalow he and Paul shared in the Islands. Paul was found passed out drunk in an alley outside a bar two blocks from their home, his hands covered in the same exfoliant that Edward had applied around his neck and face that night. The defense insisted that Paul's fingerprints were not found on Edward's neck, that the investigators were relying on the unscientific measurement of Paul's hands and circumstantial evidence.

Maxim never believed that Paul had killed Edward, even after the verdict was announced. Paul had sobbed throughout the interrogations and in his chair while he awaited his sentence. He had the face of a man consumed by sorrow and misery, not the face of a cold killer. Maxim looked onto the prosecution with contempt as they committed what Maxim believed to be character assassination. They painted Paul as a philandering drunk, a predator who chased young gay men whenever he had too much to drink. They contended that Paul had wanted to rid himself of Edward to be with some unknown lover.

Maxim wanted to give testimony in Paul's defense, but he was barred from doing so. There had been a backroom deal, he later found out, and even the defense attorneys dropped the chance for Maxim to take the stand. Maxim could only suspect the reason why. Paul openly wept, crying out for his innocence as they dragged him out of the courtroom in chains.

"He didn't do it, I know he didn't do it," Maxim told Detective Catinella over the phone.

"I'm retired, Mr. Porter," Catinella said with a sigh. "I know that my podcast is about murder, but it is not my professional background."

"I will pay you double. Triple!" Maxim pleaded. "Please Fred. Paul loved Edward."

"I can't help you, Maxim."

"Please!" Maxim insisted.

Detective Catinella declined to help. Maxim did not know how to proceed. Jamie was dismissive. Maxim searched for other detectives, but they returned only disinterested replies. Maxim became depressed, choosing to remain confined to Gwenshill's library. He would not eat, and only left the house to visit Edward's grave at the city cemetery. Maxim would stare at the headstone; its pink granite engraved with a Wordsworth quote just below Edward's name. He remembered Edward telling him about this plot, about how he wanted to be buried with Paul at this spot facing the river because of how peaceful it was.

A lingering dread crept into Maxim's mind. Could Jamie have been responsible for Edward's death? Of course he couldn't prove it, and the little anachronisms he had found could be explained away. An unaccounted-for bottle of herbicide in a receipt, sprigs of a toxic flower in a bouquet . . . people lose things, many houseplants are toxic. Maxim could only imagine the ridicule he would receive for thinking there was some conspiracy that swirled around him hiding danger in household objects. It must be paranoia, he rationalized yet again—his classic overthinking combined with the trauma of a tragic death. Jamie had no reason to go after his friends and family, as much as he had no reason to go after Maxim himself.

CHAPTER 26

I

Papain is a protease enzyme that is common to papaya and mountain papaya fruits grown in Central and South America. Papain is used for industrial, medical, and cosmetic applications. Papain enzyme has been found to temporarily remove fingerprints from subjects whose hands have been exposed to high concentrations of the enzyme found in the latex of the papaya plant and in unripe papaya fruits proper.

>Delete Browsing Data<

II

It was February again. Maxim's sixty-fifth birthday was only a few weeks away. Maxim did not know how to feel about this milestone. He could only view it through the lens of other people's lives. He remembered his father's sixty-fifth, and the celebrations of other men in Maxim's family and class. There was always a party to celebrate, but they never seemed to carry the same meaning as the birthdays of men in the lower ranks, men who had to work to survive. The end of toil, that is what it means to turn sixty-five. The government minimum to say that you had given your best years to . . . what exactly? To finally live without effort? Edward had continued to work after he turned sixty-five, his AARP card merely a quaint badge of honor. *Has it been eight years already?* Maxim reflected, looking back at photos as he scrolled through his phone.

To the men on both sides of Maxim's family, sixty-five was no meaningful milestone, no threshold to be crossed. Those men hadn't stopped working until their very last days. Extreme wealth only enabled them the freedom to pursue work as an addiction rather than a burden. It was a restless masochism for work and ambition that had consumed most of the men in Maxim's family like a toxin. Maxim was the outlier, an impostor. He was not working at his age; he truly had never needed to work. He had the means to live his life leisurely and carefree, but in that freedom, he felt shame around men who constantly demanded work. Damned for being free from slaving away, equally damned for not chaining yourself willingly to satisfy the egos of others.

Jamie was already up and working in his office. Maxim struggled to arise from bed himself, his body regularly sore now even if he was no longer exercising the way he used to. He stood up, disrobing as he walked to the mirror to examine himself as he always had. That morning, the wrinkles in his face, the stains, and pitting appeared more pronounced. Of course they hadn't appeared overnight, but Maxim had finally come to the realization that he was truly growing old. The muscles of his body were softening, the skin appearing thin and riddled with more marks. Maxim no longer looked like a terrifying visage of his grandfather, but had grown sadder, more resigned, and more fatigued.

"Now you truly look like shit," Maxim told himself.

He accepted that his regular ritual had lost its usefulness. Every imperfection Maxim believed he had, real or not, had caught up with him. He had wasted his mornings searching for a reason to find defeat in existence, and now defeat returned the favor. He stepped away from the full-length mirror for the last time, embittered, yet somehow content in his distorted self-effacement. Even though he believed himself uglier than other men, they would all grow old and die just the same.

Maxim's medication lay neatly on the counter beside his mirror, the various pills prepared and organized for him by Judith. The number of drugs before Maxim gave him pause; he would usually take them from their bottles not thinking how much medication he was swallowing. See-ing them all neatly arranged on a plate made him question why he was taking all these pills, only to remember his fear of what would become of his mind without them.

Maxim in his pajamas and robe headed to the dining room for breakfast. Once Maxim sat down in his chair, Judith appeared with his meal on a tray.

"Good morning, Mr. Porter," Judith said somberly, depositing the tray before Maxim.

A plateful of oatmeal and a bowl of fruit. Maxim sighed. For so long he had not objected to eating the food before him; he would choose to eat healthily, denying himself the meals he actually enjoyed just to keep himself in shape. But now his diet was regulated, not by the doctor but by Jamie, and Maxim detested not having control over his own body. But this was nothing new: grumbling about his bodily autonomy felt as useless as grumbling about his mental autonomy. His brain was regularly and randomly sabotaging itself; Maxim had no control over how his mind was short-circuiting. Jamie's solution was to make him take ever more dosages of creatine, in order to combat his mental deterioration, but the more Maxim was made to drink the supplement, the more he felt his symptoms worsen.

"Judith, I am not eating oatmeal and fruit again," Maxim complained.

"Mr. Porter, Master James instructed me that you're to remain in a modified diet until your condition improves," Judith replied sternly.

"And may I remind you that *I'm* your employer, and that it is my name on your fucking paycheck," Maxim scolded angrily.

"Mr. Porter, I am under the ins—"

"Judith. Tell the kitchen I want something else to eat or you're fired!" Maxim shouted.

"Yes Mr. Porter," Judith relented, nervously taking a step back. "What should I have prepared?"

"I would like . . . I would like . . ." Maxim knew what he desired, but the words eluded him. His mind tripped over itself so that he couldn't recall either the image or the construct of letters that spelled out what he wanted. He stared blindly into space, confused and irritated. He looked back at Judith and back at his plate of oatmeal.

"Just forget it. Just forget it!" Maxim shouted again, accepting defeat as he sunk the spoon into the warm food. After one bite, he barked another command: "Bring me some honey if the goddamn prison warden allows it!"

Maxim ate his breakfast of oatmeal and fruit, returning to his bedroom to shower and properly dress. *Pancakes!* Maxim finally recalled, standing under the hot shower that pelted his face. Maxim forgot he wanted pancakes. The realization that he had forgotten what pancakes looked like felt like the most crushing of mental corruptions. Why? Of all the absurd and dark memories Maxim wished he could forget, his mind had to forget that he liked pancakes. Maxim took a deep sigh, leaning against the cold marble wall. Water streaming down his body, he wept softly for a few minutes before standing up again to continue washing himself. This was a torment he felt he had no choice but to endure alone.

III

"Happy birthday Maxim!" Jamie cheered, presenting a wrapped gift to his husband.

"Oh my dear Jamie, you didn't have to." Maxim returned a smile to Jamie and unwrapped the gift, revealing a box with an ornate leather-bound book within. Inscribed on the cover was written in gold *Deauvillier: A Family.*

"Jamie, what is this?" Maxim asked.

"I had a researcher create a book on your family history. Do you like it?"

"But why just my mother's family name? We are Porters after all."

"Well, it turns out your father's family history was fairly generic. Peasant Scottish family, all from the same village, made their money in logging," Jamie shrugged. "But your mom's side was fascinating!"

Jamie began showing the book to Maxim, flipping page after page of family history. Maxim was both impressed and uneasy listening to Jamie explaining its contents with near-complete knowledge of every aspect of the Deauvillier family. At the end there was a chapter on Magnus, followed by a chapter on Maxim's mother, filled with images of her life: dozens of photographs of Karine as a debutante, a wife, a socialite, and a mother. Maxim paused briefly at a picture of Karine with a young George on her lap and Maxim by their side.

"Jamie, where did you get all of this?" Maxim asked.

"I searched through your family photos, while the researcher looked through state archives. Your family is like the Carnegies or Vanderbilts back in France."

"Well yeah, but it doesn't mean anything anymore. It's like being the prince of a monarchy that no longer exists."

"Max, in many circles a name and legacy is more important than just having money."

"Says the son of a billionaire," Maxim blurted out without thinking. He hoped that Jamie would not pick up his slip of the tongue.

"Still," Maxim continued, "I'd prefer you had included my father's family in here. Without Henry there would truly have been no money left from my mother's side."

George and Isabel had sent a birthday card, the two of them now traveling the country for George's presidential campaign. Charlotte had been sent to a boarding school to keep her away from the public eye. Maxim had sent her a book on Alice Roosevelt on her birthday, thinking she could find comfort in learning of another fiercely independent daughter. He wondered if she was feeling isolated and lonely like he was, but Maxim had far more faith in his niece overcoming the odds than he had for himself.

Maxim's birthday proved to be a lonesome one, even with Jamie by his side. He missed Edward and was unable to leave the house to visit Paul in jail; he lamented that there was no one around close to his age. Jamie, meanwhile, had grown into the peak of his adult form: his body strong and lean, regularly covered in tailored suits that kept his form svelte and elegant; his hair cropped short; his face now sporting a moustache and a five o'clock shadow that helped define his jawline. Jamie's youthful exuberance was now tempered by the patina of maturity and responsibility, but in Maxim's mind, Jamie still looked like the young man he had met years ago.

"But you still like the gift?" Jamie asked uncertainly.

"Oh I do, I love the gift. The section just on my mother was very sweet of you," Maxim assured him.

"Okay." Jamie smiled warmly. "We have reservations in the city for brunch. I have a video call this morning and I'll drive us there when it's over."

"Okay, my dear Jamie," Maxim agreed.

While Jamie worked in his office, Maxim returned to the bedroom to plan his outfit for the outing. He did not want to wear the usual subdued clothes he was accustomed to, searching through his closet for an outfit that was purposefully colorful and garish for celebrating. Maxim remembered receiving a Hawaiian-style shirt from George and Isabel a few years back as a holiday present, but when he searched through the various racks of hanging shirts he didn't find it.

Maxim wondered if the shirt had been hung in Jamie's closet by mistake. He walked into the closet, a far larger space than Maxim's own, filled with row after row of colorful clothes stacked neatly on shelves and hanging from racks. Maxim scanned the closet slowly, hoping to see the shirt hanging somewhere among the other designer garments. Maxim could not remember Jamie owning so many articles, particularly the neatly stacked rows of dress shirts and dozens of pairs of shoes. Maxim began to think he would never find the shirt, or that he may have donated it without thinking, or remembering. He gave one last glance at the closet, finally noticing the bold print of the shirt he was looking for. He pulled the shirt from the rack, but it snagged against a blazer jacket beside it, which dropped to the floor.

He leaned forward, grabbing the fallen blazer and its hanger to place it back on the rack. He noticed something in its breast pocket, either a wallet or a thin book of some kind. He pulled the object from the jacket, seeing that it was a passport. Strange; Maxim was sure Jamie's passport was with his own in the safe. Looking more closely, he realized that this was not an American passport, but a French one. Maxim had dual citizenship, but Jamie had never showed any interest in obtaining a French passport.

Maxim swiped through the pages of the passport, stopping when he recognized the American immigration stamp. Jamie had returned to the country the day prior to Edward's death, but through a different airport several hours' drive away, which didn't make any sense.

Then Maxim had a dreadful epiphany: it took only one hour to get to the Islands from this airport. He began to hyperventilate, gripping the passport tightly in his hand, his psyche spiraling with panic.

"Why did Jamie return early? No! He would have been noticed . . . but wait, he was! There was the beach bum! Or was there? Why would the police want to speak with Jamie if he had not been noticed? No! No! This is absurd!" Maxim mumbled to himself, anxiously trying to piece together what he knew. Maxim's legs felt weak and achy. No longer able to remain standing, he knelt on the floor of the closet, then toppled to the floor on his side, still hyperventilating with stress. He tried to calm himself before Jamie could appear. He had to take the passport to the police, he had to remain collected, otherwise Jamie would suspect something.

Maxim's stress soon began to induce his hallucinations, the room spinning with shadows appearing and vanishing before him. He remained huddled on the floor, shouting at the shadows to leave him alone. It only made them appear more voracious, more ominous, like a swarm slowly enclosing itself around Maxim until he felt he was in a full-on nervous breakdown, screaming and panicking on the closet floor.

"Max! Max! What is the matter?!"

Jamie's shouts broke Maxim from the hallucinations, the shadows disappearing like blips in a camera flash. He found himself on the floor, confused and afraid. He turned to face Jamie in horror. Jamie looked at Maxim on the floor, at first concerned, then turning pale when he realized Maxim was gripping the passport.

"Maxim, I can explain. It's not what you think . . ." Jamie's voice trembled as he slowly stepped toward Maxim who began to crawl to the back of the closet.

This was it, Maxim thought; Jamie was going to kill him right here in the closet. Maxim looked around him, scanning quickly to find something to use as a weapon; he felt around under the fallen clothes until his hand gripped an old cane. He held on tightly, waiting for Jamie to step closer.

"Help me Jamie, I can't get up!" Maxim exclaimed, extending one hand in Jamie's direction. Jamie took the bait; he extended his hand and Maxim used all his strength to pull Jamie to the floor. With his other hand, he struck Jamie in the head with the cane, then pulled himself up to run out of the closet.

Running on pure adrenaline, Maxim hurried to the staircase down to the front entrance. Jamie came rushing to catch up to Maxim, holding his head and yelling for Maxim to come back. Maxim turned into the staircase at speed, not seeing Judith walking up to the top of the stairs.

They collided, Judith gripping the handrail while Maxim fell, screaming as he tumbled down the steps, hitting his head as his body went still on the central landing. Jamie rushed to the scene, halting at the top of the stairs, seeing Judith clinging onto the handrail in shock and Maxim's body huddled unresponsive. As other alarmed staff members emerged from various rooms, Jamie kneeled over Maxim to check if he was alive. Maxim was unconscious but breathing.

"Someone call an ambulance! NOW!" Jamie shouted.

IV

Maxim was rushed to surgery, having suffered a broken hip and lacerations to his rib cage. He remained on the operating table for several hours, losing a lot of blood. Maxim awakened a few days later, his condition still critical. As he slowly gained the ability to move his head, he looked around the room, noticing get-well cards and flowers on one side of his bed and a sleeping Jamie slumped over in a chair on the other. At the sight of Jamie, Maxim's anxiety began to spike, his heart racing. He saw the remote with the nurse call button just beside his hand, but his arms were still numb, and he could not move to reach it.

Maxim fixated his mind on the unmoving arm, staring at it intently as he tried to summon the mental energies to move his hand. His heart rate continued to increase, the heart monitor beeping rapidly as Maxim willed his arm to act. His arms felt unbearably cold, the anesthesia rendering his body as frigid as a corpse in a freezer. Maxim kept forcing himself to move his hand, his heart beating faster, his blood pressure rising. He failed to recognize the monitors connected to him beeping and buzzing warnings, waking Jamie who started to mumble Maxim's name.

Maxim turned to face Jamie, his eyes widening in fear, his heart feeling like it was about to burst from his chest. As he slipped back into unconsciousness, he heard the sound of nurses rushing into the room and Jamie crying out before everything went black once more.

V

Maxim remained at the nursing facility for several months of treatment and recovery, not wanting to return to Gwenshill until he was capable of walking around the house with the assistance of a cane. George and Isabel had come to visit Maxim early in his stay, but soon had to return to the campaign trail. Jamie came to visit Maxim whenever he could, and Maxim received flowers almost every day from Jamie's clients and social media followers wishing him a quick recovery. The outpouring of support and well wishes was not enough to sway Maxim; he kept his physical and emotional distance from Jamie, only trusting him in public spaces. For the first few weeks, Jamie and Maxim avoided speaking of what had happened in the closet. Jamie would only make small talk, his expression penitent and somber; Maxim was more gruff, his painful recovery made more difficult by a reduced allotment of pain medication. They interfered with his current regimen, and Maxim opted to be in greater physical pain than to suffer more nightmares and hallucinations.

"Hey Maxie. How was physical therapy?" Jamie asked timidly after one of Maxim's sessions, a small sympathetic smile illuminated by his twinkling eyes.

"It was fine," Maxim replied tersely. "I'm in constant pain, manageable but constant."

Maxim sat on a bench in the courtyard; Jamie hesitantly sat down beside him, his shoulders drawn close, his hands clasped, avoiding direct eye contact. He had allowed his hair to grow, the gentle locks partly covering his pouting, remorseful face. Maxim marveled at Jamie's uncanny capacity to still come across as a boyish rogue looking for forgiveness, as if he had broken a vase or was caught smoking a cigarette.

"The garden back home is ready to burst with color. It will be nice for you to see it," Jamie was saying. Maxim looked out at the courtyard beyond him, ignoring Jamie's comment. Mention of the garden only made him worry about what new poison might be hiding in plain sight.

As Maxim remained silent, the tension in the air grew until finally Jamie gave a long sigh, realizing that Maxim would continue to give him the cold shoulder unless he told the truth.

"The passport was mine from before we married," Jamie said, his voice trembling with trepidation. "My grandmother was born in

French Algeria, my father got it for me so I could be shipped to boarding school in Switzerland."

"Wasn't she from California?" Maxim said indifferently, expecting another lie.

"No Max, my *real* grandmother. I know you know that Isidor is my real dad."

Jamie paused, his eyes affixed to the ground, his face solemn with genuine emotion.

"How long you have known?" Maxim asked.

Jamie told Maxim that the rumor had been floating around him for as long as he could remember. Jamie always knew he was different from the rest of the Grenvills, but his real father sheltered him from the truth for years. He received only coldness and apathy from the people he believed were his parents and siblings, with his grandfather being the only person who showed any interest in Jamie's well-being. Jamie said he'd kept this a secret from Maxim at first because he feared he would be rejected for being a bastard. But after the betrayal with Paul, and the separation, he was sure Maxim would have found out the truth in the divorce filing.

"Then why did you fly back to the United States that night?" Maxim asked.

"Lilliput sent me to pick up a fucking pie," Jamie admitted.

"What?"

"Lillian wanted to have this stupid cream pie from this bakery; you know, the one that was all over social media then? They did not have international delivery so she literally sent me on her private jet to get it."

Jamie pulled out his phone to show Maxim the proof of his story. "I had to use the French passport because I forgot the American one was with Lillian. When you called and told Edward had been murdered, I knew that I was going to look suspicious to the police."

Maxim's resolve crumbled and the burden of suspicion gave way to a pardoning relief, a relief that only circled back to Maxim's own feeling of guilt. He gently placed his hand over Jamie's. Maxim could only feel sorrow that he had once again allowed his paranoia to hold sway over reason. Jamie was an innocent party, Maxim thought, a victim of coincidence. Maxim looked into Jamie's eyes, remorseful yet twinkling—those beautiful eyes were not the eyes of cold-blooded murderer.

"Oh my dear Jamie, why is it you keep hiding these things from me?" Maxim asked.

"I don't know Maxie, it's just how my mind works," Jamie confided. "I promise I want to do better."

Jamie and Maxim sat together, their trust precariously mended.

From then on, Maxim's recovery proved more expedient than expected, and he was able to leave the nursing facility a month early. He could walk with a cane with minimal discomfort, though he was no longer allowed to engage in any of his strength training. When Jamie walked alongside him back home at Gwenshill, propping him up securely, Maxim could feel how much stronger Jamie had become.

Maxim realized that his mind felt clearer, more alert, and his memory had not suffered as erratically during his stay at the nursing facility as it usually did in Gwenshill. Maxim reasoned that he needed to leave home more frequently, that his symptoms were exacerbated when he remained homebody. Maxim proposed to Jamie that they could go on a long trip, maybe even a few months away from Gwenshill; but Jamie pointed out they would miss out on his garden's ever-changing blooms. Jamie's garden had come out so beautifully that year. Especially now that the grounds were awash with rolling mounds of daffodils.

CHAPTER 27

I

To Monsieur Maximillian Deauvillier Porter,

We are mailing you this courtesy receipt for the approved transfer via electronic wire of **$9,396,486.78** from the MaximDPorter Trust S.A. Luxembourg to the James-Maxim Foundation LLC effective September 3rd of this year.

Tax documentation has been forwarded to your accounting firm and to Baldwin-Crane & Co. London United Kingdom per the request of the trustees of James-Maxim Foundation LLC.

For a breakdown of total values and assets affected, please view your private account documents with your digital client key at BambergerFreres.lux.

With utmost service,

Michel Pascale Kiers

Private Banker

Bamberger Frères

Banque Privée

Luxembourg

II

Maxim stared at the letter, confounded by the amount sent over to . . . the James-Maxim Foundation? He had no memory of approving this wire transfer, or for that matter, changing the name of the foundation.

"James, do you have something to do with this?" Maxim asked, handing the letter to Jamie as the two of them ate breakfast. Jamie glanced at it with little concern.

"What about it?"

"Jamie, when did the name of the foundation change? Also, I don't remember when I agreed to forward this much money to it."

"Oh no, the old foundation still exists. This is a new one."

"What?" Maxim asked in confusion.

"I had a new accounting firm look over the books and they told me that too much of the funds we transferred were being eaten up by fees and taxes."

Jamie handed back the letter to Maxim, returning his gaze to his food. Maxim grew more confused and indignant.

"James, this amount is almost ten times higher than we would usually send. It must be a mistake."

Jamie remained dismissive, explaining away Maxim's concerns without actually answering any of his questions. Maxim had already grown concerned with the reforms that Jamie had taken as head of his foundation; Jamie had broken ties with agencies, closed down the city office, and laid off staff with the explanation that there was too much "bloat" in the way Maxim had run things. Too much money was being wasted on expenses and causes that were not sustainable, Jamie had argued, constantly reassuring a reluctant Maxim that all his efforts would result in a greater impact on the causes they both cared about.

"Maxim, you gave me your blessing. You signed all the documents yourself," Jamie reminded him firmly.

"James, I would have remembered having agreed to transfer over nine million dollars!" Maxim insisted, growing frustrated at Jamie's indifference.

The men stared at each other in a stalemate. Jamie remained composed and collected, but his calm gaze twinged with irritation. Maxim glared indignantly until Jamie rose from the table and headed for his office. He returned to the dining room shortly after with a collection of documents in his hands, tossing them onto the table in front of Maxim.

"You don't remember this?" Jamie sniped. "Legal documents? Certifications? Incorporation filings? Tax filings? Your signature and mine are all over these papers!" he exclaimed.

Maxim scanned through the various sheets, dumbstruck. There was no disputing that they were all signed by him, but he still had no memory of doing so.

"This is absurd! I don't remember signing any of this!" he protested. "I know I would remember having gone through all this paperwork, let alone approving this transfer!"

Jamie threw his hands up in frustration. "Max, you can barely remember where you are in the house some mornings! You would have drowned in our pool if I had not jumped in to save your ass!"

"Stop bringing that up! And you did not save me, Edward did!"

"Oh! So you can remember that, but not this? Maximillian, this is childish!"

"Oh yeah? Where is my money going to, James?" Maxim retorted angrily. "Because for months all I ever seem to get in my inbox are emails of all the charities I've always donated to, asking why the rug was pulled from under them!"

"I am the one who's out there reaching out to charities that make a difference!" Jamie shouted. "All you ever did was throw money at leeches who keep coming back to beg year after year! You know what we got from all that money we threw in their faces? Nothing!"

"You treat every cause like it needs to pay out by the end of the quarter! Nothing gets done that way, James!"

"You're right, if I'm committing a dime to fucking parasitic beggars then there better be fucking results to show for it!"

"But how does burning bridges result in anything James? How?!"

"They've got to earn the right to have our money!"

"It's MY money, James!" Maxim screamed. "Not . . . not . . . n—" Suddenly he was overcome with dizziness, clasping his head as he slumped back into his chair.

"What are we doing?" Jamie cried in disbelief as he saw his husband's distress. "God! Max, do you need help?"

Maxim looked up at Jamie, his frail mind warping and distorting what he saw, his husband's expression flitting between a worried gaze and a malevolent grin. Maxim just wanted all of this rage to stop.

"I'm fine," Maxim replied with a deep breath. Shakily, he grabbed his cane to rise from his chair. "I don't want to fight . . . if I signed the documents then I had to have trusted you with the money to begin with."

Jamie nodded anxiously. "Thank you, Max."

III

"How tragic it all turned out with Paul and Eddy," Elliot Newsham was saying.

Maxim had invited Elliot out for a drink after a New Mattachine meeting. They walked a couple of blocks to a piano bar where they talked over cocktails; any time relationships and marriage came up, conversation invariably turned to the dramatic events of the previous year.

"I still think Paul was innocent," Maxim commented, taking a sip from his drink.

"Unfortunately, you are in the minority my good friend," Elliot responded.

"Oh please. I know Paul was a drunkard, but he never had a violent bone in his body."

"Everybody knew of his backstory Maxim. Trauma has an ugly way of unfolding as you get older . . . and in our generation it can get *very* ugly."

"Not for Paul," Maxim insisted. "Eddy was always a positive influence for him. They knew how to balance each other's temperaments."

"I wonder if the balance was simply mutual enabling more than anything else?"

"Bullshit."

"It's true; look at myself and my husband. It took many years of therapy for us to realize that just because we could recognize our own demons in each other doesn't mean we should be apathetic about it."

"Elliot, Eddy did not enable Paul to become an alcoholic. If anything, Edward recognized that Paul was self-medicating with the bottle and pulled him back to a place where he could find closure, and still enjoy being an active gay man."

"I disagree, Maximillian . . . I disagree," Elliot replied, ordering another drink for himself. "Though it is a moot point now."

Maxim sighed at the morbid truth. "I know. I know."

"So, how are things going between you and James?" Elliot asked to change the topic.

"We are doing okay; we have our ups and downs but nothing we couldn't overcome." Maxim paused and then confessed, "The separation was the lowest point in our relationship."

"Yeah I remember that. How long have you two been together?"

"It's been . . . eight years? Our ninth anniversary is in April."

"Did you guys open the relationship after you got back to-gether?" Elliot asked casually.

"No, though sometimes I wonder why he's still with me," Maxim reflected, rubbing his thumb along the rim of his glass.

"Why do you say that?"

"Oh, you know, just life, I guess. I know he would probably prefer to be with someone younger and in better shape."

"I don't think so, Max. When I first met him, he seemed only interested in older men."

"You mean back at that gala I planned?"

"Actually, now that you mention it, yes. God, that was a while back!" Elliot chuckled. "He hit on me that night, but I wasn't interested. I told him about you and your background, so I guess I was your inad-vertent matchmaker."

"Really? How funny."

"Yeah, instead he convinced me to invest in his fund after you got married."

Maxim was surprised to think of Elliot being the catalyst for his relationship with Jamie. Jamie had never mentioned it, but, Maxim thought further, it did explain why Jamie had been carrying two drinks when they had their first botched encounter. Jamie also had never told Maxim that he had taken on Elliot as an investor, which made him won-der how many of his circle had ties to Jamie's investment fund that he was not aware of. But then, Maxim had never prodded too deeply into his husband's business affairs.

"Are you still investing with Jamie?" Maxim asked curiously.

"Oh no," Elliot shook his head. "I was convinced by another Mattachine member to just put my money in an index fund instead. Though to Jamie's credit, he did save my investment before the latest downturn."

"That was clever of Jamie. How much did you have invested? If you don't mind me asking."

Elliot took a sip of his drink, taking a brief pause to recall the amount in his head before replying nonchalantly, "I think it was around . . . nine million and change? There was a delay in the wire transfer, but I got the funds back in September."

CHAPTER 28

I

"Oscar Wilde? And his boyfriend?" Jamie queried skeptically.

"Why not? Our height difference is not dissimilar to theirs, and with your moustache, you'd look very handsome," Maxim persisted, trying to convince Jamie.

"But Max, everyone knows who Oscar Wilde is. Will anyone besides you and some theater queens know who his boyfriend was?"

"Of course people know who his boyfriend was."

"Who was he then?"

"Lord Alfred Douglas. You know, Bosie!"

Maxim and Jamie had been invited to a private Halloween party being held by George and Isabel at a hotel in the city. Jamie had suggested they do a couple's costume, and Maxim was enthused by the suggestion. Maxim knew of a tailor who specialized in historical costumes, and Maxim was attempting to convince Jamie for the two of them to go as the great Irish poet and his aristocratic lover.

"Max, if we're going to do a couple's costume, I want to do a famous couple. Like Bonnie and Clyde, or Romeo and Juliet. Hell, maybe even JFK and Jackie."

"Jamie, most famous couples are straight. The only iconic gay couple I know is Jack and Ennis. I saw the movie and from what I remember, it didn't end well," Maxim protested.

"At least we can try the reverse cowboy later," Jamie teased with a coy smile. "How about Alexander the Great and his boyfriend?"

"Two gay men half naked in Greek dress? Jamie, that's too on the nose even for you."

"You may have a point. Then let's just go as a man and woman," Jamie suggested. "My friend Casey is a drag queen; he can dress me up in drag for the party if we have to."

"James, the last thing I want is to see my husband in a dress and lipstick," Maxim groaned.

"It'll be just for the party Max, I promise you I don't intend to keep it past Halloween night."

"Absolutely not."

"Oh, come on Maxie!" Jamie begged, aiming his twinkling blue eyes at Maxim. "Tell you what, next year we can do a famous writer's theme here at the house. Then we will hire that professional costume designer and make you the spitting image of Oscar Wilde."

Maxim mulled over the proposal, still reluctant to see Jamie transform into a woman.

"Jamie, my brother is on the brink of winning the election. The last thing I want is for there to be a scene because of your costume. No way."

"Max, your brother is a Democrat for fuck's sake—heaven forbid he can't stomach being around the people who will vote for him. So, what if I'm in drag? It's a Halloween party! Your brother knows who I am, and that I am the last person to want to make a fool of himself for attention."

Jamie had a point, though Maxim knew that George would not be happy with the idea.

"Fine," Maxim conceded. "You can do drag for the party as long as Isabel and my brother agree to it."

"Thank you handsome," Jamie said, kissing Maxim. "I know we'll look great together."

"But then who do you want to be? We went from few options to almost anyone."

"Hmmm, let me think it over. We have a few weeks to think of an idea still."

Jamie took to mulling over their options, writing down the names of couples he thought of on a notepad, weighing the pros and cons of the costumes and the time it would take to make them. Meanwhile Maxim was struggling with another bout of symptoms. His short-term memory loss and fatigue were severe, to the point that Maxim was taking long naps during the day and afternoon, ruining his sleep cycle. He began to take notes in his own notepad, carrying it with him around the house to write reminders to himself, though by the beginning of the weekend he found himself back in a more stable mental state. On Saturday afternoon, Maxim and Jamie lounged in the library reading when Judith approached Maxim with the house telephone in hand.

"Mr. Porter, there's some confusion with the instructions for the wine supplier," she reported.

"How so?"

"I am not sure, Mr. Porter. I have the supplier on the line. He speaks limited English, and I do not speak any French."

"That's not a problem, let me talk to him." Judith handed the phone to Maxim, who spoke with the man for a few minutes before handing it back.

"Thank you Mr. Porter," said Judith. "My apologies for the inconvenience."

Maxim waved away her apology. "It is no inconvenience, Judith. The shipment will arrive two weeks from now. Inform the kitchen that James and I are going out for dinner tonight."

"Yes Mr. Porter," Judith nodded, returning to the service wing.

"It is so sexy when you speak French," Jamie teased.

"It's a bit rusty; I've been told I have an American accent," Maxim responded modestly.

"Beats learning Mandarin. With French there's passion in every syllable. Mandarin however, ugh," Jamie shuddered. "I only learned it to please my family."

"Good to know my French drives you wild with desire, *mon petit Jamie*," Maxim laughed.

"*Oui.*" Jamie chuckled back.

"Well Gomez, we better get ready to head out. Our reservation is at seven and we want to beat traffic." As they got up to head upstairs, Jamie got a sudden flash of inspiration.

"Maxie, that's brilliant!"

Maxim turned back with a curious look.

"Morticia and Gomez Addams. That's what we'll be for Halloween!" Jamie enthused.

"From the old TV show?"

"I was thinking more the movie from the nineties. Oh, I love Angelica Houston! Casey will love dressing me up like her."

"Gomez and Morticia?" Maxim asked once again, a bit skeptical.

"Why not? It's spooky, sexy, funny . . . and there's no more romantic a couple I can think of. It'll be perfect for Halloween," Jamie continued, grinning excitedly at the idea.

Maxim laughed, finding Jamie's enthusiasm infectious. With George's reaction still in the back of his mind, he knew he would only be fully convinced with the costume if he had George and Isabel's blessing, but otherwise, Maxim figured this idea was tame and inoffensive enough for them to wear out in public.

"Why not? Let's see what our hosts think," It was all in good humor after all, Maxim reasoned.

II

"Really? That sounds like a fun idea," Isabel said over the phone.

"So you don't think George would object?" Maxim queried, half hoping that George's objection would sabotage the idea.

"George will be okay with it. James is the one dressing up as Morticia, right?" Isabel asked with trepidation.

"Ha, of course," Maxim replied. "He's the braver one out of the two of us."

"Then your brother will be okay with it, I think," Isabel said.

Maxim confirmed Isabel's blessing to Jamie, who immediately called up his friend to inform him of the plan. When Maxim asked Jamie if his friend would make Maxim look like Gomez Addams, Jamie dismissed him.

"No need, all you have to do is slick back your hair and wear a pencil moustache."

"I suppose . . ." Maxim replied, though he had to figure out where he had seen a pin-striped suit stored in the house.

III

Maxim's old office computer had given out. Maxim remembered that they had hired a company to install Jamie's computer systems, and called them once more to provide Maxim with a new machine. The technicians came to Gwenshill, transferring what they could from the old computer into the new device. As they finished setting up his new computer, the technician approached Maxim.

"Mr. Porter, would you like to reconnect the computer monitoring system to your new device?"

Maxim was confused. "I'm not sure, what is it?"

"It allows you to view and record the screen activity of other computers," the technician replied. "Employers use them to make sure staff members are not fooling around on the internet during work time."

"I don't understand; you're saying this was set up on my old computer?"

"It was. Some private households have them installed, though it is not very common."

Maxim knew he hadn't asked for this software to be installed on his computer, but he remembered that at one point while Jamie's office was being set up, he had let Jamie use his computer to figure out how to connect to the house server. It had seemed an innocuous request at the time, but now Maxim became suspicious.

He asked the technician, "Can you tell me what computer is looking at my screen from the other end?"

"The computer upstairs," the technician confirmed. "Your husband requested to be able to see the monitors of his employees and this one as well."

"Did he give a reason?"

"We only install and maintain the systems, Mr. Porter," the technician replied. "Though I did inform your husband that you could also use the system to check on your employees."

Maxim was frustrated that Jamie had kept yet another secret from him, though he couldn't be sure of Jamie's reasoning so many years after the fact. Jamie must have been using the system to track the work of the foundation staff, but why would he need to monitor Maxim's computer? He asked the technician for the password and account information, feigning forgetfulness in order to obtain the credentials. With the computer installed and Maxim's files restored, the technicians left Gwenshill. Later that evening Maxim found the information he needed, but he didn't reveal it to Jamie.

Jamie had been acting increasingly abrasive and secretive over the last few months. Maxim suspected that it had something to do with the downturn in the stock market that Elliot had told him about back in September, but Jamie only ever gave the same excuse of overwork and stress. Jamie always gave the impression that he was doing well with his day trading, but his behavior made Maxim suspect that he was having trouble with his investments again.

"How is your trading going, Jamie?" Maxim asked him over dinner at home.

"It's fine; some volatility but nothing I can't manage," Jamie replied indifferently.

"Well, I was with Elliot after our society meeting, and he—"

"What did he tell you?" Jamie snapped suddenly. Startled by the blunt response, Maxim looked up to face Jamie with apprehension. Jamie's eyes were affixed to Maxim with a cold and defiant stare, and he gripped his steak knife tightly in his hand, its tip pointing in Maxim's direction.

Maxim took a deep breath to collect himself. "Nothing Jamie, only that he was glad you pulled out his money before the downturn," he replied sincerely.

Jamie's expression returned to indifference.

"Well, that old fag was very impatient. He thinks he can make more money just sitting on his ass," Jamie said tersely.

"Now Jamie, don't use that kind of language. It doesn't suit you."

"That's rich, considering you call me that all the time when we're in bed. Though now that I think about it, it's been months," Jamie retorted bitterly.

Maxim remained silent; he had long since lost the desire to spar with Jamie over that matter. They both knew that Maxim could not confer his duties as a husband with Jamie because of his medications. With the increased dosages, he found himself devoid of any carnal desires.

Maxim looked onto his plate, a spartan meal of chicken and grilled vegetables, thinking what he could say to Jamie about the matter. A thought came to his mind, that he couldn't quite believe he was going to suggest until he actually said it out loud.

"Why don't we open up our relationship?"

Jamie gaped at him in astonishment.

"What for?" Jamie asked, incredulous.

"I am clearly not satisfying you. You're at the prime of your life, stuck with me out in the country," Maxim stated matter-of-factly.

Jamie sat back against his chair, wiping his mouth with a napkin. He looked away from Maxim, pausing briefly before responding.

"Maximillian, I may have been unfaithful in the past. But I have no desire to sleep with anyone else. If I wanted to fool around, I wouldn't be married to begin with."

"But you have needs too."

"And only you can meet them. For fuck's sake Maxim, there's Viagra! Every gay man your age is doing hormone therapy in one way or another. But you keep putting your medications above everything else. Is that how you want to keep living your life?"

"Jamie, I can't quit my regimen. I have been on it for so long I can't just give it up. Please consider this, I want to give you permission to enjoy your life."

"And I am declining it!" Jamie replied angrily, rising from his seat. "That's just what I need! A reason to make everyone think I'm only with you for the money when you're the one passing up this ass!"

They both sat back silently after this outburst. Jamie ate a few more bites before excusing himself, leaving Maxim to finish his meal alone. Maxim felt regretful and guilty for not living up to Jamie's expectations; once again he was failing his husband like he had failed so many others in his life. He sat slowly eating his food until the plate was cold, then remained in his seat for another few moments of silent reflection before finally calling Judith to remove the dishes from the table. He retreated into the library to read for a while before heading up to bed.

Jamie was not in their bedroom, having chosen to sleep in another room. Maxim changed into his pajamas and lay on the bed alone, its cold sheets no match for his husband's comforting warmth. Maxim could not fall asleep, tossing and turning in bed even though he felt tired. He forced himself to remain still, closing his eyes and trying to clear his mind. Breathing slowly and deeply, he listened to the quiet stillness of his bedroom, broken only by the rustle of the leaves outside. Just when Maxim was finally surrendering to the serenity of sleep, an intrusive thought rushed into the foreground of his mind to blast his consciousness awake with further anxiety.

"Fucking *great!*" Maxim griped to himself. Seeing that it was 1:00 a.m., he got up from bed and looked out the window. Tonight was a full moon, the grounds of Gwenshill rendered luminous under the clear night sky. Maxim decided to walk the grounds for a bit, hoping the cold night air would clear his mind and help him sleep soundly. He put on a thick wool coat and a pair of boots over his pajamas, grabbed his cane, then walked about the house, its inhabitants fast asleep. He exited through the terrace doors off the living room and walked along the terrace down to the grounds beyond.

The lawns and gardens shone dimly in the moonlight, the forests around them rendered pitch-black in the shadows with only the tips of the trees recognizable. Maxim walked along the trail that descended from the hill, keeping an eye out for movement coming from the forest. It was common for the occasional deer to wander through the grounds, but the threat of something more dangerous was always a concern at night.

Maxim felt a strange thrill at the idea that danger could appear in the darkness of nature. He could not fault the animals for occupying a place that their ancestors had inhabited for thousands of years before humans had come along to impose their will upon nature and its balance of life and death. Maxim had been taught to fear the forests at night, but at the looming sight of his family's home in the darkness, he pondered why he should view that edifice as a haven from the beasts outside; after all, the shadows that haunted him resided in Gwenshill, formless wraiths that danced ominously in his presence while those around Maxim continued on oblivious. Gwenshill itself resembled a monstrous shadow, its darkness menacing and foreboding, seeming to call to Maxim softly to come in from the cold night back to its warm but dark embrace.

Maxim walked the trail, hearing the call of a lone crow echoing in the night. He took the sound as a sign to return to the house, opting to enter through the service entrance. He had stepped onto the stone path just a few yards from the entrance when he saw the light of the kitchen window turn on. Maxim at first stood frozen in place, but realizing he could be seen, he hid behind a nearby hedge. As he peeked out, through the window of the kitchen, he once again saw Judith pulling something from the cabinet and standing over the counter. Maxim stepped closer, keeping himself hidden from the line of sight of the window.

There were various jars and bottles spread on the counter and a pot heating on the stove. It seemed that Judith was cooking, but none of the items she used looked like food; Maxim tried to look at their labels but couldn't read them clearly. Judith added various ingredients into the pot, mixing and cooking the mixture before pouring it into a mold. She set the mold in the fridge, collecting the various bottles she had used and turning off the lights as she left the kitchen.

Maxim stood still for a moment, waiting to hear her walk away before he entered through the service door. The kitchen smelled like a perfume shop; an almost sickening scent of lavender permeated the air. Maxim opened the fridge door to look at the mold Judith had placed inside it. It was still warm and reeked of lavender and lemongrass. Maxim realized what he was looking at—this was a mold used to make soap.

Why was Judith making soap, let alone in the middle of the night? Maxim thought to himself, placing the mold back in the fridge. Jamie had the habit of requesting organic soap for the house bathrooms, but he never recalled Jamie asking Judith to physically make it herself.

Maxim stood alone in the kitchen, his mind abuzz with a suspicion that he could not rid himself of. Judith's behavior was odd, and the encounters Maxim had with her in this room never felt organic or spontaneous, especially that night when she had stumbled in the kitchen with an empty bottle of aspirin. Just to be sure, he checked his pot of creatine in the cabinet, but the white powder looked undisturbed. He realized he couldn't think any further while so consumed by the strong smell of lavender. He opened a small window to vent the kitchen and returned to his bedroom, but the smell seemed to follow him. Remembering he still had residue from the soap on his hand, he rubbed his fingers and smelled the scent once more.

The lavender and lemongrass were strong, but Maxim recognized a hint of another scent alongside them, faint but unmistakably present. As Maxim closed his eyes, and began to finally drift into sleep, it occurred to him what it was: the faint smell of almonds.

IV

The Halloween party was being held at the Park Savoy. Because the presidential election was only days away, Secret Service members had been dispatched to ensure the safety of George, his family, and the hundreds of guests who would be attending the party. Spirits were high for the Porter family; George was ahead in the polls, and there was an optimistic feeling that victory was within their grasp. Maxim stayed at Gwenshill to dress, while Jamie chose to get ready in a suite at the hotel. Maxim hadn't seen Jamie's costume, but he wasn't expecting to be too surprised; after all, it would just be Jamie in white makeup and a black wig.

Maxim had found the perfect pinstripe suit inside an old trunk. He wondered if the suit had been his at some point that he couldn't remember; it fit his frame so well it was as if it had been made for him. He trimmed his moustache and swept back his hair with mousse, looking into the bathroom mirror to check his appearance. Maxim was unsure if his costume would work, but he reasoned that as long as he stood next to Jamie people would get it. He found a dark bowtie in his closet and kept a cigar in his breast pocket to complete his costume.

Maxim lounged in the living room with a tumbler of cognac while he waited for the car George was sending for him.

"Mr. Porter, you have a telephone call from Master James," Judith announced, walking into the living room.

"Why wouldn't he call my cell phone?" Maxim asked.

"Master James says there's some problem with your number," Judith replied. "He's on the line in the library."

Maxim placed his undrunk tumbler of cognac on the cabinet and went to talk to Jamie, who explained he kept getting a busy signal on Maxim's cell, though Maxim saw no missed calls from him. Jamie said that his costume was taking longer than expected and he'd be late to the festivities. When they hung up, Maxim returned to the living room and took up his glass of cognac, then noticed Judith still standing there.

"Judith, you are dismissed." Maxim commanded, taking a long drink. It tasted very bitter and wasn't worth the wait.

A black SUV arrived for Maxim, who was silent for most of the journey.

"What are you supposed to be?" the driver asked. "A gangster?"

Maxim, caught off guard by the question, meekly nodded yes without explaining further. He had no reason to feel unsafe, but still feared the driver's judgment if he knew that Maxim's husband would be dressed as a woman.

When Maxim arrived at the hotel, he found the ballroom decorated with black and purple papier-mâché trees wrapped in orange string lights, creating a moody and ghostly forest dotted with pumpkins carved out with slogans from George's campaign. High above the mezzanine that ringed the ballroom, Maxim could see the various security guards with high-powered rifles overlooking the ballroom below. The fantasy forest reminded Maxim of his walk through the grounds of Gwenshill at night, only instead of worrying about beasts hidden in the shadows, he worried about self-aggrandizing guests hiding behind colorful masks.

Maxim meandered through the costumed crowd, finding George and Isabel in a corner of the ballroom talking with some of their guests. George was dressed in ancient Greek garb with a fake white beard, while Isabel wore a Victorian-style costume, her hair piled high on her head and a sash that read "Votes for Women."

"Well, if it isn't Susan B. Anthony and Plato? Or are you an emperor waiting for his laurel wreath, George?" Maxim joked as he approached the couple.

"Hello Maxim! Wow, you look great in your costume," Isabel enthused.

"Thank you Isabel. Your costume also looks amazing."

"For your information Maxim, I am dressed as Aristotle," George corrected him in jest. "And why am I not surprised you chose to show up in that suit?"

"What do you mean? I found it buried in a trunk," Maxim told him. "Funny that it fits me, I don't recall ever buying it."

"You really don't remember, do you?" George continued. "Max, that's Grandpa's suit."

"Wait, Grandpa Magnus?" Maxim asked.

"Who else? We have a picture of him back at the house wearing that exact suit," George replied, pulling out his phone to find the image. When he found the picture, he paused in disbelief, looking back and forth between it and Maxim.

"You look like the spitting image of Magnus!" he said, showing the image on the screen to Maxim and Isabel.

Maxim at first could not see the resemblance, but the more intently he looked at the photograph, the more the similarities emerged, right down to the glum scowl. He couldn't believe he had effectively dressed himself to look like his grandfather, the man who had made him feel inadequate for most of his life. He'd known they looked similar, but in this getup, he was more like a mirror image.

"Cheer up Max. Let's be honest, Gomez Addams was modeled on men like your grandfather," Isabel consoled him. "And Gomez was a good and loving husband to his wife."

"Now that you remind me . . ." George smirked, rolling his eyes. Maxim glowered at him.

The party continued. Jamie had yet to arrive, still texting updates that his makeup was taking longer than planned. Maxim broke away from George and Isabel to try to find Charlotte. Walking through the multitude of guests, he encountered what looked to be a young boy dressed as Charlie Chaplin.

"Kid, have you seen Charlotte?" Maxim asked.

"Uncle Max, it's me, Charlie!" Charlotte's voice echoed from underneath the bowler hat and pencil mustache. Maxim laughed warmly at the unexpected reveal. Charlotte told him she'd wanted to dress up as Chaplin to stand out from the other girls at the party, much to her father's chagrin. Maxim told her how proud he was of her and left Charlotte with her friends, returning to George and Isabel with a grin.

"Charlie's costume is very good; I'm surprised you went along with it, George," Maxim commented.

"Well, better than the costumes some girls are wearing these days," George grumbled. "So long it doesn't become a habit."

"Calm down, George," Isabel soothed her husband. "It's Halloween."

Maxim stepped away from his brother and sister-in-law, looking for the restroom so he could take his medication. Maneuvering his way through the crowd, he was overwhelmed by an old feeling of foreboding. The ballroom's light seemed to glow more dimly, the shadows more pronounced, the room growing darker. Maxim worried that his mental state was waning, though the medication's effects had never dissipated so quickly in the past. He stopped at the bar for a glass of water and entered the restroom. He pulled out his pills from his coat pocket and began to swallow each pill with a gulp of water. Maxim waited for the medication to take effect, but the room just seemed to grow even darker. He looked at the mirror in front of him, his reflection looking bright and normal at first, but Maxim realized that the person was not himself. It stood still and unmoving, its gaze fixed and angry. It must be a hallucination; he was not looking at his reflection but his grandfather.

"You're not real," Maxim said aloud. "I know you're not real."

"I am real, you fucking disappointment," the reflection boomed back in Magnus' thundering voice.

"You're not real . . . you're not real!" Maxim cried.

"Will you stop yelling you goddamn fruit! Act like a man!"

Maxim snapped out of the hallucination back into reality. The room was bright once more. Maxim hoped it meant his medication was finally working. He saw a text on his phone from Jamie that he was waiting for Maxim in the ballroom. Maxim was nervous to leave the restroom, wondering if this hallucination was a single event or the beginning of something worse, but he looked away from the mirror, took a deep breath, and ventured out into the ballroom. The sound of guests talking and dancing dissipated the closer Maxim got to where Jamie had said he was. The music of the band sounded like a distant muffle, the white noise of chatter dissipating around George, Isabel, and someone Maxim could only assume to be Jamie.

As Maxim stepped forward, the crowd of guests cleared to reveal the tall dark figure. George looked on with discomfort, Isabel with apprehension. The figure turned to Maxim, covered in white face makeup, deep red lips, and dark eye shadow under a long black wig. Jamie's smile was made sinister by the layers of makeup.

"My dear Gomez," Jamie cooed.

Maxim's hallucination had indeed only primed his mind for something far more disturbing. As he stood immobile, looking back at Jamie, Maxim's mind began to warp reality, twisting Jamie's smile into something wicked and perverse, fragmenting and distorting what he saw into what he feared most to see: a corrupted distortion of his mother in her infamous black dress. He saw a debased phantom, an infernal apparition that took hold of his psyche all the way down to the innermost core of his trauma. Maxim was trapped in a waking nightmare.

"Hello handsome, you like?" Jamie asked coyly, unconcerned by Maxim's frozen stare.

George and Isabel recognized the same horrified stare they'd seen on Maxim all those years ago. They tried to pull Jamie away from Maxim, but it was too late; Maxim with one quick movement gripped Jamie's throat with both hands, squeezing the life out of him with all his might. The other guests looked on in shock at the sight of a struggling and breathless Jamie caught in Maxim's unflinching grip. George forced himself between Maxim and Jamie to pry them apart.

"Maxim! Let go of James! Let GO!" George shouted. The Secret Service guards came rushing in their direction.

With one swing of his arm, Maxim threw George on the floor. A guard jumped in to pull George away from the threat while the snipers engaged their weapons, aiming their sights at Maxim.

"Don't shoot! MY GOD DON'T SHOOT!" shrieked a hysterical Isabel.

Jamie tripped on the skirt of his costume, pulling both himself and Maxim onto the floor. Maxim did not let up, keeping his hands tightly on Jamie's neck, pressing with all his body weight, slowly crushing Jamie's windpipe. Maxim's mind was no longer processing what was going on; he could think of one thing only: punishing Jamie for making a mockery of his dead mother. Half a dozen officers piled on top of the two men, at last pulling Maxim away from a nearly blue Jamie. It took four men to subdue Maxim, who by then was apoplectic, jerking his body wildly and screaming at the top of his lungs, before his mind went completely black.

CHAPTER 29

I

The winter season at Gwenshill had been mild; while the wind was cold, the storms of December and January had only brought rain rather than a blanket of snow on the ground. The sky was gray and bright, the light of the sun refracting in the clouds to render the world monotone and sterile. Maxim took to walking along his trail again, following the edge of the hill from the terrace and returning to the house through the service entrance. Maxim trekked the path in the same wool coat and boots, no longer bothering to dress up as he once had. He grew out his facial hair, an old fedora covering his shaven head.

He had taken to shaving his head with a razor blade every morning, running his hand over his scalp multiple times to make sure all the hair had been removed. Maxim shaved his head, brushed his teeth, and trimmed his five o'clock shadow before the bathroom sinks without ever looking at the mirror, a towel draped over its frame to ensure that Maxim could never look at his reflection. He could not look at his own face without feeling shame, without feeling numb, without feeling alone.

The wind blew against Maxim's body, his legs taking the brunt of its winter chill under the thin sweatpants he wore. Maxim would often forget to put on his scarf, relying only on the high collar of his coat to protect his neck.

Maxim walked the same path every day after his meals, never deviating. The sense of routine and the cold weather soothed his mind in a way his new medications didn't. The nightmares and hallucinations that had been suppressed by his old regimen had burst forth like an exploding pressure cooker. The new drugs did not truly prevent the intrusion of these painful memories or eliminate the visions that haunted Maxim day and night; they simply kept him sedate and numb, so that he no longer felt anger or fear, joy or sadness. He was imprisoned in a dull detachment from his emotions, even if his mind continued to bombard him with visions and delusions that tormented his every moment.

Walking the quiet trail alone was the only control Maxim still had over his mind and body, because everything else was now mandated by others. Maxim did not remember what happened on Halloween night, or what had happened after. He had woken up in a padded cell in a psychiatric hospital; at first confused, then mortified at what his confinement meant. There were whispers of scandal, but Maxim was never placed before a court or judge. He sat in his cell for several weeks before receiving the news that he was to be placed under house arrest. A plea had been arranged while Maxim was locked up. He was never made aware of the exact terms of the deal; he knew only he would not be prosecuted for assaulting Jamie and George during his psychotic episode. A psychiatrist would be assigned by the state to check on Maxim on a weekly basis, and Maxim was not allowed to leave Gwenshill's grounds for a minimum of five years unless for medical attention. The trail was the safest distance Maxim could walk around the grounds without setting off his ankle monitor.

He completed his walk around the grounds, heading back to the house to sit by the fire. Arriving at the service entrance, he heard once again the call of a crow in the distance. He wondered where the bird was calling from. Maxim walked into the kitchen, finding a cup of hot tea on the counter. He called out to ask if anyone had left their drink unattended. He grabbed hold of the mug's handle, only to see its contents turn black and putrid as he looked at its surface; the hot handle burned his hand and he dropped it on the floor. As it shattered, the spilled contents returned to their original form of harmless tea. Maxim would have once found such a sight frightful and disturbing, but under his new chemical stupor, he felt only apathy.

Judith walked into the kitchen, seeing the broken porcelain and spilled tea at Maxim's feet.

"Mr. Porter, that tea was not for you," Judith said sternly.

"I'm sorry Judith, I only picked it up and it slipped from my hand," Maxim apologized.

"That is alright Mr. Porter. Master James has returned from his trip. He is expecting you in the library."

"Oh, James is here! Wonderful!" Maxim replied, delighted.

Jamie had forgiven Maxim for what had happened at the party, though he had never revealed to Maxim what had transpired. He took to going on long trips, only returning for a few days at a time after several weeks abroad. When Jamie returned to Gwenshill, he would lavish all his attention on Maxim.

"Hello handsome!" Jamie said sweetly, giving Maxim a warm smile as they met in the library.

"Hello my dear Jamie," Maxim replied, stepping forward to kiss his husband. "How was your trip?"

"Oh Maxie, it was good, I convinced the clients to keep investing in my fund."

"Good! You're the smartest investor I know." Maxim smiled as they embraced. Jamie was at his sweetest and most caring when they were together, but when Jamie departed, Maxim's longing for him only increased the madness that roamed free in his mind.

"That's a nice scarf, Jamie. Did you buy it recently?"

"Oh, this old thing?" Jamie replied cautiously, checking carefully that his bruises were still concealed. "You bought it for me, remember? It was back in Hamburg."

"I must have forgotten. You look very nice."

"Why thank you, handsome."

Maxim hallucinated effigies of Jamie; cursing, screaming, attacking Maxim with the deepest of Maxim's insecurities. Maxim knew they were fabrications of his mind, because in all of them, Jamie's neck was purple and bruised as though Jamie had been strangled. Maxim could never hurt Jamie . . . he would rather die than hurt Jamie.

"Are you done with your trips for the time being?" Maxim asked.

"Unfortunately, no; Lilliput and I are going on a cruise in Tahiti and we'll be gone for two weeks."

"Oh pity, this house feels so much colder without you," Maxim bemoaned.

"Why don't you sleep in our room? At least while I'm away."

Maxim no longer shared the main bedroom with Jamie. Maxim did not object to sleeping in another room; he wanted to avoid the mirror that hung in the main bathroom because it was too large to cover up easily.

"The room I'm in is pretty warm, it's just that I miss you, that's all," Maxim said.

"I'm going to be with you for this whole week to make it up to you. And after my trip, most of my work will be from home."

"Good . . . I love you Jamie, I'm so proud of you."

"Thank you Max, this matters so much to me."

Maxim and Jamie sat by the fireplace in the library, holding each other close while the embers glowed with comforting heat. Jamie was now the only family Maxim had; he had not heard from or seen George, Isabel, or Charlotte since that night in October. Maxim was not permitted to talk to them as a condition of his house arrest, and even if he could, he did not want to. He loved his family deeply, but his soul harbored a shame and guilt that could not be overcome. Like the mirror, Maxim did not want to face his brother again after all the disgrace he had brought on his family. Only Jamie understood Maxim's failings; only Jamie remained by his side.

II

The physical symptoms that Maxim suffered waned with time. The fatigue, confusion, mental fog, and lightheadedness were no longer happening with the frequency that used to render Maxim infirm. Maxim could focus on the books he read, watch movies without his mind skipping forward, and he could remember what he ate for breakfast that morning. His thoughts were clear, his stream of consciousness uninterrupted and concise. However, this unexpected turn of good mental health was but a consolation prize for Maxim, as physically, his body had grown frailer; he could not exercise, or swim, or exert any strain at all. He could feel the pronounced wrinkles on his face, the skin of his hands thin and riddled with spots. Maxim's body ached, and walking with his cane became a difficult task on some days. He felt like he had aged a decade in the span of four months. Maxim could read novels to pass the time, but his restless nature kept prompting him to walk the grounds of the estate, to avoid spending all his time within the walls of Gwenshill.

The visits from the psychiatrist were an exercise in futile indifference. Maxim, of course, had delayed seeking help and counseling all his life. Maybe now that he had imploded his reputation, he could find someone to listen to his story. But the more he spoke to the psychiatrist the less he felt he was being heard. A man only a few years younger than Maxim, the doctor would jot down on his notepad what he observed, speaking only a few words before issuing another prescription for pills. He did not appear to show much interest in Maxim's story, or in the traumas and experiences that had led him to this point. The man was only there to make sure Maxim would not pose a threat to others in the house. Maxim did not feel disappointed in the apathy of the state-appointed doctor. He took the ambiguous advice of his father to heart: life was about choices. Maxim had the choice to seek someone who may have shown him empathy and understanding, and he hadn't taken it; now he was living with the consequences of his inaction. Although, Maxim thought to himself, he had not made the choice to suffer from the anguish and pain that festered in his mind. He did not choose to be born to a family and legacy that demanded so much from him.

"Thank you Doctor, I'll see you next week," Maxim responded. The psychiatrist departed for the day, handing the latest prescription to Judith.

Their weekly appointment was held in the family office away from the staff. After each session, Maxim would open the internet on his computer to read the news and watch history lectures. Beyond his walks along the grounds and reading his books, it was another means by which Maxim's mind could escape from its imprisonment. Maxim found himself delving deeply into the most random of topics, burrowing through pages of websites to learn more on topics that he found interesting but had never bothered to look up. He wondered if the old medications he had taken for those many decades had been the reason for his strange symptoms. He remembered their names by heart, and began to type their names into the search engine.

> **Selective serotonin reuptake inhibitors (SSRIs)** are part of a family of antidepressants used to treat depression, anxiety, and panic attacks. It is not recommended to combine SSRIs with other medications such as anti-inflammatory drugs (aspirin, ibuprofen, acetaminophen) or with first-generation allergy medications such as diphenhydramine.

> **Serotonin and norepinephrine reuptake inhibitors (SNRIs)** operate similarly to SSRIs while blocking norepinephrine neurotransmitters along with serotonin. Not recommended to be taken with first-generation allergy medications such as diphenhydramine, leading to increased side effects such as drowsiness, dizziness, confusion, and impaired thinking.

> **Prazosin** is a medication used in the treatment of high blood pressure and nightmares related to post-traumatic stress disorder. Prazosin not recommended to be taken with aspirin due to its ability to interfere with the drug's efficacy.

Maxim read through the descriptions in detail, a bit confused by the interactions and potential side effects. He didn't take aspirin, though he had the faint recollection of Judith taking it. Then it dawned on him—what did diphenhydramine look like? It took him less than a minute on his computer to find the image of the small pink pills, similar in color to the dissolved clump he had found in his creatine. Could it be that his mental fog and fatigue had been the outcome of his mind being poisoned by these drugs without his knowledge? Maxim suspected tenuously that his antidepressants had not failed him, that his mental state was being deliberately tampered with.

"Hello handsome." The sound of Jamie's voice scared Maxim, who was so distracted by what he read on his computer he hadn't heard or seen Jamie walk into the room.

"What are you looking at?" Jamie asked sweetly, giving an uneasy half smile. Maxim remembered with dread that Jamie could monitor him from his computer upstairs. Could Jamie have seen what Maxim was searching? Could Jamie know what was going on? Could Jamie . . . ? Maxim could not reveal that he knew he was being watched, so he played dumb and lied.

"Oh, I was just reading the news. The war is so destructive it makes you think how precious life is," Maxim replied.

Maxim's new medication had suppressed his emotions to such a degree that he hoped Jamie would accept his monotone delivery without suspecting any falsehood. As Jamie began to walk toward Maxim's desk, Maxim shut down his internet browser before Jamie could see the screen. Maxim remained seated on his chair, Jamie wrapping his arms around Maxim and sitting on his lap. Jamie kissed him firmly, pressing their lips together. Maxim did not feel tenderness or love from Jamie's lips locking onto his, only a forceful dominion over Maxim's being. There was an uncomfortable tension; now weaker than Jamie, Maxim could not push away from Jamie's embrace. Jamie pulled away, still sitting atop Maxim, and gave a smile that seemed sinister underneath its pretense of warmth.

"Maxie, I am going to miss you, you know," Jamie said sweetly. "I know that I haven't been as present as I used to be. But at one point all this effort will pay off."

"Is that right?" Maxim replied.

"Of course! Soon it will be you and me going around the world traveling and enjoying life."

"Jamie . . ." Maxim paused apprehensively. "You would never do anything to hurt me. Would you?"

Surprised at the question, Jamie sat back, his arms still holding onto Maxim.

"I would never hurt you Maxie. You are the only person in the world I care about," Jamie replied, kissing Maxim on his cheek before getting up from Maxim's lap.

"I have to head upstairs and pack, I'm leaving tomorrow for Tahiti. I'll bring you a cute Polynesian guy as a souvenir," Jamie teased, walking toward the door of the office.

"You don't need to bring me anything, my dear Jamie," Maxim said timidly. "Send well wishes to Lillian for me."

Just before Jamie stepped through the door, Maxim's mind lit up with another suspicion.

"Oh Jamie, can you tell Judith to buy creatine? It occurred to me that I haven't taken any since I came back."

Jamie gripped the door handle, but gave Maxim a casual smile.

"Oh, I told her to stop buying it. It did its job, now it will just make you retain water." Jamie walked out of the office, closing the door behind him.

Maxim felt in the pit of his stomach that something had changed. There was something dangerous and frightening in Jamie's words, his eyes, his lips. Jamie knew what was going on, and Maxim was now in effect a prisoner of his own making because of Jamie. Maxim had been domineered by his emotions: his paranoia and insecurity had made him susceptible to his mental extremes. Now that his mind had leveled, he could finally see the real threat, and it wasn't a monster or a demon lurking in the shadows, it was right in front of him. But he still could not understand what Jamie's motive could be; they had been together for almost ten years, and Jamie seemed to be doing well with his investments. There had to be something that Maxim was missing. Maxim sat in front of his computer, looking at the screen, when it came to him that he had the means to see what was on Jamie's monitor.

He found the account credentials the technician had given him, using them to open the monitoring software. Jamie was not tracking his coworkers' computers after all; only Maxim's. With a few keystrokes, he could now see Jamie's screen. There were tables and charts showing Jamie's trading activity, millions of dollars' worth of securities and other financial instruments. Maxim realized that he could only see one of Jamie's monitors, and he did not know what else his husband was doing on the others, but he still looked carefully at what he could see before him. Jamie was losing money, lots of money. Maxim would need to access Jamie's computer in person to see the rest, but he had to wait until Jamie had left the country.

Just then Judith walked into the office, carrying a glass of water and his new medication.

"Thank you Judith, you can leave it there on the table," Maxim instructed her.

After Judith left the room, Maxim looked at the pills before him, wondering what he was taking. He looked at the markings on their surface and typed them into his computer. Sure enough, an answer: benzodiazepine. As he swallowed the pills with a gulp of water, he equally began to suspect that Judith was involved. Could she and Jamie be working together? Why?

III

When Jamie had been gone for three days, Maxim waited late into the night before creeping quietly and determinedly to Jamie's office. His mind battling the visions that haunted the shadows, he first checked the service wing to see that the lights in Judith's room were off and her door locked. He paused just outside the room, listening for the sound of movement. Satisfied that she was asleep, he continued on to Jamie's office. He inserted the key into the lock and tried to turn it, but couldn't. Jamie had changed the locks.

The following morning Maxim sat at his desk trying to think of a way to get into Jamie's office. He called the computer technician, who revealed that Maxim could access the files on Jamie's computer through the house server. All this time, Maxim had access to Jamie's secrets but was too oblivious of how his own computer worked to notice.

He found dozens of files with hundreds of documents, dating back to when they had married and to when Jamie had started investing on his own. Jamie kept duplicate files of invoices and tax statements; he had been hiding losses for years. He would lose the money of his investors, only to win it back through aggressively risky bets on the stock market. When Jamie became head of Maxim's foundation, he had used his position to dip into the organization's funds to cover his shortfalls. Maxim's money was not going to charities at all, but to keep Jamie's reputation afloat. Jamie owed money to dozens of clients, from Mattachine members, to friends, to Lady Wendell, and to supporters of George's campaign. Maxim found that Jamie had even lied to Henry, showing false invoices of his returns. Most damning was the amount of money Lady Wendell had entrusted to Jamie, about twenty-seven million dollars. Only a fraction of it remained, Jamie paying off fake dividends with Maxim's trust fund.

Distraught was too weak a word to describe what Maxim felt. The hallucinations intensified around him as he sat before this evidence. Jamie was a fraud, and Maxim was his pawn. The effigies of Jamie manifested before him in full vigor. Laughing at his stupidity, his igno-rance, his weakness, they mocked Maxim maniacally. Maxim wanted to break down into tears—his life had been a lie, his marriage had been a lie, Jamie's professed love for him . . . all a great lie. But the medication stripped him of his full emotions, keeping him numb and sedate. Perhaps it was for the best it did so. This was his punishment, Maxim thought, for believing anyone would have loved him for anything else other than his money. Maxim was locked in a different level of mental anguish and could not even express it.

IV

London Evening News – February 2nd – Society section:

Lady Lillian Elizabeth Montesquieu Wendell (neé McLaidlaw), mother of the eighth Baron Aysgarth and heiress to the McLaidlaw shipping for-tune, has passed away at the age of sixty-three. Her body was discovered by her traveling companion, the American socialite James Grenvill-Por-ter, while on holiday at a private resort in French Polynesia. French au-thorities ruled the death accidental. Lady Wendell suffered a severe aller-gic reaction to a bar of soap she had used the night of her death. The soap in question had been bought from a local vendor in Hong Kong during a layover en route to Tahiti from London, Mr. Porter informed the authorities. Lady Wendell's net worth was estimated to be in the amount of 470 million pounds.

CHAPTER 30

I

Jamie inherited thirty million dollars after the death of Lady Wendell. Her will had stipulated that the money she had invested in Jamie's fund now belonged to him. His fraud remained concealed. To Maxim it was clear that Jamie had tricked the poor woman into thinking he was a great investor, and she had died believing in the lies he crafted. Maxim could not stop suspecting that Lady Wendell's death was no accident—that Jamie knew his fraud was about to be discovered and killed her to hide his secret. There was no doubt in his mind that he could not trust Jamie. He could see that Jamie's only true skill was to use his charms and looks to con the people around him.

Although the curtain of enchantment had been pulled away, Maxim found that he could not rid himself of his feelings for Jamie; his love for his husband was too deeply engrained in his soul and psyche.

Maxim wondered if there had been a time when Jamie had loved him truly, or whether their whole relationship had been an act. He imagined that Jamie had been drugging him all this time in order to take advantage of his mental state, to help hide his schemes, to drive him into insanity, so that Jamie could finally take over his inheritance. Maxim entrenched his mind in bitterness, blaming himself for letting that smile and those twinkling eyes ruin his life. Maxim, now a prisoner in his home, could only count the days until Jamie's debts would grow so large that Jamie would need to reap Maxim's life to carry on with the charade. What a fool Maxim had been, to allow his lonely heart to bring an angel of death into his home.

April showers kept Maxim from his walks around the grounds of Gwenshill. Jamie had ceased his travels and took to working in his office, still unaware that Maxim was spying on his activities from his tablet. Jamie spent days and nights working, Maxim watching the activity from the seclusion of the library and his own bedroom. When the two of them met for their meals in the dining room, Maxim remained quiet, stealing glances at Jamie from across the table as they ate. Stress was taking away Jamie's looks; the wrinkles around his eyes were visible from afar, his hairline was receding. Or maybe Jamie just looked ordinary to Maxim now that his illusions of enchantment had been shattered. Maxim looked down at his plate with disgust, unable to stomach his food in the presence of the man across from him.

"Something wrong with the food, Maxie?" Jamie asked sheepishly, breaking the silence that hung in the air.

"I lost my appetite," Maxim replied, placing his utensils down on the table. "I'm going to go read in the library."

Maxim stood up, leaving Jamie at the table by himself. Maxim walked slowly along the long gallery to the library, the sound of his shoes and cane echoing on the stone floor. Soon he heard other steps following behind him and turned back to see Jamie standing before him. Jamie's eyes teared with sadness and he embraced Maxim, burying his head in Maxim's shoulder. Jamie began to cry inconsolably. Maxim hadn't expected such emotions to come from him after so many weeks of stoic silence. Maxim recognized those tears. They were the tears of loss, the loss for someone close to him. Maxim gently wrapped his arms around Jamie, holding him tenderly as Jamie continued to weep.

"I failed her," Jamie said, pulling his head away from Maxim. "I failed her."

"Who, Jamie?" Maxim asked softly.

"Lillian. She was the closest thing to a mother I ever had, she cared for me, she loved me like I was hers. And I lost her."

Maxim rubbed Jamie's back softly. "Oh Jamie. She may be gone but it doesn't mean she stopped loving you."

"What am I going to do? I don't want to keep doing this," Jamie declared, wiping tears from his eyes with his hands. "I can't keep going like this, I don't want to keep failing at life."

Maxim looked at Jamie with confusion as Jamie began to confess.

"I lost all of the money Lillian invested with me . . . all of it!"

Maxim's eyes widened, nervous as to why Jamie was revealing this now. Jamie confessed that the reason why he inherited his investment from Lady Wendell was because he told her about his losses. He had begged Lillian to forgive him and promised he would work hard to get her money back, and she forgave him and told him that it was not his fault. Maxim did not believe this, but held his tongue while Jamie continued.

"I just don't know how to trade anything! I try and try . . . and no matter what I do I just can't be the trader I tell everyone I am. The only time I ever make anything is out of fucking dumb luck!"

"But Jamie, you have so many clients. You must be doing something right."

"And I keep losing all of their money . . . including yours," Jamie sighed. Maxim could not believe that Jamie was confessing this so openly.

"James, what did you do?"

"I used your foundation to pay off my debts. I'm sorry."

Maxim pulled back as Jamie turned away. Maxim had only one thought in his mind: Jamie knew that Maxim was spying on him, and he was coming clean to get Maxim's sympathy. Maxim remained calm, not saying anything. There was a miniscule fragment of hope that Jamie was telling the truth, that his emotions and his remorse were genuine—a desperate, hopeless romanticism that clung like a vine to a wall during a violent tempest. Maxim cleared his throat and spoke in a stern and serious tone to Jamie.

"That party we had. The one where Liam's watch disappeared. Why was it in my pocket?"

Jamie took a deep breath.

"I was heading onto the terrace when that argument broke out. When I saw you distressed, I had to do something to diffuse the fight. As I sneaked behind the crowd, I noticed the watch on the ground and picked it up. The chain was broken, so I assumed it belonged to one of the guests. But after Connor left I completely forgot I had the watch on me. Those were not your pants in the bathroom, they were mine. We were wearing the same color."

"Then why did you run out of the room when I asked you?"

"I don't know! I don't know what came over me! I got scared in the moment."

Maxim continued to look at Jamie, taking measure of Jamie's answer. It seemed truthful, but Maxim still had doubts, so he kept on.

"What was the real fallout you had with the Grenvills? What did it have to do with your mother?"

Jamie looked down at his feet.

"They did not want to tell me who she was. And I found out they bribed her with my birthright."

"Your birthright?" Maxim asked in confusion.

"My half-brothers told my mother that I would only inherit my share of my father's estate if she never revealed who she was, or that I was born out of wedlock."

"But your father went to jail, his assets were seized. Is there even anything to inherit?"

"No, there isn't, but my mother never came forward," Jamie continued, his voice full of shame. "She abandoned me, and my family kept her identity secret out of spite. Lillian was my mother as far as I'm concerned, and she died before I could prove to her I wasn't a disappointment."

Jamie leaned against the wall, sliding down until he sat on the floor. He returned to weeping, clasping his hands to his face. Maxim's stance softened, partly out of love for the man who wept like a little boy wishing for a mother's tenderness. But Maxim could no longer fall for Jamie's excuses or stories. There were too many secrets buried, too many suspicions unanswered, too many lies to refute. Maxim could not prove Jamie was responsible for the deaths of Luisa, Henry, Edward, Lillian . . . but he had to finally break away from the chaos Jamie carried with him.

"James," Maxim huffed, his patience exhausted. "I can't do this anymore."

Jamie looked up in confusion.

"I'm done. From the moment I met you, all you seem to do is lie to my face and others, play roughshod with people's lives and money. I kept telling you not to play these games, but you never seem to change. I'm done with you taking my support for granted. I'm done with the enabling. I'm just . . . done."

Jamie's face grew incredulous as he saw that Maxim meant what he was saying.

"I am going to pay off your debts, and you will close your fund. I will give you an allowance, and I want you out."

"I don't understand. Max, I—"

"I want you gone," Maxim repeated. "I don't care what you do with your life going forward but I don't want to see your face again."

"You don't love me anymore?" Jamie cried.

"I just stopped hating myself. I lost everything that mattered trying to uphold other people's idea of what I should be. To meet the expectations of people who only cared about power, money, and control. I want to find out what it means to be happy with myself. And to be happy alone."

"But Max, I didn't do this to hurt you! I'm sorry! I just need you to be proud of me! Please, I love you!"

"I'm done, James. That's all there is to it."

"But you can't be serious. What about us? Our home? You can't even leave!" Jamie exclaimed, his sorrow and tears turning to indignant disbelief.

"True, but I can control who I want around me. This is still my house, after all."

Jamie stood, looking at Maxim in stunned silence. Something changed in Jamie's demeanor; the mask had slipped. He kept looking at Maxim, but Maxim only returned indifference. Maxim had for the first time stood up for himself without needing to use his strength, his size, or the threat of violence.

Maxim continued onward to the library, picking up a book from the shelf. He settled in his chair and began to read, listening to the gentle tapping of rain against the windows. Jamie walked into the library, but Maxim did not lift his head to acknowledge him. Jamie picked up a book for himself and walked out.

II

Maxim walked through the grounds of Gwenshill. The gardens were overgrown, the lawn untrimmed, dandelions sprouting whichever way Maxim looked. Spring had come, but a cold wind still swept across the expanse, a last hangover of winter that stubbornly remained. Maxim listened for the sound of the crow that cawed somewhere on the property. Its sound echoed in the distance, seeming to come from everywhere and nowhere. A pair of black wings soared above him, and when he turned in the direction of the crow's flight, he saw the bird land atop the roof of the mansion.

Maxim followed the bird back up the hill, his aching joints slowing his progress. He stepped back onto the terrace, observing a nest perched in an alcove high above his bedroom window. The crow had made itself a home atop Gwenshill. Though this looked like an old nest, its branches and twigs bleached and gray from several cycles of sunshine. Maxim had brought along with him a packet of peanuts for the crow, and he tossed them on the ground, wondering if the bird would descend to the terrace to partake in Maxim's offer of friendship.

He went back inside the house through a door that had been left unbolted. Cloth covered the furniture; keepsakes were stored in boxes in the corners of the rooms. Gwenshill sat empty, no staff members left to clean the house or cook meals. Maxim had also dismissed them, along with the groundskeepers and gardeners; only Judith remained, as she had been assigned by the court to look over Maxim, and a nurse to assist her.

Jamie had left, taking Maxim's offer and paying off all of his investors. It cost Maxim a vast portion of his own personal wealth to keep Jamie's frauds concealed, and now there was no longer an income large enough to keep the estate running with people. Jamie packed his luggage, the SUV he had rented piled deep with bags. Maxim met Jamie in the motor court, not to see Jamie off, but to confirm that he had left the grounds never to come back. Maxim and Jamie did not speak; they only exchanged glances, Maxim solemn, Jamie aloof. The last bag was tossed in the back passenger seat; the car door closed firmly with a resolute clunk.

"That's all," Jamie announced. "I guess this is it."

"I guess it is," Maxim replied.

"I'm sorry it ended like this." Jamie pulled his sunglasses from his face, fiddling them in his hands. Biting his lip, he said finally, "I don't know how, but I will make it all back, Maxim. I promise."

Maxim did not speak. He wanted to say he still loved Jamie but refrained from doing so. He knew he needed to stop being the enabler to Jamie's whims.

"I think you better be going," Maxim stated, his mind unmoved, his heart aching.

Jamie gave one last glance at Maxim, his eyes holding a faint glimmer of penitence, but Maxim held firm. Jamie got into his car and drove off. Maxim headed to the terrace, watching the car speed away.

"Is there anything I can do for you, Mr. Porter?" Judith asked.

"Have my belongings been returned to the main bedroom?"

"Yes, Mr. Porter."

"Then that is all, the nurse will be taking me to my doctor's appointment. I will be in my room while I wait."

Maxim returned to his old bedroom, cleared of all traces of Jamie's presence. Maxim paced about the room, eventually sitting on the bed he had reclaimed from his departed lover while he pondered what to do next. He thought of calling Victor, but too much time had passed. Maxim had kept his own set of secrets from Victor. He would be no better than Jamie if he pursued another relationship built on a foundation of deceit.

Maxim curled himself into a ball, the deafening silence proving too much for his mind to handle. He was met with a hallucination of a shadow that stood at the foot of the bed, its profile distinct but unrecognizable as a person that Maxim knew. It did not speak, or move, it only stood there looming over Maxim as he lay on the bed.

"What do you want?" Maxim called out to the shadow in frustration, yet the shadow did not respond. It walked away from the bed and vanished into thin air. Maxim remained in bed, looking out the window. The sky was a brilliant blue, no clouds dulling the intensity of its color. He remembered the crow, moving to the window and looking out to the terrace to see if the bird had taken up his gift. The crow was old and grizzled, its coat dull with a few missing feathers. Maxim felt a kinship with the crow. An intelligent creature of great complexity, typecast as a harbinger of death and darkness. Maxim watched the bird peck at the peanuts, then fly back up to the nest just above Maxim's room. He heard its caws as it perched itself in its nest.

The nurse knocked on the door ready to take Maxim to the hospital. Judith had called the police to notify them of Maxim's travel, but he still had to listen to his ankle monitor beeping until they arrived at the hospital. Maxim was taken to the doctors for tests and bloodwork.

The doctor approached Maxim and the nurse, his face and voice somber under the weight of the diagnosis that he revealed to Maxim. They had discovered abnormal protein clumps in Maxim's brain. He was in the early stages of Lewy Body Dementia. The doctors told Maxim he had to cease taking the medication he had been prescribed by the psychiatrist. The doctors petitioned the court, but the judge refused, reiterating that Maxim had to remain sedated as part of his plea deal or be sent to a medical institution.

Maxim remained quiet, too numb to be depressed or sad at the unexpected news. He resigned himself to his fate; he just wanted to go home. While he still had clear thoughts, Maxim decided he was going to write his final directive. He would take time to plan for what he wanted to be done to his body upon his death. Meanwhile, he would keep his diagnosis to himself. He did not want anyone to know; not his brother, not even Jamie.

That evening, Maxim sat at the writing desk in his bedroom and began to write his instructions. He knew he should also think about changing his last will and testament, removing Jamie from inheriting what was left of his fortune. He pulled the will out of the safe, looking it over on the desk. He remembered his lawyer advising him that even in death, Jamie would not automatically inherit his money without the will telling so. That task could wait; in the meantime, his focus would be to decide whether to be cremated or buried, to be embalmed, what flowers he wanted, what photo of himself he wanted displayed. He thought he would leave that last choice up to George and Isabel.

Judith knocked on his bedroom door, entering with a tray of tea and scones she left beside Maxim on the table.

"Mr. Porter, it is time for you to take your medication. The doctor said that it should be taken with a meal," Judith informed him with a brief glance toward his desk.

"Right. Well, I need water to drink it with. Never mind that, I'll just go to the sink and pour from the tap," Maxim replied coolly.

"Let me grab it for you, Mr. Porter." Judith walked briskly into the bathroom, grabbing a glass of water for Maxim.

"Thank you, Judith."

"Mr. Porter, will Master James be returning any time soon?" Judith asked.

"James is not coming back. He is no longer welcome on the premises," Maxim replied bluntly, taking his pill with a sip of water and returning his gaze to his desk. "Why do you ask?"

Judith hesitated briefly, her eyes shifting between the floor and Maxim's direction.

"He—he had such a positive presence. This house does not feel the same without him."

"It does not, but his presence became a poisoned one. He abused my trust, and now he has been cast out."

Judith rested her hand on Maxim's shoulder in an unexpected show of emotion.

"Love covers a multitude of sins," Judith said softly, "1 Peter, Chapter 4 verse 8."

"Not these sins, Judith; not for this atheist anyway." Maxim sighed, turning to his tea and scones. "What flavor tea is this?"

"Dandelion and mint, Mr. Porter."

"I see. Thank you Judith, you may go."

Judith left the room, closing the door behind her. Maxim moved the glass of water away so he could pull the tray closer to him. He placed it beside a lamp, the moisture from the cold glass showing his finger-prints. He was about to grab the tray when he noticed its smooth surface, unblemished by his own hands. He realized the final truth, the confirma-tion of his suspicions as to why his life had unraveled in such an unfor-tunate way. He only needed to know why. Maxim could feel it coming closer, the end to his suffering, the end to his loneliness, the end to his shame over his wasted existence. He turned back to the documents on his desk and continued to write the plans for his death.

III

The months passed. In the middle of summer, a heatwave descended upon the county. Gwenshill's windows remained closed and curtained to combat the excessive heat, keeping its interiors dark. A portable air con-ditioner was installed in Maxim's bedroom, but he still suffered, even at night. Judith sequestered herself along with the nurse in the service wing, where the windows were smaller and the walls thicker.

Maxim remained confined to his bed, his health deteriorating. He felt weak, not able to walk farther than his own bathroom without having to rest. He found a cold bath helped him cool off, but he had to rely on the nurse to help him get in and out of the tub. Maxim awakened one night dripping with sweat, his sheets soaking; the air conditioner had stopped at some point during the night and only the fan remained work-ing. Maxim could feel that his time was approaching, the hallucinations around him flowing uninterrupted from waking to dreaming states.

Maxim could hear the piano in the ballroom playing when there was none. The sound of laughter and merriment echoing through the house from a phantom party that lived only in his head. The voices call-ing Maxim, the ghosts of his past inviting him into the ultimate end. Maxim fought the call, struggling to keep himself present and lucid. He did not want to surrender to the past just yet, when there was still a present that remained unsolved. The plans for his death were complete, sealed in an envelope to be sent to his lawyers. He held onto it, waiting for the moment he was sure.

Relief finally came with a summer downpour, the heavy rain driving out the heat, the air cleared of its stifling humidity. Dark and forbidding clouds dropped brief showers upon Gwenshill. Maxim pulled himself from his bed, looking out of the window to see if the summer storm had passed. He looked out to the still-gray sky and caught a glimpse of the terrace below. There, in a heap of twigs and sopping branches, lay the old crow. The venerable bird had not survived the heatwave; the nest containing its weathered body had fallen off the roof and into the terrace below. Maxim looked on with pity, wondering why it hadn't flown away to shelter in the trees. Perhaps the crow had felt trapped in his nest the same way Maxim was.

The nurse walked in then, catching sight of Maxim standing beside the mirror.

"Oh Mr. Porter, you're up! Good thing the rain came to end this heat. How are you feeling?" asked the nurse, setting down the tray with Maxim's medication.

"I'm okay," Maxim replied, looking out the window. "I'm sorry for making your phone fall into the tub. Did putting it in rice work?"

"Unfortunately, no, Mr. Porter—"

"Please, just call me Max."

"Max. My phone has stopped working completely, I have to go into town to get a new one."

"Oh, if you are . . . then could you do this favor for me?" Maxim asked, stepping slowly toward the writing desk. The nurse went to his side, holding his arm for support. He leaned forward to the desk, grabbing a small envelope and handing it to the nurse.

"Stop by the post office to send this? It must be shipped overnight to the funeral home right away."

"Oh dear, is it serious?" asked the nurse anxiously.

"No, no, no, my dear. I'm just doing some planning. Don't worry, I still have plenty of years ahead of me," Maxim reassured her with a smile.

"I see. Sure, Mr. Por—Max. I will stop by after the phone store."

"No, please." Maxim tried to stay calm. "I'm sorry to impose, but if you don't send it out now it will not get there until Monday. It shouldn't take you long."

"Okay, Max. I'll pop out to Gwendolyn and be right back, and Judith will bring you your lunch in a bit. Let's get you back to bed." The nurse helped Maxim back onto the bed, propping his pillows so he could sit up, and Maxim took his medicine in front of her.

"Thank you nurse. Could you leave the door open?"

The nurse nodded, walking out of the room with the envelope. He could hear her footsteps walking away down the corridor, then another set of steps approaching, the resonating thuds up the staircase announcing an incoming Judith with Maxim's food. She appeared before the door to his room holding a breakfast tray with a sandwich, a bowl of fruit, and a glass of juice. She placed the tray before Maxim, and he noticed how the glass looked foggy.

"What did you put in the juice, Judith?" Maxim asked.

"Your creatine, Mr. Porter." Judith replied.

"Creatine? I haven't had that in a while."

"I don't know what you mean, Mr. Porter." Judith replied, feigning ignorance. She looked at his desk. "You wanted me to deliver a document for you?"

"Yes actually, it's in the drawer of the desk." Maxim pointed and Judith pulled out a large manilla envelope.

"I will have this document sent out, Mr. Porter. I will leave you to your meal." Judith nodded and turned to leave.

Maxim looked down at the tray, then back at her, his mind certain, his eyes fixed and defiant.

"You know Judith, for as much as James vouched for this new style of house staffing, I never cared much for how you conducted yourself as our butler. I'm sorry . . . I meant house manager," Maxim corrected himself smugly.

Judith rolled her eyes. "I'm sorry you feel that way, Mr. Porter. Though the fact that I am still under your employ must prove some merit."

"You're under my employ as a court-ordered prison warden," Maxim quipped, halting Judith in her tracks. She stared coldly at Maxim as he heard the faint sound of a car engine starting outside.

"I am willing to listen to any suggestions you have, Mr. Porter. After all, I could learn how to better serve old families like yours," Judith remarked. He saw her mask of propriety slip.

"Well in that case, I will give you this advice," Maxim said. "In fine houses and with old families, it is customary for senior staff to wear gloves when handling silver to avoid leaving fingerprints. You are not wearing gloves."

Judith nodded impatiently and took a few steps toward the door. Maxim continued, finally hearing the car engine fade away in the distance.

"And yet," Maxim continued, "there are no fingerprints on this tray. I see the outline of your hands, but no ridges or marks, as though your fingerprints are not there, as though they didn't exist."

Judith froze in her stride. She looked back at him.

"Why did you kill my best friend and frame his husband?"

"Mr. Porter! That's absurd." Judith laughed nervously. "Where did you get such an idea?"

"Edward was sent a bottle of an exfoliant before he was killed. At first, I didn't recognize it from the products James would use in our bathroom. Then it dawned on me—James didn't send it to Edward, it was sent by you on his behalf."

"Really Mr. Porter? A bottle of lotion?" Judith scoffed.

"The homeless man claimed to have seen James the night of Edward's murder. The man didn't actually see James, but someone whose eyes looked like his. You had been out of town at the same time James was in England."

Judith sneered dismissively, "Really Mr. Porter, I think your hallucinations are starting to loosen your grasp on reality. Master James and I have the same eyes?"

"It took me too long to realize, but that unnerving cold stare you give looks just like James when he is upset. His eyes were so warm and welcoming, so full of sparkle and light . . . I would get lost in his gaze, forgetting where and who I was. When his mood soured, they would turn frigid and distant, to the point I avoided looking at them directly. And they reminded me of someone else's eyes—yours."

Judith pulled the door closed and flicked the lock. She turned to Maxim, pulling something out of her pocket and placing it on the nightstand beside him. It was a bottle of Benzodiazepines, only with Judith's name on the label.

"I suffer from insomnia. When I was prescribed these, I noticed that they had the effect of stripping me of all sentiment during the daytime. When you work with rich families, showing little to no emotion helps keep you invisible," Judith said, and began to pace around the room. Maxim looked at her, incensed but silent.

"I killed your friend Edward, though it was not my original intent. I drove to the Islands to take Paul out of the picture. I believed it would be easy, given the drunkard he was; I could slip these pills in his drink and make it seem like he either fell intoxicated from the stairs or drowned in the ocean. I had submerged my hands in that papaya lotion for weeks to be sure I could erase my fingerprints completely. But when I arrived, he and Edward were in the middle of a bitter fight. Paul stumbled out of the house and came face to face with me. He didn't recognize me in his drunken stupor."

Judith turned to Maxim with a smirk of satisfaction.

"He was holding a bottle of beer which I dropped the pills into. He drank the alcohol and proceeded to walk into an alley behind a nearby bar where he blacked out. I had my own bottle of the exfoliant, so I smeared it on Paul's hands to make it look like he was the one who squeezed the life out of your friend. In fact, it was Edward who opened the door to me. I lied and told him something had happened to you. Afterward, I smeared lotion on the doors and walls as I left the scene to add to my deception."

"But Eddy had done nothing wrong!" Maxim protested angrily. "You killed an innocent man."

"Paul had a reputation as an alcoholic that chased around young men. It is not hard to imagine that he got drunk and angry and took his rage out on your friend for not letting him have his way. Killing a man for love is one thing; lust, quite another," Judith continued. "Paul never got over James, even after you discovered them. James may have put up with Paul's obsessive infatuation, but I didn't."

"But how does that concern you?!" Maxim exclaimed.

"I had to protect James's marriage to you. You were going to divorce him over the affair," Judith said with a steely glare. "After the stupid boy signed that prenup, the only way he could get ahold of your money would be if you had written him into your will. If you died or divorced before then, he'd get nothing."

"That's why you killed my best friend? So James could get my money?"

"Something had to be done; your kind has no self-control."

"You bitch!" Maxim barked. Judith remained unmoved.

"James's father promised he would have everything, that he would be secure even if he had to put up with that god-awful family of his. But no, Isidor destroyed all of that. His sons remained rich and James was left penniless!"

"So that's it? You two were in on this together the whole time?"

"Of course not," Judith huffed. "James is not aware of what I have been doing, of what I have sacrificed for him."

"But what do you gain from all of this? Are you in love with him?"

"In *love* with him? That's preposterous," Judith interrupted.

The moment the question escaped Maxim's lips he realized what Judith's true motive was. Now all the disparate pieces began to fall into place.

"But you do love him . . . you're his mother."

Judith's eyes widened anxiously. She felt exposed, with nowhere to hide as she paced about the room.

"The agency that James contacted sent me. I had applied for the position when he first fired Luisa." She paused in front of a framed photo of Jamie that was still by the desk.

"You can't imagine what it was like for me to see him after so many years. He was three years old when I last saw him, those twinkling little eyes and that happy little smile of his. He was the most beautiful little boy in the world. And seeing that handsome young man before me, all I could see was that little boy I parted with. I could never sleep after they took my son from me, and it had been so long that he had forgotten what his mother looked like."

Looking at Judith, Maxim knew that something had snapped inside her long ago. He could now fully see the madness that she had concealed behind her stony gaze.

"When you intervened to maintain your housekeeper, I had already learned enough about the running of the house to know where the tea was kept and where she bought it from. It was the tea she drank most, otherwise I would not have taken the chance," she boasted.

"She had given *me* that tea," Maxim snapped angrily. "You could have killed me that night."

"I miscalculated that," she admitted. "Though from how I've seen you treat my poor James over the years, I wish I hadn't."

She sneered at the surprise on Maxim's face. "I knew something was wrong with you the moment I saw you. Violent, unstable, histrionic, and cowardly. You were equally too proud and too insecure of yourself to admit it. I would spike your food in the beginning, but the idea of tampering with your creatine proved more useful. I knew Jamie did not take it, so I was sure you would be the only one who would willingly poison himself just to make my son happy."

"You're insane!"

"Me? You're the one who concealed your madness! You took your insecurities out on Jamie. You fought, you threw things at each other, you hurt my son!"

"Murder is indefensible!" Maxim bellowed. "You poisoned my mind for years! You only added to my madness! My paranoia! My nightmares! I spent my entire life terrified that the world was out to get me, only for you to prove it true! You made me think my dear Jamie was a killer!"

The two of them stared each other down, Maxim breathing heavily as his fury drained his body of its energy.

"And I suppose you killed Lillian too?" Maxim said accusingly.

"I did not kill *Lady Wendell*," Judith sniped scornfully. "I saw you spying on me when I was making those bars of soap. She got lucky . . . but sooner or later that woman was going to pay for taking my child for herself."

"You took my family, my friends, my home, and what is left of my sanity," Maxim said with disgust. "Were you just going to keep poisoning me until I dropped dead?"

"I needed to protect my son's future. But now poisoning you won't be necessary anymore," Judith said, holding up the manila envelope still in her hand. "You sent your final directive to your funeral home—perhaps it's time you fulfill your final wishes sooner than you would have liked." She motioned to the glass of hazy juice on Maxim's tray.

Maxim scoffed in disbelief. "And what if I refuse? What if I tell the nurse you are trying to kill me?"

She walked slowly toward him, her face breaking into a smug grin as she softly spoke, leaning close to him.

"Who would believe you? You are talking with people who are not here . . . you are seeing things that are not there . . . I have taken everything and everyone that mattered away from you. All that is left for me to take is your life."

In truth, all Maxim wanted to do was live. Live to see another sunrise, another spring, another birthday. But Maxim thought of the reality of his diagnosis, and he knew that he was being given a choice that he soon wouldn't be able to make for himself: to pass away with his lucidity intact, or watch himself devolve into a husk of the person he used to be. He sighed, grabbed the glass, and held it close to his mouth. He looked back to Judith.

"If I'm expected to do this, then I need to know the truth. Will you tell me the truth?" Maxim asked.

"What do you want to know?"

"Did Jamie love me?" Maxim asked sincerely.

"He did." Judith paused. "I never understood what he saw in you, but he was happiest when you were together. He cared about you, he believed he understood you, and he put up with you because of it. Nothing broke his heart more than when he thought you were disappointed in him."

Maxim sighed.

"I was never disappointed," he said solemnly. "I only wanted him to find his own happiness, rather than to chase the happiness of others. I only wish I had come to this truth sooner." He tipped back the glass and drank the fatal liquid to its end.

Judith smiled with relief, her final goal achieved. She turned toward the door, holding the envelope in her hand.

"Thank you, Maximilian, I think you made the right decision. Jamie will now have a future, and I can't wait to finally become a part of his life again."

"At least you can continue to keep this house in the family," Maxim told her.

"Oh, I don't know about that. This house is so stuffy and out of date." Judith laughed. "I think Jamie and I will prefer something out west. He's still young, maybe he can find someone more age-appropriate."

"Well, it's up to you. You are the mistress of this house now." Maxim broke into a laugh of his own.

"What is so funny?" Judith asked, furrowing her brow in confusion.

"I wrote an amendment to my will. I wanted to bequeath Gwenshill and its grounds to you. As a symbol of my gratitude for your many years of service."

"Why are you laughing at that? Jamie gets your money still, right? *Right?*"

"Well, unless the poison pill my attorneys put in my will gets triggered. It was written so long ago I forgot about it! The copy I keep at home is out of date."

"What poison pill?" Judith asked nervously.

"Oh, that's in the event of my death under suspicious circumstances," Maxim said casually. "My will is rendered null and void if it's triggered. Me suddenly dying of an overdose not long after an amendment is added would certainly count as suspicious. Especially when there are no other witnesses to testify to how I died, since beneficiaries don't count. But if you don't want this house, you don't have to send the envelope you're holding."

"Very theatrical coming from someone about to—" Judith began to rip the envelope open, turning pale with shock at the first pages she saw.

"WHAT THE HELL IS THIS?!"

Maxim leaned over with an expression of pained satisfaction.

"Oh, that's my final directive. I must have given the amendment to the nurse instead. Yeah, you're going to have to find her. Otherwise, you don't get anything, and neither does James."

"I have your directive! It's as good as a suicide note!" Judith scoffed, but Maxim could tell she was panicking. She pulled out her phone, trying to call the nurse, but not getting through.

"Are you sure about that?" Maxim smirked, gripping his torso in pain. Judith raced to the locked bedroom door, dropping the documents onto the floor as she unjammed the lock and ran out to the corridor.

"YOU MISERABLE QUEER!" Judith screamed back toward Maxim as her frenzied footsteps echoed through the house.

Maxim listened for the sound of Judith's car driving away. He looked down at his hand, the pills from the nurse still closed tightly in his palm. He swallowed them now, confident that he could depart from his life with Gwenshill completely deserted. He hoped his ploy had worked, that the nurse had gotten enough of a head start to drop off his letter before Judith found her. Maxim prayed for the deliverance of that envelope, and for his end to bring justice. Judith's bottle of pills remained on the table. Maxim swatted the bottle onto the floor, where it rolled under his bed.

Maxim sat on the bed and waited calmly and quietly; there was no longer a need to feel pain, resentment, anguish, or regret. He thought back to the funerals he had attended in his life, those of his father, his grandparents, uncles, aunts, even some cousins. He could now put himself in the place of the deceased, wondering what those who would come to their funeral were so sad about—their loss was a temporary one. If there was an afterlife, there would be no need to shed tears and leave flowers. Family would be reunited again on the other side, arriving to a grand and never-ending welcome party. But then again, Maxim reasoned, even crows hold wakes for their deceased. Maybe those intelligent beings mourn because they know the real terms of existence: that there was no next stage, that this was it.

He wondered why no other crows had come to see the body resting on the terrace. Maxim wondered if that lonely bird had friends or family. Maybe when the storm ended, a murder of crows would arrive to honor it. He looked out the window from his bed, waiting to hear the caw of other birds, and wondered if anyone would come to see him either. Would George and Isabel? Would Charlotte? He hoped Paul would come. Maybe even Victor. Now in these final moments, all he thought was whether he had burned all his bridges, even if some had burnt unwittingly and unknowingly.

A numbness began to take root in Maxim's body, traveling gently up his fingers and toes, slowly spreading up his arms and legs, turning into a tingling feeling as his nervous system began to shut down. His breathing grew heavy, his heartbeat racing to keep his blood pumping. His mind continued to fight against the slow cessation of his motor functions. The end was approaching, yet the brain continued to fight on, battling to remain alert, remain lucid, to simply remain. Hallucinations materialized and vanished rapidly, blips and bursts of objects, people, and places Maxim had known flashing and then disappearing. Maxim struggled to focus, his brain refusing to go out with a whimper, but wanting to fight with a bang. Maxim could not take the chaos anymore.

"Enough!" He shouted into the empty room, the sound of his own voice halting his spiraling consciousness. He was still there, alive, his hands and legs numb and unmoving. Maxim worried the drugs had not killed him but only paralyzed him from the neck down. He could hear footsteps slowly walking through the corridor toward his room. Maxim held his breath—could his plan have failed? Was Judith back to finish him off? Maxim heard the door creak open.

"Hello handsome."

Maxim turned his face to the door. There stood Jamie in his midnight-blue suit.

"Jamie . . . you're home." He felt only relief.

"I came back to see you. I didn't want you to be alone when it was time," Jamie said softly.

He walked to the foot of Maxim's bed, his eyes soft and glittery, his smile gentle and serene.

"I'm sorry I was so terrible to you," Maxim said. "I let myself spiral into thinking the unthinkable."

"I forgive you. I'm sorry for the secrets. I didn't want to fail. I was overwhelmed, and I didn't know how to handle it. I was afraid you would stop loving me."

"Oh Jamie, I just wanted you to be happy. I forgot my own father's wisdom and let my paranoia take over. I forgive you."

"I loved being with your family, your friends, the home we had together. I would never want anything to happen to them or you. I love you . . . I always have."

As the light of the sun parted the clouds outside, Maxim shed a tear that ran down his weathered face, a quiet token of joy that Jamie was there in his last moments.

"At one point I will have to go my dear Jamie. I'm scared, but I can't stay much longer."

"Don't worry Max, I'm going to stay here until you're ready."

Jamie sat beside Maxim on the bed. They continued to look at each other, and in their mutual gaze there was a love that still burned warm and tender. Maxim's battered and weakened body no longer bothered him; it was merely a vessel that anchored him into existence. His hesitation to depart only lingered because he did not want to leave Jamie behind. In the serene silence, music began to play from the ballroom. Slowly the sound of the piano gave way to strings and brass, the melody growing alongside a low roar of people dancing and laughing. Here was a sound so familiar to Maxim: the sound of the past. The band played the music he most fondly remembered, and he could hear those he had lost, merrily calling him to the party.

"I think your family is waiting for you. It sounds like a fun party," Jamie remarked, also hearing the calls from the ballroom.

"I don't want to. I don't want to leave you," Maxim cried gently.

"I will be there. I'm just not invited yet."

"And what if I invite you? Come to the party, Jamie."

"I can't go just yet Max. But I will see you again. Will you wait for me there?"

"I will, I will wait for you Jamie. My dear Jamie."

As the music played softly, Maxim finally heard the one voice from the past that he most needed.

"*Maxime, Maxime mon soleil!* Come dance! Come dance with me!"

Maxim looked out at the door, and then back to Jamie. A tear ran down his face.

"I must go now." Maxim sighed. "Let me just look at you . . . one . . . last . . . time."

Jamie nodded, holding his hand to Maxim's face. They looked at each other as the light of the room began to fade. The music played on, growing louder as the room grew darker; not even the light of the sun could brighten the darkness that enveloped Maxim. The only light that remained came from Jamie's eyes. Jamie's twinkling, glittering eyes were the only light Maxim wanted to see as he disappeared into the darkness.

Maxim no longer regretted his final instruction.

The casket was to remain closed.

THE END

A debut novel

GLORIA LAMBSTEAD

Instagram @undersuspiciouscircumstances

TikTok @undersuscircumstances